After the War is Over

Also by Maureen Lee

After the War is Over

Maureen Lee

First published in Great Britain in 2012 by Orion Books,
an imprint of The Orion Publishing Group Ltd
Orion House, 5 Upper Saint Martin's Lane
London WC2H 9EA

An Hachette Livre UK Company

1 3 5 7 9 10 8 6 4 2

A CIP catalogue record for this book is
available from the British Library.

ISBN (Hardback) 978 0 7528 7668 9
ISBN (ebook) 978 1 4091 4024 5

Typeset at The Spartan Press Ltd,
Lymington, Hants

Printed and bound in Great Britain by Clays Ltd,
St Ives plc

The Orion Publishing Group's policy is to use papers that are natural,
renewable and recyclable products and made from wood grown in
sustainable forests. The logging and manufacturing processes are expected to
conform to the environmental regulations of the country of origin.

www.orionbooks.co.uk

For Juliet Burton, my friend and agent

Chapter 1

Bootle, Liverpool
December 1945

'*After the war is over, After the fighting's through, Now that the lights are shining, What shall we do . . . ?*'

Maggie stopped singing and grinned at her friends, eyebrows raised in a question. She looked incredibly pretty, with her black curls, no longer hidden beneath an army cap, tumbling on to her shoulders. She tossed her head to shake the tiniest curls off her forehead and out of her unusual violet eyes. 'What *shall* we do?' she asked. 'Now that the war is over and we've been demobbed?'

'I'm only going to stay at home till the new year,' Nell said. 'Then I'll be off to live in London. I'll find a job, a nice room somewhere, and live happily ever after like they do in stories.' Nell was very tall, very clumsy and almost plain, but she had the kindest and most innocent eyes in the world, like soft brown velvet.

'It's only fairy stories that end happily,' the third member of the group remarked darkly.

'Iris Grant, you old misery-guts!' Maggie snorted. 'Nothing could be further from the truth! 'Tis my experience that stories always end happily.'

'You haven't lived long enough to know otherwise,' Iris sniffed. She was going on for thirty, whereas Maggie and Nell were only twenty-one and had been friends at school. They had joined the army together three years before. Iris had joined up much earlier, just after the war had started. She had nothing

I

in common with the girls other than the fact that they all came from Bootle. Not only that, she was a sergeant and they were privates; sergeants weren't encouraged to mix with other ranks, so she always wore civvies on the rare occasions they went to the pictures together. As the years passed, she'd grown fond of the girls. She noticed that other passengers in the carriage were listening with amusement to their conversation.

They were on the electric train, the final leg of their journey home from an army camp not far from Plymouth in Devon. It had taken two days to get from Plymouth to Liverpool. In London they'd slept overnight in the ladies' waiting room on Euston station. Maggie had remarked that it would probably be the last time they would sleep on a wooden bench and find it fun. There were women there from the other services who'd been demobbed like them, and they had sung songs, danced a bit, laughed a lot, cried occasionally, and slept hardly at all.

'I feel sad,' Maggie announced, grinning from ear to ear.

'You don't look it,' Iris and Nell said together.

'Maybe not, but I still feel it. In another two stops it'll be Marsh Lane station, and we'll get off and nothing will ever be the same. The war's finished, we're no longer soldiers, we'll never wear our army uniforms again.' She looked briefly sober for a change. 'I already feel dead peculiar not wearing a cap.'

'You can always wear a different sort of hat,' Nell said sensibly.

'Oh Nell.' Maggie hugged her friend effusively. 'You are such a lovely human being. How will I ever get used to waking up and not find you snoring your head off in the next bed?'

Nell looked embarrassed. 'I'll miss you too,' she conceded. 'And I don't snore.' Privately she wondered if she would manage to exist in London without Maggie. In Bootle they lived in the next street to each other. Ever since she could remember, they had waved to each other out of their back bedroom windows every night before they went to bed and first thing each morning.

The train was drawing into Marsh Lane station.

'Good luck, girls,' a man said as they were about to get off.

'Good luck to yourself.' Maggie patted him on the head and he looked pleased.

One thing she wouldn't miss, Iris thought, was Maggie's outgoingness, her forever patting people and kissing them, hugging them for no reason at all, telling everyone very loudly how much she loved them. Tears sprang to her eyes when she realised that despite this she would miss Maggie terribly, as well as Nell's lovely nature, her patience, her inability to say a bad word about anyone.

They stood in a little huddle underneath the railway bridge in Marsh Lane, shoulders touching, suitcases at their feet. It was a dreary afternoon, almost dark yet it was only two o'clock. Being Wednesday, half-day closing, there weren't many people about. A mist hung in the air and they could feel the moisture on their faces. It smelt of smoke and coal.

'I had my first kiss in the army,' Maggie said. 'Went to my first dance.'

Nell blushed. 'So did I.'

'And I had my first shower,' Maggie went on. 'Used a telephone and a typewriter for the first time, rode a motorbike – only as a passenger,' she added, not wanting to make herself sound more experienced than she actually was.

'I cooked meals every day for over a hundred people.' Nell spoke. 'I peeled thousands and thousands of potatoes, baked hundreds and hundreds of pies. The thing I made best of all was Swiss roll.'

'I loved your Swiss roll,' Iris remarked. She was married and had kissed and danced and baked before she'd joined the army, where she'd become a driver and had chauffeured important people to their important destinations. She'd been happy in

3

the forces, happier than she'd been in a long time. She was glad the war was over, but would miss being happy.

Maggie grabbed her and kissed her on the cheek. Nell kissed her more gently on the other cheek.

'Let's meet on Saturday morning for a cup of tea in Jenny's Café on Strand Road,' Maggie suggested.

They agreed to meet at half past ten. Iris pulled away, not wanting them to see she was crying, and went home.

'She was close to tears, poor Iris,' Nell said. She and Maggie linked arms as they walked towards the streets where both had been born.

'You'd think she'd be thrilled to bits seeing her husband again. That's a lovely posh house they've got in Rimrose Road.' Maggie pulled the collar of her coat over her ears. 'Is it as cold here as it was in Plymouth? Or colder?'

Nell sniffed and announced it colder. 'The temperature of the Irish Sea is lower than the English Channel.'

'How on earth do you know that?' Maggie asked.

'I've no idea. I must have read it somewhere.'

They turned into Amber Street, where Nell lived. Further down there was an ugly gap where two houses had been hit by a bomb during the Blitz. 'Once we go inside, our lives in the army really will be at an end.' Maggie stopped by a lamp post they'd turned into a swing with a piece of rope when they were little. She unhooked her arm from Nell's and stood in the middle of the street, her hands on her hips, her lovely eyes scanning the line of small terraced houses on each side. Some properties still had blackout curtains at the windows; one had the Union Jack painted on the front door; decorations were up in some ready for Christmas – the first war-free one for six years. 'No one will ever call me Private O'Neill again, we'll never wake up to the sound of a bugle, go to a dance in uniform. Everything's going to be completely different.'

'We'll soon get used to it,' Nell said comfortably, not at all sure that it was true.

Maggie danced back on to the pavement and grabbed her friend's arm. 'Of course we will. And we'll have memories, won't we? Really gear memories of the wonderful times we had. And sad memories too.' Her violet eyes narrowed. 'All those lovely young lads that died. I promised to marry quite a few, only so they could tell their mates they had a girlfriend back in Blighty.'

Nell blushed again. 'One proposed to me. His name was Jim Harvey, and he was a lance corporal.' It had happened so quickly, and there hadn't been time to fall in love before he was killed in Italy, the victim of a sniper's bullet.

The girls walked another few feet and stopped outside the Desmonds' house.

'Home!' Maggie said. She pushed Nell towards the front door. 'Home at last. Shall we meet tonight? Come round our house whatever time you like. Me mam will be dead pleased to see you. Ta-ra, Nell.'

Maggie disappeared around the corner, leaving Nell feeling desperately lost and alone. She swallowed, took a deep breath, and pulled the key on a piece of string through the letter box. The first thing she noticed was that the hall had been redecorated. The shoulder-high Anaglypta paper had been freshly varnished and the wall above distempered dark green. A new picture hung there of a bowl of fruit that looked too perfect to be real. The parlour door was open and Nell peeped inside. The room was empty, and it too had been freshly painted the same dead miserable colours as the hall. The furniture was smart and well-polished, the cushions and curtains looked expensive and there was a new rug in front of the brown-tiled fireplace. Nell threw back her shoulders and went into the living room. Compared to the parlour, this room was neglected and shabby. The curtains were threadbare and the linoleum, which had been there for as long as she could remember, was full of holes that could be lethal if you didn't look where you were going. A sparse fire burned in the grate.

'Mam?' she said. Her mother was asleep in the easy chair beneath the window, thin and pale and helpless. She opened her eyes, then her arms, when she saw her daughter.

'Nellie, luv. Come here!' she cried.

Nell knelt and allowed her mother to embrace her. Eight years ago, Nell's father, Alfred Desmond, had quite openly taken up with another woman, who owned a hairdresser's in Strand Road and lived in the flat above; Rita Brannigan, red-haired, green-eyed, with a voluptuous body, was frequently compared to her namesake, the film star Rita Hayworth. Alfred only spent his evenings and Sunday afternoons with Rita, preferring to live the rest of his time in his own house, where he was better fed and better looked after altogether.

Overnight, Mabel, Alfred's wife, had become an invalid. She was no longer well enough to do the housework, too weak to do the shopping – and too ashamed, what with everyone knowing about Alfred's whore and laughing at his poor wife, sometimes to her face. She'd hardly moved out of the chair since, except to go to bed or use the lavatory at the bottom of the yard.

The Desmonds had five children, four girls and a boy, Kenny, who was the baby of the family. Nell was the next to youngest. One by one the older girls had taken their mother's place: Gladys first, then Ena, followed by Theresa when her older sisters had married and left home.

'I've missed you, luv,' her mother sobbed now. 'Really missed you.' She paused to wipe her tears on the pinny that she used as both a handkerchief and a towel. 'And our Theresa asks every day when we can expect you home, 'cos she wants to move in with her friend Joan Roberts from Chaucer Street. Well, now you're back, and she can move out. It's your turn to look after us now. You'll never go away again, will you, Nellie?'

'No, Mam,' Nell said weakly, while inside a voice screamed, *You shouldn't have come home, daft girl. You must have known something like this would happen.* The dream of living in London that she'd been nursing for almost a year had been shattered within minutes of being back.

She supposed she had known in a way; after all, it *was* her turn, like Mam had said, so how could she possibly not have come home? Theresa had served her time and was due her independence. But Nell was the youngest girl – who would take over when the time came for *her* to move on?

The front door opened and her dad came in, pausing to hang his overcoat and hat in the hall – Nell knew it was him by the way he stamped his boots on the doormat, making the house shake.

Alfred Desmond was a fine figure of a man, almost six feet tall, broad-chested, with the beginnings of a beer belly. He wore a pinstriped suit, a blue shirt and a red and blue striped tie. There was a red handkerchief in his breast pocket and he smelt strongly of a mixture of beer, tobacco and cheap cologne. His eyes were the same brown as Nell's, but there was no warmth in them, and his whiskers stretched almost as far as his ears, stiff and bristly.

Alfred looked what he was – a crook. He could get anything for anybody – at a price: petrol coupons, clothes coupons, food coupons, cigarettes and tobacco, alcohol, lipstick and dead posh scent. Name it, and from somewhere or other Alfred could get his hands on it. The reason why the hall and parlour were so well decorated compared to the rest of the house was because it was there that he did his business, saw his customers and took their orders.

He looked Nell up and down. 'So you're home. See y'haven't got any smaller while you were in the army,' he sneered.

'There isn't an ounce of fat on her, Alfred. She's tall like you, that's all. You can hardly expect her to have shrunk.'

'Shurrup, Mabel.' He gave his wife's feet an idle kick, then clapped his big hand on Nell's shoulder. 'Make us a cup of tea, there's a luv.'

The hand stayed where it was, getting tighter and tighter. Nell gritted her teeth, determined not to let him know how much it hurt. But in the end it became so painful that she had to shrug the hand away, and her father laughed.

'It's due on the first of May,' Sheila O'Neill said modestly. 'I didn't tell you, I thought I'd make it a surprise.'

Maggie laughed. 'Well it's a surprise all right. I didn't think people you and me dad's age got up to that sort of thing.' Ryan, her brother, was twenty-three. After Maggie had been born, Mam and Dad had gone for nearly twenty years assuming they weren't meant to have more children, so it was a pleasant shock when, at forty-one, her mother found herself expecting again and Bridget had come along. Now here she was, two years later, having a fourth child.

'Are you all right, though, Mam?' Maggie frowned. 'You're a bit old to be in the club.'

'Dr Reynolds said I'm as healthy as a horse,' Sheila boasted. She looked it, with her rosy cheeks and glorious smile. She was an older version of her daughter, just rather more care-worn and already with a few grey hairs. 'Anyroad, I always wanted a little playmate for our Bridie.'

Bridie, a pretty little doll of a child, was sitting on Maggie's knee. She had arrived after her big sister had joined the army, so the two hardly knew each other, but there was a big photograph of Maggie in her uniform on the mantelpiece and Sheila had reminded Bridie of her sister every day.

A cat strolled into the room, a massive tabby with an arrogant bearing. On seeing Maggie, it leapt on to the back of her chair and began to play with her curly hair.

'Tinker!' Maggie gasped. 'You horrible cat. You gave us a fright.' She shook her head and the cat slithered down and rested itself precariously on the arm of the chair. 'What time will me dad be in?' she asked. She tickled Tinker under his chin and he began to purr. She felt very much at home with the cat beside her and her little sister on her knee.

Mam looked at the clock. 'Any minute now. The morning shift finishes at two o'clock, but it takes a while getting home on the bus.'

Maggie's dad worked in a marine engineering factory that had turned to manufacturing munitions during the war. It had recently gone back to producing ship's parts. Her brother had started in the same factory as an apprentice. It meant both men had been regarded as essential workers and avoided being called up to fight, much to her father's relief and Ryan's frustration, as he'd badly wanted to join the navy.

'I'll make some tea.' Sheila struggled to her feet. 'Stay there!' she commanded when Maggie made to lift Bridie off her knee so she could help. 'I've got five months to go yet. Your father would have me permanently stuck in bed if he had his way, and your Auntie Kath brought in to look after Bridie. I told him I'd go stark raving mad, stuck in the same house as our Kath while she lectured me on women's rights and why we should get rid of the monarchy.'

Maggie sighed blissfully. It was the gear to be home again. She'd badly missed her family during her stint in the army, though the heavy bombing of Liverpool was over by the time she'd joined up in 1942, so at least she didn't have that to worry about. Knowing they were safe had meant she could take advantage of the glorious freedom and at the same time put up with the tight discipline of army life.

She looked around the warm room. Her mother had a way of making pretty things out of bits of this and that. There was a crocheted runner on the sideboard on which stood two jars covered with seashells painted in pastel colours, a vase filled with paper flowers, and an old wooden clock that had been painted white and decorated with flower transfers. The Christmas decorations were home-made too – Maggie and Ryan had made the tree fifteen years ago, out of green crêpe paper.

This was going to be a really smashing Christmas without the clouds of war hanging over them. There was so much to celebrate. Maggie thought about the last three Christmases, spent on the base in Plymouth. There'd been a magic to them, an air of frantic merriment, a feeling of sadness too. She was wondering if she would miss those things when the back door opened and her dad came into the kitchen.

'Our Maggie's home,' Mam said.

'Is she now! Where's my big girl?' roared Paddy O'Neill in his strong Irish accent. He appeared in the doorway, big and handsome, full of smiles. 'Welcome home, darlin'! Welcome home.'

Nell remembered, a long time later, that she'd been invited to Maggie's house in the evening. She really liked Mrs O'Neill, who always made a fuss of her. Her own mother had gone to bed, her father to the pub, Kenny to play billiards, and Theresa had gone to the pictures with Joan Roberts and two French sailors.

She wasn't used to quiet after the noisy life on the base. She put on her coat and walked around to Coral Street. For nearly six years a blackout had been in force, with everyone obliged to close their curtains so that not even a chink of light showed. Now, like a sign of belated defiance, curtains were being left wide open with lives exposed for all to see.

The O'Neills were in the parlour. Maggie and her brother Ryan – Nell had had a crush on Ryan for as long as she could remember – were jiving in the middle of the room. Mr and Mrs O'Neill were seated on the settee with their arms around each other, the little girl, Bridie, squashed between them nursing Tinker, the cat. And Auntie Kath, who oozed politics from every pore, had just come into the room with a tray of tea.

There was no place for Nell in that happy scene. No one would want to see her long face. She turned and went back to her own silent house, wondering if it was always going to be like this now that she was home.

The men had gone to the pub more than an hour ago: Tom, Iris's husband, his brother Frank, and their father, Cyril. Their wives were sitting in front of the first-floor window of Iris and Tom's house overlooking Bootle docks, admiring the view. Iris was aware of her own reflection; out of uniform, she looked small, pale and insignificant. She had natural blonde hair and a quiet face – people didn't properly notice her until they'd met her two or three times, when they suddenly realised how attractive she was.

As it had gone ten and the pubs had closed, the husbands, all doctors, were expected home any minute.

'I don't know why alcohol tastes better when they're standing knee deep in sawdust, rather than sitting at a table drinking from a crystal glass,' Constance, who was married to Frank, had said earlier. 'It must be something to do with their caveman instincts.'

'Did cavemen have pubs?' Adele Grant queried idly.

'Oh, you know what I mean,' Constance snapped.

Adele, Iris and Constance's mother-in-law, plump and motherly, was one of Iris's favourite people. She had no close family herself, and Tom's mother had proved a perfect substitute for her own, who had died not long after she was born. Her father had gone to meet his maker a short time afterwards, and Iris had been raised by a rather distant aunt and uncle until she had left home at eighteen. She had only seen them about half a dozen times since.

It was Adele who'd had the idea of making a special dinner to welcome her daughter-in-law home. She must have been saving her meat coupons for several weeks in order to buy the tender sirloin steak, and Lord knows how much the two bottles of ten-year-old French wine had cost – or where it had come from. Despite the war having ended, rationing was still very much in force.

'It's been an exceptionally pleasant homecoming,' Iris said. She had expected to spend it alone with Tom. 'And this is a wonderful sight: the lights and the glowing water.' She nodded at the window. Perhaps it was the full moon that made the water shimmer the way it did. During the day, the view was nothing to write home about: cranes, a ship or two with goods being loaded on or off. But at night, with lights burning on the ships, the docks and the street itself, it was quite enchanting. 'I still can't get used to there not being a blackout,' she said.

'I can't understand why it took so long for you to be demobbed.' Constance always managed to sound a touch bad-tempered, suspicious almost, as if Iris had been getting up to no good in Plymouth since the war had ended, which to a large extent was true, though Constance had no way of knowing.

'The camp couldn't be closed down overnight,' Iris said patiently. Constance might be bad-tempered, but she had a good heart. 'There was still work to be done, meetings to be held, furniture and equipment to be transported to other camps, put in storage or sent somewhere to be sold. I got my Heavy Goods Vehicle licence,' she said proudly, 'and drove lorries all over the country.'

'Did you really, darling?' Adele remarked, impressed. 'How clever.' She patted Iris's knee. 'I'm ever so glad you managed to be home for Christmas. Don't think of trying to get food together for a meal on Christmas Day – you and Tom must come to us.'

'And to us on Boxing Day,' Constance put in. 'Beth and Eric are really looking forward to seeing you. They badly wanted to come tonight, but I told them it was only for grown-ups.'

'Thank you both. And I'm really looking forward to seeing my niece and nephew again.'

Downstairs, the front door opened and the husbands came in singing the Eton Boating Song. All had gone to exclusive schools, but not as exclusive as Eton.

Adele laughed. 'They sound a bit the worse for wear. Three inebriated doctors! They should be ashamed of themselves.'

The visitors had gone. 'Were they all right?' Tom asked anxiously. 'I hope Constance didn't get you down. She can be awfully abrupt.'

Iris was pushing the armchairs back into their proper places. Instinctively she closed the curtains. 'She was fine, if a bit blunt. Not that I mind. Your mother was lovely, but then she always is.' She sank into one of the chairs with a sigh.

Tom gave the fire a poke and came and sat in the next chair. 'I wish I could have gone in the forces too and we could have both come home together.' A broken leg as a child had left him with a slight limp and he'd been rejected by all three services. He was a very ordinary, dependable-looking man, with straight brown hair and a whimsical smile. He wore horn-rimmed glasses. His patients loved him, but Iris wasn't sure if she still did. 'It seems a bit strange not to have seen my own wife for the whole of last year,' he said stiffly. The smile had disappeared.

'We hardly ever got passes for longer than forty-eight hours,' Iris informed him. 'It wasn't possible to get from Plymouth to Liverpool and back again in such a short time.'

'I wouldn't have minded not seeing you had I been in the forces too.'

'That wasn't possible, was it?'

He shook his head. 'I wish I wasn't hopeless in so many ways.' His shoulders sagged.

13

'You're not hopeless in any way that I know.'

'I couldn't give you a baby.'

'You gave me a baby. It's probably my own fault I can't have another.' Iris closed her eyes, seeing her baby, Charlie, six months old, smiling at her, cooing, falling asleep in her arms. She imagined his bulk pressed against her, his mouth tugging at her breast, and remembered the morning she found him cold in his cot, his face as white as a ghost, lifeless and stiff. Her little boy was dead and she would never get over it for as long as she lived. If it hadn't been for Charlie, she wouldn't have joined the army, but she'd needed to get away. Once there, she'd told no one that she'd once had a child.

Now, perhaps because she was home, in the house where it had happened, it seemed terribly real. 'Is his cot still here?' she asked Tom.

'No, I hope you don't mind, but Mother took it away some time ago. Even if we had another baby, I wouldn't want him or her to sleep in it. We put the toys and baby clothes in the loft, just in case you wanted them kept.'

'I don't think I do any more. I'd sooner they were given to another baby.'

'I'll ask Mother to see to it.'

'It's all right, Tom. I'll do it myself.' He'd also lost a son, and it shouldn't all be left to him.

'Shall I put more coal on the fire, or will we be going to bed soon?' He was probably unaware of the longing on his face.

Iris would have preferred to stay up, but Tom would be hurt. She stretched her arms. 'I'd sooner go to bed,' she lied.

'It's time we started trying for another baby.' He stood and pulled her to her feet.

Iris nodded, but didn't speak. Tom would never know, but she had been trying desperately for another baby since she'd joined the army six years ago, losing track of the number of men that she had slept with. What she would have told Tom had she fallen pregnant, she had no idea. She would cross that bridge when she came to it, she had told herself. As things had turned out, there was no need to tell Tom anything.

On Saturday, Iris was already in Jenny's Café when Maggie burst through the door, creating a terrible draught. She wore a bright red coat and a fur tippet around her neck. The café was full – Iris had acquired the last table. Her camel coat was draped over the back of her chair. Her rather severe matching hat sported a speckled feather.

The chatter in the café was deafening. Everyone was in a good mood for this very special Christmas. A strip of white material hung in the steamy window with 'Happy Yuletide' cut from red crepe paper stuck to it. The wireless was playing Christmas carols sung by a children's choir.

'Is that fox?' Iris enquired of the tippet as Maggie more or less threw herself on to a chair.

'No, me dad swears it's rat. I got it off me Auntie Kath. Mam sprinkled it with talcum powder and gave it a good shake in the yard. It's lovely and warm.' She created an even bigger draught by removing her coat and flinging it backwards over the chair, laying the fur on her knee. 'Eh, you'll never guess,' she said breathlessly. 'Me mam's only expecting another baby. It's due in May. She doesn't care whether it's a boy or a girl.'

'You must give her my congratulations,' Iris said, keeping the envy out of her voice. 'Where's Nell? I thought you two lived right by each other.'

'I called for her, but she was busy and promised to be along in a minute. Oh, and don't ask her about going to London, poor thing. She's had to give up on the idea and look after her mam and the house instead.'

'But that's not fair!' Iris was outraged. She knew how much Nell had wanted to go to London. She had grown very fond of both girls, but Nell was such a vulnerable young woman, easily hurt. In her unquestioning willingness to help, she was often taken for a fool. Iris had always felt the need to protect her. She could imagine how easy it would have been to persuade the girl that her duty lay in Liverpool, not London.

A waitress came, and Iris ordered a pot of tea for three and three scones. 'Do you have butter?' she enquired.

'I'm sorry, madam, but we only have margarine.'

'Then can we have jam as well, please. It'll disguise the taste,' she said to Maggie when the waitress had gone. 'I can't stand margarine.'

'Even before it was rationed, we only had butter on Sundays,' Maggie told her. She smiled. 'We're not dead posh like you.'

Iris rolled her eyes. 'That was very tactless of me. I'm sorry.'

'It's all right,' Maggie said generously.

'But it really is about time we were able to get butter again. The war's been over for more than seven months, yet rationing is as tight as it's ever been. Same with so many other things. I couldn't buy a lipstick anywhere in town yesterday. Not one of the big shops had any in stock, nor did they have cologne for my husband, apart from in Woolies, where it costs sixpence a bottle and can't be any good. Oh, look, here's Nell now.'

In contrast to her friend, Nell almost crept into the café. Her eyes were downcast when she joined them at the table. 'Hello, Iris,' she whispered.

'Hello, love.' Iris seized her hand and squeezed it. 'How are you?'

'All right.' She raised her eyes and they looked terribly sad.

'I've been thinking, why don't both of you come round one day before Christmas for afternoon tea?' She had already bought them presents: boxes of handkerchiefs embroidered with a flower in the corner – there'd only been three boxes left in Owen Owen's and she'd bought the third for Constance. 'Have you found a job yet, Maggie?'

'No. I thought I'd start looking for work in the new year. It was me dad's idea. He said I deserved a bit of a holiday first.'

'My husband said more or less the same. I'm not going back to being his receptionist until January. My mother-in-law has been doing it in my place and she doesn't mind sticking it out for another week or so. And you, Nell love?' she asked. 'What are you up to?' The girl looked as if she'd died a little since Iris had last seen her.

'I've put off going to London for a while and I'm helping at home instead. In fact, that's where I should be, home, like. I told me dad I wouldn't long. And I've got shopping to do, we're out of bread.' She jumped up and almost ran out of the café.

Iris gasped. 'But she hasn't touched her tea or scone!'

'I'll pop in and see her later,' Maggie promised. 'I'll make sure we come to your house, and she's coming to ours on Christmas Day when we're having a party. Me mam's sister'll be there and some of me dad's friends from work. And our Ryan's bringing his new girlfriend. I've invited Nell. If she doesn't come, I'll go to their house and drag her there.'

It was then that Iris made up her mind that she had to do something about Nell.

Iris couldn't stand Tom's brother, Frank. The two men couldn't have been more different, in either body or brain. Tall and sharply thin, Frank had dark, piercing eyes and an eternally bitter expression on his long face. Iris wouldn't have wanted him for her doctor. After dinner on Christmas Day, he denounced the planned introduction of a National Health Service in the strongest possible terms. The adults remained at the table and the children, Beth and Eric, had gone into the parlour to listen to the wireless and examine their presents, mainly books.

'I shall never join,' Frank insisted forcefully, 'even if it means I'm the only doctor left in England who's not part of it. I intend to go on choosing my own patients, thanks all the same, and treating them in the way *I* consider best without interference from the socialist crowd that make up this useless government. The idea that people will no longer have to pay to see a doctor is an insult to our profession.'

'We'll be paid by the government,' Tom said mildly. He was an ardent admirer of the new scheme and already treated his poorer patients free of charge.

'You'll probably end up without a single patient,' Constance said to her husband. The pair didn't get on and argued relentlessly. 'No one in their right mind is going to pay to see you when they can be treated for nothing by another doctor. They will even be getting their medicine for free, as well as spectacles and bandages and cotton wool and stuff like that.'

Frank spluttered. 'It's disgraceful.'

'What's disgraceful about it?' Adele glared at her elder son. 'I think a National Health Service is a marvellous idea. Poor people can have the most frightful things wrong with them, yet they can't possibly afford to see a doctor. I didn't vote for Mr Attlee, the prime minister, but I shall from now on. He's a wonderful man.'

Frank opened his mouth to splutter again, but Adele banged her spoon on the table. 'No more arguments, if you don't mind, Frank. It's Christmas, and from now on we will only talk about nice things.' She turned to Iris. 'I'm so sorry I barged in on you the other day when you had invited your army friends to tea. They were such lovely girls; one so incredibly pretty, the other with the face of a saint. I was really taken with them.'

Constance frowned. 'You had them to tea, Iris?'

'Yes, what's wrong with that?'

'It looks like the class system is coming to an end.' Constance smiled ruefully. 'It's the war, I suppose. We fought together, went hungry together, did without the same things like coal and cigarettes. In a way, it's made us all equal. Our lot can't very well look down on poor people any more.'

Not far away, in another part of Bootle, Christmas Day was being celebrated in a happier vein, though just as argumentatively.

Paddy O'Neill, Maggie's dad, was a stalwart of the Labour Party, as was her Auntie Kath, an attractive woman in her mid-thirties who had the same black curls as her sister and niece, though her eyes were more blue than violet. Labour had won the 'khaki election' held in July, so-called because it was the troops returning home after the long fight against fascism who were demanding social reform, a country that was fair for all its citizens, not just a favoured few. Labour had promised change in the form of nationalisation of the utilities, the gas and electricity companies, the railways and coal mines, and, of course, the provision of free medical care for everyone. The election had been won with a huge Labour majority.

Maggie's dad thought there was enough in the pipeline to please most of the electorate, whereas her aunt considered Labour ought to nationalise virtually everything that moved, including properties with five or more bedrooms, which would solve the housing shortage at a stroke.

'It's a great idea, Kath,' Paddy said, nodding his head approvingly, 'but the people won't stand for it. This isn't an extreme country. The population prefer things done by halves, not wholes. Unlike the last war, this time men are returning to a land genuinely fit for heroes. They fought to protect their country and it's time they had a share in it.'

'Hear, hear,' Kath said enthusiastically. 'But don't forget it's men *and* women who are returning, including your own daughter.'

'I hadn't forgotten.'

'And what about the monarchy?'

Paddy wanted to laugh. 'What about the monarchy, Kath? Do you want them taken into the countryside and shot, like the Russians did with their royal family?'

'Well, no, but they could just live in an ordinary house like this one.'

This time, Paddy really did laugh. 'There isn't enough room here for the Queen to keep her furs.'

They were standing in the kitchen and he took Kath's arm. 'If we don't go in the parlour soon and join the gang in there, girl, our Sheila'll come looking for us and we'll be in trouble.'

He pushed her out of the room, through the living room and into the parlour, already packed with friends and relatives dancing a polka. He took his sister-in-law in his arms and they began to dance. 'Don't you ever think of anything except politics, Kath?' he asked.

'What else is there?' she said simply, spreading her hands.

'There's clothes and jewellery,' Paddy suggested, 'films and books, there's listening to the wireless, going for walks.'

'I go for walks sometimes on the shore,' Kath said, ignoring most of the suggestions, 'but then all I do is think about politics.'

Paddy thought it was about time she found a feller, got married, had a few kids and thought about something else for a change, though it was more than his life was worth to suggest it.

When it got to eight o'clock, Maggie slipped on her coat, went round to Amber Street and knocked on the Desmonds' front door. Nell's sister Ena opened it. She was smaller than Nell and nothing at all like her.

'Hello, Maggie. Come in, girl, out the cold. The chaps have gone to the pub, our mam's asleep in the living room, and us girls are in the parlour with the kids, who are nearly asleep. We're all a bit merry if the truth be known, apart from our Nellie, who only drinks lemonade.'

'You're in the club again!' Maggie remarked. Ena was about six months pregnant with her third baby, yet had only been married two years. The first must have been well on its way when she promised to love, honour and obey Billy Rafferty on their wedding day.

'Yeah, I'm really looking forward to it.'

The parlour looked as if a battle had just taken place, with bodies sprawled everywhere, large and small. Maggie nearly fell over a baby lying on a pillow half tucked beneath the sideboard.

She was met by a chorus of 'Hello, Maggie' from Nell's other sisters, Gladys and Theresa. From across the room, Nell met her eyes and smiled, and Maggie felt a sense of relief. Clearly Christmas Day hadn't been so bad with her sisters there. Perhaps her loathsome spiv father had spent the day with Rita Hayworth.

'Are you coming to our party?' Maggie asked. 'They were doing the polka when I left.'

Nell nodded and picked her way over the bodies. 'Will someone please put our mam to bed.'

Gladys, who looked totally sozzled, said thickly, 'It's about time she started putting herself to bloody bed. There's nothing wrong with her, you know, Maggie. She's just pretending to be ill to get people's attention, try and make our dad feel guilty, like, but nothing could make him feel guilty, not even if the bobbies raided our cellar and found all the stuff stored there.'

'Shurrup, girl,' Ena snapped. 'Walls have ears, or so it says on that poster.'

Gladys made a show of looking around the room until her neck creaked. 'Well I can't see any bloody ears on these walls.'

'How are you getting on?' Maggie asked as they walked round to Coral Street.

'All right,' Nell assured her. 'I only wish me sisters could come round every day.'

There were quite a few parties going on with sounds of merriment coming from many houses. They sang mainly war songs: 'Run Rabbit Run', 'It's a Long Way to Tipperary', 'We're Going to Hang out the Washing on the Siegfried Line'.

'Was there a Siegfried Line?' Maggie asked Nell, who seemed to know lots of unexpected things.

'It belonged to the Germans and was opposite the French Maginot Line. Neither was any use. The enemy just went round them.'

Maggie wondered what was happening in the silent houses, the ones with dark drawn curtains. Either the people who lived there had gone to someone else's party, or the war wasn't something they wanted to celebrate, over or not. Enough men had been killed in the fighting, enough people lost in the Liverpool Blitz. Some of those people might have lived in these very houses, and the ones left behind were inside mourning the loss of their loved ones, wondering how they would live the rest of their lives without them.

She rested her open hands on the door of a silent house and could almost feel the sorrow seeping out. 'Oh Nell, it's all so sad,' she said softly.

Nell didn't say that the occupants of the house had gone to London to celebrate Christmas with their daughter. But that didn't stop other things from being sad. 'I know it is, Maggie.'

Maggie stepped back and looked at the sky, which was the deepest of blues littered with a million or more stars. 'But that sky is truly beautiful.' She turned to her friend, eyes shining. 'Despite everything, Nell, it really is a wonderful world.'

Chapter 2

A few days into the new year, Maggie went for a job interview. A secretary shorthand typist was required at Briggs & Son, a roofing firm in Seaforth, only a short walk from Bootle. She presented herself in her best red coat, the tippet from Auntie Kath and a Juliet cap knitted by her mother.

The manager, Ignatius Reilly, middle-aged, overweight and suffering from a long-term hangover due to excessive celebrating over Christmas and the new year, felt rejuvenated by the sight of Maggie's broad smile and rosy cheeks. He imagined a perfectly shaped body hidden beneath the red coat. 'How many words a minute shorthand can you do?' he enquired.

'I've never counted,' Maggie confessed, beaming. 'I learned shorthand and typing in the army of me own accord, as it were. I started as a clerk, then worked me way up to shorthand typist. I suppose, in a way, I invented me own shorthand. It's not Pitman or Gregg. Would you like to see me write something down?'

'No, luv, it doesn't matter. When can you start?' To have such a pretty, happy face in his office was better any day than perfect shorthand. And he would try and keep his distance from this one. Too many girls had left giving his roving hands as the reason.

'I could start Monday,' Maggie told him. 'Or tomorrow, if you're desperate.' She felt dead lucky to have found work so easily. What with thousands of troops home again and wanting jobs, replacing the women who'd replaced them in factories when the war had started, there were often dozens of applicants for every vacancy.

'I'm desperate,' Ignatius Reilly said. 'Tomorrow will be fine.'

In January, Iris resumed her position as Tom's receptionist. Until she'd come home, she hadn't realised just how many patients he was treating these days, most of them for free. First thing in the morning, long queues would form outside the house well before the surgery was due to open. Not everyone waiting was on Tom's panel of patients, but even people who didn't have a wireless or read newspapers were aware that an era of free medicine was on the cards, and Dr Grant in Rimrose Road was at the forefront. Tom had always been a popular doctor; now he was working himself into the ground. It was rare that a night went by when he wasn't called out to treat a patient who was sick. He had arranged that his father, who was semi-retired, would shoulder some of the load.

'Some people come with the slightest complaints,' he grumbled when that particular morning's surgery had come to an end, 'like they've cut their finger. All it needs is iodine and a plaster. A chap lost his temper today because I wouldn't take his rotten teeth out. I don't think he'd heard of dentists.'

'Did you tell him where the nearest dentist is?' Iris asked.

'Of course,' Tom said impatiently, regretting it straight away. 'Sorry for being so ratty. I think some of them like the idea of having a doctor at their beck and call. Anyway,' he said reflectively, 'there's all the good things, like prescribing penicillin for someone who has a permanent cold or a wound that just won't heal. People are so grateful; it almost makes me want to cry. And the babies! You don't know how good it feels to send a baby to hospital when you suspect they might be on the verge of getting something really serious, like

24

diphtheria, or even meningitis. I'm saving lives. I don't think I've ever saved lives before.'

'I'm sure you have, Tom.' He was a good doctor who really cared about his patients. 'Shall I make lunch now?' It was time he had a break after such a busy morning.

Iris went into the kitchen and began to spread margarine on six rounds of bread – four for Tom and two for herself; there was still no sign of the butter ration being increased. She opened a tin of Spam, cut the meat into wafer-thin slices, placed half on the bread and smothered Tom's share with brown sauce. The rest she put in the larder for tomorrow. She made a pot of tea, and took that and the sandwiches into the waiting room, where a coal fire burnt. To save fuel, the fire in the upstairs living room wasn't lit until evening.

'Tom!' she called. 'Lunch is ready.'

She sat down with a tired sigh. She'd been on her feet herself for most of the morning, but today, Wednesday, the surgery only opened half a day. The afternoon she had to herself. She kept meaning to suggest to Tom that they change to another day. Wednesday the shops closed at lunchtime, and, tired or not, she would love to have gone into the city centre and done some shopping. Tom spent his free time ensconced in his surgery reading *The Lancet*, leaving her to her own devices.

There'd been a time before the war when she'd had friends, loads of them. One had married an American soldier and gone to live in Minneapolis, another had been posted to London and stayed there. Others had got married and moved away. There were still a few left in Liverpool, but Iris couldn't be bothered looking them up, in particular the ones with children.

She heard Tom cough. He was opening drawers and cup-boards, putting things away, letting his tea get cold. He was incapable of allowing the surgery to look even faintly untidy.

Every surface had to be clear or at least the things neatly arranged before he would leave the room.

Did she really want to continue doing this for the rest of her life? Listen to Tom tidying his office, take the patients' names, show them in and show them out. It was why, six years ago, she'd joined the army, to get away from the tedium of her life, to fill it with other, more interesting things, and hopefully get rid of the ache she felt, the sense of loss over the death of her baby that was just as painful as any illness it was possible to have.

She didn't feel jealous of other women's babies. If she couldn't have Charlie, then what she wanted was another baby of her own. She didn't care if it was a boy or a girl, just a baby, *her* baby. It didn't even have to be Tom's baby. Any man's would do.

In the army, she'd been busy, but it was a different sort of busy to how she was at home. If she wasn't driving senior officers to their destinations, then she was going to dances, watching films, listening to lectures, gossiping with friends, drinking in the sergeants' mess. She supposed she should add 'sleeping around' to the list, because she'd done enough of that during her time in Plymouth. It had been pleasant enough, but throughout the entire procedure she had been obsessed with the thought that this might be the one, the time, the man who would give her another baby.

Lunch over, Tom returned to the surgery and, since it was Wednesday and the waiting room wouldn't be used again that day, Iris went upstairs to light the fire in the sitting room, but discovered she'd forgotten to bring a firelighter with her.

'Damn!' she muttered and ran downstairs to fetch one. She was on her way back again when the doorbell rang. 'Damn!' she said again. She hoped it wasn't a patient insisting on seeing Tom. Some seemed to think he wasn't entitled to any time off at all. But when she opened the door, she found Nell standing nervously outside.

'You invited me and Maggie for afternoon tea,' Nell explained when Iris had stared at her without comprehension for a rudely long time.

'Oh, I'm sorry, Nell. Come inside, please. I was miles and miles away just then. I'd forgotten all about asking you – but I would have remembered any minute,' she assured the girl. It was when she'd had them both to tea at Christmas that she'd suggested they come again in four weeks. 'Where's Maggie?'

'She's started work. She's got this job in Seaforth with a roofing company. She doesn't finish until half past five. Look, I'll go away again, shall I?' She turned on her heel and was halfway down the path before Iris could grab her.

'Don't you dare leave, Nell Desmond. I'm simply longing for company and you are the perfect companion. We'll sit in the kitchen – the stove's lit and it's lovely and warm out there – and have an interesting natter.'

Nell blushed. 'Are you sure? You're not just being nice?'

'I'm positive, Nell. Do come in, please.'

'This is a lovely big kitchen,' Nell remarked when they went in. 'Our kitchen at home would fit in here about four times. We've got no room for a table.'

What Iris's kitchen needed was a family, one to sit around the long wooden table for their meals. Iris imagined herself making rounds and rounds of toast and imaginary children passing jars of home-made jam and marmalade to each other. And there would be a whole brick of best butter in a special dish.

'One of these days you'll have a family, won't you?' Nell said in that comfortable, complacent tone she used when making such remarks.

'Hopefully.' Iris did her best to smile. In fact, she had never liked any part of the house. The rooms were too big, the ceilings too high, the decoration much too gloomy. Perhaps she could immerse herself in having the main rooms wallpapered in bright colours, buy new curtains, some attractive rugs. The idea appealed, and she hoped she wouldn't have gone off it by tonight, when she would discuss it with Tom. It would, at least, give her something absorbing to think about for a while. Her enthusiasm quickly paled when she remembered there was a shortage of virtually everything in the shops, including wallpaper, curtains and rugs.

'How are you getting on?' she asked Nell, who looked terribly unhappy, as if some of the blood had been drained out of her. The girl had always been quiet, never with much to say, but had always seemed contented with her lot.

'Not so bad,' she said listlessly. 'What about you?'

'I'm not getting on so bad either.' Iris laughed, and for some reason, so did Nell. Perhaps it was their shared misery that made them reminisce about the army, the good times they'd had, the laughs, the tears, the joy towards the end when they'd listened to the news and Britain and her allies had just won an important battle. The kitchen disappeared; they were no longer in Bootle, but in the camp in Plymouth where they'd felt so much more alive.

'Those were the days,' Nell said with a sigh.

'For goodness' sake, Nell, you shouldn't be talking like that, not at your age. What are you – twenty-one?'

'Well, you're not much older.' The girl's eyes grew dark and her face emptied of expression. 'Does it ever worry you,' she said quietly, 'I mean, I know we're only young, but that we've already lived the best years of our lives and from now on we'll never be that happy again?'

It was going on for half past five. Maggie was typing so fast she half expected the typewriter to puff steam. She wanted to finish the rather complicated quotation for roofing work before she left work for the night.

Ignatius Reilly prowled around the office, glancing surreptitiously at his newly acquired secretary. She was alluring even from the back. Her black curls shook from the effort she was putting into the typing, her white neck twisted slightly as she glanced from the paper in the typewriter to the notebook on the desk full of overlarge scribbles that purported to be shorthand though she seemed able to read it. He visualised her full bosom shaking with the neck movements. Unable to resist, he crept up behind her and embraced the soft breasts in his big fat hands.

'Ouch!' he screeched seconds later, clutching his stomach, into which Maggie had shoved a very sharp elbow. 'That really hurt.'

'It was meant to hurt,' Maggie said severely. 'You're disgusting, that's what. If you dare do that again, next time it'll hurt even more. If you're not careful, you'll end up with me paperknife stuck in your gut. And it wouldn't be counted as murder, but self-defence.'

'You've got no right to speak to me like that,' Ignatius grumbled.

'You've got even less right to touch *me* like that.'

'I could sack you any minute.'

'And I could leave even quicker,' Maggie retorted. 'This very minute, in fact.' She looked even more desirable when she was angry. 'The thing is, I could get another job in a jiffy, but you, you're not likely to find a secretary in a million years who'll willingly let you maul her. In fact, if you carry on the way you do, I'll tell me dad, and him and me brother will come and batter you to within an inch of your miserable life.'

Little did Maggie know that Iggy was finding these threats terrifically exciting. She pulled the quotation out of the typewriter with a flourish and laid it on his desk, then collected her hat and coat.

'Good night,' she cried cheerily.

★

'He's an octopus,' she told Nell on Saturday night. 'It's as if he's got eight hands that come at you from different directions when you least expect it.'

'I don't know why you stay there, Mag.' Nell was horrified. 'Me, I'd've left like a shot.'

'He's all right, I suppose,' Maggie conceded. 'He pays good money and never moans when I'm late. What's more, I give as good as I get. One of these days I'll knock him out. If I did, I suppose I *would* have to leave.' She smiled at the thought. 'Come on, let's have a rest before the next dance starts. It's time for a tango, and you know I'm hopeless at tangos. '

They were in the Grafton ballroom, where they'd been every Saturday since coming home – Fridays they went to the pictures. Tonight, Phil Jones and the Jonesmen, the resident orchestra, were playing. Maggie was just as good at dancing tangos as she was at every other dance. It was just an excuse to sit upstairs with Nell, who wasn't asked to dance all that often because she was too tall for most men and looked shy and wasn't remotely glamorous.

'I'm dying for a lemonade,' Maggie said when they reached the balcony. 'Sit down a mo, Nell, while I fetch them.'

Nell sat on a maroon velvet settee. She didn't mind not being asked to dance, as she loved the Grafton, with its smoky atmosphere, gold lights and ever-moving bodies. She admired the ingenuity of some of the women's outfits, so obviously made out of old curtains and decorated with tassels and odd bits of ribbon or net. One girl's dress was clearly blackout material covered with a white lace tablecloth. Most of the clothes, though, were quite ordinary, like Nell's own drab green frock, which was made out of the minimum amount of material and had a utility label in the back.

Oh, but she loved the music, particularly the tunes that had been played in the camp, where she'd been asked up for every dance like all the other girls in uniform. 'I'll Be Seeing You', 'Yours Till the Stars Lose Their Glory', 'There's a Boy

Coming Home on Leave' – and her favourite song of all, 'Goodnight, Sweetheart'. She began to sing it quietly to herself.

Maggie came back with the drinks. 'I love that song,' she said. 'The last time we sang it, we were halfway through when you collapsed in a heap on the floor. It was at that victory party in the sergeants' mess.'

Nell looked shamefaced. 'Someone gave me a glass of dandelion and burdock and it had rum in it. It was really hot there and I drank the lot. You know alcohol doesn't agree with me.' She hadn't found out until she'd joined the army, as she normally never allowed alcohol to pass her lips. She'd had to leave the dance early and go to bed, where she'd slept like a log for hours and woken up as sick as a dog.

'There's no need to be embarrassed about it, Nell. It wasn't your fault.'

'Hello, girls.' A man had stopped in front of them and was regarding them with interest. At least he was regarding Maggie with interest, having given Nell merely a brief glance. Maggie looked desperately pretty in her blue taffeta dress, which had been made years ago when she was a bridesmaid at someone's wedding. It had since been shortened.

'Hello.' Nell could tell from the tone of Maggie's voice that she was interested. Her admirer was quite tall, with a thin, handsome face and dark green eyes. His brown wavy hair could have done with trimming and his grey suit badly needed a good press. Despite his shabby appearance, Nell couldn't help but admire his elegant stance; one knee slightly bent, one hand in his pocket, a cigarette in the other. You'd think he was a lord or something. He was quite old, about twenty-seven or twenty-eight.

He came forward and shook hands with Maggie. 'Chris Conway,' he said.

'Margaret O'Neill, but most people call me Maggie.'

'How do you do, Maggie?' He was still holding her hand.

Without waiting for an answer, he released her, turned and offered his hand to Nell. 'And you are?'

'Nell Desmond,' Nell stammered. His hand was strong and lean. She felt herself blush.

Without bothering to ask if it was all right, Chris Conway fetched a chair and placed it in front of them. He stubbed out his cigarette and sat down, crossing his legs.

'And what do you girls do?' he enquired. He was well-spoken, but not posh.

Maggie told him she worked for a roofing firm as a secretary, but didn't mention Iggy Reilly's disgraceful behaviour. Nell was wondering how to describe her own occupation, but her friend did it for her. 'Nell looks after her invalid mother, but she was a cook in the army, the best there was.'

'A cook!' Chris turned his green eyes on Nell. 'In the army!' She was aware of the intensity of his gaze, the glow of his eyes, and felt as if she was being hypnotised, brought under his spell. 'I've never met a cook before. How do you do, Nell?'

Despite knowing for certain he was only there because of Maggie, Nell could tell he was going out of his way not to make her feel like a gooseberry. She couldn't help but warm to him.

'I'm very well, thank you. What did you do in the war?' It was the question everyone asked of each other these days when they first met. The band had started to play 'You and the Night and the Music'.

'I was a second lieutenant in the Royal Air Force.' He paused to light another cigarette. 'I've not long been demobbed. My plane was shot down during one of the last raids over Berlin and I suffered internal injuries.' He slapped his stomach. 'Nearly better now. I'm so sorry, I should have offered you both cigarettes.' He removed the silver case from his inside pocket and snapped it open.

'I don't smoke,' Maggie said. 'Neither of us do.'

'You are two extremely sensible young ladies. Maggie, would you like to dance?' He smiled at Nell. 'Don't go away.'

'I won't.' Nell felt as though she was glued to the settee. Leaning forward slightly, she watched over the balcony until Maggie and Chris came into view. They were only dancing one step to everyone else's two and their bodies seemed to fit quite snugly together, as if they'd been made for each other.

She sighed wistfully, remembering the proposal of marriage she'd had in the army. There'd never been the opportunity to dance like that with Jim Harvey, who she'd met at the pictures in Plymouth – she'd gone by herself because there'd been an emergency in Maggie's office and she'd had to stay late. Afterwards, she and Jim had gone for a walk. In those dangerous days, it had been possible for people to feel they'd known each other all their lives when they'd only met a few hours before.

'Will you marry me when this is over, Nell?' Jim had asked. Nell had promised that she would, though she knew the chances of him taking her up on it were most unlikely. Even if he returned all in one piece, he would almost certainly have forgotten about it by then, perhaps wouldn't even remember her name.

Maggie and Chris were out of sight. They appeared again dancing in exactly the same way as before. Nell drank some of her lemonade. It was warm and had lost its sparkle. She contemplated hiding in the ladies' for the rest of the evening, or going home by herself claiming to have a headache. She felt certain that Chris would invite her up for the next dance, and she would sooner be a gooseberry any day than dance with a man who'd only asked out of a sense of duty.

She'd hardly been home five minutes when someone tapped on the front door. It could only be Maggie, who she'd left with Chris Conway on the back seat of a taxi barely five minutes ago. She let her friend in.

'He's a real gentleman,' Maggie whispered. 'He only kissed me the once. I thought he'd expect a long snog – not that I would've let him, mind.' She sat in the easy chair in which Mrs Desmond spent most of her life. 'He just told me the truth about himself.'

'The truth! Does that mean that what he told us before was a lie?'

'Yes.' Maggie made a face. 'He was in the RAF, but not as an officer. He was an aircraft engineer and only had a single stripe. He wasn't injured, either.'

Nell was puzzled. 'But why did he come out with all that other stuff before?'

'He wanted to impress me. It's what he tells all the girls, but with me he said it was different.'

'Different in what way?'

Maggie looked at her, her remarkably coloured eyes wide with wonderment. 'Because he wants to marry me one day. "I don't want us getting off on the wrong foot," he said.'

'But there's nothing wrong with being an aircraft engineer.' Nell was annoyed. 'I didn't think any better of him when I thought he was an officer than I do now.' In fact, he'd gone down in her estimation.

'That's because you are such an honest person, Nell. I've never known you tell a lie.'

Nell contemplated the last statement. It was flattering, but made her sound like a prim old maid. 'Are you going to marry him?' she asked gruffly.

'I don't know.' Maggie looked dazed, as if she wasn't sure if she was dreaming or not. 'Anyroad, he's taking me to the pictures on Wednesday night. 'We're going to the Forum to see *Buffalo Bill* with Joel McCrea.'

'What sort of job does he have?'

'I don't know.' She shrugged. 'I didn't think to ask.'

'Well, it must pay well if he can afford a taxi all the way from the Grafton to Bootle.'

'Maybe.' Maggie leapt to her feet. 'I'd better be getting home. Look, don't tell anyone about Chris, will you, Nell? I'm not going to tell me mam or anything, not yet at least.'

'All right,' Nell said reluctantly. 'But can I tell Iris?'

'Yes, it's all right to tell Iris. Perhaps we could meet in Jenny's Café one Saturday for a chat.'

After Maggie had gone, Nell went into the kitchen to find the sink piled high with dishes and dirty clothes thrown on the floor. She ran the water, which was still warm enough for the dishes. When she'd finished, she filled the kettle and made tea. There was no sugar left, but she'd stopped taking it in the army. The dirty clothes she'd put in the wash house in the yard when she went to the lavatory before going to bed.

She shivered. It was freezing in the kitchen, where there was no heat at all except when the gas was lit. It was like one of those buildings made out of snow that Eskimos lived in. She wondered how they were kept warm. They couldn't light fires, surely.

She took the tea into the living room, where a few embers in the fire were still red. In the street, two men walked past arguing violently. 'I'll bloody kill you,' one of them shouted. People could be heard singing outside the Queen's Arms in Pearl Street. 'Bless 'em all,' they bellowed. 'Bless 'em all.'

Monday, she thought gloomily, she'd have the washing to do, stacks of it. Mam, who loathed any sort of physical activity, was inclined to leave her visits to the lavatory until the last minute – or well after the last minute – and the washing usually included several pairs of knee-length bloomers that really stank. Dad wouldn't dream of giving his dirty clothes to Rita Hayworth to launder, so there'd be his to wash too. Kenny didn't leave much, but the moleskin trousers he wore for clearing up bomb sites were difficult to get clean, and it was impossible to get the heavy material through the mangle.

It was so different to what she'd been planning for herself

35

during her last months in the army. Nell closed her eyes and indulged in the delightful daydream that kept her mind occupied during the long, tedious days that made up her present life. She was living alone in London in a big room overlooking a tree-lined street. The room was on the first floor and she was able to see inside the top deck of the trams and buses that went past. Occasionally people would wave and she would wave back. Weekends, a Salvation Army band played on the corner. The Catholic church was only a few minutes' walk away, so she could go to Benediction as well as Mass on Sundays.

In her imagination, the room always remained the same, but her job would change. Sometimes she worked behind the counter of a posh shop – the scent counter, for instance, or the department that sold handbags. Or she might have a job in a cake shop – a confectioner's, it was called, or a bakery. Or a nice little tea shop like Jenny's on Stanley Road.

She was designing her uniform in her head, when the backyard door opened and someone came in. It could only be their Kenny. She heard him put his bike in the wash house.

'Would you like some tea?' she asked when he appeared. She was fonder of Kenny than she was of any other member of her family. He was a slight, delicate lad with butter-blond hair and long dark eyelashes, who'd shot up over the last year or so until he was at least six feet tall. For a boy, he was undeniably pretty, prettier than all his sisters. It must have been the reason why, when he was only a little lad, their father had needed only the slightest of excuses to beat the living daylights out of him, ashamed perhaps of his pretty son, wanting to make a man of him.

'I'd love some tea, Nelly,' he said now.

'Don't call me Nelly; it's Nell,' she remonstrated. She lit the gas underneath the kettle. It started boiling straight away.

'You always used to be Nelly,' he argued.

'Not any more.' Nell was much nicer. Nelly made her feel old. 'What's your new bike like to ride?' she asked. Dad had come up with a Raleigh racing bike he'd probably taken in payment for something like a wireless or an electric fire that was worth far less. Very little of Dad's way of making a living was on the right side of legal. There was always the chance that the bike had initially been stolen.

'It's the gear, sis, but I'm terrified of it being robbed. Me dad's threatened me with death by a thousand cuts if I lose it. I think I might stop using it. It's not worth the worry.'

Maggie's mam and dad rarely went to bed before midnight. When she reached home, the wireless was on, Dad was writing letters at the table and Mam was knitting a cardigan for the new baby. Tinker was prowling the room looking for something to do.

'Can't you ever sit down normally?' her mother asked when Maggie threw herself into a chair. 'You fling yourself about like a football.'

Maggie ignored the comment. 'Is our Ryan in the parlour with Beattie Doyle?' she enquired. Dad normally used the parlour as an office. He was secretary or chairman of several organisations such as the Labour Party, the Workers' Educational Authority and the Fabians, which meant having to write loads of letters. That he was writing them in this room meant the parlour was being used for another purpose.

'Ryan's in the parlour,' her mother replied, 'but Beattie's been given her marching orders. He's with Rosie Hesketh. She only lives in Amber Street, opposite the Desmonds.'

'I liked Beattie, she had lovely nails.' Rosie Hesketh had been in the same class as Maggie in school, and was the most argumentative person she'd ever known. On impulse, Maggie seized her mother's scissors and began to cut bits off her hair, while her mother watched, frowning.

'If you cut that curl off, you're going to have a gap in your forehead,' she said. 'Put them scissors down and tell me about tonight. Did you have a nice time?'

'It was the gear, Mam.'

'Did you meet anyone?'

'No.'

'How about Nell? Did she have a nice time?'

'It was the gear for Nell too, but she didn't meet anyone either.'

'It sounds to me as if it was nothing but a waste of time,' her father grunted, lifting his head.

'How can it be a waste of time, Dad, if it was the gear?' She and her father stared at each other, trying not to blink, until they both started laughing. Maggie said, 'Don't forget I can type those letters for you if you want. I can do them in me dinner hour when Iggy goes to the pub. He usually stays two hours at least.' He often returned as drunk as a lord, but she hadn't told Mam and Dad that. Her mother already disapproved of Iggy without having so much as set eyes on him.

'It doesn't seem proper,' she said now, 'your employer allowing you to call him by his first name. You should address him as Mr Reilly, or sir.'

'Sir!' Maggie snorted. 'He'd laugh his head off if I called him that.'

'That seems a very strange attitude for an employer to take.'

Maggie went to bed. Tinker came with her and fell asleep on her feet. She lay there, listening to Mam and Dad talking downstairs and her little sister Bridie breathing softly in her bed on the other side of the room. After a while, she heard Rosie Hesketh in the hall saying good night. Ryan said in a loud voice, 'See you in five minutes,' and the front door closed. Five minutes later it opened again and Ryan came back in. Not long afterwards, he went to bed. He slept in the next room and made a terrible noise as he got undressed. The bed creaked violently when he got in, as if he'd dropped on it from a great height. Then there was silence, though she could still hear the murmur of her parents' voices downstairs, and Tinker's loud purring.

Feeling content that her family were all safe and sound under the same roof, she prayed for everyone she knew, snuggled beneath the clothes and thought about Chris Conway.

He both disturbed and fascinated her, and she didn't know what to make of him. What was his background? She hadn't thought to ask any of the numerous questions she wished she could ask now. She must try to memorise them so she could ask on Wednesday.

She fell asleep with the memory of them dancing and his arm in the small of her back; their cheeks pressed together and his breath on her ear. She had a feeling that he'd actually kissed her ear.

Am I in love? she asked herself, but didn't get an answer.

'Maggie met this dead funny chap at the Grafton on Saturday,' Nell told Iris on Wednesday. She'd got into the habit of calling early on Wednesday afternoon, when she and Iris would have a pot of tea and a sarnie together. She told her mother, who didn't like being left alone, that she was going to church. To save it from being a lie, she always called in at St James's on the way and lit a candle.

'What's his name?' Iris asked.

'Chris Conway.'

'And what's funny about him?'

'Well, it's funny peculiar, not funny ha ha. He told us he'd been an officer in the RAF, then later on, after he'd brought us home, he told Maggie that was a lie and he'd been an aircraft engineer. The reason he told her the truth was because he wants to marry her.'

'Good heavens!' Iris put the teacup in the saucer with a crash. 'And is Maggie going to marry him?'

'I think she's a bit gobsmacked, if the truth be known. She's seeing him tonight and he's taking her to see *Buffalo Bill* at the Forum in town. I'll let you know next week what happens. Oh, and Maggie said it was all right to tell you, so I'm not spreading gossip, like.'

'That's good. I'd love to know how she gets on.'

There was a real Red Indian actor in *Buffalo Bill* called Chief Thundercloud, as well as Maureen O'Hara, who Maeve McSharry from Amethyst Street swore had lived next door to her when she was a child in Ireland.

'I always knew she was going to be a famous film star,' Maeve claimed, though not a single soul believed her.

After the film, Chris took Maggie to the Lyons in Lime Street for a cake and a cup of tea and proceeded to tell her his life story. He was every bit as handsome as she remembered, perhaps even more so this week than last. There was something terribly romantic about his green eyes and slightly-too-long hair. He could easily have been a poet. The knot on his tie was askew, only adding to his rakish charm.

His parents had been in show business, he told her. They were dancers and called themselves Antonia and Antonio. 'There are loads of stage pictures of them at home. They danced in theatres all over the country, from the very top ones to the very bottom. They never had a proper home, so when my father dropped dead on the stage of the Rotunda Theatre in Liverpool, my mother found a flat and stayed here.'

'Whereabouts in Liverpool is the flat?' Maggie asked, wishing she could feel more certain that she believed him.

'Everton Valley. Nowadays she makes clothes for dancers. You should see some of the dresses she turns out.'

'I'd really like to see them,' Maggie said.

'Then you shall,' he said grandly. 'I'll ask her to invite you to tea.'

'And what do you do?' she asked.

He sold a lotion called Kure from door to door, he told her, in such a dramatic, impressive way that it made him seem as if he was on his way to curing the entire world of every known disease, internal and external, starting with Liverpool. 'It only costs one and ninepence a bottle.'

He insisted on accompanying her back to Bootle on the tram. Outside the front door of her house, he kissed her on the cheek and invited her to the Grafton on Saturday.

'Only if Nell can come too,' Maggie said. 'Saturday, we always go dancing together.' She couldn't possibly desert Nell.

'I would love to see Nell again,' he assured her, with the utmost sincerity.

Chapter 3

'I think she's going to marry him,' Nell said.

Iris gasped. 'Really! Has she said anything to that effect?' Sometimes she felt as if she and Nell were like leeches, using Maggie's fascinating life to provide excitement to their own dull ones. Unlike them, Maggie had put army life behind her and become absorbed in the world as it was now.

'Her actual words were,' Nell continued breathlessly, ' "We're going to get married one day *soon*." They're waiting until Chris gets a better job and they've got somewhere to live.'

'Well, both the job and the house could take a while.' Male unemployment was increasing as more and more men were demobbed and returned to civilian life. Not only that, due to the air raids having destroyed so much property, there was a desperate shortage of houses. 'Once we have the National Health Service, Chris isn't likely to sell any more of that dubious medicine,' Iris went on.

Iris hadn't met Chris, but she had a picture of him in her mind; rather bohemian, with laughing eyes and a daring expression. Sometimes she imagined him wearing a short black cape and a wavy hat, not exactly the uniform of a door-to-door salesman.

'Anyway,' Nell continued, 'they're considering getting engaged at Easter.'

'That's only a few weeks off,' Iris mused. 'What sort of ring does she fancy?'

'A diamond solitaire. Apparently, Chris's mother said she can have hers.'

Iris examined her own diamond solitaire engagement ring. The day Tom had bought it had been tremendously exciting. She recalled going to lunch at Frederick & Hughes afterwards and waving her hands all over the place in the hope that people would notice the way it sparkled. These days, she often forgot to put it on. 'Oh, Nell, there's something I must tell you: Tom has agreed to make Thursday the day he has his afternoon off, so you and I can go into town to the pictures or the theatre and afterwards have afternoon tea.'

Instead of looking pleased, Nell's pleasant, good-natured face fell. 'That's nice,' she mumbled, though it was obvious she didn't mean it.

'What's wrong?' Iris asked gently.

'Well, I haven't got any money, have I? I mean, not enough for cinemas or theatres or meals in restaurants. Me dad only gives us half a crown a week.'

'Half a crown! But that's disgraceful. It'd cost him at least fifteen shillings to get a woman in to do what you do.' Iris had conjured up a picture of Nell's father in her head too. He looked very much like Charles Laughton in *The Hunchback of Notre Dame*. In other words, as ugly as sin. She remembered at Christmas having vowed to do something about Nell. Now seemed to be the time.

She discussed her idea with Tom that night. He was the most easy-going of men. As long as it didn't interfere with his duties as a doctor, he was inclined to agree to anything Iris suggested, leaving her to wonder why she didn't love him considerably more.

'It sounds as if it's something that will be of benefit to both you and Nell,' he said when she told him what she had in mind. He had met Nell and liked her very much. 'Go ahead, by all means,' he finished with an approving nod.

'I'll have a word with her when she comes next week.'

'What we would like,' she said to Nell the following Thursday, when they were both seated at the table in the kitchen over a pot of tea, 'is for you to come and make our evening meal for us five afternoons a week, and sometimes on Sundays when we have Tom's relatives to lunch or dinner. You'd only have to be here at the most two hours a day. The pay would be ten shillings, and extra if you came at the weekend.' Ten shillings meant little to her and Tom, but was a small fortune to someone like Nell.

To her dismay, Nell frowned. 'You're asking because last week I said me dad only gave us half a crown,' she said crossly. 'That's charity, that is. I don't want charity off nobody, thanks all the same.' She jumped to her feet, knocking over the chair and making a terrible clatter. 'I think it'd be best if I never came again.'

Iris wanted the floor to swallow her up. 'If you didn't come again, I don't know what I'd do, Nell. You are the person who keeps me sane. I can talk about things with you that I can't with anyone else, certainly not Tom. I can't discuss with him the lovely time we had in the camp at Plymouth. And I *do* want a cook, honestly I do. I'm hopeless with food; I really hate cooking.' She burst into tears and buried her face in her arms.

'Oh dear, Iris. I'm sorry. Of course I'll cook for you, but you don't have to pay me.'

'To have making dinner taken out of my hands is worth a fortune to me,' Iris said passionately. 'But I don't want you to come if I can't pay you.'

Nell shrugged helplessly. 'Oh, all right, I'll do it. But I'll have to ask me dad first. Y'see, I'm not supposed to leave me mam for all that long.'

Maggie didn't know whether to laugh or cry when Betty Conway showed her the engagement ring. Of course, she did neither, just took it politely and thanked her extravagantly.

'It's beautiful,' she said in an awed voice, 'absolutely beautiful.' It was also incredibly tiny, little more than a pinprick in the narrowest of gold bands. Thank goodness she hadn't mentioned the ring to her family. She'd feel too embarrassed to let anyone see it.

'Try it on,' Betty urged.

Maggie did so, hoping it would be much too big or too small and she could refuse it, but it fitted perfectly. 'I can't thank you enough,' she said, in the same awed voice.

'It looks magnificent, darling,' Betty said huskily. This must be one of her Marlene Dietrich days. She also had Greta Garbo and Katharine Hepburn days. Once Maggie married Chris, she would have the most interesting mother-in-law in Liverpool, except Betty was moving back to London and bequeathing Maggie not only her ring, but her flat and her handsome son.

Since her husband, Antonio, had died on stage in Liverpool and her own dancing days had come to an end, Betty had lived on the top floor of a four-storey house in Everton Valley. From the window, the tops of ships could be seen on the distant river. The main room had a sloping ceiling and was at least thirty feet square, while the two bedrooms, the rough-and-ready bathroom and the kitchen were exceptionally small.

About a quarter of the main room was taken up by a large table heaped with glorious dresses. Because there was a shortage of material in the shops, along with everything else, Betty was turning old dresses into beautiful new ones by taking yards of net off one to put on another, switching frills and bows, adding sequins here and fancy buttons there, and coming up with a differently styled garment altogether.

According to Chris, she had become as well-known and

successful in the dancing world as a dressmaker as she had been as a dancer.

There were posters of Antonia and Antonio on the walls, including an overlarge one, a painting showing a magnificent couple dancing the flamenco, the woman wearing brilliant scarlet and the man with a black mask over his eyes just like Tyrone Power in *The Mark of Zorro*. Whilst this wasn't an exact likeness of the pair, it had been on show outside the theatre the only time they'd been top of the bill.

'It was in a place called Stoke Newington,' Betty had told her.

Betty was about fifty and still magnificent. Today she wore a long navy silk gown patterned with orange poppies, an orange sash around her narrow waist, bangles on both wrists, and glittering earrings that skimmed her shoulders. Her brown hair, liberally streaked with grey, was piled untidily on top of her head.

There were footsteps on the stairs. 'Ah, here is Chris now,' she said.

Maggie had been invited to tea, and Chris had been sent to buy fish and chips. There were bottles of wine and vinegar on the table – a different table to the one with the costumes on – along with three highly ornamental glasses, three beautifully embroidered napkins and an assortment of fancy cutlery, none of which matched.

Chris entered the room and Maggie could have sworn that her heart stopped beating. She was so much in love that she could hardly concentrate on anything else, not her family, not her work, not her friends. He smiled right at her and her heart stopped again. One of these days she was sure she'd have a heart attack, or her heart would stop beating altogether.

'I like him,' Maggie had heard her mother say after the first time she'd brought Chris to the house. She'd been sitting on the stairs quite shamelessly eavesdropping on her parents

46

discussing her new boyfriend. 'He's a bit out of the ordinary, just right for our Maggie.'

Dad had begged to differ. 'He's a funny sort of bugger. Hasn't got a trade. I can't figure out a man without a trade.' Paddy O'Neill was a centre lathe turner and proud of it.

'He's interesting,' Mam claimed. 'We talked for ages about Fred Astaire and Ginger Rogers. He's seen every one of their pictures.'

'So have a lot of people. That's nothing to boast about,' her father growled. 'It might be a good idea if he found something more useful to do with his time, like earn a proper wage instead of selling that vile mixture that's probably ruining the health of the nation.'

'I had a letter today from my friend Susan in London,' Betty said now, waving a sheet of mauve notepaper. 'She's really looking forward to us living together in Crouch End. She's been a theatrical agent for years, but started off as a dancer like me and Antonio.' She always referred to her husband by his stage name rather than his real one, which was Gordon.

Betty had wanted to move away for a long time, but Chris was attached to Liverpool and not at all keen on London. She didn't like the idea of leaving him behind, but now he had met Maggie and would have a wife for company when she went.

Maggie was thrilled. 'I'd love to live here. It's so *bohemian*. Oh, but I'll really miss you, Betty,' she added fulsomely.

Later, after Betty had gone to the pub on the corner with her friend Eunice, Maggie and Chris lay together in the room where he slept, which was just about big enough for a single bed and a chest of drawers.

'I love you,' he whispered.

'And I love you. I love you so much it hurts.' She could actually feel an ache in the bothersome heart that kept switching itself on and off these days.

He stroked her neck, then her breasts through the thin

material of her blouse. She didn't protest when he pulled the blouse out of her skirt and slid his hand beneath it and her bra until he was touching her naked flesh. Everything inside seemed to explode in great spasms of pleasure, but when he reached under her skirt and his hand touched the skin at the top of her stockings, she made him stop, though it took an enormous amount of determination.

'No,' she said firmly, if a trifle shakily. 'No, not yet. Not until we're married.' She struggled to a sitting position and pushed his hands away.

He groaned. 'Lord knows when that'll happen.'

'Now we've got somewhere to live, all you have to do is get a better job – a proper one.'

His face lit up. 'I met a chap today who said that a new picture house is opening in Walton Vale. Actually, it's an old one being done up and reopening, but showing nothing but foreign pictures. It'll be called I Continental. As soon as I find out who's running it, I'll apply for the job of manager, though assistant manager would do for the time being.'

'Oh, Chris! That'd be the gear.' She got up and went into the big room, away from the dangerously enticing bed. Having spent three years of her life in an army camp and emerged still a virgin, she wanted to stay that way until she and Chris were married.

She glanced at the glowing fire, the table full of gorgeous materials, the posters on the wall, and the gas lamp with its multicoloured glass shade that cast a rainbow of colours over everything. It was like a stage set for the most wonderful play ever written, a play that would never end. And she and Chris would be the stars.

She hadn't imagined it was possible to be so monumentally happy.

The man wore a grey worsted overcoat with an astrakhan collar, a grey trilby hat and a navy suit, and carried a walking stick with an ivory handle. The effect was spoilt rather by his brown boots. He was tall, with a red face, a vast moustache and a straight, imperious stature, and Iris could tell he was the sort of man who didn't suffer fools gladly.

'Yes?' she enquired when she opened the door. He didn't have the apprehensive expression of a patient. If it hadn't been for the boots, she would have thought him a salesman.

He lifted his hat. 'Mrs Grant?'

'That's me, yes.'

'I'm Alfred Desmond. I've come about our Nellie, me daughter.'

It took Iris a moment to realise he meant Nell. He didn't look anything like she'd expected. She had thought Nell's family were poor, but this man looked relatively prosperous. Nell didn't mention him often, but when she did, it wasn't in exactly admiring tones, which was why she'd built up a picture in her mind of him looking very different.

'You'd better come in,' she said tersely. It was early afternoon and surgery was due to begin soon. In fact, a woman carrying a baby was walking through the gate. Iris took Alfred Desmond into the kitchen, returning briefly to show the woman into the waiting room. She left the front door on the latch so that from then on people could let themselves in.

'What can I do for you?' she asked when she went back into the kitchen. He had undone his coat and was nursing his hat and stick on his knee.

'About this job you've offered our Nellie, I'd like to know more about it.' He actually sounded suspicious, as if Iris intended selling his daughter on the white slave market.

'It's just preparing dinner for my husband and myself. I know what a good cook Nell is from the army. As I'm hopeless at cooking, I thought I'd ask Nell to do it for us.' Iris considered it, but decided not to offer him a cup of tea. There was something about the man that she didn't like.

49

'Do you consider ten shillings sufficient recompense for that?'

He's after more money! She imagined how upset Nell would be if she knew. 'Nell would only be here for at the most two hours a day for five days,' she pointed out. 'Ten shillings works out at a shilling an hour. That seems a fair wage to me, considerably fairer than the money she gets from you.'

He didn't look annoyed, just paused and considered the matter. 'I suppose you're right. Her poor mam'll be left by herself while Nellie's out, and we'll all have to wait for our own dinner, but we'll just have to put up with it.'

'Nell's entitled to a life of her own.'

He got rather ponderously to his feet. Iris had a strong feeling that he hadn't really come about the money, but to inspect her and have a look inside the house. 'I'll call round Friday dinner time for our Nell's wages.'

'You'll do no such thing!' Iris slammed her hand on the table and he jumped. 'Nell will have earned it and I shall give it to her and no one else.'

He looked mildly surprised, but Iris reckoned he'd only said it to irritate her. 'But I'm her da.'

'True, but you won't be making me and my husband's dinner; Nell will, and she's the one who'll be getting paid.'

He had the nerve to smile, even if it was only a flicker, as if he admired Iris for standing her ground. 'Is there anything you need?' he enquired.

'Need?'

'I've got quite a collection of stuff at home,' he said boastfully. 'Max Factor make-up, sugar, a china dinner set decorated with rosebuds, umbrellas, a selection of size six leather court shoes in a nice tan colour – brand new, of course – a coffee table. Oh, and I managed to get me hands on a whole dozen bottles of scent the other day, *Shalimar*. I understand it's dead expensive, but I'm only charging ten bob a bottle.' He winked. 'Anything you fancy – I could have it back here within the hour.'

Iris shuddered with desire. She would have given her eye teeth for a bottle of *Shalimar* and a Max Factor lipstick, any shade would do. As for the dinner set . . . ! 'No thank you,' she said stiffly. He was a spiv, a horrible, revolting spiv selling stuff on the black market. She'd known people who were of the view that spivs should have been strung from the lamp posts when the war ended, just like Mussolini. She wondered if she would have had the willpower to turn down a pound of butter!

She showed him out. He lifted his hat and strode down the little drive. Once on the pavement, he lifted his hat again and winked. Iris shuddered for the second time. She had a horrible feeling that he rather liked her.

Iris's mother-in-law telephoned on Tuesday morning sounding desperate. 'Darling, can we possibly come to dinner on Saturday night?'

'Of course, Adele. Tom and I aren't doing anything.' They *never* did anything. She had been out of the army for three months, and all they had done was have his parents and his brother and his wife to dinner – and gone to dinner at their houses. She wondered if she could ask Adele the reason for her desperation without sounding rude, when her mother-in-law explained.

'It's just that odious friend of mine from across the road, Beatrice, has invited us to dinner at their house,' she said in an accusing voice, as if Beatrice had committed some sort of crime. 'Apparently her brother, who we have met before, is staying, and he is the most revolting man in the world, with abominable table manners. Cyril can't abide him. I declined, of course, said we were having dinner elsewhere, but if we stay in and Beatrice sees the light on, she will know I lied. We can't very well sit at the back in the kitchen all night long, not on a

Saturday, and you know how hard it would be to get Cyril to a restaurant.'

'What time should I expect you both?'

'Oh, Iris, you are an absolutely perfect daughter-in-law. I just knew I could rely on you. Half-seven say?'

'Half-seven it is. I'll invite Constance and Frank, shall I?' They usually had dinner together once a month, and this could be counted as her and Tom's turn.

Iris discussed the menu with Nell when she came on Thursday. 'I haven't bought this week's meat ration yet, but whatever I get, there won't be enough for six.'

'Have you got a couple of tins of corned beef?' Nell asked.

'Only one, but my mother-in-law is bound to have another. Since the war started, she and my father-in-law have become fond of corned-beef hash.'

'Can you get a pound of haricot beans and a cabbage?'

'I should imagine so, yes.'

'Would you like me to come and make dinner for you?' Nell offered kindly.

'Oh Nell, would you?' Whenever they had people to dinner, Iris usually spent the entire day in the kitchen getting herself worked up into such a state that Tom was scared to approach her. Inevitably, something would burn or not be cooked enough. 'I'd love you to come,' she said, emotionally. 'What are you going to make?'

'Potato soup, followed by haricot beef casserole, and dripping cake with mock cream for afters. I used to make that at camp when we got short of rations. Oh!' Nell said, delightedly. 'I'm already looking forward to it. All we have at home is scouse. Me dad always manages to get a bit of meat from somewhere, but it worries me what sort of animal it came from.'

On Saturday, Nell arrived at five o'clock. She put a small parcel on the table. 'Me dad's sent half a pound of best butter,' she said. 'The other day I told him how much you missed it. He likes you. He keeps asking questions about you.' She grinned. 'It's not often me dad likes anybody apart from Rita Hayworth.'

'Rita Hayworth!' Iris said faintly. She tried not to visibly recoil from the idea of being sent a present by Alfred Desmond, despite it being butter. After all, the chap was Nell's father.

'She's his woman,' Nell said in a matter-of-fact way. 'Me mam's his wife and Rita Hayworth is his woman. 'Course, she doesn't look a bit like the real Rita Hayworth, but she's got the same red hair.'

'Doesn't your mother mind?' Iris asked, possibly even more faintly.

'Mind! Of *course* she minds, but what can she do about it? Me dad's a law unto himself. She just sits in the chair all day and pines. She's lovesick, according to me sisters. She doesn't like being left on her own for long, so our Kenny's staying at home with her tonight.'

'Poor woman.' Iris wondered if Nell's mother would appreciate a visit, but she would ask about that some other time.

'Anyroad,' Nell said, 'did you manage to soak the beans for twenty-four hours without getting yourself into a tuck about it?' Having made meals three times a day for up to a hundred people in the army, she found Iris's inability to cook for two highly amusing.

'They're in the larder,' Iris told her.

'Well, now they have to be boiled for an hour in the same water.' She giggled. 'Can you do that yourself, or would you like me to do it for you?'

'I can do that by myself, thank you.'

The beans boiled and suitably tender, Nell placed them in layers in a dish along with the crumbled corned beef, the cabbage and sliced carrots, covered with half a pint of thin gravy to which she had added two teaspoons of mustard powder, to 'give it a tang'. 'Now it needs to cook for three quarters of an hour.' The potato soup had already been made. 'I'll start on the dripping cake as soon as I've drunk the tea you're in the middle of making.'

While this magic was going on, Iris was able to make the table look attractive for a change with the addition of two silver candlesticks – though without candles; they'd been almost impossible to buy for years – and white napkins folded to look like swans. The wine glasses sparkled and the smells coming from the kitchen were mouth-watering.

Tom came in. 'That smells good. What are we having?'

'Haricot beef casserole, though it's corned beef, not the proper sort.'

'Really!' He came and put his arms around Iris from behind. 'I'm glad you've got Nell for a friend. Does she remind you of the army? I know how much you miss it.' He didn't seem to mind.

Iris nodded. 'She misses it too. Life was so intense then.'

'And it's anything but intense here.' He kissed her neck. 'In fact, it's dead boring. Maybe we could go on holiday somewhere interesting this summer. The only place in Europe fit to visit is Paris, which is at least still standing. Or how about Spain?'

'Not with that awful chap Franco in charge,' Iris reminded him.

'No, of course not. I'd forgotten about him. I know,' he said brightly. 'We could go to the States – sail there, it takes five days, spend five days in New York, and sail back again. How do you fancy that?'

'It sounds wonderful.' It was no good explaining to him that what she wanted more than anything was another baby, for what could he do about it? They could make love till the cows came home – he would be very keen on that idea – but Iris felt in her bones that it was a waste of time.

Nell called from the kitchen and Iris looked at her watch.

'Everyone's likely to arrive any minute,' she said, slipping out of Tom's arms. 'Will you please see to the drinks?'

In the kitchen, Nell was stirring the soup. She looked up, eyes shining. 'I know it's only for six people, but it's a bit like being back in the camp.'

Nell had insisted on waiting on them. 'I can be getting the next course ready while you eat,' she said.

She turned out to be the perfect waitress, and Iris knew already that she was a perfect cook. She served the food with smiling politeness, wearing a plain brown dress and a little white apron that she'd made especially for the occasion out of an old pillowslip. Her hair had grown a little since leaving the army and had acquired a suggestion of a wave in front. Iris noticed Frank, her brother-in-law, regarding Nell with interest. Frank was a notorious ladies' man, and his relationships with other women were the source of much bitterness between him and Constance. Iris was never sure if they were genuine affairs or merely flirtations, and had never liked to ask. She must make sure that Frank didn't get his hands on Nell. The poor girl wouldn't know how to cope.

'How on earth does she do it?' Adele asked when the meal was over and they were seated around the table lazily finishing off the wine. The men smoked. Iris was actually enjoying herself for once. At this point of a meal, she was usually longing for the guests to go home so she could go to bed, where she would lie and think what a disaster the meal had been. 'Such basic food, but she made it taste delicious.'

Cyril agreed, but Constance looked suspicious, as if she'd been tricked in some way and the meal had contained secret ingredients that had made it exceptionally nice.

'Perhaps Nell could come and cook for us next time we have guests for dinner,' Frank suggested.

Constance glared at him. 'I can make my own dinners, thank you,' she snapped.

'I shall definitely ask her to make mine in future,' Adele enthused, while her husband nodded his approval. 'She's such a lovely young woman. Not so much in looks, but gentle and ladylike. Do you think she would agree, Iris?'

'I should imagine she'd be only too pleased,' Iris confirmed. 'She loves cooking. I'll ask her, shall I?'

In the kitchen, Nell had removed her apron and was wearing Iris's old green pinafore while she dried the dishes.

'There's no need to do that,' Iris protested. 'I know I'm a hopeless cook, but I can manage to wash and dry dishes.'

'I thought I may as well.' She dried the final plate and put it on the dresser shelf. 'I'll be off now. I hope everyone enjoyed their meal.'

'They did indeed. In fact my mother-in-law would like it if you'd do the same for her next time she has a dinner party. She'll pay, of course.'

Nell confirmed that she'd love to. 'I'll save the money up for when I go to London. I'm bound to get there one of these days.'

'I hope you do, Nell.' Iris squeezed her arm. 'Oh, but what will I do without you!' It wasn't just the cooking, but the friendship too. In a curious sort of way, she needed Nell more than she did Tom.

Maggie hadn't meant for them to go all the way, but she couldn't help it. Their kissing had become more heated and abandoned, his hands touching her in the most intimate places, making her body quiver with delight. She couldn't remember taking off her clothes and was amazed when she realised that Chris was undressed too. It didn't seem possible that the feelings she had could become even more passionate, but they did, because by then Chris had slipped inside her and it didn't hurt a bit, when all along she'd been told the first time was really painful. She screamed with pleasure and delight. What seemed like ages later, though turned out to only be minutes, ended like an orchestra building up to a grand, overwhelming climax. She lay back on the bed, exhausted, while Chris collapsed beside her.

'Whew,' he gasped. 'Let's get married soon.'

'How soon?'

'Next week.' He sat up and laid his hand idly on her breast. 'Tomorrow? How about now?'

They were in his mother's place in Everton Valley. Betty had gone to London the day before, accompanied by most of her possessions in a trunk. Soon, she would come back for the last of her things. In a few weeks she would be established in Susan's flat in Crouch End and her own flat would belong to her son, whose name was already on the rent book. Chris had approached the man who was opening the picture house in Walton Vale and applied for the post of manager. He had been assured the job would eventually be his. As from now, there was nothing to stop him and Maggie from getting married.

Thinking about this now, Maggie had no idea why she should suddenly feel apprehensive. Despite having been so close to Chris, as close as a man and woman could be, thereby putting a seal on their relationship, she was aware that she didn't know all that much about him. They hadn't discussed all sorts of important things; politics, for instance. Because of her father, Maggie was more aware of politics than most women. For which party had Chris voted at the last election? Another thing, did he want children? Maggie wanted at least four and didn't care what sex they were. One thing was for sure, it would be impossible to raise four children in a fourth-floor flat with two small bedrooms, so where would they live when their babies began to arrive?

Why hadn't she thought about all these things before?

She slid from underneath Chris, who seemed to have fallen asleep, picked up her clothes and went into the main room. There were no lights on, but the curtains were open and a pale moon was visible through the window; the nights were gradually getting lighter. As she dressed, she listened to the traffic on the road below; horns sounded, people shouted, tram cars trundled past.

What was she to do now? Should she tell Chris she wanted to wait a bit longer before they got married? It was also essential that she discuss it with Mam and Dad before a date was set. They'd met him, Mam liked him, Dad didn't, but they had no idea that their daughter getting married so soon was on the cards.

'Oh!' Maggie sat down, feeling sick. What a terrible mess she'd got herself into. People were always saying she was too headstrong. Only minutes ago she'd been soaring through blissful heaven; now she felt panic-stricken and full of worry.

In the bedroom, she heard Chris stir, and next minute he walked into the room completely naked. She wasn't prepared for it. He should have worn something, even if it was only underpants or a towel, she reasoned. She had never seen a naked man before.

Oh, Jaysus! I'm a madwoman, she thought. Chris was coming towards her. She could tell by his face that he wanted to kiss her. But he had nothing on!

Maggie grabbed her coat and handbag and fled from the room. She ran downstairs with Chris shouting, 'Maggie, Maggie, what's wrong?' from the fourth-floor landing. 'Come back,' he called plaintively as she raced through the front door.

She waited on Scotland Road for a tram, half expecting Chris to come running around the corner, having forgotten he hadn't any clothes on. But the next tram that came was heading for Bootle. Maggie got on with a relieved sigh and a racing heart, thankful that she was going home.

Angry voices were coming from the parlour of the house in Coral Street. The loudest voice belonged to Auntie Kath, who always shouted when she argued about politics with people who disagreed with her.

'What's going on in there?' Maggie asked her mother, who was in the living room. There was no sign of her brother, and Bridie would have gone to bed hours ago.

'Phelim Hegarty has decided to resign, so there'll be a by-election. Our Kath is trying to talk your dad into standing for the seat,' her mother said tiredly. 'There's half a dozen Labour Party members in there, all sticking their oar in.'

'Me dad, go into politics!' Since before Maggie was born, Phelim Hegarty had been the Member of Parliament for the Bootle Docklands constituency in which the O'Neill family lived. A few weeks before, he'd had a heart attack. 'Flippin' heck.' She dropped on to a chair with a bang. 'That's a desperately good idea.'

'Oh, I do wish you'd sit down in a normal way, girl,' Sheila said tetchily. 'One of these days, you and the chair will go right through the floor. And I don't meself see anything good about your dad going into politics.'

'Are you all right, Mam?' She noticed how pale her mother was and how weak and tired she looked. The baby wasn't due for another two months and the pregnancy was wearing her down. She was anaemic according to the doctor, who'd pre-scribed an iron tonic that didn't seem to have done any good at all.

'I'm just a bit weary,' she said now. 'I won't half be glad when this baby is born. Anyroad, you're home early. We weren't expecting you back until gone ten.'

Maggie had no idea what time it was. The clock on the sideboard chose that moment to strike, announcing that it was quarter past nine. She was trying to think of a reason to explain why she was home so early when Auntie Kath shouted, 'You've got no guts, you useless man. If I thought they'd elect a woman, I'd bloody well stand meself.'

'That's your poor dad she's talking to.' Sheila pulled herself to her feet and made to go into the kitchen. 'They'll be out in a minute. I'd best make some tea.'

Maggie pushed her mother none too gently back into the chair. 'You'll do no such thing. I'll make it.'

Not long afterwards, the tea made, the parlour door opened and Auntie Kath came into the room. 'Paddy's agreed to stand for Labour at the by-election,' she said triumphantly. 'I'll be his agent, naturally.'

'You're nothing but a bully,' Sheila told her sister. 'Since when did Paddy ever say he wanted to go into Parliament?'

Kath grinned. 'Just now, Sheil, in your very own front parlour.' She rubbed her hands together gleefully. 'He's bound to get elected. Your Paddy's one of the most popular men in Bootle. Once Phelim Hegarty makes a statement to say he's resigning, we'll tell the *Bootle Times* about Paddy.'

'How many cuppas do you want?' Maggie shouted from the kitchen.

'None.' Auntie Kath poked her head around the door. 'There's still some of that sherry left that I got your mam and dad at Christmas. We'll finish it off with a toast to your dad.'

'No sherry for me, thanks. I've already got a splitting headache,' Sheila said sourly. Once again she attempted to struggle out of the chair, this time successfully. 'I'm off to bed. It doesn't matter about wasting a whole pot of tea, by the way,' she finished crossly.

Auntie Kath frowned worriedly at her sister as she lumbered out of the room. 'I'll come round and see her tomorrer after-noon,' she muttered after she'd gone. 'Bring her some flowers or summat.'

Maggie waited until her mother had got into bed before going up herself. Her previous worries had returned to haunt her and she wasn't in the mood for drinking sherry. Anyroad, after thinking about it for a bit, the idea of her dad becoming a politician seemed too far-fetched for words. It was up to the entire membership of the local Labour Party to choose the candidate, not just Auntie Kath, even if she was the biggest bully on earth.

★

Once in bed, Maggie tossed and turned, knowing there was no chance of falling asleep. Bridie was well away, and she could hear her mother breathing heavily in the next room. She was worried about Mam and felt guilty for being out with Chris so much that she hadn't noticed how exhausted she was. From now on, she'd help every day with the housework. As for Chris, tomorrow was Saturday and she'd go and see him first thing and apologise for behaving the way she had. They would have a proper discussion about getting married, name a date – later in the year, say, after Mam had had the baby. She felt uneasy that marrying Chris, which that morning had seemed an infinitely desirable thing to do, now seemed terribly wrong.

She turned on her back and gazed at the ceiling. Downstairs, Auntie Kath was laughing loudly – well, someone was pleased that Phelim Hegarty had had a heart attack!

Ryan came in. He was still going out with Rosie Hesketh, who wasn't at all his sort of girl. Maggie had tried to tell him, but he'd just laughed and told her to sod off.

It was at this point that she fell asleep. When she woke again, it was early morning and the house was completely silent. For some strange reason, she'd been dreaming about Edna Wilcox, who'd joined the army at about the same time she had, but had left after a year.

Why had she left? And why dream about Edna Wilcox out of all the other girls that she'd known for much longer?

Maggie racked her brains. In the dream, Edna had been digging a garden – not a garden that Maggie recognised, but that was the way with dreams. She couldn't remember if they spoke, but the reason why she'd left came to her quite clearly. Edna had discovered she was having a baby.

'It's just not fair.' The tearful words carried over the years. 'After all, we only did it the once.'

Her father, a small, square man with tight, bad-tempered

61

features, had come into the hut to collect her. He stood over her while she packed her bag.

'Bye, everyone,' Edna had said when she left. Her father said nothing. The other girls stood staring at the door after Edna had gone, feeling desperately sorry for her.

Maggie and Chris had only done it the once. The possible consequences of that act hadn't crossed her mind until now, though there must have been some sort of awareness or she wouldn't have dreamt about Edna Wilcox.

She knew little about the inner workings of a woman's body. Her imagination took over, and she visualised Chris's seed already inside her womb, in the process of turning itself into a baby.

She was pregnant. She was convinced of it. It would kill her mother and ruin her father's political career. The entire family would be disgraced. 'I see Paddy O'Neill's girl is up the stick,' people would say. In no time at all, it would be all over Bootle.

The only thing to do was to marry Chris after all – as quickly as humanly possible.

Chapter 4

Next morning, Maggie burst into the Desmonds' back yard and through the door into the house.

'Nell!' she yelled.

'She's not here, Maggie luv.'

To her amazement, Mr Desmond was seated on a pouffe in front of the living-room fire, a skein of wool stretched between his thumbs, while Mrs Desmond, who had spoken, wound the wool into a ball. 'She's at her friend's house in Rimrose Road,' Mrs Desmond went on, adding a touch smarmily. 'The one that's married to the doctor.'

'Is it all right to go out the front door?' Maggie asked, wondering what on earth Nell was doing at Iris's so early in the morning – it had only just gone nine o'clock. Another mystery was why Nell's mam and dad were getting on so well when they were supposed to be mortal enemies.

Mr Desmond nodded towards the hallway. 'Help yourself, luv.'

'Ta.'

Maggie ran in the direction of Rimrose Road until she got a stitch in her side and had to stop. She leaned against a wall, panting hoarsely and waiting to get her breath back. Nell was the only person in the world who she could confide her troubles in and not be criticised or blamed, but told that everything was going to be all right. She knew it was un-reasonable to expect her friend to be at her beck and call, but she couldn't help feel put out that she was with Iris just when Maggie needed her.

'Are you all right, luv?' A woman stopped and took hold of her arm. She wore a georgette headscarf over a head full of metal curlers. 'Why, you're Sheila O'Neill's girl, aren't you? How's your mam these days? Last time we met she was having a bit of a hard time. It's not good for a woman to be having a baby at her age. Mind you, me own mam had our Derek at forty-eight.'

'She's a bit run-down,' Maggie gasped. 'The doctor's given her iron tablets.'

'Iron? The trouble with iron is it can make a person constipated. I remember when . . .'

The woman looked set for a long jangle. Maggie broke in claiming an emergency, though it was nothing to do with her mother, she then had to explain. She and the woman went their separate ways, Maggie more sedately this time.

There was a small queue outside Iris's house and the front door was open. Maggie didn't know whether to join the queue or knock on the door. After a while, a woman came and waited behind her, a crying baby in her arms, and she realised she was in a queue to see the doctor. She went inside and shouted for Iris, who appeared out of the kitchen looking harassed.

'Why, Maggie! How lovely to see you,' she exclaimed. 'As if Tom hadn't got enough to do, he's started a Saturday-morning surgery. Come in the kitchen and have some tea. Nell's here. There's an Easter carnival or something this afternoon at the school she went to, and we're making cakes to go with the refreshments.'

As Maggie had gone to the same school as Nell, it must be St Joan of Arc's carnival. It wasn't Easter until next weekend. She entered the kitchen, where Nell was beating a bowl of cake mixture with a fork.

'Carrot buns,' she said when she saw Maggie. 'They're

supposed to have currants in, but we haven't got any. There's rock cakes in the oven. We're going to put jam in them.'

'I think we might have some currants at home. Auntie Kath always gives us the rations she doesn't use.' Maggie could have sworn she'd seen some sort of dried fruit last time she'd looked in the larder.

'It'd be best to leave little treats like that for your mam, Mags. How is she today, anyway?'

'Not so bad.' Maggie hadn't realised that Mam was poorly enough to have attracted the attention of half of Bootle. Being Saturday, her father had been making tea and her mother was still in bed when she'd left the house.

Iris was attending to the queue outside the door, taking people's names and putting them in the waiting room. She came into the kitchen and washed her hands. 'That's the last for now,' she sighed. 'The poor child had impetigo. Maggie, do sit down. I've got time till the next patient to make tea. I wouldn't mind some myself and I've never known Nell turn down a cup. What brings you here anyway?' She smiled and her eyes gleamed. 'Have you got some really interesting news to impart?'

'Well, no.' Maggie sat down, feeling uncomfortable. Iris probably thought she'd come to invite them to her wedding or ask Nell to be a bridesmaid. 'Chris has got a job in a picture house in Walton Vale,' she told them, just for something to say.

'That's good,' Iris said encouragingly. 'And what with his mother letting you have that nice flat of hers in Scotland Road, there's nothing stopping you from getting married, is there? You're awfully lucky, Maggie. Isn't she lucky, Nell?'

'Dead lucky,' Nell agreed. She began to put spoonfuls of the cake mixture into a metal tray, the sort that Maggie's mother used to make fairy cakes. She looked searchingly at her friend. 'You're unhappy about something, aren't you? I can tell. What's wrong, Mags?'

As if Maggie could tell her there and then that she and Chris had made love the night before, that she thought she might be pregnant, that she wasn't too sure if she wanted to marry Chris after all but would have to if she *was* pregnant. She couldn't confide all those intimate things, not with Iris there, a room full patients close by, and the doctor in his surgery only a few feet away. The doctor, Tom, chose that moment to stick his head around the door and demand a packet of cotton wool.

'There's none in my drawer,' he complained, completely ignoring or not noticing Maggie.

'It never has been in your drawer,' Iris told him patiently. 'The cotton wool has always been in the cupboard on the wall behind you.' She rolled her eyes, but didn't appear to be annoyed. 'I'll get it for you.'

'There's something up, isn't there?' Nell said when Iris had gone.

'It's not important,' Maggie assured her. She hadn't realised how friendly Nell and Iris had become, how close they were. Nell's *my* friend, she thought jealously, yet she knew in her heart she'd been neglecting her. It was weeks since they'd been to the pictures or the Grafton together.

'Are you seeing Chris today?' Nell enquired.

Maggie had no idea when she was seeing Chris again. 'Not till tonight,' she mumbled.

'Then why don't you come to the carnival with us this avvy?' Nell suggested. 'It'll be dead busy, but we're bound to have time to ourselves after all the cakes have gone.'

'Will Iris be there?'

'No, She's going shopping with her mother-in-law, Adele, in Southport. Isn't Adele a pretty name? She's ever so nice. I'm only doing the baking here because it's easier than in our house. Have you noticed the cooker's got six rings and two ovens?'

Maggie hadn't. She wasn't interested in anything to do with

66

kitchens, and hadn't noticed either how big Iris's kitchen was, or that the pine table could easily have seated ten.

There was something she *could* talk about, though. 'Your mam and dad seemed to be getting on remarkably well when I called in on me way here.'

Nell grinned. 'Apparently Rita the hairdresser's got engaged to a ticket inspector on the trams, and me dad's been shown the door. I think she must have been wearing him out, 'cos he seems perfectly happy at home, particularly with Mam smartening herself up a bit. Let's hope it stays like that, eh?' She chuckled. 'Mind you, I think he's already got his eye on some other woman.'

'Do I know this other woman?

Nell's grin grew even wider. 'Of course you do,' she said. 'It's Iris. I can't see him being lucky there, can you?'

Not wanting to bring on another stitch, Maggie walked home at a normal pace. She was feeling very much out of things. Nell had met Iris's mother-in-law; Iris had met Nell's father! Not that it was anyone's fault but her own. She'd been wrapped up in Chris to the exclusion of everyone else in the world.

To her astonishment, Chris was there when she got home, Bridie sitting on one of his knees, Tinker purring madly on the other, and her mother looking infinitely better than she'd done recently. Maggie met his eyes across the room and felt no more certain about her feelings than she'd done the night before.

They'd been talking about pictures, Mam said. 'Chris told me about this little British girl who's become a Hollywood star, her name's Elizabeth Taylor. She went to America as a refugee to avoid the air raids and has made this lovely picture called *National Velvet* about wanting her horse to run in the Grand National. I'd love to see it, Maggie. You know I love pictures about animals.' Her face was pink and animated.

'I've promised to take her,' Chris put in. 'We'll sit in the best seats with the biggest box of chocolates I can buy.'

'I'm really looking forward to it,' Mam said.

'I bet you are, Mam.' Maggie knew there and then that she was going to marry Chris Conway, who had cheered her mother up no end. They would get a special licence – during the war it had been possible to marry at only a few hours' notice, and she supposed the law still stood. Unfortunately, it would have to be in a registry office, not a church, but she had no choice.

If she announced it now, Mam would absolutely insist they wait until she'd had her baby and everyone would support her – dad and Ryan, Auntie Kath – but by then Maggie just knew she herself would have been pregnant for two or three months and her own baby would be born much too soon.

Maybe she and Chris could make a great big do out of their first anniversary, invite everyone as they would have done to their wedding. And although Mam wouldn't approve of a registry office wedding, she wouldn't mind too much if she was getting married to Chris, who she clearly thought was the gear. And if Mam came round, then so would Dad.

But, but, but . . . Maggie felt literally sick with confusion. There were too many buts. Too much that was wrong. For no particular reason, her mind went back to the day she, Nell and Iris had returned to Bootle from the camp in Plymouth. 'From now on, nothing will be the same,' she'd announced, or something like that, when they got off the train.

If only she could go back to that time, she thought wistfully, and follow a different path.

That afternoon, after most of the races were over and all the carrot cakes and rock cakes had been sold and eaten, Nell went outside and sat on the grass behind the marquee, where it was quiet. Maggie hadn't come, so they couldn't have the talk that she'd so obviously wanted. Something was seriously wrong.

Later, on her way home, she'd call at the O'Neills' and maybe they could go for a walk and have a talk then.

But when she went to the house later, she was told that Maggie was out. 'With Chris,' Mrs O'Neill said. 'I'm not exactly sure where they've gone, only that they caught the tram into town about half an hour ago.'

It was a lovely sunny Wednesday afternoon a few days later. Maggie and Chris were getting married in Brome Terrace Registry Office in West Derby, rather than in Bootle where Maggie might be recognised. She wanted to break the news to Mam and Dad in her own time, and it wouldn't be today. She'd told Iggy she was going to a friend's wedding in Southport, and he'd given her the day off.

The place was crowded. This was where births and deaths were registered as well as where marriages took place. Sad-looking women – it was mainly women – queued clutching bits of paper, and babies cried.

She and Chris were due to get married at three o'clock. They were shown into a large, shabby room where two other couples already waited. Both had members of their families with them: mothers, fathers, possibly friends. Maggie wanted to cry, because she and Chris had no one. Two members of staff, both strangers, would act as their witnesses. It was all so different from how she'd imagined her wedding day would be.

A door opened, names were called, and one of the couples went through the door with their noisy entourage. The woman who seemed to be the bride wore a smart dress made out of parachute silk and an enormous cortege of artificial pink flowers. 'Here comes the bride,' a man sang. 'Forty inches wide.'

'Shurrup!' someone hissed.

Another door opened, the one they'd come in by, and a man entered. To Maggie's surprise, he laid his hand on Chris's shoulder.

'Will you come with me, please,' he said curtly.

Chris had gone surprisingly pale. 'But why?' he asked.

The man's hand tightened on his shoulder. 'Just come with me,' he repeated.

To Maggie's further surprise, Chris got obediently to his feet and went without saying 'I'll be back in a minute' or 'Won't be long' as she would have expected.

In a while – it seemed like hours but was only about ten minutes – she heard the first wedding leave noisily and the second couple were called in.

Twice Maggie got up and looked into the corridor, but there was no sign of Chris and she had no idea where he'd gone. All she knew was that something serious was going on. Her head was buzzing, her stomach hurt and her legs were trembling.

Another couple had arrived; two couples, actually, one middle-aged, one young. Maggie might well have wondered which couple were getting married had she not been so worried about Chris.

A woman entered the room. She wore a badly creased black costume and a white blouse with a soiled collar. Her hair was cut like a man's. She nodded at Maggie. 'Miss O'Neill, will you come with me, please?'

'What's going on?' Maggie asked. Her voice was shaking in a way it had never done before. 'Where's Chris – Mr Conway?'

'Come in here and I'll explain. I'm Mrs Slater, by the way.'

'Explain what?'

Mrs Slater led her into a tiny, dusty room lined with shelves full of files. She sat behind a metal desk and indicated that Maggie should take the chair on the other side.

'Were you aware that Christopher Conway already has a wife?' she asked. She looked at Maggie closely, waiting for her reaction.

'*No!*' She wanted to be sick, to faint, to scream, to die. 'No,

I didn't know.' Her throat felt swollen and she could hardly speak.

'Would you like some water?' Mrs Slater asked. She was being quite kind and sympathetic.

'No thank you – yes, yes, I would, please.'

'Here we are.' There was a tray with a jug of water and a glass on the desk. Mrs Slater filled the glass and put it within Maggie's reach. She took a few sips; her mouth was completely dry. The woman continued. 'He married Beryl Martha Cameron in Manchester on the fourth of October nineteen forty-two. It was during his time in the RAF. One of our officials recognised him, the reason being that his name is also Christopher Conway. He has since moved to Liverpool, the official, that is.'

Maggie had no idea what to say to that. 'Can I see him?' she asked after a while.

'Not while he's being interviewed by the police. I suggest you go home and talk to someone, your mother, perhaps, or a friend.'

'Will he go to prison?' After all, bigamy was a crime.

'He hasn't done anything wrong, has he?' Mrs Slater stood. 'Although he was about to. Whether that's a crime or not, I've no idea. Me, I'm just a clerk.' She moved towards the door. 'I'm sorry, dear, but I'm very busy today and I really must get on.'

Five minutes later Maggie was on the tram back to Bootle. She found it hard to believe that the last few hours had actually happened, that she hadn't just lived through a desperately real nightmare. The sun had gone in, leaving a gunmetal sky that matched her mood.

She couldn't go home, not yet. It was much too early. She'd lied to Mam, as well as Iggy, telling her that she was going straight into town after work to meet Chris. 'We're going to the pictures and it starts at half past six,' she'd explained, anticipating spending the evening in Chris's flat, which would have been *her* flat too, though this would have had to be kept a secret until she revealed that she and Chris were married.

It was with almost a sense of relief that she realised she wouldn't have to do that now; she and Chris *weren't* married, the flat belonged to him and him alone. She, Maggie, was still a single woman who lived at home with her mam and dad. And, you never knew, there was always the chance, just the slightest chance, that she might not be pregnant.

She decided to go home at the normal time, as if she'd been at work, and tell Mam that Chris had telephoned the office saying he was unable to meet her. In a few days, she would reveal that she wasn't seeing him any more. At least she hoped so. Everything was so unpredictable, including herself.

Next day at work she felt almost light-headed. 'You had a nice time then yesterday?' Iggy remarked when he noticed her extra-bright eyes.

'Not really,' she replied. How could she describe yesterday? As possibly one of the worst days of her life?

The following day was Good Friday. She went to St James's church with Nell and they did the Stations of the Cross. After-wards they went into town. The shops were closed but they looked in the windows, then walked down as far as the Pier Head, where they caught the ferry across to New Brighton and back again.

'At the camp,' Maggie remarked on the boat back, 'Sundays and holy days were hardly noticeable. After all, the war couldn't grind to a halt because it was Good Friday. I hate it when the shops and picture houses and theatres close down and everywhere is as dull as ditchwater.'

Nell was shocked. 'But Maggie, Good Friday is the day Jesus died for us on the cross. It wouldn't seem right to go dancing when you think of the way He suffered.'

Maggie sniffed. 'I'm sure He wouldn't mind, not now, nearly two thousand years later.'

When she woke the following morning, she discovered she'd started her period and had lost an unusually heavy amount of blood, which she continued to do for the rest of the day. It was accompanied by a dull pain in the pit of her stomach. For the remainder of her life, Maggie was convinced that on that day she had a miscarriage. Her feelings were confused: sadness if she was in fact losing a baby, yet wholehearted relief that she was no longer pregnant.

On the same day, a letter arrived from Chris. He pleaded for her forgiveness, claiming he'd only married Beryl Cameron because she said she was having a baby, which turned out not to be true. He loved *her*, Maggie. She would always be the love of his life. Could they please start again? He would instigate divorce proceedings that very day.

'Blah, blah, blah,' Maggie said under her breath as she ate her breakfast.

'What was that?' Ryan asked.

'Nothing,' she sang. 'Absolutely nothing at all.' She didn't reply to Chris's letter. Perhaps he wasn't expecting her to, because a few days later he wrote another, asking for the return of his mother's ring. He put in brackets that Betty had known nothing about Beryl Cameron. Maggie sent the ring back by registered post. He didn't acknowledge it and she never heard from him again, so never knew if he was punished for attempting to get married a second time. A continental cinema didn't open in Walton Vale, and she wondered if it had only existed in Chris's imagination.

Over the Easter weekend, the O'Neills' house had been as busy as a mainline station. Small meetings of the Labour Party were held in the front parlour and larger meetings in the party's offices on the Dock Road. Phelim Hegarty had announced to the press his intention to resign as Labour Member of Parliament for the Bootle Docklands seat, by which time the party had chosen Paddy O'Neill as their prospective candidate. The by-election would be held in a few months' time, before Parliament closed for the long summer break. A statement would be given to the press before the end of the week. The idea of a Conservative being elected to a seat in Bootle wasn't even debatable, and only a fool with money to burn would have put a bet on Paddy not winning.

It was during this week that Maggie arrived home from work in the best mood she'd been in for a long time. It was only ten days since her life had been turned upside down and back again, but it felt like ages. The idea of her father becoming a Member of Parliament was like something out of a film or a novel, and she was really looking forward to it.

Only her mother was in. Bridie was having tea with her friend Shirley, who lived in Pearl Street; Dad and Ryan had yet to arrive back from work.

'Hello, Mam!' Maggie had burst into the living room full of smiles, unaware that the next hour would go down as the worst in her life. She bent to give her mother a kiss, but was none-too-gently pushed away.

'Sit down,' her mother said in a hard voice. 'I've got a bone to pick with you.' Maggie sat, too surprised to ask what was wrong. 'Remember that friend of mine from school called Alice?' her mother began. Without waiting for a reply, she went on. 'She got married to this lovely young feller in the Merchant Navy at around the same time as I married your dad. His name was Felix, but they called him Faily – Faily Walters. Poor young man, he died within a few months of the wedding, washed overboard in the Barents Sea, or somewhere like that up in the Arctic. She never married again, did Alice.'

'Why are you telling me this, Mam?' Maggie was longing for a cup of tea.

'Just shut up and listen,' her mother snapped. Her skin was

74

yellow, her expression sour. Her stomach was swollen to the extent that she could have been expecting two or three babies. Maggie had never seen her in such a state before. She wondered if her mind had slipped just a little bit because of the pregnancy. 'Faily was already dead,' she continued, 'when Alice discovered she was having a baby. She had a little girl, Lily – isn't that the prettiest name? I think I might well have called you Lily if Alice hadn't taken it first. Anyroad, she had a hard struggle bringing up a baby on her own. When the war started, she moved to the other side of Liverpool and I haven't seen much of her since.'

'She came to our house the Christmas before I joined the army,' Maggie said warily, worried that the words might irritate her mother, though they wouldn't have done normally. But in this strange mood . . . 'I remember her well.' She was a tall, sad-faced woman with prematurely grey hair.

'She remembers you well, too.' Sheila O'Neill gave her daughter a look that could well have been described as one of dislike. 'She came this avvy to tell me she saw you recently in the registry office in Brome Terrace with a very nice-looking young man who sounds very much like Chris Conway. It's where she works. She thought you must have been guests at a wedding, never believing that you yourself were getting married in such a heathen place. And even if you were, that your mam and dad and all the rest of your family wouldn't have been there as guests. It was only later she learnt that the young man was a bigamist and you hadn't got married after all.'

'He's not a bigamist,' Maggie said faintly, but her mother, this odd, unpleasant mother, wasn't interested.

'Are you pregnant, girl?' she asked in a hoarse voice.

'No, Mam. I just thought I was.' She wasn't sure if discovering she'd been thinking of getting married for that reason would make her mam less upset or more. On reflection, it probably made no difference.

'You're a bad girl, Margaret O'Neill.'

The tone was so bitter and unforgiving that Maggie shivered. 'Mam,' she said tearfully. 'Don't talk like that. I was wrong, but I didn't know Chris was already married, did I?'

'You should've thought of that before you were so free with your body.' Tinker came and jumped on to Sheila's knee, but leapt off straight away as if sensing he wasn't welcome. 'I expect in the army you made yourself available to any old Tom, Dick or Harry.'

'Oh, Mam,' Maggie cried, 'I did no such thing. Honest. Chris was the first, the only one.' She got to her feet. 'Let's make us a cup of tea,' she said brightly. 'It'll do you good. You know you always say the world looks better after a cuppa.'

Her mother said nothing, so Maggie went into the kitchen and put the kettle on. She winced when she heard the hard, brittle voice again, a voice nothing like her mother's normally soft one.

'You know what's cut me up the most,' the voice said. 'I never realised before how much Alice hated me. I thought we were good friends all these years, but this avvy, when she was telling me about you, I could see she was enjoying it. Her eyes were all feverish like, as if she'd always resented me and your dad being so happy and she was really glad she was making me as unhappy as herself.'

There was a long pause. Maggie peeped into the room. Mam was staring at the empty fireplace. 'I'll not be telling your dad,' she muttered. 'And Alice won't let on to anyone else. It was me she wanted to get at, her old friend.' She leant back in the chair and her head fell to one side. 'Oh, Paddy luv,' she whispered. 'I'll really miss you.'

It was quite a few seconds before Maggie noticed that her mam was no longer breathing, and more seconds before reality dawned and she realised that her mother was dead.

★

Sheila O'Neill's heart had been shockingly weak. The doctor hadn't realised. No one had. The baby she'd been carrying turned out to be a boy, and he was dead in her womb.

Paddy O'Neill swore that once the funeral was over, he would never set foot inside a church again. He wanted no more to do with the God who had taken away his beloved wife, who'd never harmed a hair on the head of anyone in her entire life.

'Where's the fairness of it?' he wailed. 'My Sheila was a saint, a living saint.' He cross-questioned Maggie as to what his wife had said during her last conversation on earth.

'She talked about you and Bridie, about Ryan, the new baby, all of us,' Maggie stammered. It tore at her heart having to invent her mother's last words. Was it her own behaviour that had caused her mother to die? How could she ever forgive herself?

'What else? What else?' her father demanded, greedy to know everything, even the sound of Sheila's very last breath.

When reminded of it, he announced that he wanted nothing to do with the by-election. He didn't want to be a Member of Parliament without his wife at his side. 'She was really looking forward to it,' he claimed.

As for Maggie, she was storing up secrets: the almost wedding, the almost baby, and now knowing that these two things might well have been the cause of her mother's death. The knowledge had literally broken Sheila's fragile heart, and it was something her daughter would have to live with for the rest of her life.

She gave Iggy a week's notice. 'But I've got to take me mam's place, you see,' she told him when he said she could take as much time off as she wanted; she didn't have to leave. 'Someone's got to make the meals and do the housework and look after Bridie. Me dad and our Ryan both earn decent wages; there's no real need for mine.'

*

Auntie Kath was as upset as anyone that her beloved sister was dead, but the world didn't stop turning no matter how much you had loved the person who had died. There was the serious matter of who would replace Phelim Hegarty now that her brother-in-law had turned the job down.

An emergency meeting was held and Auntie Kath was adopted as prospective parliamentary candidate for Bootle Docklands. She was well aware that many people, and not just men, didn't approve of women meddling in politics, but she was determined to show them bloody politicians down in London a thing or two, particularly the Tory ones.

Chapter 5

Iris had never met Maggie's mother, but she ordered flowers for the funeral; miniature daffodils and violets mingled with trailing ivy and tied with a blue satin bow.

'Why don't you come with me?' Nell suggested. 'I'm sure Maggie will appreciate it.' Privately, she didn't think Maggie capable of any feelings just now apart from grief, which Nell found surprising. Naturally she would be horribly upset that her mam had died, but she was the sort of person who would normally have subdued her grief and consoled her dad who had fallen apart. According to Ryan, who was holding the family together, Paddy O'Neill spent every evening in the parlour talking to his wife, who lay in her coffin with rosary beads threaded through her white fingers.

'I never thought I'd say this, but I'll be glad when me mam's in her grave.' Ryan made the Sign of the Cross in case the words sounded blasphemous.

'I don't blame you.' Nell squeezed his hand, glad of the opportunity. Since she'd been able to tell the difference between men and women, she'd wanted to marry Ryan O'Neill. But she wasn't pretty or glamorous enough. Ryan's girlfriends always looked as if they had stepped out of the pages of a women's magazine; perfectly made-up, beautifully dressed, drenched in expensive scent. Mind you, lately he'd taken up with Rosie Hesketh, who'd been at school with Nell and Maggie. Rosie had been a sturdy, argumentative little girl with

79

ringlets, who'd done well in cookery and needlework and poorly at everything else, though if there'd been a prize for arguing, she would have won hands down.

'I don't know what he sees in her,' Maggie had said flatly only the other day. 'She hasn't a brain in her head and she's not exactly pretty.'

'She's got a determined chin,' Nell pointed out.

'Well, a determined chin isn't anything to write home about.'

Nell, being no beauty herself, felt obliged to stand up for Rosie. 'It was enough for your Ryan to ask her out.'

'Humph!' was all Maggie said.

Rosie wasn't at the funeral, but she turned out to be in the O'Neills' house when everyone went back for refreshments, having prepared sandwiches and baked cheese straws the night before. Bridie, Maggie's little sister, was also there.

'I would have helped with the refreshments,' Nell said when they met in the O'Neills' kitchen. Since leaving school, Nell and Rosie had done no more than nod at each other in the street.

'S'all right, Nellie. I could easily manage on me own,' Rosie said in a friendly manner. 'Anyroad, Bridie here gave us a hand. Didn't you, darlin'. She patted the little girl's head. 'Would you mind helping Nell take the sarnies around? Ryan's seeing to the hard stuff,' she remarked to Nell, 'and there's tea if folks want it.'

'Me mammy's gone to heaven,' Bridie told Nell.

'I bet she'll be happy there.' The poor child didn't understand what had really happened, that her mammy was dead.

In the parlour, Iris was talking to Auntie Kath, congratulating her on being a candidate in the forthcoming by-election. 'I do envy you,' she remarked. 'Being in Parliament must be incredibly interesting. I wish I could do something like that.'

'Well what's stopping you?' Auntie Kath asked pugnaciously. She had Maggie's dark curls and her pretty face sparkled with life and intelligence. She wore a black dress that was much too long, and clumpy-heeled shoes.

'For one thing, I have a husband,' Iris stammered, slightly taken aback by the woman's attitude.

'Does he keep you locked up or something?'

'No, but he's a doctor and I'm his receptionist.'

This was greeted with a contemptuous 'Huh! Did you want to be a doctor's receptionist when you were growing up?'

Iris was obliged to shake her head. In the manner of most little girls, she'd wanted to do all sorts of exciting things.

Auntie Kath seemed determined to prove her a total failure as a woman and a human being. 'But your husband wanted to be a doctor and just assumed that you, his wife, would be his assistant. If you were the doctor, would your husband agree to being *your* receptionist?'

'I doubt it very much,' Iris was forced to concede.

'It's just so unfair,' her tormentor raged. 'Men automatically assume their wives will be on hand to provide free labour. It doesn't cross their minds that women have ambitions too. And I bet your husband doesn't even pay you a salary.'

'No, he doesn't.' She would demand one as soon as she got home.

Auntie Kath was slightly more impressed when Iris told her she'd been a sergeant in the army, which was how she'd met Maggie, her niece. 'What did you do there?'

'I was a driver.' Iris wanted to laugh, but remembered she was at a funeral. 'I'm awfully sorry, but all I ever did was chauffeur officers around, and not a single one was a woman.' She finished by offering to deliver leaflets leading up to the election. 'And I'll put your poster up in our window.'

Auntie Kath thanked her kindly, and when they shook hands, Iris felt as if she'd made a friend.

★

Wakes never seemed to be all that sad, Nell mused as she carried round another plate of sandwiches, this time in the street outside the house, where the mourners had spread when it became too crowded indoors. There was no sign anywhere of Maggie or her father. At the cemetery, they'd stood by the grave, the despairing husband of the deceased, and the devastated daughter, drained of life, neither recognisable from the dignified man and laughing girl they'd been this time last week.

Now, hours later, conversations were animated. People who hadn't seen each other for ages were catching up on old times, sharing experiences they'd had during the war. There was even laughter here and there. Sheila O'Neill was remembered with affection, and instances of her kindness were described with real warmth.

Perhaps it was only to be expected that someone would start to sing, starting with *Oh, Mary, this London's a wonderful sight, with people here working by day and by night* . . .

Inevitably the sound carried and people from nearby streets came to join in. It's a celebration of a life, Nell thought, much better than everyone weeping and wailing. If it had been her own funeral, she would have far preferred songs to hymns, and jokes to tears. She said this to Iris when she went back indoors and they came face to face.

'If I'm still around in another sixty years, I'll remember that, Nell,' Iris said with a grin. 'These sandwiches are nice. Is it real salmon in them?'

'It came from me dad,' Nell informed her. 'He got a big tin from somewhere.' A tin that size couldn't possibly have been acquired legally; it had probably fallen off the back of a lorry.

When Irish eyes are smiling, people were singing now.

'Your dad is very generous,' Iris said.

'That's the first time I've ever heard anyone call him that. He's usually referred to as a bloody criminal.' Nell took the empty plate into the kitchen and found Ryan O'Neill and Rosie Hesketh locked in a passionate embrace.

'Ah well,' she sighed. It looked as if her long-held ambition to marry Ryan was no longer on the cards – if it ever had been.

At five o'clock, Ryan O'Neill ran upstairs and banged on the door of the bedroom where his dad was, then on his sister's. 'Everyone's gone,' he shouted. 'Me and Rosie are going round to their house. She's dead tired. She's been in the kitchen since early this morning and was baking stuff till nearly ten o'clock last night. Me and Nellie Desmond saw that everyone had a drink. Now someone needs to come down and look after our Bridie.'

His voice was only slightly accusing. It was a black business, his dear mam dying long before she should, and he was as upset as anyone, but he considered that his dad and their Maggie were laying it on a bit thick. What if he too had decided to go into a virtual coma and expect someone else to see the day through?

He banged on the doors again, this time louder. 'Will at least one of youse come down and see to Bridie. She's also lost her mam and it needs to be explained to her.'

Both doors opened at the same time. 'I'm coming, son,' his father said.

Jaysus! Paddy's face looked as if it had caved in and his eyes were glazed. Then Maggie came out and she looked just as bad. Ryan hoped he hadn't sounded too hard. Maybe there was something wrong with him, that he wasn't sensitive enough, that he didn't feel things as badly as his dad and Maggie.

He put his arms around both of them. 'I think our Bridie needs a cuddle,' he said. 'She keeps asking where her mammy is.'

★

It was Saturday afternoon a few weeks later and Iris was trying on hats in Owen Owen's, her favourite shop. She couldn't make up her mind between the blue linen halo and the pink straw shaped like a pie with a frilly veil. In the end, she chose the pie, paid for it, and went upstairs to the restaurant for a coffee and a cake.

She'd brought a novel with her, mainly to read on the tram: *The Razor's Edge* by Somerset Maugham, her favourite author. She took it out of her bag and began to read now as she sipped the coffee. After a while she became conscious that a man in a loud tweed sports jacket two tables away was staring at her fixedly. She frowned deliberately, hoping to put him off, but he continued to stare. Lifting the book, she held it in front of her face and he disappeared from view. When she'd finished the coffee, the cake, and the chapter she'd been reading, she put the book down and the man had gone.

Back home, Iris made tea and continued reading *The Razor's Edge* in the kitchen. Tom, Frank and their father had gone to a football match – Liverpool were playing a London team, she couldn't remember which. Going to the football was something they did three or four times a year. The match over, they would buy fish and chips and eat them out of the newspaper, then spend the rest of the night in a working-class pub singing along with the clientele. They would all go home mildly drunk, so she wasn't expecting Tom until about ten o'clock.

Not that she minded. In about an hour, Nell would arrive, possibly bringing Maggie with her. The plan was to have tea and afterwards go to the Palace in Marsh Lane to see *Mr Skeffington*, with Bette Davis and Claude Rains. If Maggie came, it would be as if they were in the army again – it was the first time all three of them had gone out together since they'd left.

It would seem Maggie was finding it hard to get over her mother's death; it had really knocked the stuffing out of her.

Nor was she enjoying having taken over Sheila's role in running the house. She was a hopeless cook with no interest in housework of any description, and the O'Neill household was a complete mess according to Nell, who helped out a bit. Poor little Bridie cried for her mam every night, but Maggie was no help, too easily giving in to tears herself.

There was a knock on the door. Iris laid down her book and went to answer it. It might be Nell arriving early, or a hopeful patient looking for emergency treatment. If the second, they would be unlucky. She would direct them to the nearest hospital.

But when she opened the door, she found it was neither. Instead, the man she'd seen in Owen Owen's restaurant was outside. It was the sports jacket she recognised first: black and cream houndstooth, really dreadful.

He smiled, but she didn't smile back. 'Yes?' she asked abruptly.

'You don't remember me, do you?' His smile became wider. 'Sergeant Grant, isn't it? Iris to her friends.' He spoke well, with a classy southern accent.

'Who are you?' Her heart seemed to shrivel inside her body. He had actually followed her home, boarded the same tram.

'Major Williams, Matthew to *my* friends.' He made to walk into the house, but she stopped him. 'Now that's no way to act with a friend, is it, Iris?' he said, smiling still. 'Because we *were* friends in Plymouth, close friends if I remember rightly. *Very* close,' he emphasised. 'I would like us to have a little talk about those times, if you don't mind.'

'I do mind, actually.' Iris stayed where she was, blocking his access.

The smile vanished and his blue eyes narrowed. He was a good-looking man, about forty, quite tall. She noticed that the collar of his pale grey shirt was slightly frayed and the button-holes on his sports coat needed repair. There was a weary, almost shamed expression on his handsome features. This was a man down on his luck, she realised.

'Then maybe I should talk to your husband about our friendship,' he said. 'I'm sure there are episodes of your life in the army that he would find fascinating. I'll come back tomorrow, shall I? After Sunday lunch should be a good time. Or is your husband available now?'

Iris stood to one side and let him in. 'My husband is out,' she said quietly. She took him into the waiting room. No way would he be allowed upstairs where she lived with Tom.

He glanced around the room with its four rows of metal chairs. 'I noticed the brass plate outside saying your husband is a doctor.' He managed to raise another smile. 'In which row should I sit?'

'Anywhere you like.' She sat at the end of the back row. He turned the chair in front round so they were facing each other.

'I'm not going to beat about the bush,' he said. 'I need cash and I need it straight away. I'm only in Liverpool because I came for an interview for a job that I didn't get. It was like manna from heaven when I saw you in that shop earlier and remembered what we'd been to each other in the army – lovers, were we not? Quite passionate lovers, if I remember rightly. How many nights did we spend together in that hotel?'

'I can't recall.' It had been four, she remembered quite clearly. And they *had* been passionate. He hadn't been at the camp for long. He'd been posted to India and she had taken it for granted that she would never see him again.

'I wasn't the only one, was I, Sergeant? You were well known in that place. "Keep an eye out for the sexy sergeant," I was told by one chap when he knew I was bound for Plymouth. I think "camp bike" is the appropriate description.'

'How much do you want?' Iris asked baldly. She had no alternative but to pay him.

He shrugged. 'Fifty quid should do for now.'

She gasped. 'Fifty! Do you seriously think I can lay my hands on fifty pounds at the drop of a hat? I would have to go to the bank, and they aren't open until Monday.' What did he mean, 'for now'? Was it his intention to come back again? She was doing her utmost to stay calm, but inwardly she was screaming and badly wanted to be sick. Now that he had found where she lived, she was trapped. He might never leave her alone.

She said, 'On reflection, even if the bank was open, I couldn't withdraw fifty pounds. My husband would have to sign the cheque and I couldn't possibly ask him.' She had a bank account of her own, but it only contained about ten pounds, maybe even less.

'You must think of a reason to get him sign a cheque. Tell him you want a new fur coat or something.'

'But he'll expect to see the coat!' He'd also think it very strange that she'd want a fur coat at the start of summer. And it was out of character for her to buy something so expensive without discussing it with him first.

'Then say you want jewellery, buy cheap stuff instead and show him that,' he said impatiently, as if it was something she should have thought of herself. 'It's what my wife used to do.'

'Does your wife approve of you blackmailing other women?' Iris asked sarcastically.

Anger flared in his nice blue eyes. 'She left me for my brother while I was in India fighting for my country,' he said bitterly. 'When I got home, she'd moved into his house and our house had been let to someone else. I had no job, nowhere to live, no wife.'

Iris wasn't going to say she was sorry for him. 'So you decided to take up blackmail as a career.'

She'd made him angrier, which was a foolish thing to do. He leant forward in the chair and grasped the top of her arm, squeezing it hard. 'Look, I'll be here at half past ten on Monday morning and expect to be given fifty pounds – no,

87

more like midday; you need time to get to a bank. If it's not forthcoming, I will sit in this room and wait until your husband is free and inform him of his pretty wife's sideline while she was in the army.'

'And do you expect *him* to give you fifty pounds?' Iris said, not without irony. She wondered how she was managing to stay so outwardly calm when her insides were in turmoil.

The man shrugged and released her arm. 'You never know, if I put it a certain way, offer him my sympathy, say my wife did more or less the same, tell him just how hard up I am, the good-hearted doctor might find it in him to help me.'

Knowing Tom, that could possibly turn out to be true, but it would mean the end of their marriage. Iris rose from the chair. 'I think you'd better leave,' she said. 'Where will you be staying in Liverpool?' She wasn't sure why she asked, because she didn't care if he was sleeping in the street. Perhaps it was because she already had the germ of an idea.

'The Sloane Hotel in the city centre. I don't suppose,' he said with a sly grin, 'there's any chance of renewing the exciting relationship we had in Plymouth for half an hour or so? As you can imagine, I have plenty of time to spare.'

'You must be joking.'

Nell and Maggie arrived not long after the major had gone. Nell remarked that Iris looked terribly pale. 'Are you feeling all right?' she asked.

'Just a bit off,' Iris confessed. 'Do you mind if I sit upstairs while you make the meal?'

Maggie asked if she would like a cup of tea brought up, and Iris agreed that she would. Maggie was looking a bit brighter. It seemed Ryan's girlfriend Rosie had started to come at weekends and look after things, so Maggie could have Saturday and Sunday off.

'She *loves* housework,' Maggie said incredulously, as if

Rosie had a rare disease that marked her out from the rest of society. 'She and our Ryan are talking about getting married.'

Iris went upstairs and could hear them chattering away. They were such innocents, the pair of them – well, Nell was. Lord knows what Maggie might have got up to with that Chris character she'd been going out with, had been about to marry but had finished with in a quite mysterious way.

The camp bike!

'Oh Lord!' she whispered, burying her face in her hands. If only you could rub out the past and start again. What a stupid thing to think. The past was set like concrete and could never be changed. She wondered if Major Williams would get fed up with Liverpool and return home before Monday. If he had a home. But he must live somewhere, even if it was only a bed-sitting room in London, or even one of those hostel places where men slept in dormitories.

Perhaps she should have been nicer to him, Iris thought, much too late, instead of rubbing him up the wrong way, making it likely he'd return on Monday and tell Tom purely out of spite.

She should have cooked him a meal, explained in a reason-able way how impossible it would be to obtain money without Tom knowing. She could have offered him the money out of her own account as proof that she was genuinely sympathetic and wanted to help. She could even have gone to bed with him . . . She dashed the thought from her mind.

Since coming home, she'd not felt sure of her feelings for Tom, but the prospect of losing him filled her with horror. He wouldn't throw her out, but their marriage would be over. No man would be willing to tolerate his wife behaving like a whore.

'But all I wanted was a baby,' she imagined herself saying.

'You still behaved like a whore,' Tom would say back.

Nell came in with a cup of tea. 'How are you feeling now?'

'Much better,' Iris lied. 'Almost back to normal. I'll be down in a minute.'

'You stay here and have a nice rest,' Nell insisted. 'I'll give you a shout when the meal's ready.' They were having mock duck – made with sausagemeat and covered with cheese sauce that didn't require cheese. It was absolutely delicious.

Iris drank the tea quickly, then went downstairs. Just now, she preferred not to be left alone with her own thoughts.

It appeared Alfred Desmond had spent the afternoon at the police station.

Iris gasped. 'What's he done wrong?'

'Nothing,' Nell said. 'He's friendly with some of the coppers; takes them whisky and biscuits and stuff, to keep on their right side, like. Me da's got irons in an awful lot of fires. He could get away with murder if he wanted.' She'd brought a large box of Cadbury's chocolates for the girls to eat at the pictures, a beautiful round box with yellow roses on the lid, a gift from her father.

It was then that the seed that had been planted in Iris's mind earlier that afternoon began to sprout. She would think about it in the pictures and see what developed.

The plot of *Mr Skeffington* was highly dramatic, but Iris was too busy creating her own plot to concentrate. Bette Davis and Claude Rains were two of her favourite actors, and she hoped the opportunity might come to see the film again.

'What's the name of the pub where your father drinks?' she asked Nell when they were outside, the picture over.

'The Queen's Arms in Pearl Street,' the girl replied. 'Why d'you want to know?'

'Like I said before, Tom's spending the evening in a pub for a change. I just wondered if it might be the same one as your dad's.'

Nell chuckled. 'Liverpool has about a million pubs. It

wouldn't half be a coincidence if your Tom and my dad ended up in the same one.'

'I just wondered.' Iris shrugged.

They said good night, and Maggie and Nell went home. Instead of going home herself, to pass the time Iris walked slowly in the direction of the river. It was impossible to get close to the water because of the docks that lined the road. Lights shone beyond the tall wooden gates, and there was the sound of people working. At this hour, there were few people in the Dock Road and a sensation of aloneness pressed heavily upon her. She shuddered at the idea that this sensation could stay with her for ever if Major Williams told Tom about their relationship on Monday morning.

By now, the girls would be in their own houses and there was no chance of bumping into them. She squared her shoulders and walked swiftly back the way she'd come, into Marsh Lane, where there was rather more life. The chip shop was open and people were gathered outside, as well as outside a pub she didn't know the name of. She walked further until she came to Pearl Street. The Queen's Arms was situated about halfway down, and once again the customers had collected outside, some sitting on the pavement, leaning against the pub walls. She couldn't imagine Alfred Desmond occupying such a demeaning position. He would be inside, on one of the best seats in the parlour. She visualised him surrounded by admirers and hangers-on, the centre of attention.

Well, she wasn't going inside to find out. A man emerged in his shirtsleeves, no collar, and tattered braces holding up his working trousers. His hands were stuffed in his pockets and he was whistling 'It's a Long Way to Tipperary'.

'Is Alfred Desmond in there?' Iris asked. She had on a headscarf rather than a hat, thinking that it made her less noticeable.

'He is indeed, missus,' the chap replied chirpily.

'Would you ask him if he'll come out and speak to me, please?'

'Who shall I say it is? He's not likely to come out without knowing who wants him.' He grinned. 'You could be a member of the criminal underworld luring him to his doom.'

Iris made a face. The chap had far too much imagination. 'Tell him it's the doctor's wife.'

Barely a minute had passed before Alfred Desmond emerged from the building. 'What's up?' he enquired, wiping his beer-soaked moustache with the back of his hand.

'I'd like you to do me a favour,' Iris said. 'If it's possible, that is.'

He put his hand beneath her elbow and led her around the corner into Garnet Street, where it was quieter. 'And what can I do for you, Mrs Grant?'

'I have a problem,' Iris stammered. She should have rehearsed what she was going to say. 'There's a man – I knew him in the army – and he came to the house this afternoon. He's threatening to tell Tom, my husband, all sorts of things about me that aren't true. There's no way Tom will believe him, but it will upset him terribly. Nell will have told you how hard he works on behalf of his patients. I just don't want him troubled, that's all.'

'And what would you like me to do about it, Mrs Grant?' He sounded vaguely amused. He'd probably guessed what she had in mind, but wanted to hear her put it into words.

She swallowed nervously. 'He's staying at the Sloane Hotel in Liverpool tonight and tomorrow night, with the intention of coming to see Tom on Monday morning. His name is Matthew Williams and he was a major in the army. I just wondered if you could possibly persuade him that it's not such a good idea and to please go away? I can pay you up to ten pounds – more than that if you're prepared to wait a little while.'

'I'll do that favour for you, Mrs Grant,' he said pleasantly. 'I don't want your money, but there's a condition.'

'What's that?'

'That you do something for me one of these days.'

'What sort of something?'

'I dunno.' He squeezed her elbow. 'We'll just have to wait and see.' He gave her a little shove. 'I think you'd best be getting home now, Mrs Grant. It's late and you'd be better off tucked up in bed than wandering round Bootle at this time of night.'

'Thank you, Mr Desmond. Good night.' She had only walked a little way when she turned around and called, 'Please don't hurt him,' but there was no sign of Alfred Desmond; he had disappeared.

Chapter 6

Tom had got home before her. He was making tea in the kitchen when Iris arrived. She felt a surge of tearful affection that took her by surprise.

'Did you enjoy the picture?' he enquired.

'It was exceptionally good.' She could tell from the silly look on his face that he was mildly inebriated. 'Have you had a nice day?'

'We had an excellent day, my darling.' He came and took her in his arms. Another time, Iris would have pushed him away and insisted he get on with making the tea, but tonight she threw her arms around his neck. 'Oh Tom!' she sighed, resting her head on his shoulder. 'Oh Tom!'

'What's the sigh for?'

'Sometimes I forget how much I love you.' She felt ashamed that she'd only remembered when their marriage was under threat – all due to her. 'Let's go to bed now,' she said, 'and forget about the tea.'

Tom grinned as he led her out of the kitchen and up the stairs. 'I've already forgotten about it,' he said.

She felt on edge when she woke up on Sunday, half expecting Major Williams to turn up at some point, not only to expose the relationship they'd had in Plymouth, but also to accuse her of trying to have him run out of town by a gang of criminals. She was pleased when Tom suggested they go to Southport in

94

the car – as a doctor, he was allowed a petrol ration – and drop in on some old friends they had remained in touch with. Their children were away at boarding school.

On the way home, they stopped in Formby and went for a stroll on the sands. Iris took off her shoes and wiggled her toes in the sand. Her emotions were in turmoil and she couldn't have described how she felt.

'Oh, by the way,' Tom remarked. 'You know it's Mum and Dad's ruby wedding anniversary in September? Frank and I wondered if we should throw them a party.'

'What a good idea. Shall we have it in our house? It's bigger than Frank's.' She watched a man throw a stick into the water for a dog, who skidded after it and returned to its owner shaking itself energetically. She wondered about getting a dog for themselves; medium size, not so small it would be treated like a baby, or big enough to hog the fire when it was cold.

'Frank and I had already decided on our house, subject to your approval, of course.'

'I do approve. I could ask Nell to make the food – oh, and invite Maggie's auntie as a guest.' She rubbed her hands together, already looking forward to the occasion.

Tom raised his eyebrows. 'Maggie's aunt?'

'Kathleen Curran. Surely you've noticed her poster in our front window? She's standing for Labour in a by-election the first Thursday in May, which is only a few days away. I hope Frank and Constance won't mind, you know, a Labour MP.'

'It's not their wedding anniversary, is it? It's Mum and Dad's and *they* won't mind a bit. In fact, I think Mother's quite likely to turn into a good Socialist one of these days.'

At noon the next day, Iris telephoned the Sloane Hotel and asked to speak to Matthew Williams.

'You mean the major? He left yesterday,' she was told by a male employee. 'His friends came to collect him.'

She wanted to ask if he'd looked all right, had he gone

willingly, but surely the man would have said if something out of the ordinary had happened. She just said, 'Thank you,' and rang off. She wasn't sure how long it was that she sat on the stairs, her head in her arms, feeling almost sick with relief. It was over.

Kathleen Curran won the by-election hands down. The result was announced on the BBC news on Friday morning and in the national press the day after, accompanied by a flattering photograph of the new MP.

On the whole, Bootle was delighted. Despite most of the men disapproving of women having important jobs, it made their little town seem out of the ordinary in the nicest possible way by adding a female Member of Parliament to the handful already there.

After the votes had been counted in Bootle Town Hall, the exuberant members made their way to the Labour Party offices on the Dock Road. One member, though, was noticeably absent. There'd been no sign of Paddy O'Neill all day, and people reckoned he was still mourning the loss of his missus. Someone was sent to call on him and impress upon him how badly he was missed.

Ryan O'Neill and Rosie Hesketh were a sensible couple. Ryan had had enough girlfriends to realise that Rosie was one in a million and would make a perfect wife. She held opinions on pretty nearly every topic on earth and they enjoyed arguing. While her face was never likely to launch a thousand ships, it was nevertheless a nice face and he liked it very much. He would trust Rosie with his life. He loved her, though he wasn't *in* love with her. He sensed that she felt the same, and thought their sort of love was more likely to stand the test of time than the other.

As for Rosie, in her wildest dreams she had never imagined Ryan O'Neill asking her out, let alone kissing her, let alone continuing to ask her out and, by some sort of miracle, asking her to marry him.

She thought she knew why. His mam was dead, his dad had fallen to pieces, his sister Maggie was making a pig's ear out of running the house. And his other sister, little Bridie, who Rosie loved to bits, was dead miserable, poor lamb. Rosie's heart went out to her. Ryan wanted Rosie not only for a wife, but as a replacement for his mam, and she was more than willing to oblige.

When he proposed, she snapped him up. At home she was just one in a family of ten, but with the O'Neills she would become a wife, a daughter-in-law, a sister-in-law, and a mother to Bridie. She couldn't wait.

They decided to get married the following month, June. The announcement was unexpected and the date was early enough for people to take it for granted that Rosie was in the club. She looked forward to proving them wrong.

Maggie bought herself a new dress from C&A Modes for the occasion, pale blue linen with three-quarter-length sleeves and a pleated skirt. Rosie made her a sort of hat by covering a cheap Alice band with blue velvet and attaching a narrow circle of net. She made a similar one for Nell, except it was red to match her own new dress, which was dead straight and sleeveless with a black patent-leather belt. Iris had talked her into buying it, saying it made her look incredibly smart.

'You're slim enough to be a model,' she added.

Rosie made her wedding dress out of white rayon lining, though hardly anyone guessed that the material had cost a mere eleven pence a yard. Her only bridesmaid was little Bridie, who looked pretty in a pink frothy creation decorated with rosebuds. Rosie had no doubt made it out of old dish-cloths, Maggie said sarcastically.

Nell, assisted by Iris, had made the cake: three eggless sponges joined together with layers of jam and covered with chocolate butter icing It was both utterly delicious and a little bit sickly.

The fact that the wedding was on a Wednesday instead of a Saturday like most weddings rather took the shine off in Maggie's eyes. Nevertheless, when she woke up that morning, it was the first time in ages that there'd been a lift in her heart. It came partly from knowing that her brother would be happy with the bossy, rather nice young woman who quite clearly loved him to death, and who was taking over Maggie's role in the house when she and Ryan returned from their honeymoon in Blackpool, which meant Maggie could go back to work. She couldn't wait!

Although most of Rosie's family came to the wedding, at least half had to go to work once it was over, so the number of guests who came to the reception held in a room over the Queen's Arms was small. It was a pleasant, if sober occasion. Getting drunk on a Wednesday afternoon didn't hold the same appeal as getting drunk on a Saturday. Everything was over by three o'clock, when the guests went home and the bride and groom left for their honeymoon.

Maggie and Nell returned to their own houses to change out of their new dresses. They arranged to meet afterwards and visit Iris, who would be interested to know how things had gone.

Paddy O'Neill had changed out of his best suit for his workaday clothes when Maggie went into the sitting room. Bridie had had a tiring day and was asleep upstairs. Maggie was about to go up herself, but her father asked her to stay. She sat at the table and he in his armchair – as yet, no one could bring themselves to sit in Sheila's chair in front of the window, apart from Tinker, who enjoyed having it all to himself.

'It's about your mam, luv,' her dad said tiredly. 'I've never told anyone this, but on the morning of the day she died, me and her, we had a fight, like.' He put his hand over his eyes, unable to go on.

'What about, Dad?' Maggie asked softly.

He shook his head, still shielding his eyes. 'She didn't want me going into politics,' he said eventually, in a raw voice. 'It got dead heated. She thought I'd be spending all me time in London, that we – the family, like – would hardly see each other. She seemed to think I wouldn't be around when the new baby was born, though I insisted that I wouldn't miss it for worlds. She got in a terrible state, Maggie luv. There was nothing I could do to calm her. Christ!' He lay back in the chair, an expression on his face of such naked misery that Maggie wanted to weep. 'I should've given in, been more gentle with her, but I thought she was just being awkward. Up until then, she hadn't seemed to mind the idea. That was an awful pregnancy she had, luv.' Tears were running down his cheeks now. 'It was my fault for putting her in the club. Oh, Maggie girl, sometimes I feel as if I want to kill meself.'

'Dad!' Maggie knelt beside her father and laid her head on his breast. She contemplated telling him about her own confrontation with her mother, but the truth of her association with Chris and the way it had ended was likely to upset him as much as it had done Mam. Instead, what she told him was close to the truth. 'Her friend Alice came that afternoon and was really horrible. It turned out that over all these years she'd been dead jealous – apparently her husband was killed a few months after they'd got married and she was pregnant with their daughter. She was dead spiteful, Alice, and it upset Mam no end. So it wasn't your fault, not at all, Dad. I mean, you and Mam had had rows before, but it didn't cause her any harm, did it?'

Even as she watched, it appeared to her that her father's brow became smoother, and his face didn't look so gaunt.

'Is that really true, Maggie?' he asked.

'As if I'd make up a story like that! I bet Mam really liked the idea of you going into politics, but she was feeling dead lousy that day and Alice really got under her skin in the afternoon.'

'Mebbe.' He stretched his arms and yawned. 'Y'know, I wouldn't mind half an hour's kip.'

Maggie got to her feet. 'It'd do you good, Dad. I'll just get changed and call for Nell.'

Nell had gone when she called at the house. Mrs Desmond was ironing on the dinner table when Maggie went in the back way.

'She said to tell you to meet her at the doctor's. She makes their tea, you know.' Mrs Desmond was desperately proud of her daughter's relationship with Iris.

'You're looking well,' Maggie remarked. It was hard to believe this was the same woman who'd spent years stuck in a chair being waited on hand and foot. With her husband no longer in the clutches of Rita Hayworth, Mrs Desmond was her old self again, and Mr Desmond no longer gave the impression of being the devil incarnate either.

As she walked towards Iris's, it occurred to Maggie that there was no need for Nell to stay in Liverpool. With her mother on her feet again, she could live in London as she had originally planned. And what was more – Maggie caught her breath – *they could go together!* Rather than hunt for a new job in Liverpool, she would look for one in the capital, where she would find something far more interesting than being a typist in a roofing firm with someone like Iggy for a boss – a receptionist in a dead-posh hotel, for example, an extra in films, secretary to a millionaire. The list was endless. With Rosie installed in the O'Neills' house, Maggie wouldn't be missed.

It was still horrible to think of Mam dying virtually before her eyes, but her poor sick heart must have exhausted her and the visit from Alice had been the last straw.

As soon as she could get Nell to one side, she'd bring up the idea of them both going to London. She just knew that Nell would jump at the chance.

'I suppose I've gone off it, that's all.'

'But Nell, you were *mad* to go to London,' Maggie gasped.

'I know I was, but I couldn't, could I,' Nell said reasonably, 'not with me mam the way she was. Now she's better, but I don't want to go any more. Y'see, Mags, I'm really enjoying getting me little business going. I've already made a few lunches and dinners for people, mainly Adele's friends. I get paid really well, and Iris gives me ten bob a week for making her and Tom's tea. And it's *so* interesting,' she added, with such enthusiasm that Maggie winced – fancy getting enthusiastic about *cooking*! 'Iris thinks I should have menus printed, like, and cards with me name on.'

'How exciting,' Maggie said, hoping she didn't sound as underwhelmed as she felt. 'Where do you get all the food from?' she asked in an attempt to show some interest. 'Everything's still rationed.' Nell was her best friend and she should be pleased for her, not bored.

'The customers provide the ingredients,' Nell said. 'All I do is cook it for them and serve it up nicely. Anyroad, not everything is rationed.'

'Oh, I see,' Maggie said lamely.

Well, she thought in bed that night, if Nell wasn't prepared to go with her to London, she'd just have to go by herself!

'Your bed will always be here for you,' Rosie assured her, which Maggie thought was a bit of a cheek, seeing as she'd been born in the house and Rosie had hardly been there five minutes.

'It's a gear idea, sis,' Ryan said. 'You're obviously fed up to the teeth here. Go and have a good time.'

'Lucky old you.' Nell gave her a hug. It was a ridiculous

thing for her to say: she could easily have gone to London too, so what was lucky about it?

Iris bought her a tan leather handbag. 'It's nice and big. You need a big bag in London to hold all the things you'll take to work each day, like a book and make-up and a rain hat and stuff.'

'Thank you.' Maggie wished someone would say they were sorry she was leaving, that she'd be missed. She got the impression everyone would be glad to see the back of her, including her father.

'Well, it's not the first time you've left home, is it, luv?' Dad said. 'But this time you'll be on your own. Now,' he gripped her by the shoulders and gave her a little shake, 'I want you to promise to come back straight away if you're not happy down in London. It's a big place with lots of people living there and it's easy to feel lonely in a crowd. Promise now!'

Maggie nodded. 'I promise I'll be home like a shot.'

Maggie wasn't happy in London, but she didn't go home. She didn't want anybody to think she was a failure. And she wasn't *desperately* unhappy, just not particularly happy. She was no longer crying herself to sleep every night, and hopefully it would stop altogether soon.

She'd got herself a nice room on the fourth floor of a big house in Shepherd's Bush, an attic room with sloping ceilings and a lovely view of hundreds and hundreds of roofs. She had never thought that roofs could be so colourful: black, red, orange, all different shades of grey, a single roof with green tiles. Some appeared white in the moonlight or gleamed like black satin in the rain. When the sun shone, they looked like a multicoloured chess board. Chimneys, stubby and tall, puffed smoke from early morning till late at night. When it was foggy, the smoke and the fog combined, casting a pall on the part of the city that was visible from Maggie's window.

Realising that it would take time before she found her ideal job, when she'd first arrived she had registered as a shorthand typist with an employment agency in the city and had worked in a series of little Dickensian offices, full of dusty ledgers and wooden filing cabinets that were so jammed full of papers they were difficult to open. The typewriters she'd worked with were genuine antiques and incredibly hard to use, the keys sticking, the print barely readable. She was usually the only female there; the men were ancient and had worked there all their lives. Occasionally there'd been an office boy, bored witless by the utter tedium of his life. What had he to look forward to? one boy asked Maggie, who was unable to provide an answer apart from recommending that he leave and find another job with prospects and a more cheerful atmosphere to work in.

It was advice she'd eventually taken herself when a girl she'd spoken to on the tube advised her to register with an agency in the West End. 'They'll send you to more modern places.'

Since then, she had been working as a temporary typist for Thomas Cook, the travel agent, in their head office in Berkeley Street just off Piccadilly. After a week, she was offered a permanent post, but turned it down. She'd sooner wait until the job of her dreams turned up and she'd be able to start straight away.

Shepherd's Bush was only a few stops on the Underground from Bond Street, where Maggie got off each morning and walked through the Mayfair streets to Berkeley Square. Lunchtimes she sat on a bench in Green Park or wandered along to Piccadilly Circus and joined the tourists who were beginning to return to London now the war was over. As in Liverpool, the boarded-up bomb sites were an ugly reminder of the Blitz that had so recently been the curse of British cities.

Although she enjoyed working at Thomas Cook's, there were no women of her own age in her part of the office, and Maggie badly wanted to make friends. In July, it was her birthday and she turned twenty-two. Almost that many cards fell through the letter box downstairs, but not a single one bore a London postmark.

She had never known what it was like to be friendless, had never thought that one day she would discover how it felt to be lonely. In the army, she'd been one of the most popular girls in the camp with both men and women. Until now, never in her entire life had she gone to the pictures or a dance on her own. In her darkest moments, she imagined collapsing in the street and being taken to hospital in an ambulance, and being unable to give the name of a single friend or relative who could be contacted.

Sundays were the worst days. An elderly foreign couple lived in one of the ground-floor rooms. Every weekend, dozens of relatives would turn up armed with food: casserole dishes, tureens of soup, and large tins of other food. They would spend the afternoon there, and their busy conversation and laughter could be heard four floors up. It used to be rather like that in the O'Neills' house in Bootle. Not quite so many people, not nearly so much food – Sheila O'Neill would have been outraged had people brought their own – but all sorts of friends and Irish cousins who spent the rest of the day there, staying for tea and supper too.

That was what Maggie missed most of all, the sense of belonging and being surrounded by family, in particular Mam, something she hadn't appreciated when she'd had it. She continued to cry at odd moments thinking about her mother, wondering if it would ever stop.

As she sat contemplating the hundreds of roofs and thousands of windows visible from the attic room that, as yet, showed little sign of anyone living there, she was conscious of the odd tear slowly trickling down her face. She would angrily brush it away before settling down to write a letter to someone, usually her father, telling him that she felt absolutely fine.

There are so many things to do in London, she would write, *and I am making loads of friends . . .*

Nearly every day Nell and Iris made yet another list of the refreshments to be served at Adele and Cyril's ruby wedding celebration. It was now nearing the end of August and the party was three weeks away. Iris had made a list of twenty names to be invited, a list that was quickly doubled when Adele got her hands on it. It turned out she had tracked down a number of guests who had been at the original wedding forty years ago, and Cyril wished to invite some of the members of his golf club.

'Forty!' Nell was stunned. 'How on earth can we make enough food for forty people in a single day?'

'For goodness' sake, Nell, in the army you catered for a hundred, maybe two hundred hungry people. Have you forgotten how efficient you were?' Nell was a lovely person, Iris thought, but she was inclined to dither.

'You must think me dead stupid,' she said. 'It's just that it didn't seem to matter in the army as much as it does now.'

'Well, that doesn't say much for your comrades in arms.' Iris briskly clapped her hands. 'Look, let's start with things like potato cakes that will keep for a while in the larder. Do you know, in America they have things called refrigerators or ice boxes where food can be kept for weeks, even months?'

Nell looked impressed and sighed longingly.

'We can make big cakes too,' Iris continued. 'How about that nice moist apple cake you made once, and the eggless ginger cake? We could make little trifles the day before – I managed to get a tin of peaches in the Co-op the other day, did I tell you?'

'No, but that's the gear, isn't it? We can cut the peaches up in bits to go in the jelly. Have you ordered the invitations yet?'

'Yes, I ordered fifty, just in case Adele came up with more names. Are we inviting Maggie?' The invitations were costing more than Iris had expected. She would have asked Nell's father if he could obtain them cheaper, but he might expect to be invited.

'Shall I draw up another list of what food to make and when we should make it?'

'That would be very helpful, Nell.' They both loved making lists and the house was littered with them. 'Do you think Maggie will come to the party? After all, it's a long way from London, and there's the train fare.'

Nell shrugged and spread her hands. 'She might, or she might not. I know she's not happy in London.'

'How do you know she's not happy?' Iris frowned. 'In the letter she sent me, she said she was having a wonderful time.'

'Yes, but she never mentions names, does she? She doesn't say "I went to the pictures with so-and-so" or "I had dinner with someone else". No, Maggie's finding London a bit hard to take.'

Well, at least she had someone to go to the pictures with – and not on the crowded tube, either.

Mrs Ivy Morrison, who lived on the ground floor of the house in Shepherd's Bush, arrived home in a taxi one Tuesday evening at the same time as Maggie came home from work. Maggie carried her bag of groceries into the house for the woman, who looked well into her seventies, waiting while she unlocked the door to her flat. When she had, Maggie was invited in for a cup of tea and a piece of cake.

The large room smelled delightfully of lavender and was like a Victorian museum, full of little tables laden with photos in elaborate frames, lacy cloths, velvet-upholstered furniture, home-made rugs, a piano, and a dining room suite with the curliest legs Maggie had ever seen. The walls were so covered with pictures that the wallpaper behind was hardly visible. Mrs Morrison lit a gas lamp with a heavily fringed shade, then disappeared behind a curtain at the end of the long room and emerged with two cups of tea and a cherry cake on a plate.

'I made the cake this morning,' she announced, 'so it's very fresh. I won the cherries at a whist drive.'

'It's the gear,' Maggie said with her mouth full.

'Shall we have some music while we chat?' Without waiting for a reply, Mrs Morrison removed an embroidered cloth to reveal a Bakelite wireless underneath and switched it on; Frank Sinatra was singing 'All or Nothing at All'.

'I love Radio Luxembourg,' she said. 'I listened to it all during the war.'

'So did I – I mean we. I was in the army,' Maggie explained. 'We had a wireless in our hut.' She felt as if she was in a time warp; two different worlds, the Victorian one and the modern one, but with the same tunes.

'The army! How exciting. Do tell me all about it. I was a nurse in the Boer War at the beginning of the century,' Mrs Morrison said proudly.

'That sounds dead exciting too. Perhaps you can tell me about that after I've told you about the army.'

'You start, dear, and in a little while I'll make more tea.'

On Saturday, Ivy Morrison and Maggie went by taxi to he Globe Electric Theatre in Wandsworth to see *Anchors Aweigh* with Frank Sinatra and Gene Kelly. The old lady needed help going into the cinema, then with finding a seat.

Maggie fell instantly in love with Gene Kelly, who she'd never seen before. Do I love him more than I do Fred Astaire? she asked herself, but couldn't decide. Frank Sinatra sang 'I Fall in Love Too Easily', and Mrs Morrison hummed it in the taxi all the way home. She invited Maggie into her flat for a glass of sherry.

All in all, it was a really enjoyable evening. Maggie promised that she would go again in a month's time. But she still felt lonely, still wanting to make friends, preferably ones who weren't four times her age.

★

The day of the party was getting closer and closer and Iris and Nell were becoming more and more nervous. It was such an important anniversary, celebrating forty years of marriage; very happy years, Adele emphasised.

Iris had found a box of a dozen candles. On the night, she placed them strategically in glass jars in the parlour. Once lit, the perfectly ordinary room turned into one full of secrets and mystery. The music of Cole Porter and Irving Berlin was being played on the gramophone, so headily romantic that Iris felt her heart beat a little faster.

The nights were already starting to dim. When the guests first arrived, Nell handed round tiny Welsh rarebits as an aperitif. Tom was in charge of the wine. He had prepared a bowl of fruit punch for Nell, who was still unable to drink alcohol.

He had diagnosed her as suffering from something called 'alcohol intolerance'. 'It's a well-known condition. Some people can't break the stuff down in their stomach. It can cause palpitations, headaches, excessive sweating and other complications.'

The whole house took on a special quality, as if it was alive and responsive to the people enjoying themselves within its walls. They danced in the candlelit parlour, held long, highly intellectual conversations in the dining room, ate in the kitchen and on the stairs, were sick – just one or two – in the bathroom.

Other than that, it was a very decorous party when compared to the ones Iris had known in the camp at Plymouth, where the men in particular partied as if it might possibly be the last one they would go to – which sometimes it was.

Frank, Tom's brother, was keeping a close eye on Nell, who looked exceptionally attractive in her red dress, waiting for her to finish serving the food so he could ask her to dance. In turn, Iris was keeping a close eye on Frank, who she didn't trust further than she could throw him. Nell was too young and vulnerable where men like Frank were concerned.

Kathleen Curran was a popular guest. Few people there other than Nell and Iris had voted for her in the recent by-election, but she was a woman with such an effervescent personality that she was hard to dislike. Her loud, distinctive voice with its broad Irish accent could be heard echoing through the house offering quite shocking opinions on some of the things people held most dear, such as the royal family, the Church of England and the great Winston Churchill himself. She had brought Paddy O'Neill, Maggie's father, with her. Paddy had given in his notice at his old job and would soon be the agent in charge of the Labour Party office in Bootle.

'The food's gorgeous,' Adele said happily. 'Everybody loves it. I shall mention who is responsible for it when Cyril and I thank everyone later for our presents. Nell will be inundated with people wanting her to prepare the food for *their* parties. Where *is* Nell?' she asked, looking around.

Iris shrugged and said, 'Somewhere.' It wasn't for another half-hour that she discovered Nell was nowhere to be seen. Worried, she looked in the waiting room, Tom's surgery, the bedrooms. She eventually found her in the spare bedroom fast asleep on the bed, her breathing raw and uneven. Her face was almost as red as her dress, and when Iris touched her forehead it was burning. She fetched Tom immediately.

'The punch has been spiked,' he said angrily. 'Cyril's just told me. I've poured it down the sink.' He bent over Nell. 'She's got a temperature. It can only be that bloody stuff. I saw her drink some.'

'What shall we do? Does she need to go to hospital?' Iris felt the urge to panic.

'No. It's best for her to be left to sleep it off.' Gently he pulled the eiderdown over the girl. 'She's going to be all right. We'll look in on her from time to time and I'll put a glass of cold water and some aspirin by the bed ready for when she wakes.'

'But we can't just continue with the party!'

'Yes we can, darling.' He led her from the room. 'Nell's in the best place. I don't want to spoil Mum and Dad's night. They'll never have another fortieth wedding anniversary, will they?'

'No,' Iris said miserably. 'Should I sit with Nell, do you think?'

'There's no need.' He closed the bedroom door quietly behind them. 'You might disturb her. Go and make yourself some tea. It's not far off midnight and people will start going home soon.'

'Oh, all right.' She still felt unhappy about things. As she was going downstairs, there was a knock on the door and she opened it to Ryan O'Neill, who she had met just once, at his mother's funeral.

'Hello, Iris.' He smiled. 'I promised me Auntie Kath I'd come and help fetch me da home, on the assumption he might not be up to it himself.'

'Your father's upstairs.' He was in the room with the candles. As far as she knew, he hadn't moved out of his chair. She had no idea how much he'd had to drink.

'You'd better go upstairs and look for him,' she said. 'Oh, and help yourself to a drink while you're at it.'

'Ta. Is Nell here? I thought she might like to come with us.'

'She's lying down with a headache.' Nell had told her father she might not be home until morning.

Ryan bounded up the stairs and Iris thought what a remarkably handsome young man he was.

It turned out that Paddy O'Neill had spent the evening getting quietly drunk. It wasn't until an hour later that Ryan helped his father out of the house with his Auntie Kath supporting his other side and singing 'The Red Flag' in a loud voice.

'What a remarkable woman,' Cyril said as he watched her leave. 'If I'd been in her company for much longer, I might well have joined the Labour Party. I think quite a few people would agree with me. Mind you, there's also a few who wanted to strangle her.'

It was quarter past two and everyone had gone. Iris found Nell sitting up drinking the water Tom had put on the bedside table. 'How are you feeling, love?'

'All right.' The girl smiled sleepily. 'Something dead funny happened – though I might have dreamt it.'

'What was this dead-funny thing?'

'I'll tell you some other time.'

Iris forgot to ask again, and it was months before she discovered what the funny thing was. When she did, it was to change her life and the lives of others in the years to come.

Chapter 7

Maggie went home for Christmas. It had always been her mother's favourite time of year, and this, the first Christmas without her, was particularly hard on the family she had left behind. But Rosie – Maggie was beginning to genuinely love her sister-in-law – had made great efforts with the food and decorations, even checking that her new family hadn't forgotten to buy each other presents, so that the gap left by Sheila O'Neill was at least partially filled.

On Boxing Day, Maggie had tea with Nell and Iris. Not for the first time, she marvelled at what close friends they had become. For herself, she knew it would be a wrench to return to London, though by now she had got to know a few people.

Philip Morrison was Ivy Morrison's youngest son – she called him her baby. At thirty-five, he was considerably older than Maggie, but they enjoyed each other's company. He had lost his fiancée during the war, he told her on their first date.

'Oh dear, I'm dead sorry,' Maggie exclaimed. 'Was it the Blitz?'

Philip had given a wry smile. 'No, I lost her to a first lieutenant in the navy. Silly of me, I know, but I've not been able to trust a woman again – present company excepted,' he said with a smile.

'I expect it was the uniform.' People were dazzled by uniforms. In the army, men had far preferred girls wearing their horrible khaki ATS outfits, including thick unflattering stockings and flat lace-up shoes, than the most glamorous dresses. She explained this to Philip, who said he could well believe it.

'I'd like to think I am better-looking than the chap Margery went off with,' he said gloomily. 'He was a most unattractive individual, with a face like a pig. If it was the uniform she was impressed by, I feel sorry for her when he gets demobbed and is back to wearing ordinary clothes.' He had spent the war as a statistician working for the government, and had worn an ordinary suit.

Maggie assured him he was extremely handsome. The Morrisons had Welsh blood, and Philip was dark-haired with smoky grey eyes. If he hadn't been so ancient and, let's face it, a trifle old-womanish, Maggie might have been smitten.

She described him to Nell on Boxing Day evening when they went to a dance at the Grafton. 'We've been to the theatre together a few times. We saw *The Winslow Boy* with Emlyn Williams. Remember him in *Hatter's Castle*, except this time he was in the flesh. Oh, and we saw Vivien Leigh in a play called *By the Skin of our Teeth*. You know, the actress who played Scarlett O'Hara?'

'Of course I know who Vivien Leigh is,' Nell said. 'This is Liverpool, Maggie, a big city, not the back of beyond. You might have noticed we have theatres here, if not as many as in London.'

'I'm sorry, Nell.' Maggie hugged her friend. 'In London, it's like living at the hub of the universe.' She was exaggerating a bit. She regarded Nell critically. 'Are you all right?'

'I'm fine,' Nell assured her. 'What makes you think I'm not?'

'You look different somehow. Your cheeks aren't usually so rosy and you look incredibly happy.'

Nell laughed. 'So you think there's something wrong because I look happy and have rosy cheeks?'

'The cheeks could mean you have a temperature. Are you in love?'

'No, I'm not. But I am happy; happy with my life.'

'That's good.' Maggie had been hoping that Nell might change her mind about London after hearing what a wonderful place it was, but it seemed it was not to be. Nell was perfectly contented with her lot in Liverpool, which was a shame.

They were on the balcony in the Grafton – sitting on the same seats they'd been when Chris Conway had approached them all those months ago. Neither girl had mentioned Chris.

Maggie said, 'Shall we stay up here and watch the jitter-bugging?'

'Okay,' Nell said dreamily.

'I have to go back tomorrow,' Maggie sighed. 'It's work again on Monday.'

'Poor old you.'

'Lucky old you! It must be nice being self-employed and able to please yourself whether you work or not.' Maggie watched as a young man threw his partner over his shoulder. The girl landed unsteadily on her feet and continued to dance, obviously not caring about showing her knickers to the world.

'I had loads of dinners and parties to cater for in the run-up to Christmas,' Nell pointed out. 'I've got another big party on New Year's Eve. I think I'm due a rest.'

'You'll make so much money, you'll end up like Barbara Hutton, the Woolworth heiress,' Maggie said.

'I hope not.' Nell shuddered. 'She's desperately unhappy, poor woman. If I make too much money, then I shall give it away.'

There'd been a postcard on the message board in Thomas Cook's asking for new members for a club for ex-service-women who met fortnightly in the West End for a meal and a chat. Maggie had joined, but was disappointed to find herself the only one who'd been a private. Another woman had been a sergeant in the WAAF, but the rest, about ten altogether, were ex-officers. Most were unmarried. The leading light, Alicia Black, a nursing officer in the WRNS, had started the club, and ruled it with a rod of iron. Maggie felt obliged to make sure her shoes were well polished before they met, and was conscious of her posture. A few times she had almost saluted, but stopped just in time.

She had nearly left the club after the first meeting, when she'd found the other women cold and unfriendly, but in her experience, no matter what tensions might exist at the start of a friendship, they would disappear as time passed.

On New Year's Eve, the women were eating in a restaurant in Covent Garden and afterwards making their way to Trafalgar Square to let in the new year with the crowd.

Maggie had promised to have dinner with Philip Morrison and his chess club on the night. She knew how keen he was to turn up with a woman on his arm, and couldn't bring herself to desert him for her new women friends. As the chess club intended breaking up at about eleven so the members could celebrate the new year at home, Maggie arranged to meet the ex-servicewomen afterwards in Trafalgar Square, outside the National Gallery.

She thought about Nell while having dinner with the chess club. The meal was served in a pub off the Old Kent Road that was decorated with paper streamers faded with age and a Christmas tree that had lost most of its needles. There were gaps in the floorboards and it was also exceedingly cold. Draughts blew up her skirt and down her neck. She would have liked to put on a scarf, but it would have looked rude.

In fact, it had been an unusually cold December and the country was hoping that the new year might see an improvement in the weather. Maggie's room in Shepherd's Bush had only a small, inadequate gas fire. She had been sleeping with her coat on top of the bedclothes and had bought bed socks, yet still felt cold.

The reason she thought about Nell was because she wished she had been there to make the dinner. The steak was so tough she could have soled her shoes with it, the cabbage hadn't been properly cooked and the roast potatoes didn't look very roasted and were limp and tasteless.

Philip introduced her to his fellow chess players as 'My *very* good friend, Miss Margaret O'Neill' and squeezed her hand a lot. Maggie got into the spirit of things and flirted with him madly. After a while, she was able to see the funny side of the evening and enjoyed herself from then on, though she was relieved when the meal was over, a final drink was ordered, and everyone wished each other happy new year.

Outside, she kissed Philip on the cheek and caught an Underground train to Trafalgar Square, probably the noisiest place on earth that night. Men – women wouldn't have been so stupid – were throwing themselves in the fountain and wading through the icy water soaking wet and dripping. Different songs were being sung in different places. 'Lily Marlene' was being played on a piano accordion, and an entire band in uniform blasted out a military march. A man in evening dress was making a passionate speech, throwing his arms about. Maggie listened and discovered he was arguing that the world was flat. Another man vomited in her path and she had to skirt round him.

'Can I kiss you, girl?' a soldier pleaded. Maggie refused with a laugh.

Trumpets were being blown. People danced, either with each other, or in a long conga line without an apparent end. They stood in circles and did the hokey cokey.

'Put your right leg in, your right leg out, in, out, in, out, shake it all about, do the hokey cokey and you turn around, that's what it's all about.'

'Oh, *hokey cokey cokey*,' Maggie sang as she made her way towards the National Gallery. *'That's what it's all about.'*

They'd always done the hokey cokey at dances in Plymouth, usually at the beginning of the proceedings, along with the Gay Gordons, the conga and the Lambeth Walk. As the evening had worn on, the dances became slower, the lights dimmer, the smoke thicker, the music more romantic. 'Who's Taking You Home Tonight?', 'Goodnight, Sweetheart', 'You'll Never Know', 'We'll Meet Again' . . . She began to hum the last song.

She'd reached the National Gallery and was sitting on the steps, but soon got to her feet when she discovered they were freezing. For a while she marched up and down, hugging herself as she tried to keep warm, jumping up and down. She looked at her watch and saw it was ten to twelve, but there was no sign of Alicia Black or any other member of the club. Surely she wasn't about to face the advent of the new year on her own? She looked wildly around the crowded square and couldn't see one other person by themselves, not a single one.

'Where are you?' she cried. Her voice sounded pitiful and desperate. She wanted to get away, hide in one of the neighbouring streets in a doorway, where she wouldn't look out of place on her own. But someone might still come. Anyroad, she'd never make her way through the hordes in time. Already people had begun to count down. She looked at her watch again and it was almost midnight. Not far away, Big Ben began to toll.

'Twelve, eleven, ten,' people were chanting. 'Nine, eight, seven.' Maggie put her hands over her ears. She sat down on the steps again, not caring if she froze to death. Why had she come to London? Back home in Liverpool, they'd be listening to Big Ben on the wireless. The house would be full; it would be warm there.

'Six, five, four,' the crowd shouted. 'Three, two, one.'

It was 1947, and a tremendous cheer erupted. Everyone

began to sing 'Auld Lang Syne', apart from Maggie who was in tears and had no one's hand to hold. Previous New Year's Eves flashed through her mind, and on every single one she was with loads of friends, being kissed, being hugged, laughing, feeling happy, oh so happy.

'Young lady. Young lady, why the tears on such a night?' She was being pulled firmly to her feet. She opened her eyes and looked into a pair of calm grey ones. Until then she had never believed in love at first sight, but now she changed her mind immediately.

'What's your name?' he asked. He had a strong, yet gentle face; not handsome, but attractive. His hair was hidden under a woollen hat, but blond tufts stuck out on his neck.

'Maggie O'Neill,' she sobbed.

'I am Jacek, Maggie, but over here people call me Jack. Jack Kaminski.'

Maggie was beginning to feel better. At least she wasn't standing out like a sore toe, so obviously by herself.

Another man came bounding up, very young, very boyish. 'Jack, people were wondering where you'd gone.' He grinned at Maggie. 'Who's this?'

'This is my new friend, Maggie O'Neill. She is not so happy with the new year. I was about to invite her to our party. Maggie, this is my friend Drugi Nowak. We are Polish and there is a party going on in a restaurant in Soho, not far from here. Would you like to come back with us?'

Maggie nodded vigorously. 'Yes. Oh yes please.'

'What are you doing here by yourself?' Jack asked.

'I was supposed to be meeting people, but they didn't come.'

'Maggie!' a voice screamed. 'There you are. I've been looking for you everywhere.'

Maggie didn't recognise the woman running towards her until she'd skidded to a stop in front of her. Daphne Scott, one of the club members, was terribly posh and had an army general for a father. She wore a full-length grey fur coat and a hat to match, and looked like a Russian countess.

'Alicia and co. are waiting for you in the restaurant,' she said in her beautifully refined voice. 'A couple of the women aren't feeling well, so they decided not to come to the square. I offered to come and get you.' She looked extremely puffed. 'We couldn't very well let you down, could we?'

'That's dead kind of you,' Maggie said gratefully, but Daphne had come too late. Jack and Drugi were waiting politely, and she much preferred the prospect of their party to the restaurant in Covent Garden. 'I hope you don't mind, but Jack and Drugi have invited me to a party and I said I'd go.'

'A party! Oh, can I come too?' Daphne laid her lemon kid-gloved hand on Jack's arm. 'You look far more interesting than Alicia and her lot.' She fluttered her lashes. 'My name is Daphne Scott.'

Jack gave a little bow. 'I am Jacek Kaminski, but you can call me Jack.'

'It's nice to meet you, Jack.' She linked his arm. 'Shall we go?'

Maggie was left to walk with Drugi, who seemed very nice, except she much preferred his friend.

Nell only agreed to provide food at an event if she was able to leave by half past ten. On New Year's Eve, she had packed up her kit, as Iris called the various tins, boxes and dishes she carried around with her, and was on the tram from Orrell Park back to Bootle before eleven o'clock, having left behind an assortment of savoury and sweet biscuits to be eaten later. The party had gone well. She had been congratulated on the food, and the payment, plus a large tip, was in her bag. She had given her card to several of the women there. Her father, who appeared to be dead chuffed about having such an independent daughter, was looking around for a small car for her to buy.

'You'd be allowed a petrol ration,' he assured her, 'being in business, like. It'd look really professional, you turning up with your own transport. And your friend Iris can teach you how to drive, her having been a driver in the army, like.'

It was the gear having money. She'd bought some really nice presents for her sisters, their husbands and their kids, and a lovely checked jumper for her brother Kenny, who'd started courting a girl from Chaucer Street called Myra Hammond.

The tram stopped at the terminus at the end of Rimrose Road. Nell got off and crossed the road to Iris and Tom's house, where she let herself in using her own key. The couple had gone to a party in Waterloo.

In the kitchen, she put the tools of her trade away on the bottom shelf of the dresser – she preferred to keep them here. Back home, things could well disappear and she might never see them again.

It was just after half eleven according to the clock on the wall. Her sisters were coming round tonight, so there'd be plenty of company at her own house. And she'd been invited to a party at the O'Neills', to which she would have gone had Maggie still been home.

Being alone at the onset of the new year didn't bother Nell. She'd stay where she was until Iris and Tom came home. They were unlikely to be late, as Tom's surgery was opening in the morning, and there was something important she wanted to say to them. She made tea and took it upstairs, where the remnants of a fire glowed in the living room. She curled up in an armchair, drank the tea and promptly fell asleep.

She didn't wake until almost one o'clock, when she heard the front door open and Iris and Tom's footsteps on the stairs.

'Hello!' she called.

'You're still here.' Iris came into the room. She looked really lovely in a new pink satin frock that she'd had made by a dressmaker from Pearl Street. The material had once been a bedspread with frayed edges. 'I thought you'd have gone home by now. Were you very late back?'

Nell unfolded herself out of the chair and stood up. 'No, it's just that I wanted to talk to you about something, that's all.'

'That's nice.' Iris kissed her on the cheek. 'Happy new year, Nell.'

'Did you have a nice time at the party?'

Iris made a face. 'No, it was horrid. The host and hostess, only a young couple, fought all night long, and the food was dire. I shall send them your card tomorrow.' She sat on the settee. 'Sit down and tell me what you wanted to talk about.'

'I want Tom to hear too.'

'Tom!' Iris called. 'Nell wants to talk to us.'

'Just a minute.' Tom came in seconds later carrying two drinks. 'Sherry for you, darling, whisky for me, and nothing whatsoever for Nell here – unless you want lemonade or something?' He raised his eyebrows.

'No thank you.'

'If you're about to tell us you're going to live in London with Maggie,' Iris told her, 'then I positively refuse to listen.'

'I'm expecting a baby,' Nell said.

Iris choked on her drink.

Tom looked at Nell in total surprise. 'When?' he enquired after a pause.

'At the end of May, I've worked it out,' Nell replied.

'That means,' Tom said slowly, his brow furrowed, 'that you became pregnant around the beginning of September.'

Nell nodded. 'That's right.'

Iris opened her mouth to say something, then closed it again.

'Was it the night of Mum and Dad's party?' Tom asked.

Nell nodded again. She had to tell the truth as far as she could. She didn't want them thinking that she'd got pregnant in some back entry like her sister Ena.

Iris found her voice at last. 'Who was it?' she demanded

angrily. 'Was it Frank? Did he rape you? If he did, I'll kill him. I'll report him to the police, doctor or no bloody doctor.'

'Iris!' Tom spoke calmly. 'You're jumping to conclusions. Nell will tell us what happened.' He turned to Nell. 'Go on.'

'I wasn't raped.' Nell looked first at Iris, then at Tom, allowing no expression on to her face. She didn't want to put on a show, turn things into a drama. 'And that,' she said, 'is all I'm willing to tell you. What happened that night isn't something I intend to talk about – not ever. I'm only telling you I'm having a baby because I want *you* to have it – the baby, that is.'

Iris burst into tears and Tom looked totally stunned. Neither spoke for several minutes, because they had no idea what to say.

Eventually it was Nell herself who broke the silence. 'I know how badly you want a child, Iris. I've noticed how upset you are when someone brings their baby to see Tom, and Adele told me you'd had a little boy, Charlie, and that he'd died.'

By now, Iris was able to speak, though her voice was raw and hardly recognisable. 'I can't believe you're saying this, Nell. How can you possibly give us your baby? Just hand him – or her – over. You have no idea how much you will love your baby when it arrives.' Her eyes shone with passion. 'I couldn't have given Charlie away to save my life.'

'That's different, darling,' Tom muttered, 'completely different.'

Nell looked at her friend. 'It is, you know.' She patted her stomach. 'I know this baby isn't going to be mine. As soon as I realised I was in the club, I made up me mind to give it to you. I don't think of it being mine. It belongs to you and Tom. He can put on your medical notes that you're pregnant, then when it's born the birth certificate can have you down as the mother and Tom as the father.' She frowned. 'I don't like referring to the baby as "it", but we won't know if it's a boy or a girl until it's born, will we?'

Perhaps it was the way Nell said '*we* won't know' that gave Iris real hope that what she was proposing could actually happen. After all, she was a single, pregnant Catholic girl. For someone of her faith, having an abortion was akin to committing murder, yet to have the baby would create a scandal that Nell – possibly the entire family – would never live down. The child would be regarded as a bastard for the rest of its life, an extremely miserable life. Another alternative would be for Nell to go into a home for unmarried mothers. Afterwards, her child would be passed to strangers, but how much better for it to be given to her and Tom . . .

'Oh Nell!' She threw her arms around the girl, overwhelmed by the generosity of her spirit and the kindness of her heart. 'But how will we go about it?' she asked. 'Do we both go away until after the birth, or hide here, in this house? And what about your family, Nell? Surely they'll suspect something odd is going on if you disappear for months?'

'We can sort things like that out later.' Tom still appeared to be stunned by Nell's offer.

Iris shook her head. 'I want them sorted out now. I don't want us finding out in a month's time that it can't be done, that it can't be arranged. I'd like to know right now that it's going to be possible.'

'I've thought about it,' Nell said. She appeared to have planned everything in her head. 'It's going to be difficult not telling Adele and Cyril and Constance and Frank the truth, but I think we should try to if we can. I'd sooner just us three knew I was the real mother.'

'And how will we do that?' enquired Tom. He had brought the bottle of spirits upstairs with him and now refilled his glass.

'Well,' Nell drew a deep breath, 'I'm already almost four months gone and it hardly shows. Another month, February, and people will begin to notice, so I'll have to go away before then. Iris can come with me, or she can stay here and pretend to be pregnant.'

'I couldn't possibly do that!' Iris gasped. 'I mean, that's taking misleading people a bit too far. Adele would make a great big fuss of me and I'd feel awful. Anway, Nell, I want to be with you. You can't possibly go through this all on your own.' She leant back, closing her eyes. The other two watched, waiting for her to come up with an idea. About half a minute later, she opened her eyes again. 'I know,' she said. 'Let's tell people I'm pregnant but have high blood pressure and need to spend the next few months in a nursing home, and that you, Nell, are coming to keep me company.'

'Does that mean I'll go in a nursing home?' Nell asked.

Iris shook her head. 'Tom and I have a little cottage in a village called Caerdovey on the Welsh coast. We used to stay there, mainly at weekends, before the war. During the war, the army requisitioned it for their own use. Perhaps we could all drive there on Sunday and see what sort of state it's in.'

'Good idea,' Tom said crisply. 'We'll just have to think of a way of putting people off if they decide to come and see you. Oh, and we'll need fresh bedding and dishes and other essential items.' He reached for Nell's hand. 'The new year couldn't possibly have got off to a better start. Thank you, Nell.'

Iris squeezed Nell's other hand. 'I can't thank you enough,' she said softly.

'Do you really think it will happen?' Iris asked Tom later when they were in bed. 'That by the time summer comes, we'll have another baby?'

'I don't think Nell will change her mind,' Tom said thoughtfully, 'but I wouldn't bet on something else happening to spoil it.'

'Such as?'

Tom shrugged. 'A miscarriage, her family finding out, *our*

family finding out, something completely unexpected occurring that doesn't come to mind at the moment.'

'It seems too good to be true,' Iris sighed.

Tom kissed her. 'Don't get your hopes up too much, darling. We'll just have to keep our fingers crossed for the next five months.'

Soon afterwards he fell asleep, and Iris lay for a long time wondering who the father of Nell's baby could be. Frank was at the top of her list – Constance would have a fit if she knew Iris regarded her husband as a potential rapist. Though Nell had said it wasn't rape. The faces of the men at the party were lined up in Iris's head like an identity parade in a police station, mostly elderly faces, friends of her in-laws. Some she couldn't remember. Paddy O'Neill had been there, but hadn't moved out of the parlour as far as she knew. Ryan O'Neill for the last hour or so. And what about Tom, who'd been there longer than anyone and was the only person who knew Nell was ill in bed?

'I wasn't raped,' Nell had said. Did that mean a man had intercourse with her and she didn't mind? It was hardly what Iris would have expected of the Nell she knew.

In the end, she gave up. All that mattered was that Nell was giving her baby to the Grants. Iris closed her eyes and tried to sleep. For a change, it was happiness and excitement that kept her awake.

Just after lunch on the second day of January, Maggie, seated in front of her typewriter at Thomas Cook's, became aware that waves of horrible pain were spreading over her body and she felt an overwhelming desire to vomit. As the afternoon wore on, she came to the conclusion that she must have the three-day flu that was doing the rounds. She made her excuses to the woman in charge of her section and went home, managing to reach her flat in Shepherd's Bush on the tube, feeling sicker with each mile. Once in the house, she dragged herself upstairs, collapsed on the bed fully dressed and fell into a horrible, restless sleep.

Some time later, when it was dark outside, she woke up freezing cold and shivering so much that her teeth really did chatter. She groaned loudly and wished she were back in the army. She'd never been a patient in the little hospital with just four beds in the women's ward, but she had visited sick friends there. It was always warm, a wireless played all day long, and the nurses were friendly and caring.

Right now, she would have given anything for a hot drink and a cool hand on her brow, but there was no chance of either. The only hands available were her own rather clammy ones – she'd begun to sweat horribly – and she wasn't up to making her way down to the kitchen on the floor below to boil water.

Oh God! She felt so *miserable*. She buried her head in the pillow, determined not to cry. It had been her own decision to come to London, and she must put up with the fact that there wasn't a soul to look after her now she was ill.

She sat up, removed her coat and immediately felt cold again. Fortunately she hadn't made the bed that morning, so it was easy to wriggle under the blankets still wearing her furry boots. She was trying to kick them off when there was a knock on the door.

'Come in,' she wheezed, realising too late that she should have asked who was there. Lord knows who she had invited into her room. It was a relief as well as a big surprise when the door opened and Alicia Black, leading light of the ex-servicewomen's club, came in.

'Darling!' she gasped. 'Oh, just look at you, you poor soul.'

Maggie couldn't help herself; she burst into tears.

'There, there!' Alicia soothed. She knelt by the bed and removed the boots, smoothed the bedclothes, lifted Maggie's head, shook the pillow and carefully laid it back again. She enquired where the kitchen was and went to make tea.

'The milk you said was yours was sour, so I used someone else's,' she said when she came back with two cups on a tray. 'Could you bear to be propped up a little so you can drink this comfortably? When you've finished, I'll help you change into a nightie.'

'Thank you.' While she was being propped up, Maggie remembered that Alicia had been a nurse in the WRNS. She was an attractive woman of about thirty with the most beautiful skin and dark red hair. 'How did you know I was ill?' she managed to croak.

'I went looking for you at work, darling,' Alicia said in her dead-posh voice, 'and was informed you'd gone home feeling rotten. Daphne told me only this morning that she'd met you the other night in Trafalgar Square and you'd both gone to a party, where she'd met this delightful Polish gentleman called Jack and fallen in love. All thoughts of why she'd gone to the square in the first place, to fetch you, were forgotten. As for your address, it's on our list of members.'

Maggie was still cross that Daphne had managed to nab Jack Kaminski when it was she who'd seen him first – he'd actually *spoken* to her, in fact. She'd been landed with Drugi, who was much too young and boyish. All four were meeting again on Saturday and going to another party. Maggie hoped she'd be better in time.

There was a further knock on the door. This time Alicia leapt to her feet and went to answer it.

'My mother saw Maggie come home earlier and said she didn't look a bit well. She wants to know if there's anything she – or I – can do?' Maggie recognised Philip Morrison's voice.

'Come in, please. I'm Alicia, by the way.'

'How do you do? I'm Philip. Hello, Maggie.' He came in, gave her a cursory glance, then turned what could only be described as an admiring gaze on Alicia, who gazed admiringly back. It took quite a few seconds before they remembered Maggie was there.

'Hopefully you'll be a little better by tomorrow,' Alicia said when Philip had gone. 'Would you like another cup of tea before I go?'

'No thank you.'

'About Philip, is he married?' she asked in a way that was supposed to be casual but sounded terribly contrived.

'No.'

'What does he do for a living?'

Maggie couldn't remember. 'He designs things,' she muttered. She was grateful Alicia had come to see her, but longed for her to leave so she could sleep.

Philip returned with the hot-water bottle and the drink, and shortly afterwards he and Alicia left to have dinner together and Maggie fell asleep.

News spread throughout the house in Shepherd's Bush that one of the residents on the fourth floor was ill. Maggie was brought flowers and meals and other gifts, but it wasn't these that made her feel better, but the cheery faces that appeared around her door to wish her well. It was almost worthwhile having three-day flu and making so many new friends as a consequence.

Chapter 8

The property in Wales wasn't exactly Nell's idea of a cottage, being merely the end of a terrace of nine similar houses on the edge of a coastal village. It had two bedrooms, two living rooms, and a tiny kitchen tacked on the back. There was no bathroom and the lavatory was in the yard. There was no gas or electricity in this part of the village, but the place was well equipped with paraffin lamps, and there was a paraffin stove in the kitchen.

Iris and Tom had looked doubtful when they and Nell had gone to look round the place early in the new year.

'I don't recall it being quite so *basic*,' Iris commented as she looked at the peeling wallpaper and crumbling putty on the windows.

'Nor I,' said Tom. 'It needs decorating from top to bottom – and the furniture throwing away and new stuff bought.'

The place was clean, but that was all. Iris suggested they look for a proper holiday cottage that they could rent, perhaps closer to Liverpool. 'Though we'll need to have this place done up if we ever want to use it again.'

Nell suggested they had it done up now. 'Why not see what it looks like when it's finished? You would have had it done anyway, so it's no loss. *Then* you can decide whether to look for somewhere else if you don't like it.'

'Good idea, Nell.' Tom went out to search for the local

builder, and Iris and Nell to a hotel on the high street, where they ordered tea and scones.

'I'll measure the windows before we leave so I can have curtains made,' Iris said, 'and make a list of what furniture has to be bought.'

'Why does she need you to stay in Wales with her all that time when she's married to a bloody doctor?' Alfred Desmond enquired suspiciously when Nell informed him of her plans.

'Tom can't possibly stay in Wales with her, Dad,' she explained. 'He's got his patients to look after. Iris needs peace and quiet, like; her blood pressure's sky high. And it's ever so noisy in their house; people turn up at all times of the day and night and the telephone never stops ringing. And what with the trams running right past . . .' She shook her head, as if it was sheer bedlam in the doctor's house, which indeed it was sometimes. 'Iris'll stay in the nursing home, and I'll live just around the corner and go in and see her every day. Otherwise, she'll feel dead lonely.'

'Me, I feel dead flattered that the doctor wants our Nellie to look after his wife while she's up the stick,' Mabel said.

'Are you getting paid?' Alfred wanted to know. He still looked suspicious, but then his own actions were so crooked that he found it hard to comprehend that a person could help another without expecting a reward.

'We haven't discussed it, Dad.' She had no intention of selling her baby for cash.

They moved to Caerdovey on the first Sunday in February, arriving by car at midday. It was a bitterly cold day, but the woman who lived in the house next door, Nerys Jones, who'd been engaged as a cook and cleaner, already had a stew prepared, and fires had been lit in both the downstairs rooms.

Iris rubbed her hands together. 'It's nice and warm in here,' she said gratefully. She seemed to feel the cold more intensely than most people.

Nell wandered about the house admiring the wallpaper – plain and pale, as Iris had requested. The creams and light greys made the rooms appear bigger, and the flowered curtains looked dead pretty. The linoleum was an unobtrusive mottled pattern. The Irish Sea could be seen from the upstairs windows, a not particularly attractive sight today – the water was leaden and the sky a depressing mixture of black and grey clouds.

Tom shouted that he'd like to have lunch immediately, so he could get back to Liverpool before it got dark.

'Don't forget,' Tom said after they had eaten and he was ready to leave, 'if this place isn't satisfactory, we'll find somewhere better. In case of emergency, you can ring me from the telephone in the post office.' He kissed his wife on the lips and Nell on her cheek. 'I'll be back again next Sunday,' he promised and was gone.

Nell surveyed the range of items spread out on the table, brought to keep them occupied during the forthcoming months: baby knitting wool, needles and crochet hooks, tiny gowns to be embroidered along with the coloured thread to do it, books, writing pads, drawing pads, crayons . . . There was also a wireless with an acid battery.

'I suggest we go for a walk on the sands every morning, as long as the weather is nice, that is.' Iris began to put the books in a row on the new sideboard. 'I must say,' she added, smoothing her hand along the sideboard top, 'I really like this utility furniture. I much prefer it without beading and curly bits and fancy knobs. It looks really expensive.'

'Hmm,' Nell murmured. 'Shall I make some tea?'

'Yes, but this tea is all you'll be allowed to make,' Iris said sternly. 'Nerys is going to cook all our meals except for breakfast. I must give her our ration books later, so she can register us with the local grocer.'

'I would have been happy to do the cooking.' Nell was worried she would become bored with nothing to do. She wasn't much good at needlework. She liked reading at bed-time, but it seemed self-indulgent to do it during the day.

'Tom has ordered you to do nothing but rest. Are you wearing your wedding ring, Nell?'

Nell displayed the ring on her left hand that she'd bought for sixpence from Woolworth's in Bootle. 'It's brass. I bet it turns me finger green.'

'Perhaps you should take it off at night.'

'I'll try and remember.' Nell twisted the ring around. She'd been introduced to Nerys as Mrs Nell Desmond. She said the words out loud. 'Mrs Nell Desmond.'

Iris looked up and smiled. 'I can't thank you enough for what you're doing for me and Tom, Mrs Nell Desmond.'

'Think nothing of it,' Nell said lightly. She didn't know what else to say, or how to explain that she felt just as grateful to Iris and Tom for taking her baby as they were to her for giving it to them. She'd known girls in the army who'd got into her position and had abortions, but as far as Nell was concerned, an abortion was out-and-out murder. She could never have lived with herself had she had her baby murdered. Giving it away to strangers was almost as bad, knowing that somewhere in the world she had a son or a daughter she'd never see again and who wouldn't know who its real mother was. Letting it go to people she loved was the perfect solution. She went into the kitchen. 'I'll make that tea.'

Iris had insisted that Nell sleep in the front bedroom. 'It has the best view. In fact you're to have the best of everything.'

When Nell pulled back the curtain next morning, the Irish Sea looked just as miserable as the day before and the sky just as leaden. She was about to turn away when she glanced down-wards and shouted, 'Iris!'

'I know,' Iris yelled back. 'I've just opened the curtains and seen the hills behind – they're covered in snow!'

'It's deep, *really* deep.' Nell put on her new extra-warm dressing gown and slippers and went downstairs. She pulled back the curtains and gasped. A snowdrift covered half the window.

Iris came in. 'It's been this deep down south for days,' she said.

'And now it's this deep in Wales.' Nell shuddered. 'I don't like it – it makes me feel trapped.' It was like being in a giant white coffin.

'When Nerys comes, I'll ask if she knows someone who will clear it away.'

Although Nerys only lived next door, she'd still have to battle through the thick snow to reach them. 'Can we turn the wireless on?' Nell asked.

'You can do anything you want,' Iris insisted.

Nell switched on the wireless. A cultured male voice on the BBC was reading the eight o'clock news. Heavy snow had reached the Midlands, he announced, and was due to spread further north that very night.

'I suppose it's about time the north had its share.' Iris knelt down and began to brush the ashes out of the grate. 'This still feels warm.'

Nell had only just discovered that she hated snow, this sort of snow, the sort that stopped you from leaving the house. The voice on the wireless was at least confirmation that she and Iris weren't the only two people on earth left alive. Coming from a city, she wasn't used to being isolated. She pulled the dressing gown around her as if it offered protection, not just warmth, whilst saying a little silent prayer that the snow would soon go away and never come back. 'We didn't bring wellies,' she said.

'What?' Iris sneezed. The ash must have got up her nose.

'Wellies – wellingtons, we didn't bring any. We won't be able to go out in the snow.'

'We couldn't anyway, Nell. The boots would be full of snow before we'd gone a few feet.'

The back door opened and Nerys burst in covered with clumps of white and carrying a brown muggin teapot. She was a well-built woman of about sixty, with red cheeks and a determined face, who would prove to be worth her weight in gold in the near future.

'I could hear you from next door cleaning the fireplace,' she said breathlessly. 'But that's my job, luvvies. You both sit down now in the other room and have a cup of tea while I light the fire.'

Nell hadn't thought she was frightened of anything apart from obvious things like axe murderers and escaped lunatics. The loudest thunder didn't bother her, nor the sharpest cracks of lightning. She wasn't a hypochondriac, never became hysterical, wasn't afraid of the dark, but being shut in a house surrounded by snow, unable to get out, she had discovered was quite terrifying.

'This is cosy,' Iris would say when darkness fell and they sat down to read or sew or knit.

Within a few days, it became obvious that the entire country was covered by a thick blanket of white and there was no sign that the snow would soon stop falling. Blizzards came, lasting forty-eight hours. Winds lashed the unprotected houses, screaming down the chimneys and round the edges of windows and doors.

Nothing was being delivered. There were no letters, newspapers or fuel. Nerys's son, Idris, fetched groceries from the village using a hastily made sledge, including condensed milk when the real sort was no longer available. The only meat and fresh fruit was that produced locally. Nerys made delicious soup from chicken bones, and baked bread every two days, but she would soon be out of flour. Although more logs appeared in the tiny yard, she suggested she only light one of the fires in case the supply dried up. The little village school closed down, and so did the hotel.

There was no sign of Tom, who'd promised to drive down to Caerdovey every Sunday: roads all over the country were blocked. Iris saw no point in writing him a letter, nor expecting him to write to them. The snow was much too thick to walk to the post office and use the telephone. One of the reasons for him to visit regularly was to keep an eye on Nell and her baby, but Iris was of the opinion that both were coming along famously.

Some of the snow outside the row of houses had been cleared for children to play on. Their cheerful cries were the only thing that Nell found heartening during all of that unhappy time.

The baby in her stomach began to grow at a rapid rate. Within no time at all she was huge. She went up and down the stairs dozens of times a day in order to get some exercise. She felt sick; her clothes felt too tight, even though they were loose.

Iris fussed around, fetching things, insisting that she rest, not allowing her to do so much as poke the fire, until Nell wanted to scream at her to stop, leave her alone. Let me *do* something, she wanted to cry. Yet previously she had always had the patience of Job. She'd been well known for it in the army. No matter how bad-tempered or unreasonable the corporals and sergeants in charge of the canteen were, Nell carried on working, singing serenely to herself. But now Iris's kindness, and Nerys's too, was getting her down, though Nell gave no sign of it. She never once let on how miserable she was.

'Nell,' Iris said one night in the middle of one of the worst storms, the house creaking and groaning as if the bricks might fall apart and land on top of them. 'I hope you don't mind my asking, but the night you were raped, why didn't you cry out

135

or something? I mean, it must have hurt, being the first time. But there was no blood anywhere.'

Nell smiled, not at Iris, but at something in the past. 'It wasn't the first time,' she said softly. 'My corporal, the one who was killed, made love to me. It was the least I could do when he'd asked to marry me. And he made sure I wouldn't have his baby. Oh, and Iris, I wasn't raped at the party. I did tell you that.'

Mornings, first thing, Nell would draw back the curtains in the bedroom to find that her prayers remained unanswered: there was yet more snow and the world was silent. She would wonder if she had gone deaf. Sometimes the snow would be falling, great lumps of it building up on the windowsill. She would bang the window and it would fall off, though not if it had already frozen. Like most people, she had forgotten what the sun looked like.

March arrived and nothing changed, until one day Nell pulled back the curtains to discover there'd been no fresh snow overnight. A few days later, it began to thaw and there were floods as the ice melted. Milk was restored, eggs, fruit. It was still cold outside, though, and the ground too dangerously icy to walk on.

Iris took the risk of slipping over and went to the post office to telephone Tom.

'He's coming on Sunday,' she said gleefully when she came back. 'He set off to come and see us quite a few times, but had to turn back when he found the roads were blocked.'

Tom brought a fresh battery for the wireless, scented soap from Adele, magazines, and cream cakes from Sayers' confectioners.

'And how are you, Nell?' he asked. 'You only have another nine weeks to go.'

Iris grinned. 'She's fine, aren't you, love? I've been keeping a close eye on her,' she said to Tom.

'I'm fine, like Iris says,' Nell confirmed.

Tom listened to her heartbeat, felt her pulse, looked down her throat, pressed her tummy a few times, and pronounced her perfectly fit.

April came. It was the first Good Friday, Nell announced, that she hadn't done the Stations of the Cross – there wasn't a Catholic church in Caerdovey. 'Me and Maggie used to do them together. I wonder if she's doing them in London?'

During the worst of the weather, she'd gathered from the wireless that the snow was just as heavy in London, but that workmen came out at dawn to shovel it away. Some buses and trains ran, if not all. Most cinemas, theatres and restaurants had remained open. People still went to work. Nell had written imaginary letters to her friend telling her how desperately awful it was in Caerdovey. Since then, she'd sent a real letter, less truthful than the imaginary ones, saying that everything was okay, she was enjoying her stay in the countryside, and Iris's pregnancy was proceeding well. She owed it to Iris and Tom never to tell Maggie the real truth anyroad.

It wasn't until April was nearly over that the earth was completely dry, the sun shone warmly, and there was a tingle of spring in the air. Snowdrops had managed to struggle through the hard ground and were scattered over the hills behind the cottages, followed later by yellow crocuses. There was a pretty bluebell wood nearby that they could walk to, Nerys informed them.

It was while wandering through this little blue heaven that Nell realised that she was her old self again. Both women walked carefully so as not to tread on the flowers. Birds chirruped, squirrels chased each other through the spreading branches of the trees, rabbits leapt across their path, the undergrowth rustled with creatures unseen. There was a wonderful, fresh smell.

'It's magic,' Nell whispered. For the first time in weeks, she felt glad to be alive. She looked forward to having the baby, giving it to Iris and Tom, and starting to lead her old life once again.

It had been Tom's intention to stay at the cottage for several days before the baby was due, having arranged with his father to look after the practice at home. He would deliver the child, stay another few days, then return to Liverpool with both women and the baby.

Two weeks before this plan was to be put into operation, Tom came down on one of his regular Sunday visits and proposed they all go for a drive. 'It's a lovely day. We can have lunch somewhere. You two must be fed up stuck in Caerdovey all this time. It's so dead here.'

Nell refused. She felt just a little bit sick, though she didn't tell Tom that; until now, the pregnancy had been trouble-free. Nor did she say that she quite fancied being alone for a few hours and not subjected to endless questions about her health.

Tom and Iris went off. He was right; it was a beautiful, sunny day, the sky almost cloudless. Nell strolled as far as the sands. She was feeling bulky by now, very conscious of the huge stomach that preceded her everywhere she went, as well as her enlarged breasts. She stood and studied the crystal-clear water cluttered at its edge with clumps of seaweed and little smooth stones. One stone was as big as a bird's egg and a remarkable blue colour. She bent to pick it up, her hand breaking through the surface of the water, when she felt a searing pain in her gut. She jerked upwards, much too quickly, as she immediately felt dizzy. She swayed and nearly fell.

Please, dear Jesus, help me, she prayed. But there wasn't a soul in sight to help. She eased herself down until she was actually sitting in a few inches of water, and wondered if it would be of any use to call for help. She was, very slowly, beginning to panic as the pain got worse.

Then she heard a shout, a series of shouts. She couldn't make them out at first, but the voice became clearer as it got louder. 'Mrs Desmond, Nell, I'm coming. I saw you from me window, luvvie.'

Nerys Jones was running towards her, waving her arms. 'I'm coming. Don't be frightened.'

'I think it might be the baby,' Nell cried. It was the only thing that could have been responsible for such a terrible pain, and the ones that had followed shortly afterwards.

'Well, I've delivered more babies than you've had hot dinners, so you'll be all right with me.'

Nerys was hardly out of breath. With the woman's strong arms supporting her, Nell was led slowly back to the house and upstairs to the bedroom, where she fell thankfully on to the bed.

'I'll go next-door-but-two in a tick and tell Mrs Evans to start boiling water,' Nerys said, rolling up her sleeves before removing Nell's wet clothes. 'You lie back and take things easy. I'll be as quick as I can. I've been delivering babies in Caerdovey for the last thirty years, so you've got nothing to worry about.'

Nell did her best to relax. She was breathing slowly in and slowly out when Nerys returned with a pile of towels and the woman from next-door-but-two, who was called Pauline. She had long untidy grey hair like a witch. 'Let's put a couple of these underneath you, luvvie,' Nerys said.

Before Nell could comply, another pain, as sharp as a knife, sliced through her stomach and she screamed.

From that moment on, everything became a blur of pain and screams and struggle. Someone behind the bed held her hands against the headboard. She heard a man's voice. A woman shouted, 'Push.' Her body felt as if it was falling apart. There was a delighted cry, 'Here it comes!' then, 'It's a boy!'

'Lord almighty, Nerys, he's a giant. No wonder he came

early. Another two weeks and he'd've killed the poor girl. What's she going to call him?'

'I don't know, Pauline.'

The baby began to cry, great howls of misery and despair.

Nell's face was stroked, her chin chucked. Very slowly, she opened her eyes. The witch-like Pauline was bending over her, and Nerys Jones was standing behind her nursing a baby wrapped in an old, frayed towel.

'This is your son, luvvie. Would you like to hold him?'

'Please,' Nell whispered. The plan agreed with Iris and Tom was that she wouldn't touch her baby. It would go straight to Iris, so Nell didn't have the chance to get attached to it – to him; 'bond' was the word Tom had used. But how could she refuse? In Tom's plan, Nerys wouldn't have been present, and would have been kept at bay for the next few days.

Her baby was laid in her arms. Oh my God, he *was* big! Big and tough and strong. But he was still only a tiny human being. He moved his arms and his elbow dug into her breast. Nell touched his nose with her finger and he gave a desperate sigh and stopped crying.

'Aaah!' Nerys and Pauline said delightedly together. 'What are you going to call him?' Nerys asked.

'William.' It came from nowhere, but it was a name she had always liked, a warm name with soft letters. 'Hello, William.' She laid her finger in his palm and he wrapped his own little fat ones around it.

'In a minute,' Nerys said, 'I'll give him a wash, and Pauline'll clean you up a bit, then you can give William his first feed. Well, won't this be a surprise for Mr and Mrs Grant when they get back,' she cried jubilantly.

'Sorry we took so long,' Iris shouted as she ran upstairs. 'You'll never believe, but we had a puncture and Tom had simply no idea how to fix it. Fortunately, we were quite close to a garage. Are you having a little lie—' She burst into the room where William was fast asleep against Nell's naked breast and Nerys was sitting at the foot of the bed, watching. 'Oh my God!' Iris cried. Her face went as white as a sheet.

'What's the matter?' Tom shouted. He followed his wife upstairs and into Nell's bedroom. 'It came early,' he said in a dull voice. 'We shouldn't have gone out.'

'It's a boy!' Nerys said joyfully. 'William. He suits William. I reckon he weighs a good nine and a half pounds, possibly ten. He's a beautiful baby.'

'So I see,' Iris said faintly. 'May I hold him?'

'Why not wait until he wakes up? He had quite a struggle getting out. Best not disturb him.' Nerys yawned. 'Seeing as how you're both home, I'll get back and make our Idris his tea. By the way, he had to give a hand holding this young lady against the headboard while she was giving birth, like. It wasn't easy, was it, luvvie?' She patted Nell's hand and left the room.

'It was worse than I ever thought it'd be,' Nell said when Nerys had gone.

'Was it, darling?' Iris fell to her knees beside the bed and put her arms around both Nell and William. She was crying. 'How do you feel now?'

'Tired,' Nell sighed.

'Shall I take William?'

'Not just yet.'

'Let Iris have the baby now, Nell, if you don't mind,' Tom said in a hard voice.

'Don't take any notice of him, darling.' Iris looked at her husband with burning eyes. 'Go downstairs, Tom, and do something useful. And don't dare come back unless I ask you to.' Tom left the room without a word. 'Would you like me to fetch the cradle, Nell, and put it beside your bed?' It was a wicker basket on springs suspended from a metal base, easier to transport in the car than a wooden cot.

Nell smiled. 'In a minute,' she said. 'I'd like to hold William for a bit longer.'

Three hours later, with the sun beginning to sink low in the sky, Iris and Tom left the cottage in Caerdovey. Iris resolved she would never go there again. She had baby William in her arms. He wore one of the embroidered gowns and a soft white shawl knitted by Tom's mother. The shawl kept the baby warm and absorbed the tears that Iris couldn't stop shedding.

'Will you for Christ's sake stop crying,' Tom snapped. He'd become a completely different person since they'd returned from the drive. 'You've got the baby you wanted; why can't you be pleased about it?'

'What do you mean, the baby *I* wanted?' Iris said tearfully. 'Are you saying now that you didn't want him too?'

'Of course I wanted him.' Tom shook his head angrily. 'But I don't see the need for a scene.'

'I'm crying for Nell. We've stolen her baby from her, Tom, while she was asleep. How will she feel when she wakes up?'

'It's *our* baby, damn you.' Tom sounded as if he could easily cry himself. 'It's always been our baby. It's never been Nell's; she knows that full well. And I wanted him more than anything I've ever wanted before, mainly for you, Iris. When Nell wakes up and finds him gone, she won't feel anything.'

'What a stupid, insensitive man you are.' They'd never had a row like this before. She felt almost numb with rage. 'You were stupid for suggesting we go out for a meal, knowing that the baby might arrive while we were gone. And insensitive for talking about Nell as if she was an animal, a cat or something that's just had her kittens taken away from her and will have got used to it by now.'

Tom turned a corner dangerously fast. Iris clasped the baby closer to her chest. He made a little snuffling sound. She looked closely at his face to see if there was anything familiar about it; the shape of his lips, his nose, his ears, anything to indicate who his father might be. She still suspected it was Frank who'd taken advantage of Nell, barely conscious in bed. Right now, because he was being so unpleasant, she wondered, not for the first time, if Tom was the father, though it was a really outrageous thought. Normally Tom was the nicest of men. It could have been any man at the party. It was something she might never know.

Tom said, 'Nell showed no sign that the baby would arrive today. And babies don't usually come so quickly. What happened was totally unexpected. Anyway, if you had any concerns about it, all you had to do was refuse to leave Nell on her own.' There was a long silence before he reached out and squeezed his wife's knee. 'I'm sorry, darling. I'm being a pig. I'm angry with myself more than anyone. It's just that I find all this terribly upsetting, and I know you must do too. I'd expected everything to go quite smoothly. I'd never imagined for a minute it happening the way it did.'

'I'm sorry too.' Iris hadn't the energy to argue any more. She didn't say that the person who would find it the most upsetting of all would be Nell. She wondered if that somewhere in the further recesses of the baby's mind Nell's face had been stored, and one day the memory would return and he would realise that another woman, not Iris, was his mother.

Nell knew, before she opened her eyes, that William had gone. When she did open them, she saw the cradle was no longer in the room and the house was completely silent. Next door, Nerys was singing a wartime song she couldn't remember the name of.

She sat up in bed and put her hands over her breasts; the nipples felt hard and pointed. Her son had sucked on them only a few hours ago. She would never forget the feeling, a delicious sort of churning in her stomach. But he was no longer her son; William had a different mother now.

In a way, she was almost glad he'd been taken while she was

asleep. To see him go, carried away in another woman's arms, would have broken her heart. And there was always a chance, just a chance, that she might have refused to give him up, and there would have been ructions. Yes, she was glad things had gone the way they had.

Yet she felt hurt, deeply hurt, that Iris and Tom had left without a word, taking with them the most precious thing she had ever owned. Iris had said right from the start that it was important that she didn't bond with the baby, not hold him, not even touch him. Over the few days they'd been planning to stay in the cottage after the birth, it would be best for her not to go near her baby.

Such wise advice; Nell had been all prepared to go along with it. She couldn't see any reason not to co-operate fully. But now she had touched her baby, held him, fed him and nursed him, having been given no other choice. He had held her finger in his little hand and she had felt the love flow between them.

Any minute, Nerys would come in and expect to see him. How on earth was Nell supposed to explain why he'd been taken away from her, his mother? She felt upset again that Iris and Tom had left her having to make up lies to satisfy Nerys's understandable curiosity, answer her shocked questions.

She got out of bed and tested her ability to stand, walk a few steps. Her breasts were hurting and she could feel blood running down her legs. There was nothing she could do about the first, but there were a few old but clean towels thrown on the chair that she could use to deal with the second. She found she was able to walk quite steadily – after all, she was young, and had always been fit. According to the bedside clock, it was only twenty to five – she'd thought it much later. She found a note by the clock in Tom's handwriting saying he would arrange for her to be taken back to Liverpool early on Wednesday.

It took less than half an hour to get washed, dressed and

pack some of her things in the shabby cardboard suitcase she'd used when she was in the army, leaving behind the maternity clothes. Iris had left a lot of her things too. She tiptoed quietly around the house so Nerys wouldn't hear, and crept out of the back door. There was a road behind the cottages that led to the village centre, where she hoped it would be possible to catch a bus.

She hadn't been walking long when she heard the sound of a car, and a male voice singing 'Ol' Man River'. Seconds later, the car drew up beside her.

The singer, a man with a huge black beard and laughing eyes, rolled down the window. 'Want a lift somewhere, pet?' he asked in a strong Yorkshire accent.

'The nearest bus stop, please.'

'Get in then, pet. It's only half a mile away. Give us your suitcase and I'll put it in the back.

'And where is it you're heading on the bus?' he enquired when he set off again, Nell in the passenger seat. She felt grateful to be off her feet, already feeling worn out after walking merely a fraction of a mile.

'Liverpool,' she replied. 'I mean, I know a bus from Caerdovey won't get me as far as Liverpool, but I thought it'd take me to a place where I could catch one.'

'Not at this time on a Sunday afternoon, pet, but I can take you to a place where a bus leaves for Liverpool in another two hours, at eight o'clock. In fact it's where I'm heading right now. I'm night manager at Butlins holiday camp in Pwllheli, about twenty miles away. Being so early in the season, we have guests who come just for the weekend, and an awful lot of them are from Liverpool.'

Nell told him it was the closest to a miracle that she had ever come and she would be eternally grateful. He told her his name was George Hurley and that he would eventually live in the camp when it got busier, but for now he was staying with an old army mate who'd lost a leg during the D-Day landings.

'I'm sorry about your mate,' Nell said. 'I was in the army too – the Auxiliary Territorial Service.'

By the time they reached Pwllheli, they were good friends. Nell promised to do her very best to spend a week at the camp, if not this year, then next, and George said that if he ever went to Liverpool, he'd look her up.

The bus was a dead-posh charabanc with comfortable seats, and was only half full when it left for Liverpool. The other passengers were mainly young men who were very drunk and very noisy, but Nell fell asleep soon after they left the camp and didn't wake up until the bus stopped at the Pier Head in Liverpool. From there she caught a tram to Bootle and went home.

Chapter 9

It was well past midnight when Nell let herself into the house in Amber Street. As expected, it was in darkness. 'It's only me,' she called.

Minutes later, her father came downstairs wearing maroon silk pyjamas no doubt destined for a posh men's shop, but that had fallen off the back of one of the lorries that featured so largely in his life. She'd like to bet that half the men in Bootle were wearing identical pairs.

'Long time no see, luv,' he said. 'How's the doctor's missus? Did she have the baby?' Strangely enough, Nell was really pleased to see him. He was much nicer these days. She remembered the day she'd come home from the army, when he'd been dead cruel. She reckoned the change in attitude was at least partly due to her starting her own business; he now considered her a chip off the old block.

'Yes, Dad. She's fine, she had a boy: William.'

'Would you like a cuppa or something?' He gestured towards the stairs. 'I'll wake your mam up if you like.'

'I'd sooner go to bed, ta. Is me bed made up?'

'It's never been unmade, luv. Your mam even kept a hot-water bottle in it during the really cold weather.'

'I'll just go to the lavvy, then I'll go on up.'

'Righty-o, Nell.' He patted her shoulder. 'I'll see you tomorrer. Your mam'll be dead pleased when she wakes up and finds you home.'

Next morning, Mam brought her tea upstairs after Nell had explained that she had the curse pretty bad. 'Me tummy really hurts.'

'You don't usually have trouble that way, do you, luv?' Mam said sympathetically. She'd had her hair tinted, not a different colour, but to her original dark brown to hide the grey. 'You have a nice lie-in, then. Your sanitary rags are in the drawer and there's a jerry under the bed, save you using the lavvy. Just shout if you need anything.'

Nell had little difficulty getting used to being home where she was with people who loved her, even if they didn't always show it. Their Kenny came in for a word at one o'clock when he was home for his dinner, and her sister Theresa dropped in after work.

The bed was warm, and more comfortable than the one in Caerdovey. Nell mostly lay in a dreamlike state without any idea what time it was, dozing off now and then, waking up to wonder where she was and finding she was in Bootle. Sometimes she remembered William and sometimes she forgot. The memory would come with a tug of the heart, the feeling of his body pressed against hers, his fresh soapy smell after Nerys had washed him.

She worried about Nerys, about walking out without thanking her, without saying ta-ra. When she felt better, she would write her a letter. Well, she might.

Dad was out all day. He came into the bedroom when it was dark smelling of ale. 'I've been thinking,' he said. 'Did the doctor's wife compensate you for giving up that nice little business of yours while you stayed with her in Wales?'

Nell poked her head out of the bedclothes. 'We're friends, Dad. You don't compensate friends. I willingly gave up me time.'

Dad didn't agree. 'If you're such a good friend, it'd be only fair if she compensated you,' he argued. 'But never mind. By the way, I've been offered a little Austin 7, which I wouldn't want meself, but it'd be perfect for you. I take it you intend starting up your little business again.'

'How much is it?' She had nineteen pounds, four and sixpence in her Post Office account, which she considered a small fortune.

'I've been offered it for nothing, in return for a favour, like, so it'll cost you the same.'

'Ta, Dad.' She didn't ask what the favour was.

He went away and Nell snuggled under the bedclothes. When she woke up next morning, she felt much better after a whole day in bed, though she was still bleeding and her breasts felt like concrete and hurt quite a bit. She supposed the milk was drying up.

She got out of bed and looked in her wardrobe for something to wear. It was May, almost summer, and apart from the nice red frock she'd bought for Ryan and Rosie's wedding, she possessed just one summer dress, as well as a flowered dirndl skirt and two cotton blouses. She put on a blouse and the skirt and, after breakfast, told her mother she was going to church. 'And I might go round and see Rosie O'Neill and little Bridie while I'm out.'

Mass was being said in St James's church when she went in, attended by only a handful of worshippers at the front, all women. Nell knelt at the back with her head in her hands. She remained there for more than an hour, praying and thinking in turn. She prayed for her family and thanked God for returning Dad to his proper wife and improving his temper no end. She prayed for Kenny and her sisters and their children, for Maggie, and Maggie's family. 'And please, God,' she whispered, 'make William have a really happy life.'

Although she didn't wish them any harm, she hesitated before praying for Iris and Tom. From the start there'd been no suggestion that after having had the baby she wouldn't return to their house and their relationship continue as it had done before. Nell would still make the meals and, of course, help look after the baby now that he had arrived. She hadn't anticipated having the feelings for him that she had now.

After Sunday, she didn't think she would be made welcome. She recalled the horrible way that Tom had spoken to her after he and Iris had returned to find William had already been born. It was as if *she'd* done something wrong, when things wouldn't have happened the way they did if *he* hadn't gone for a drive. And then to leave while she was asleep without saying goodbye! The idea of facing either of the Grants again made her shudder.

Her knees were hurting. She sat back on the pew and wondered seriously what to do with the rest of her life. For a brief moment she thought about demanding William back – legally the Grants wouldn't have a leg to stand on if she insisted – but her son would have a far better life with them than he would with her, his real mother.

The years in the army had been the best of her life, but, thankfully, the war was over. She'd enjoyed running her 'little business', as Dad called it, and now he'd said there was a car available if she wanted it. Nell's brow creased as she thought ahead. Yes, she did want the car, and she would start up her business again. There was still no sign of food rationing ending – in fact, for the first time bread and potatoes had joined the list of rationed foods when they had been freely available during the war.

She'd give her company a name, wear a smart white overall, have new cards made, start using a wider range of menus and have them printed too so customers could make a choice. And there was no way she could carry on the business from Amber Street. She would need to find a place of her own. Her spirits were gradually lifting as she thought ahead.

One thing, though – all her cooking utensils and other bits and pieces were in the Grants' kitchen. She would collect them now, this very minute. And once she'd got them, she would never go back to the house again. As far as she could, she would try to put her son out of her mind for ever.

Adele Grant was slightly perplexed by her daughter-in-law's behaviour since she'd returned home from Wales on Sunday with the new baby. Iris had always appeared to be an exceptionally level-headed person. Of course, she'd had a problem, very high blood pressure, the reason why she'd gone away to have the baby in the first place, to get some peace and quiet. Maybe, instead of the long rest doing her good, it had got her down, or perhaps it had been the terrible weather. Whatever it was, Iris had returned home quite obviously depressed and much too soon after the baby's birth.

At first, Adele had been worried there was something wrong with the baby, with William, but he was a lively, healthy little chap and she had fallen in love with him immediately.

She was acting as her son's receptionist once more. The Tuesday-morning surgery was extremely busy, but Tom's surgeries always were. She was so proud of him, the care he took of all his patients, overloading himself with work. She'd been run off her feet since the door had opened that morning at half past eight.

The buzzer rang again to indicate that another patient had come in, and she went out to take their name and give them a number in the queue. She was pleased when she saw Nell Desmond in the hallway, although she thought she looked a bit peaky.

'Nell!' She kissed the girl on the cheek. 'Have you come to see William?' Adele rolled her eyes, aware of her own stupidity. 'Of course, you saw him when he was first born, didn't you? I forgot for the minute that you'd been in Wales with Iris. It was awfully good of you, Nell.' She kissed her again. Nell was just about the nicest person she'd ever known.

'I've come for me equipment,' Nell said in a strangely

subdued tone. 'It's in a cupboard in the kitchen. I just wanted to take it out the way, that's all.'

'Oh, I'm sure it won't be in Iris's way, dear. I'd ask her to come down, but last time I was upstairs she was bathing William. Of course, you can always go up and have a word.'

'No thank you. If I could just have me things . . .'

'Of course, dear.' There was something really odd about this. She wondered if there'd been some sort of unpleasantness in Wales.

The buzzer went and another patient entered. By the time Adele had dealt with the woman, Nell was emerging from the kitchen carrying a cardboard box.

'Thank you,' she said, nodding.

Adele went ahead to open the door. It was then she noticed the wet marks on the front of Nell's blouse, and she came close to fainting from the shock of it. 'Dearest Nell,' she murmured. She made a clumsy attempt to hug the girl, but didn't quite manage it. 'Nell, dear,' she whispered, 'if you bind your breasts tightly with bandage, it will dry the milk up.'

Nell walked away clutching the box as if she hadn't heard.

Adele returned to the kitchen, heart racing, hardly able to breathe. So *that* was what had happened! She would never mention it to a soul, not even her husband, and certainly not to Iris or Tom.

'Nell came this morning,' Iris told her husband when surgery was over. 'Adele told me.' Adele had claimed a headache and gone home, which was very unlike her, and Tom and Iris were drinking tea in the kitchen. The baby was asleep in his pram in the corner of the room. 'Lord knows how she managed to get home from Wales so quickly. Weren't you supposed to be collecting her some time this week?'

Tom grimaced. 'I'd arranged with the taxi in Caerdovey to bring her home on Wednesday. It's not yet forty-eight hours since she had the baby and she should still be in bed. Anyway, what did she want?'

'Her equipment, that's all. She'd left it the dresser cupboard.'

'If she's collected her equipment, does that mean she won't be coming back again?'

'I reckon so. We've really hurt her. Do you understand that, Tom?' she asked a trifle shrilly. 'You shouldn't have spoken to her the way you did. We shouldn't have just taken William while she was asleep. It was terribly cruel.'

Tom studied the tea in his cup before answering. 'I didn't like the way she was holding William, as if she *owned* him, as if he was *hers*, when we'd always known he would be *ours*.'

Iris wondered how this usually soft and gentle man could sound so hard, cruel almost, when speaking of Nell, who was her dearest friend – or had been until the day before yesterday.

'What was she supposed to do when William arrived and we weren't there: ignore him, refuse to touch him, refuse to hold him, refuse to give birth until we got back?' she asked. 'You should have known better than to suggest we went out, Tom.' How could he have been so stupid, on top of everything else?

'We've had this discussion before, several times, over the last two days,' Tom said coldly. 'I was anxious for you. We both wanted a baby, but you wanted it the most. I visualised Nell refusing to hand him over.'

'So, you told her in a really horrible way to let me have him. I wonder how she must have felt.'

'Oh, for Christ's sake, Iris, can we please stop having this argument?' Tom groaned. 'What's done is done. We've got William, though if I remember rightly we'd chosen the name Christopher if it was a boy; it's still not too late to change it.'

The baby began to cry. Iris rose to her feet. 'Nell chose William and I wouldn't dream of changing it.' It was the least she could do, she thought as she lifted him out of his pram.

'Hello, darling.' It was a horrid way of acquiring a baby, stealing him away from his mother while she was asleep. It was all supposed to have been so different. She would always blame Tom for the way things had turned out.

'Is he all right?' he asked.

'Fine, probably just hungry.' We'll pay for this, she thought. One of these days William will find out the truth and turn against us.

Tom said, 'I'm sorry for the way I've behaved. But when I went into that bedroom on Sunday and saw Nell and William together, I was terrified, more terrified than I've been in my entire life, that we might lose him.'

That said, he burst into tears.

Nell's car was stored at the back of a garage in Stanley Road. After work Kenny taught her how to drive, having learnt himself while she was away. She had put her name down for a driving test. Meanwhile, she enjoyed being left to herself in the parlour to draw up menus, design cards and try to think of a name for her business.

'I can get the name embroidered on the pocket of your pinafore,' Dad said enthusiastically. 'And have it painted on the car doors if you want.'

'We'll see, Dad.'

In the end she decided to call herself Crown Caterers. She thought it sounded classy, and her father agreed. 'As if you were catering for the King and Queen, like,' he said proudly.

Halfway through June, a month after William's birth, Nell went to London to stay with Maggie. Maggie had been nagging her to come ever since she'd moved there a year ago. Just now, there was a room to let in the house where she lived in Shepherd's Bush, and she'd talked the owner into letting Nell stay for a few days while a new tenant was found.

Nell wore her red dress, a black bolero that belonged to

their Theresa and a black Greta Garbo hat that she had found on the floor of the wardrobe. She caught a train that arrived in London at six o'clock. Euston station was full of smoke and thunderously noisy. It was Friday, and Maggie had come straight from work to meet her. She flung her arms around her friend's neck, full of questions.

'What's Iris's baby like? Did you like Wales? Was the journey all right? You look awful pale, Nell. Have you really got a car of your own?'

Nell laughed. 'Last Christmas you accused me of having rosy cheeks. Anyroad, the baby's fine, Wales was okay once the snow went, the train journey was interesting and, yes, I have a car of me own. I'm taking the driving test next month. '

Maggie looked impressed. 'You're getting dead posh, Nell Desmond, particularly in that hat.'

'I'll never be posh,' Nell vowed.

'Nor me.' Maggie linked her arm. 'Shall we go to the pics and have something to eat afterwards?'

'Yes please.' Nell felt happy for the first time in ages. 'Are there any good pictures on?' She hadn't seen a picture in ages, either.

'There's one called *The Spiral Staircase*. A woman at work saw it and she said it's dead creepy.' Maggie shivered as if to emphasise just how creepy it was. 'It stars Dorothy McGuire and a woman called Rhonda Fleming who's got this incredible red hair.' She tossed her black curls, which had grown long again. 'I'd love red hair.'

'You've already got beautiful hair. I wish I could do something with mine.' She hadn't had it cut in Wales, and it lay on her collar like rats' tails.

'Have it cut while you're here, and buy some clothes too. There's this enormous C&A Modes by Marble Arch.' Maggie squeezed Nell's arm somewhat painfully. 'We'll go tomorrow. Oh, Nell. We'll have a gear time together in London.'

The Spiral Staircase was really terrifying. Maggie swore she wouldn't be able to sleep that night. Afterwards, they went to a restaurant in Soho where Nell had spaghetti bolognese for the first time and a man wearing a red bandanna wandered around playing the guitar and singing Italian songs.

Back in Shepherd's Bush, they sat and talked until almost two o'clock in the morning, and Nell fell asleep sitting up.

London was packed, a lot of the people being foreigners. It couldn't have been more different from Wales, where Nell had been living only a month ago.

She had brought food with her, basic things like tea, sugar, butter and tins of corned beef and salmon to supplement Maggie's rations. On Saturday morning, they had beans on toast for breakfast. While they were eating in Maggie's room, a young woman knocked and put her head around the door to announce that it was her birthday and she was throwing a party that night to which Maggie was invited.

'And you too,' she added, smiling at Nell.

'That's Violet. I'll buy her a present while we're out,' Maggie said when the young woman had gone.

After breakfast, they left for C&A Modes, where Nell took ages trying to choose between a knee-length white polka-dotted dress and a blue silky one with a full skirt that reached her calves. It was based on the Dior New Look that had so excited the fashion world, using twice as much material as the utility clothes available during the war.

In the end, she bought both dresses. As she said to Maggie, 'I might have to wait until the New Look arrives in Bootle before I can wear the blue one.'

'You could wear it at the party tonight,' Maggie suggested. 'I've seen loads of people wearing the New Look in London.' She looked appraisingly at the blue dress. 'In fact I wouldn't mind one meself, though a different style from yours. I like the look of that red one with the striped collar.'

Nell went on to buy white sandals and a cardy, also white, while Maggie treated herself to a new straw hat and bought a georgette scarf for Violet, whose birthday it was.

They left the shop laden with carrier bags and made their way to Maison Lyons opposite Marble Arch for lunch. The magnificent five-storey building had a different restaurant on each floor, ranging from the very expensive to the very cheap. Maggie, who'd been there before, said the second floor was the cheapest and they could have omelettes at only a shilling each.

'You're not very forthcoming about Iris and the new baby,' she remarked after the food was eaten and they were sharing a pot of tea. 'I thought you'd be going on and on about it.'

'There's not much to say,' Nell mumbled. 'The baby's lovely, I've already told you that.'

Maggie narrowed her eyes. 'Did you and Iris have a row?'

'No, of course not. Though . . .' Nell paused. She supposed it did seem odd, hardly mentioning Iris and the baby. For the briefest of moments, she badly wanted to tell Maggie everything, that William was her baby, not Iris's. But caution won the day. Although Maggie would always be her dearest, closest friend, it was only right that the truth about William should remain a secret between the three people concerned, Iris, Tom and Nell. Anyway, she suspected that Maggie had never divulged the facts about her relationship with Chris Conway, so Nell wasn't the only one keeping a dark secret.

'Me and Iris got a bit fed up with each other towards the end,' she said. 'The weather was awful and we couldn't get out the house for a lot of the time. Back in Bootle, I've had me hands full with Crown Caterers, y'know, learning to drive an' all.' Nell lifted her head. She could hear music, and in the corner of the enormous room an elderly woman had started to play the harp. 'Isn't that lovely!' she remarked. 'It sounds dead romantic.'

Maggie nodded with her usual enthusiasm. 'I love London,' she breathed.

'So do I.' It wasn't until that moment that Nell realised just how much she liked the capital city. It was full of noise, always something going on, buskers everywhere, bright lights, entertainment. Yet she wouldn't have wanted to live there. There were times when she desperately wanted to shut her eyes, not because she was tired, but she wanted to close down, think a few quiet thoughts, but that would have been impossible except in the privacy of her room. Tonight was the party, tomorrow Mass in Westminster Cathedral, then Petticoat Lane market, and a walk through Hyde Park in the afternoon . . . London was a gear place to stay, but not to live. She couldn't have stood it and far preferred life in Bootle.

At the party, Nell met Drugi, who was Polish and Maggie's sort of boyfriend.

'Why is he only "sort of"?' she'd asked earlier.

Maggie tossed her head. 'Because I've no intention of marrying him. I really fancy his friend Jack, but if I give up Drugi, I might never see Jack again.'

'Is Jack Polish too?'

'Yes. His proper name is Jacek Kaminski. He goes out with my friend Daphne Scott, but I'm not sure it's serious, though Daphne thinks it is.'

'What about the chap you were going out with at Christmas – Philip something?'

'Philip Morrison. He's courting Alicia Black, another friend. Now *that's* serious on both sides.'

It all sounded terribly complicated to Nell. She liked Drugi when they met. He was boyishly handsome and had a nice friendly personality. Maggie mainly ignored him at the party and flirted with another chap, leaving Drugi to dance all night with Nell and tell her how much he loved her friend. Nell didn't think he could love her all *that* much, else he wouldn't have laughed quite so often or so heartily.

Mass in the imposing Catholic cathedral was an experience in itself. She emerged, after praying really hard, awed by the beauty of the building and the sense of calm and peace inside.

In Petticoat Lane, she came down to earth amid the clamour and the yelling of the traders. Goods of all kinds, from clothes to cheap jewellery to fresh fruit and vegetables, were pushed under her nose. She bought three sets of cheap earrings for her sisters and a pure silk tie, or so it said on the label, for their Kenny. She'd get something a bit more expensive for Mam and Dad.

The dull morning turned into a sunny afternoon just in time for the visit to Hyde Park. She hadn't realised that they were meeting Jacek Kaminski – Jack – who Maggie confessed to be madly in love with.

Nell understood why. He was a charming man, not as handsome as his friend Drugi, but with a strong, enigmatic face. It was impossible to imagine what he might be thinking. She thought his expression lightened a little whenever he glanced at Maggie and turned to one of slight irritation when his girlfriend, Daphne, spoke to him. She decided not to tell Maggie that for fear of unintentionally raising her hopes.

Nell returned to Liverpool on Friday, having been in London a whole week. Maggie had been at work at Thomas Cook's, but they'd met for lunch, and in the afternoons Nell had wandered around the shops by herself or gone to the pictures.

The best part of her stay, though, was late Tuesday afternoon, when they went to the House of Commons, where Kathleen Curran, Member of Parliament for Bootle Docklands as well as being Maggie's Aunt Kath, was taking part in a debate on the National Health Service that was due to be introduced next year.

To think she had known this woman all her life, and now here she was, making a speech in the most important building in the land, being listened to with rapt attention and stared at with admiration by politicians from every party. After all, how could you argue with someone who was so concerned about the poor, who said forcefully that everyone had a right to a home, food, a good education for their children and medical care when they were ill?

Nell was therefore astounded when a man on the benches opposite stood to declare in an unbelievably posh voice that the Right Honourable Member was living in cloud cuckoo land. 'She needs to take her head out of the sand, realise that our country is deeply in debt due to the war. We cannot, in truth, afford to bring in a National Health Service, let alone all the other things the honourable lady demands.'

There were shouts from Auntie Kath's side of 'balderdash', 'stuff and nonsense' and 'twaddle'.

Soon afterwards, Auntie Kath left the chamber. Maggie and Nell met her at the front of the building, where, to Maggie's delight, her father was waiting too. The girls were treated to tea in the visitors' restaurant.

Auntie Kath was desperately impressed with Crown Caterers, which Nell assured her would be starting soon. 'I've got the car and all the equipment,' Nell told them in her calm, unhurried tones. 'I really need me own kitchen, but I'll just have to work at home until something comes up. Trouble is, our kitchen is really titchy, and sometimes I need to spread meself out.'

'Well, dear,' Auntie Kath said, 'if you don't mind hanging on a bit, the flat over the Labour Party offices on the Dock Road will be vacant soon.' She smiled admiringly at Nell. 'You'd be a perfect tenant, wouldn't she, Paddy?'

'Perfect,' Paddy O'Neill agreed. 'Absolutely perfect.'

Giving William up was the most awful thing to have happened to Nell, but she'd had some enormous good luck lately too: the bus to Liverpool, for example, on the day William had been born, the car Dad had acquired for her, and now the flat over the Labour Party, for which she apparently would be perfect. She'd never been there, but Auntie Kath had promised that the kitchen was a good size.

'I hope you and Jack Kaminski get together soon,' Nell said to Maggie at Euston station before catching the train home.

'And I hope you meet a nice feller soon, Nell,' Maggie said in return. 'Businesses are all right, but having a husband and babies is what women are born to do.'

'Your Auntie Kath seems happy enough without either,' Nell pointed out.

'Auntie Kath is the exception to the rule.'

'Perhaps I'm another exception.' Nell had already had a baby and couldn't visualise having another. As for a husband, the only man who'd wanted to marry her had been killed not long after proposing. She had a feeling she was destined to be an old maid, and after thinking about it for a while, she decided she didn't mind a bit.

Chapter 10

Maggie really missed having Nell in her life. Since they were little girls they had done everything together, but, she told herself, she had moved on and Nell had stayed behind. She had made friends in London, built an entirely new life, full of fun and excitement. Barely a week would pass when she didn't see the latest picture or visit the theatre. She had dinner out regularly, went to numerous parties, and bought new clothes whenever she could afford to. She didn't even attempt to save any of her wages.

The year before, she had become a permanent member of Thomas Cook's staff, having discovered that temporary workers were only paid for the hours they worked so lost money when the firm closed over Christmas and Bank Holidays. Working as a shorthand typist wasn't exactly what she'd come to London for. She'd planned on getting a really interesting job, something fascinating and rewarding. Arranging people's holidays gave her no thrill at all, it was in fact as dull as ditchwater, but the pay was good, and just then, having a good time was all that mattered.

She knew she was lucky, and so were her friends. They were single, had few responsibilities, and their out-of-work hours were their own to spend as they wished. Although the war had been over for two years, looking after a family wasn't easy. Most children under ten had never seen an orange or a banana, let alone tasted one. Women still struggled on the meagre rations to feed their families. Some of the tinned food that Nell had brought from Liverpool, Maggie took into the office to give to Rita Chase, a girl she worked with whose father had been killed at Dunkirk and who had five younger brothers and sisters, as well as a mam who'd lost her hearing in the Blitz.

In London, as in every big city, ugly bomb sites were still a feature of most streets, and it would be years before they were tidied up and developed. They remained, like the shortage of food, as reminders of the war that had cost so many precious lives. Although the lights were on again, those in the West End shone on only a handful of Londoners.

It was the first of July, exactly six months since Maggie had met Jack Kaminski and Drugi Nowak in Trafalgar Square. Frequently, she would curse Daphne for turning up and nabbing Jack for herself, leaving her with Drugi.

There was no doubt that Drugi was a generous and amusing boyfriend. One of his uncles owned a popular restaurant in Soho, where Drugi worked as a waiter. There was a whole tribe of Poles in the area, not all Nowaks, who'd come from the same village in Poland and ranged from the very young to the very old. Jack Kaminski was one, but the only person not to have any other family. A week rarely passed without a celebration of some sort: a birthday, an engagement, someone's wedding. Even the one death – Drugi's grandfather – had turned into a celebration of sorts.

Drugi seemed to have plenty of money. Maggie frequently offered to pay for herself when they went out, but he wouldn't hear of it. He professed to be madly in love with her, but didn't seem to mind that she never claimed to love him back. At the end of the evening, they would kiss, quite passionately. Maggie flatly refused to let him go further. She was worried she would enjoy it as much as she had done with Chris Conway, and had an uneasy feeling that she was oversexed, but didn't know who she could discuss it with. Nell knew nothing whatsoever about sex. She wondered if Auntie Kath might be a good person to ask, but was too embarrassed.

Daphne confessed to be head over heels in love with Jack Kaminski. She had actually used those words, 'head over heels', to describe how she felt.

Maggie wasn't surprised. She felt the same about Jack, who should have been living in Hollywood like Clark Gable or Alan Ladd and starring in pictures, rather than working in a Polish bank in the city.

'His job is frightfully important,' Daphne told Maggie in hushed tones. 'He doesn't work behind the counter, he's not just a bank *clerk*, but is in charge of foreign investments. He deals with millions of pounds.'

'Did he tell you that?' If he had, Maggie thought it rather incautious, not the sort of information that should be spread around.

'No, but Daddy said he almost certainly would, working in that department. Daddy's longing to meet him. As you know, he was in the Royal Air Force during the war, and he said that Polish pilots were the best he'd known.' Both Jack and Drugi had been in the RAF.

'Hasn't he met your family yet?'

Daphne puckered her red-painted lips. 'He's been invited loads of times, but he flatly refuses to come.' Her eyes grew moist. 'Sometimes I worry that he's not really serious about me.'

Maggie hoped and prayed he never would be. But how could she make him be serious about *her*? In the past, she had never had a problem getting any man she wanted, and she wanted Jack Kaminski more than anything on earth.

To her pleased surprise, Jack telephoned her at work one day. 'Maggie, I understand the MP Kathleen Curran is a relative of yours?' he said in his lovely deep voice – his English was almost perfect,

'She's me Auntie Kath, yes,' Maggie replied.

'Would it be possible for me to meet her? I heard her on the wireless the other evening and I was extremely impressed.'

Maggie's heart did a somersault. 'If I want to see her, I sit in the visitors' gallery in the House of Commons and wave. Once the debate's over, we meet in the lobby.'

'So if I accompanied you one evening, would you introduce me?'

'Of course.'

'How about tonight? Have you arranged to do anything?'

Maggie had genuinely been intending to wash her hair, but immediately dismissed the idea. 'Absolutely nothing,' she said.

He said he would pick her up in a taxi after work. There was no mention of Daphne. Maggie said she'd wait in Piccadilly rather than Thomas Cook's entrance in the street behind, as it would be easier for the taxi to stop, though the real reason was in case Daphne came out at the same time. She didn't want to be suspected of two-timing her friend. Not that Jack's request to meet Auntie Kath could be deemed romantic.

It was rather nice to sit within the sanctuary of a taxi and watch other people pouring down the steps of the Underground or queuing for buses. She said so to Jack, who remarked that that was just like her.

'Most people find riding in a taxi rather boring; you regard it as fun. You always manage to get the best out of life, Maggie.'

'I wasn't getting the best out of life when you found me in Trafalgar Square on New Year's Eve,' she snorted. 'I was desperately miserable.'

Jack smiled. He was dressed as she'd never seen him before, in a black jacket, striped trousers and sparkling white shirt. She was pleased he hadn't added a bowler hat or a rolled umbrella to the outfit. There weren't the words to describe just how handsome and desirable he looked.

'That's understandable,' he said. 'In the same position I would have been desperately miserable myself.'

He was clearly impressed by the grandeur of the British Parliament. They took their place in the visitors' gallery and Maggie saw Auntie Kath, dressed entirely in bright red, in her usual position in the chamber: in the back row behind where the prime minister normally sat. So far, Maggie hadn't seen Clement Attlee, the man who'd led the Labour Party to its overwhelming victory during the last months of the war. Auntie Kath had promised to let her know next time he was likely to be present in the evening so she could be there.

Her aunt nodded slightly to let her know she'd been seen. She didn't take part in the debate, a rather dull one about farm subsidies, no doubt of great importance to some people. After only a few minutes, she got up and left the chamber.

Maggie nudged Jack and they left too.

In the lobby, she introduced them. Auntie Kath wasn't as appreciative as some women – no, *most* women, thought Maggie – of having her hand kissed by the charming Jack Kaminski, though she showed keen interest when Jack explained his role as an employee of the Polish state bank. She asked him to describe in detail the economic state of his country after its brutal occupation by the Germans throughout the war years.

'Or is it too soon to ask that question, Mr Kaminski?' Auntie Kath frowned earnestly, her entire attention directed upon Poland and its economy, as happened with every matter that came her way. It was what made her such a good Member of Parliament. She put her heart and soul into everything.

'As far as I know, things are slowly getting back to normal,' Jack said. 'I haven't been back to Poland since I left to join the

RAF at the start of the war. I would not be made welcome now that we are under communist rule.'

'Do you have any family there?'

Jack shrugged. 'My parents died in a concentration camp. I left behind other relatives, but don't know their fate.'

'Are you Jewish, Mr Kaminski?' Auntie Kath asked bluntly.

'No, Miss Curran, but my mother and father were pacifists. They died for their beliefs, not their religion.'

Listening, Maggie felt ashamed. It hadn't entered her head that Jack might have a history, a tragic history. Her aunt would be understandably shocked if she knew her niece looked upon him in a purely superficial way, imagining what it would be like if he kissed her or how she would feel in his embrace.

Auntie Kath looked at her watch and said she had a committee meeting and it wouldn't do to be late. 'I'm *never* late,' she said firmly.

Jack shook her hand and said it was a pleasure to have met her. 'I hope one day that we will meet again.'

Auntie Kath smiled a little smile and looked at Maggie. 'Oh, I'm sure one day we will, Mr Kaminski. And it was lovely meeting *you*.'

'What a remarkable woman,' Jack murmured as Auntie Kath marched purposefully away, shoulders back, red skirt swishing, determined to do all she could to make the world a better place.

They left the building. It was a beautiful summer evening, the sun a huge red ball as it made its slow journey towards the horizon. The day had been hot, but now the temperature was perfect. The area outside Parliament was full of people lying or sitting on the grass or strolling along in their summer clothes. Jack commented that he wished he was wearing something more casual. Maggie suggested he take off his jacket and tie.

'I'll put your tie in me bag,' she offered.

Jack divested himself of his jacket and rolled up his

shirtsleeves. Maggie folded his navy and gold striped tie neatly and put it carefully in her handbag. She was aware that his shoulders were very broad, he was wearing a belt instead of braces and his waist was very slim.

'Would you like something to eat?' he asked.

Maggie immediately realised she was starving. 'Yes, *please*,' she said with enthusiasm. The road they were in contained only large important buildings and houses, no shops or restaurants.

'There's a hotel not far from here, just around the next corner, the Meredith; a rather grand place. I think only a grand place will do for our first meal together, don't you, Maggie?'

Maggie felt herself go hot, then cold, then faint. She almost stopped walking, feeling dizzy on top of everything else, and was scared she'd fall over. It came to her like a rocket out of the blue that Jack wanting to meet Auntie Kath was merely an excuse; that it had been a roundabout way of asking her out, that if he'd asked in the ordinary way for a date she would have refused on the grounds that he was still going out with Daphne, which would have complicated matters and made her feel she was being disloyal.

'What about Daphne?' she asked in a small voice.

'I talked to Daphne last night and she agreed our relationship was going nowhere. I told her I was in love with you, that I had been since we met in Trafalgar Square on New Year's Eve, and she agreed that it was only right that we part.' He stopped in the street and so did she. People walking by had to dodge around them, but Maggie didn't notice and neither did Jack. He kissed her lightly on each cheek, then tucked her arm inside his, and they made their way towards the Meredith.

Today was the day when her life had changed for ever. Nothing would ever be the same again. Jack Kaminski loved her and she loved him. One day soon they would get married, have children and grow old together. All the things that had happened before were as nothing compared to what would happen once she became a wife to Jack and a mother to their children.

She would never forget that night, the air touched as if by magic, every single little thing about it perfect, almost surreal. She had never eaten such a wonderful meal before, or drunk such delectable wine in such desirable company.

'Oh, Maggie, your eyes!' Jack raised his glass and drank to them. 'They are such a beautiful colour and they shine like stars.'

'It's you that's made them shine,' Maggie said shyly. Any minute she would come down to earth and find she was imagining things, or wake up and discover it had all been a dream.

But it was real, all of it. Jack Kaminski had been in love with her and she with him ever since they'd met. Within a week, they were discussing when they would get married and where they would live.

'Where would you like to live, Maggie?' he asked one night when they were in Drugi's uncle's restaurant in Soho – Drugi didn't seem to mind Maggie dropping him in favour of his friend.

'I hardly know London,' Maggie confessed. 'I'm only famil-iar with the West End and Shepherd's Bush. I'll leave it to you to choose.'

But first of all, they had another wedding to go to. At the beginning of August, Alicia Black married Philip Morrison in St Mary's Parish church in Twickenham. All the members of the Thomas Cook ex-servicewomen's club were there. Alicia and Philip had met earlier in the year at Maggie's sickbed, and as Alicia didn't have any sisters or female cousins, she had asked Maggie to be her only bridesmaid.

On the day, Maggie wore a long rose-pink dress and carried a posy of white roses. Jack had only recently bought her an engagement ring, three diamonds in a white-gold setting. It was their first outing as an engaged couple.

It was another perfect day – most days were nowadays. The sun shone, the scent of the flowers in the church was overwhelming, the choir sang gloriously. The reception was held in the garden of Alicia's parents' house and the only black spot occurred mid-afternoon when Maggie ran upstairs to the lavatory and heard a woman sobbing in one of the bedrooms.

When the weeping woman was tracked down, it turned out to be Daphne Scott, who had gone out with Jack for more than half a year. She was lying face down on the bed, her face buried in the pillow.

'You are so lucky,' she wept when Maggie attempted to comfort her. 'Only twenty-three and about to get married. I'll be thirty-one soon and I have no one. I loved Jack and I thought he loved me, but he loved you instead.'

Maggie had no idea what so say. She stroked Daphne's blonde head, muttering, 'There, there.' It was no use promising that the right man would turn up one day – what did *she* know about it? The right man for Daphne might have died in the war. Or pointing out that Alicia was thirty-three, or saying that her friend Nell in Bootle had claimed she was looking forward to being an old maid.

'There, there,' she said again. 'There, there.'

Jack took her to view a house he had found for sale in Finchley. It was semi-detached with a big square bay window in the lounge, a dining room, breakfast room, a modern kitchen with built-in units, four bedrooms, a huge bathroom, and a garage. The present owners were leaving behind the curtains and fitted carpets.

'Can we buy it?' Maggie asked when the estate agent had shown them round the spacious rooms and the neat, very ordinary garden. She was already planning a rockery, a rustic arch and dozens of rose bushes.

'If it's what you want, love. But this is the first house we've looked at. Don't you think we should look at others before we make up our minds?'

'We have a number of prospective buyers on the list waiting to view this one,' the estate agent said smoothly. He looked as if he had been polished all over, including his dark blue suit.

'I can't imagine liking another house as much as I like this one,' Maggie said.

'In that case, we shall buy it.'

Even so, over the following week Jack took her to half a dozen other properties that were for sale, only looking at them from the outside, but Maggie still preferred the first.

'The road has the nicest name too: Coriander Close, and seven is my lucky number.' She was a lucky person. Everyone in the army used to say so. Of course, that was before Mam died in such a horrible way. But she was still lucky. Hadn't Daphne told her so at the wedding only a few weeks ago?

The wedding of Margaret O'Neill, Paddy O'Neill's eldest girl, became the talk of Bootle for a while. It took place in the middle of December, with Christmas decorations up everywhere. Early on the day, a charabanc turned up outside St James's church hall, where the reception was to be held, full of foreigners, all jabbering away to one another in German, or so claimed Elsa Moody, who lived opposite and was worried Bootle had been invaded by the Hun.

'Don't talk such drivel, Ma,' her son Edgar said derisively. 'They're speaking Polish, you daft ould biddy. It's people like you that start wars.'

'So Paddy O'Neill's girl's marrying a Pole, eh! What's the matter with her, wouldn't a decent English feller have her?'

'Shurrup, Ma.' Felix had had a crush on Maggie O'Neill since they'd been at school together. *He* was a decent English feller and she hadn't looked twice at him.

★

Maggie's dress was white sculpted velvet with long sleeves and a small train. She carried a bouquet of red roses and was attended by three bridesmaids in scarlet brocade: her little sister Bridie, her friend Nell, and Rosie, her sister-in-law, who was six months pregnant. The bridegroom wore a grey morning suit, as did Drugi Nowak, his best man.

The bride, with her black curls piled on top of her shapely head, made an impressive and truly beautiful sight. All in all, it was the most lavish and striking wedding to be held in Bootle in most people's lifetime.

When the newly married couple left to catch the train from Lime Street station to Euston, and thence to Paris, the bride threw her flowers in what she perceived was the direction of her friend Nell; sensing this, Nell moved aside so that the woman called Daphne who she had discovered earlier crying her eyes out in the ladies' toilet caught them.

'That means you'll be married next,' Nell said to the red-eyed woman.

'Oh, do you really think so!' Daphne gasped.

As Nell watched the taxi drive away with Maggie and Jack waving out of the rear window, she worried a little about her friend. Jack was a decent chap, of that there was no doubt, but Maggie seemed besotted by him, hanging on his every word, agreeing with him, looking at him adoringly. Everything was perfect, she kept saying, in particular Jack, but also the house he'd bought, the furniture, the car to go in the perfect garage, the life they would lead, their future together.

Nell was only twenty-three, but one thing she had learned in her short life was that things never remained perfect for long. Sooner or later they would turn sour. She hoped for her friend's sake that they wouldn't, but she would bet a pound to a penny that at some point in time she would be proved right.

★

Eight-month-old William was standing up in his cot; without help from anyone, he had actually pulled himself to his feet by holding on to the bars. He was a remarkable child, very advanced according to Tom.

'He'll be walking soon,' Tom predicted. 'We have a very clever son, darling.'

He seemed to have hypnotised himself into thinking that William genuinely was their son, born out of his seed and her womb. She no longer bothered to remind him he was wrong, that William was Nell's son, father unknown. For the ump-teenth time she wondered if the unknown father was Tom himself. She would have liked to face him with it, see what his reaction was, but it was an outrageous, offensive thing to accuse him of if he was innocent.

'You are a genius,' she told William.

The little boy made an untranslatable noise, sat down with a thump and grinned mischievously at her through the cot's bars. Iris threw him a kiss and looked at her watch. Maggie's wedding would be over by now – or at least her and the bridegroom's part in it. No doubt there'd be a dead-rowdy party going on in St James's hall, which she would have loved to have gone to. She and Tom had been asked to the wedding, but had declined the invitation claiming a previous engage-ment. The truth was she didn't want Nell to know that she was five months pregnant. She had this stupid, unreasonable, absolutely ridiculous idea that Nell would see this as an excuse to demand her own baby back once she realised that Iris could have one of her own.

She was pleased, though, really pleased. 'How can it have happened?' she'd asked Tom when she realised she was expecting. He was just as thrilled. 'I've gone for years without conceiving.'

'It often happens,' Tom said. 'If a couple adopt a baby because they can't have one of their own, the woman will quite often conceive. I suppose it's to do with the fact that she is no longer desperately anxious for a child and relaxes.'

'It probably means that we can have more.'

Tom smiled. 'As many as you want, darling.'

'Four, I'd like four,' she said eagerly. 'I mean, four altogether, including William.'

'Then four it shall be.'

'You're going to have a brother or a sister in four months' time,' she told William.

He pulled himself to his feet again and gave a cry of triumph.

'You are a genius,' she told him again.

Of course, Nell wouldn't dream of taking him back. She wasn't that sort of person. Dear Nell wouldn't hurt a fly, let along another human being. If only Tom hadn't been so downright horrible the day William had been born. Remembering the way he'd spoken to the girl could still make Iris's stomach curl. She and Tom were getting on all right nowadays, but she would never forgive him for the way he had behaved that day. Because of it, she had lost the best friend in the world. And she would have loved to have gone to Maggie's wedding.

Maggie and Jack were drinking champagne in the sumptuous bar of the Ritz Hotel in Piccadilly in London. Tomorrow they were going to France on the ferry, where they would be staying in Paris in another hotel called the Ritz.

Why didn't I think of it before? Maggie hoped her inner turmoil didn't show on her face. *She wasn't a virgin!* Would Jack notice? Was it possible for a man *not* to notice? If only she'd thought of it earlier, she could have asked someone if it was possible for the thing – the hyphen or something – to be broken for any reason other than intercourse. Perhaps she could claim she'd had something as a child, appendicitis, say,

and it had been taken out. Where on earth was her appendix?
Was it approached through the womb?

For some inexplicable reason she giggled. She wouldn't be
surprised if Jack didn't care if she was a virgin or not. After all,
she didn't care if he'd been with dozens of women. All that
mattered was what happened from this moment on and in the
future. The past was over.

'What's so funny?' Jack asked.

'Nothing.' She giggled again. 'Everything.'

'That makes sense.' He laughed and stared at her. 'You suit
blue,' he said. Her going-away outfit was more turquoise than
blue; a plain costume with a white jumper underneath and a
little pork-pie hat with a veil.

'You suit grey. It goes with your eyes.' His suit was navy
with a subdued dark grey stripe, made for the occasion by a
Polish tailor.

He claimed never to have seen anyone with striped eyes.
'You're making me out to be a freak.'

Maggie giggled even more and couldn't stop. 'You've had
too much champagne, my love,' Jack said. 'I think it's about
time we went to bed.'

She stopped giggling. 'Bed?'

'It's what married people do,' he said gravely. 'This is
merely the first of a million times.'

'A million?'

'Or perhaps two million. And that's only the first year.' He
reached for her hand and pulled her to her feet. 'Will you sleep
with me tonight, Mrs Kaminski?' he whispered in her ear.

'Yes, Mr Kaminski, I will.'

He put his arm around her shoulder and led her towards the
lift.

Two elderly ladies were sitting in armchairs next to Maggie
and Jack's now vacant table. 'I wish I could be in that young

woman's shoes for the next few hours,' one said longingly to her friend as she watched the couple get in the lift.

'Why, Hettie?' the friend asked.

'It's their first night together. My first night was awful, Harold hadn't a clue what to do and he was a dead loss. I feel I should be entitled to another first night, and that young man,' she nodded at the empty table, 'would have done nicely. Extremely well built, couldn't wait to get his hands on the girl.'

Her friend's jaw dropped. 'Hettie Weatherspoon!' she gasped. 'You disgraceful old woman. How did you know it was their first night?'

'The girl had confetti in her dear little hat. And it was the look on their faces as well. I could tell they'd never done it before and they couldn't wait to get their hands on each other.' She glanced at her diamanté watch. 'I wonder if they're undressed yet.'

'Would you like to go upstairs and watch through the keyhole?'

'If I were capable of kneeling down, I might well have done. I say, Belle, have they only drunk half the champagne out of that bottle?'

'They have indeed.' Belle rose unsteadily to her feet. 'I'll fetch it, shall I, before the chappie comes to clear the table?'

'Clever girl,' Hettie said when Belle returned. 'Fill my glass up, there's an angel. In a minute I shall go to bed myself. If I can't actually *do* it, then I shall dream about it instead.'

Maggie had been married a month. She had left Thomas Cook's to become a housewife instead of a shorthand typist. It had been her own decision to leave; Jack hadn't minded whether she stayed at work or not. She was really looking forward to being at home during the day.

'Dusting and washing and ironing and shopping and making our dinner.' She sighed happily, entirely forgetting how hopeless she'd been at housework after her mother had died. She'd bought a *Good Housekeeping* recipe book and studied it carefully. She also wrote to Nell to enquire about simple recipes. She made pastry and it stuck to the bread board, made omelettes, using up two weeks' egg ration, and they didn't rise at all, and neither did the bread she attempted, though she didn't give up. She didn't want to become a master chef; adequate would do.

At half past ten each morning, she stopped to make tea or coffee, listened to the wireless, and read ten pages of a novel. She vacuumed the carpets every day until Jack said she'd wear the pattern off, and there was no need to clean the windows quite so often either, nor wash the bedding.

Occasionally, in the afternoon, she went to Selfridges and John Lewis in the West End to look at the curtains they would buy once they had enough coupons. Neither she nor Jack liked the curtains and carpets kindly left behind by the previous owners of their house, but every single one of Maggie's coupons, some of Jack's and some of her father's had been used up on her wedding dress and the bridesmaids' outfits.

She visualised the big square bay hung with cream chintz curtains dotted with pink rosebuds. Oh, but I'm being really selfish, she thought. Mam would have loved the rust and gold curtains that are there now. I'm too lucky for me own good.

She returned to her lovely house feeling ashamed. Life was so wonderful, what did the colour of the curtains matter?

She loved Jack so much that it hurt, literally made her throat ache each morning when they kissed goodbye and she watched through the window as he walked away towards East Finchley Underground station. Even if there'd been enough petrol, it was far more convenient to travel by tube than car in London. It would be *hours* until they saw each other again, and she wasn't sure if she could bear it. At six o'clock she would be at the window once more, waiting for him to appear, her heart leaping as he came closer and closer. Then they would shut the door and stand in the hall and kiss for ages. Sometimes they were tempted to make love there and then, downstairs on the settee, but as Maggie would point out, somewhat breathlessly and very reluctantly, the potatoes might burn or the casserole get too dry or the sponge cake collapse, if it hadn't done so already.

She had never had a telephone at her disposal before, and she spent hours sitting on the stairs talking to her friends, some of whom were pregnant: Rosie, her sister-in-law, whose baby was due to arrive shortly, Alicia, who'd only just discovered she was in the club, Iris, expecting her second baby around Easter. And of course Nell, now living in the flat over the Labour Party office on the Dock Road. Nell wasn't even married, let alone pregnant, and Maggie couldn't understand how she could be so happy.

'Don't you want a family of your own one day?' she said crossly. It irritated her that her friend didn't want what she herself had – a husband, a lovely home and the prospect of having children.

'One day, maybe,' Nell said casually. Maggie imagined her shrugging her thin shoulders. 'I love where I live and Crown Caterers is becoming more and more successful. I'm actually doing well enough to take on staff if I wanted to expand.'

'But it's not the *same*, Nell.' Maggie was exasperated. Mind you, although she wanted Nell to have what she had, there weren't enough men like Jack Kaminski to go around. In fact, she had the only one. Every other woman could only have second best.

It was on Good Friday that she noticed her period was late; only a day or two, but she was usually as regular as clockwork. She didn't tell Jack until she was a whole week late, and he took her for dinner at the Meredith hotel to celebrate. His first order was for a bottle of champagne.

'To you, to me, and to our baby,' he said by way of a toast.

Maggie's baby was due at Christmas. She would call it Noel if it was a boy and Holly if a girl. Jack approved of both names. Although there were babies being born all over the place, she just knew that theirs would be extra special.

In Liverpool, Rosie had had a boy, Patrick, named after his grandad, and in May, exactly a year after she'd had William, Iris gave birth to a girl she called Louise. Alicia's little girl, Marian, was born with a serious heart defect and was still struggling to survive three months later.

Holly or Noel Kaminski wasn't a very active baby. He or she rolled dreamily around Maggie's stomach, stretching oc-casionally, never kicking, just moving smoothly, as if having a little lazy swim. Maggie claimed her baby was waltzing, whereas other babies did the quickstep or a tango, making sharp staccato movements and giving the odd vicious kick. She sang 'Who's Taking You Home Tonight?' and 'We'll Meet Again' as she did the housework, dancing from room to room and down the garden when she went to hang the washing out. If Jack were home, he would dance with her.

The baby was born in a nursing home in London on Boxing Day after a long, excruciatingly painful labour. It positively refused to budge even though Maggie was pushing like mad, and the contractions hurt so much she almost fainted with each one.

'It's a girl,' the midwife announced at some point in the proceedings. Maggie became aware that the pain had stopped and she was so tired she could have slept for a week.

'It's a what?' she asked blurrily.

'A girl, dearie. A fine baby girl, about six and a half pounds, I reckon.'

Maggie was convinced she must have been twice that big. It had been like giving birth to a baby elephant. She was pulled to a sitting position on the bed and the baby, Holly, was placed in her arms. She was so tiny, so totally perfect, incredibly beautiful – and so utterly defenceless. Even so, there was a moment, the briefest of moments, when she felt resentful of her daughter for all the suffering she had caused, but the feeling was quickly replaced by a rush of love so fierce, it was almost like another contraction.

'Jesus!' she muttered, wriggling uncomfortably.

Jack came in. He was in tears, having listened for hours to the cries and moans of his wife. 'A few times I thought you might be on the verge of death,' he confessed. He looked down at their small daughter. 'I hope she's worth it,' he said. Then he put his arms around both of them, his wife and child. 'Maggie, my darling girl, I don't ever want you to have another baby. I couldn't stand it.'

'If I can stand it, then so can you, Jack Kaminski,' Maggie said wearily, but with a hint of steel in her voice. 'I don't want Holly to be an only child. As soon as I feel up to it, I want us to try for another.'

Jack laid his head on her lap and groaned.

She was still in the nursing home six days later, on the eve of 1949. When Jack came, she reminded him that it was exactly two years since they'd met in Trafalgar Square.

'I think I fell in love with you at first sight,' she told him.

'And me with you,' he swore. He looked at Holly, who was sleeping peacefully in a cradle beside her mother, and shook his head in wonder. 'She gets more beautiful every day,' he remarked.

'Doesn't she,' Maggie said fondly.

'And how are you feeling, love?'

Maggie felt as if various parts of her body had been torn

to pieces and were very gradually melting back together. 'Wonderful,' she lied.

She wasn't a very efficient mother. There didn't seem to be enough hours in the day to do all the things necessary for a baby, as well as for a man with a healthy appetite who liked a clean shirt every day. She often ran out of nappies and had to make do with towels till the ones she'd already washed had dried.

Jack never complained. She didn't notice until she hadn't washed a shirt for more than a week that he was sending them to the laundry.

'It won't always be like this,' she promised him one night when she'd burnt the gravy and the custard had burnt the day before. Frequently she hadn't found the opportunity all day to brush her hair before he came home, she was usually wearing the first clothes she'd grabbed that morning, and Holly might be patiently waiting for her afternoon feed.

'I know it won't, my love.' He pulled her on to his knee. 'But in the meantime, I don't care. I worship everything about you and I will send my shirts to the laundry until kingdom come.'

She cradled his head in her arms. 'You are a dead-perfect husband,' she told him before kissing him passionately on the lips.

He muttered something about not minding being perfect, but he'd sooner not be dead, thanks all the same.

Had she been the sort of person who thought using the word 'perfect' so much might be regarded as tempting fate, then perhaps Maggie might not have said it. But there was no denying that Holly was a perfect baby. She scarcely ever cried, and smiled long before the time when babies were reputed to smile. Her eyes sparkled with what could only be described as sheer happiness when her mother's face appeared over her pram or her cot in the bedroom.

'Have you been awake all this time without uttering a single word?' Maggie would say. 'You are without doubt a little angel, Holly Kaminski. I think the good lord himself must be keeping a close eye on you.' It was because she was lucky, had always been lucky, always would be.

A mere eleven months after Holly had made her painful way into the world, Grace Kaminski arrived rather more sedately, but making a great deal of noise.

'Another girl.' The midwife had to shout to be heard above Grace's lusty yells. 'That's the first time *that's* happened,' she gasped when the baby kicked her in the eye. It was a moment that became part of Grace's history, and was told and retold numerous times throughout her life.

It was November. In another six weeks it would be 1950, the start of a new half-century. Maggie and Jack invited a photographer to the house to take a photograph of the happiest couple in the world with their two beautiful daughters. A month later it was sent to their numerous friends along with a hand-embroidered Christmas card made by Drugi's Aunt Kazia.

Alicia Morrison opened it and cried when saw the photo, thinking of her own little delicate daughter who continually failed to thrive. In Liverpool, Rosie showed it to Ryan, snorting, 'Wouldn't it make you sick! They're just showing off. Pair of silly buggers if you ask me – the grown-ups, not the kids.'

Not far away, in Rimrose Road, Iris said to Tom, 'I think our two are better-looking, don't you?' She handed the photo to Tom, who merely glanced at it. 'Much better,' he said automatically. He wasn't interested in other people's children, only his own.

'Oh, what pretty little girls!' Nell remarked to herself when she opened the envelope and removed the contents. 'And what a lovely card.'

She put both the photo and the card on the mantelpiece in her flat. After Christmas, she would buy a frame for the photograph and keep it for ever.

Chapter 11

Judging by the excited whoops and stamping of feet, everyone seemed to be enjoying themselves downstairs. The music was really catchy, an Irish jig played by an Irish duo, Flynn and Finnegan, one on the piano, the other on the fiddle. Nell hadn't seen them yet, so didn't know who played what.

She spread margarine on another slice of bread. This wasn't a Crown Caterers job, just something she was doing as a favour for the Irish-night party being held in the Labour Party offices below. She had worked every day except for Christmas Day. When she'd finished the sandwiches, she would go down and join in the party herself.

Rosie O'Neill came in. She was expecting her second baby soon and was enormous. 'Shall I take them sarnies down, Nell? It'll be the interval soon. What's on this lot?'

'Grated cheese – it goes further when it's grated – and brown sauce.'

'Yum, yum.' Rosie's eyes glowed. 'I'm starving.'

'Well, you're eating for two, aren't you?'

Iris Grant was also expecting another baby, her third – or so everyone thought. Only Nell knew that the first, William, hadn't been the fruit of Iris's womb, but her own. She didn't think about it often, but sometimes, when she did, the memory hurt, and she would recall the feel of her baby in her arms, his mouth tugging on her breast. How many teeth did he have now he was more than two and a half years old? And had Iris breastfed her daughter, Louise? There'd been no chance of that with William.

'He's a fine little feller,' her mam had said a few times after seeing Iris shopping in Marsh Lane with her little boy in the pram. 'Really big for his age and full of mischief; you can tell from his face.'

Mam and Iris didn't have proper conversations, they had never formally met, but they always nodded to each other, and since William had come along, Mam would ask after him in the painfully polite voice she used when she considered that the person she was talking to was posh.

'I can't understand why you two aren't friendly any more,' she would say to Nell after she'd finished reporting on William. It was Mam who'd told Nell that Iris was having another baby. She claimed she was able to tell from a woman's face that she was expecting before the woman actually knew herself.

Rosie left with a plate of sarnies and Nell continued to make more. There were jam tarts for later, and a tin of almond cookies from America that someone had donated to the party.

This new year, 1950, was pretty significant, denoting the end of the first half of the century and the start of the second. A few nit-pickers pointed out that the new half-century didn't start until 1951, but people weren't prepared to wait that long. They were only too glad to bid farewell to the first half, which had seen two world wars, not to mention the Boer War, the Spanish Civil War and no doubt many others they hadn't heard about.

What seemed like a great leap in time made people conscious of their own mortality.

'I won't be around when the next half-century starts, that's for sure,' Nell's dad had said dolefully the other day, and her mother had agreed. Nell wondered if she would last that long herself. When the year 2000 came, she would be seventy-five.

'Seventy-five!' she said aloud. Maggie would be the same.

Gosh! What would their lives be like then? She paused over the bread and margarine and tried to look into the future, but couldn't imagine herself and Maggie fifty years older, or where they would be living or who they would be with. Why, even Maggie's little girls would have turned fifty. She shook her head. Thinking so far ahead was a bit depressing. She resolved not to do it again.

Aunt Kath came marching upstairs. 'I've come for a rest,' she announced. 'I need to sit down for a few minutes. Is there any tea made, Nell? If there isn't, I'll make some meself. Would you like a cup?'

'Please. I've nearly finished. I wouldn't mind a sit-down either. I'll just put the kettle on.'

Aunt Kath took two cups and saucers out of the wall cupboard. 'You've turned this place into a real little home from home. I like the colour you've distempered the kitchen. What's it called?'

'Eau de Nil.' It was a pale, powdery green with a hint of blue. Nell had taken over the flat more than two years ago. Before that it had been occupied by an elderly man for no one could remember how many years. The flat consisted of four small rooms: a living room, bedroom, kitchen and bathroom. Some decent second-hand cupboards had been acquired for the rather squalid kitchen, a newish sink fitted, and the bathroom updated. While Nell was wondering if she could possibly live with the old bits and pieces the man had left, her father had turned up with a collection of furniture that wouldn't have disgraced the poshest house in Bootle.

'Where on earth did it come from, Dad?' she asked. She imagined some poor soul – well, they wouldn't have been poor to have owned this stuff – returning from holiday and finding their house stripped bare.

Dad tapped his nose. 'Don't ask, girl, and you won't be told no lies.'

She felt uneasy living with the furniture until Dad confessed, somewhat ruefully, that he'd come by it in a perfectly honest way. 'There was this family emigrating to Canada; I bought the entire contents of their house dead cheap. I sold a lot of the stuff elsewhere.'

From then on, Nell was able to sit on one of the tapestry armchairs – there wasn't room for the settee – and eat at the small wooden table without feeling guilty. She made pretty draped curtains out of an old sheet dyed blue and felt really proud of her home.

The thing she was proudest of, though, was the garden she had made at the back, a small area approximately twenty feet by twelve. When she had arrived, it had consisted of waist-high weeds mixed with tough grass that had to be dug out rather than tugged. It had taken months to clear. When she had finished, she had borrowed a fork and other gardening tools, turned the black soil over and chopped it to pieces with a hoe. She'd bought grass seed and created a lawn, by which time members of the Labour Party realised what she was doing and brought bushes and flowers to create a border. A couple of benches were donated and a pretty little garden had been created behind the office to which older members were drawn in the warm weather to sit and smoke and knit and discuss politics and football in equal measure.

Auntie Kath had made the tea. Nell finished off the sarnies and arranged them artistically on a plate. Rosie appeared almost straight away and took them downstairs. The other women took the tea into the living room and sat down.

'Have you read that book, Nell – *Nineteen Eighty-Four*, by a chap called George Orwell?' Auntie Kath enquired.

'I never have much time for reading,' Nell said regretfully. She kept on top of things by listening to the BBC news on the wireless.

'You should find the time to read this. It has some pretty

terrifying things to say about the future. Would you like me to lend you my copy?'

'Yes, I would, thanks.' That way she would feel obliged to read it and perhaps learn something for a change.

They chatted until the music below stopped and they went downstairs for the interval. Auntie Kath made a little impassioned speech. She thanked everyone for coming and said what an enormous difference the introduction of the National Health Service had made to the nation's well-being, as well as the nationalisation of the railways and other forms of transport in Britain. 'It means the trains and buses are owned by you, the people, rather than the millionaires.'

There was a cheer when she said that she thought it likely that food rationing would end during the forthcoming year.

'Let's hope that by next New Year's Eve we'll be having ham sandwiches for refreshments. And by the way, please join me in thanking Nell Desmond for making the food this year. Thank you, Nell.'

'Thank you, Nell,' the room chorused.

The music started again and Nell saw Flynn and Finnegan for the first time. She had never heard of them before, but they were apparently well known in the world of Irish jigs and ceilidhs. They were a colourful pair, dressed in shamrock-green shirts and black trousers. The fiddler had a head of violent ginger curls, which shook while he played, dancing like a maniac to his own frantic music, leaping and skipping to and fro across the stage.

His partner on the piano didn't sit, but sort of tap-danced while he pounded the keys, jabbing at them carelessly, running his fingers up and down the keyboard, yet there wasn't a single note out of tune. He was tall and thin and remarkably agile.

Nell made her way towards the little stage to see better. She stood at the front, watching the wild activity. It was impossible not to smile at the antics of the duo. Where did they get the energy from? she wondered.

To her surprise, the fiddler came to the edge of the stage and bent towards her. He shouted something, but she couldn't understand. He shouted again, louder this time. 'Are you Nell, darlin'?'

'Yes.' She nodded furiously.

'Then will you marry me, Nell?' he bellowed.

Because it was New Year's Eve and she felt uplifted by the music and the crazy atmosphere, she laughed and nodded again. 'Yes!'

'I'll hold you to that, darlin',' the red-haired fiddler promised.

Just then, Paddy O'Neill came and whisked her away. He was as drunk as Davy's sow, but still able to trip the light fantastic as well as a man half his age.

It was time for the new year to arrive. The music stopped, the lights went out, a wireless was turned on and with it the sound of Big Ben ringing out the last minutes, the final seconds of 1949, followed by a cheer.

It was 1950!

'No more wars in this century!' someone yelled.

A circle of crossed arms was hastily formed to sing 'Auld Lang Syne'. When it finished, everyone turned to kiss or shake hands with their neighbour. To Nell's astonishment, she found herself in the arms of the red-haired fiddler, who was kissing her more soundly and thoroughly than she'd ever been kissed before.

'Okay, so what date shall we pick for the wedding?' he asked when he stopped kissing and grinned into her face. His own face was thin and pale and his twinkling eyes were bottle green, with gold flecks. His nose was a mite too big and his mouth a touch too wide. Nell liked him immediately.

'Don't be daft.' She couldn't help but laugh when really she should have been annoyed. He had no right to kiss her, a stranger, like that.

He pretended to look hurt. 'But you promised . . .'

'I didn't mean it.'

'You mean you lied? Oh, well, look, if you won't marry me now, can we start courting? I'm Red Finnegan, by the way, and the bloke who plays the piano is my very good friend Eamon Flynn.'

Eamon was back on stage and had started to play again.

Red gave Nell a squeeze and promised to see her later. 'Let me know what you think about it, then. Oh, and by the way, Nell, you are a vision of loveliness, a wholesome lass with the purest of hearts and the kindest of eyes that I have ever seen in the whole of me unholy life. If I can't have you, then I shall die.' He laid his hand on his chest in the area of his heart and staggered mournfully on to the stage, where he picked up his fiddle and began to play.

'Marry him,' said Auntie Kath, who had overheard everything. 'You might well have more dinner times than dinners over your life, but you'll never go short of a good laugh.'

Nell went to bed before the party was over and lay listening to Flynn and Finnegan playing their wild music as she slowly fell asleep. Maybe it was a line he used on many of the women he met at venues all over the country.

They played mainly in the north of the country and in Ireland, Rosie said when she came next day to tidy up after the party. It was their Ryan who'd booked the twosome, having had excellent reports on their performance from mates at work. They would play again at the Irish club at Easter.

And Easter, Nell assumed, was when she would next see Red Finnegan.

Instead, he arrived that afternoon while she was getting the food ready for a children's party. Lemons were available in the shops again, and she was making lemon flummery. She had bought an electric mixer and been obliged to demonstrate its usefulness in the kitchen to every woman she knew. She poured the resultant creamy mixture into little paper moulds to set and proceeded with the ginger buns and Bourbon biscuits.

Finished, and with everything spread out ready to put in tins or on a tray when the time came to leave for the party, Nell sighed, made tea and sank into an armchair in her little sitting room. She felt a trifle discontented, not quite her usual calm, unruffled self, unable to get any sense of satisfaction out of her baking that afternoon, or the comfortable chair in the cosy room that belonged to her and her alone. She knew she lacked imagination, that her contentment with her lot was a trifle unnatural in that it didn't include eventual marriage to a yet unknown man, followed by children.

She really liked her life and the way it was, but today . . . Nell knew she was no oil painting, yet men had frequently shown an interest in her over the years. The trouble was, they were often old or married or both. She remembered how Frank Grant, Iris's brother-in-law, was forever brushing himself against her or stroking her arm – she hadn't liked him a bit. It was rare she met men the same age as herself. But Red Finnegan wasn't much older than she was, and she'd liked him. It was stupid to believe he really wanted to marry her, but had he been just flirting, was he genuinely interested in her – or had it all been a joke and they would next meet at Easter and during the intervening months he would have pretended to ask dozens of other women to marry him and entirely forgotten about Nell?

Her doorbell rang. Nell had her own personal entrance at the side of the building down a narrow set of steps. She went down and opened the door.

'Good morning.' Red Finnegan raised a rather dusty-looking trilby.

For some unreasonable reason, Nell felt cross with him. 'It's afternoon,' she snapped. 'It's been afternoon for at least two hours.'

He raised his hat again. 'Good afternoon, then,' he said affably.

Nell rolled her eyes. 'I suppose you'd better come in.'

He stepped inside, clutching the hat to his chest. 'I detect that that welcome isn't exactly warm.'

How could she explain that he'd made her feel very mixed up, not quite herself, out of kilter, as it were. She wished he hadn't come if all he intended to do was play silly buggers again. 'I'm sorry,' she said, aware that she didn't sound it. 'Would you like a drink: tea, coffee, or something stronger?'

'Strong coffee would be nice; one sugar. I've a bit of a head on me this morning.'

'Afternoon,' she reminded him.

He dipped his head. 'Afternoon,' he agreed. 'It was a good night, last night. I enjoyed it. Trouble is, we get a thirst, me and Eamon, what with all the fiddling, the ivory-tickling and the jumping around. Folks insist on giving us pint after pint of ale, when we'd be perfectly content with water,' he finished virtuously.

'I'm sure you would.' She took him into the living room, told him to sit down and went to make coffee. Her heart must have taken over her entire body, because every bit of her, from the top of her head down to her feet, was thumping just a bit. She made the coffee and a milder one for herself, took them into the living room, and sat in the other armchair so they were facing.

He took a sip of his coffee and put the cup on the floor. He wore a suit of sorts, grey, except the jacket was tweed and the trousers made of shiny material. His shirt was blue and white check and his tie off-white. It was a most peculiar outfit. His red hair was wet and plastered against his skull so it looked like a baby's bonnet. 'I meant what I said last night. I'd very much like us to start courting with a view to getting married in a few months' time. I'll ask your dad, formally like, if that's what you want, like men used to do in olden days when they asked a feller for his daughter's hand in marriage. I'll even go down on bended knee.'

'Me dad'd think you were having him on,' Nell said, wanting to laugh, but managing not to. 'He'd tell you to go and jump in the lake. Anyroad, if you want to go around raising serious matters like marriage, it'd help if you could bring yourself to stop grinning all the time.'

'Sorry, but I was born grinning, or so me mammy says. I can't stop.'

'What happened when you hurt yourself; fell off your bike or something?'

'Well, I never had a bike, but when I hurt meself, I still couldn't stop grinning.'

'Excuse me a minute.' Nell jumped to her feet and rushed into the kitchen, where she leant over the sink and laughed until her stomach ached and her throat hurt. She was still laughing when Red Finnegan came in and started kissing her as thoroughly as he'd done the night before. After a while, she agreed that they should start courting as from today. By then it was time for her to leave for the children's party.

When this was explained to Red, he offered to take her as his van was parked outside. His fiddle was in the back and he came in with her to the party, where he played, sang and danced around the furniture and in and out of the rooms, much to the delight of the young guests.

The mother of the boy whose birthday it was said it was the best party she'd ever known and would Nell please bring the fiddler with her again next year?

Nell hesitated. Would she still know him next year? Would he still be around? She hoped so. 'This time next year we'll be married,' she said daringly. 'I'll bring him, I promise.'

Iris hadn't entirely forgotten that she owed Alfred Desmond a favour of sorts. He had removed Major Matthew Williams from her life – how, she had no idea – on condition that one of these days she did something for him in return. That had been nearly four years ago, and she hadn't set eyes on him since, thank goodness. She prayed he had forgotten all about it, yet knew in her heart that he wasn't the sort of person to forget unreturned favours.

She was therefore not totally surprised when, having just bought the weekly rations, she came out of the Maypole grocery shop one Friday morning in January to find him outside talking to William, who was in his chair on top of the pram. Louise was fast asleep beneath the hood.

'He said he's two and a half and will be three in May,' Alfred chuckled. 'Clever little lad you've got there. He'll be a doctor too, I reckon, when he grows up.'

'Let's hope so,' Iris said weakly.

'Earn a few bob, doctors, so I'm led to believe.' He looked at her slyly. 'More than a few bob, even.'

At first she thought he was going to ask for money as Matthew Williams had done, and she wondered if she could refuse. After all, who else would know that he'd scared the man away at her request? He could prove nothing and she could deny everything.

He lifted a paper carrier bag with a string handle and *Henderson's*, a department store in Liverpool, printed on the side, and swung it in front of her eyes. 'One good turn deserves another,' he said with a smile. 'There's something I'd like you to do for me.'

Iris swallowed. Despite her previous thoughts, she felt no desire to argue; she knew exactly what he meant. 'What?' she enquired.

'There's been a spate of burglaries in our street over the last few weeks, and I'd like you to keep this till the bobbies have caught the thieving sod.' He swung the bag again. 'Wouldn't want anyone finding what's in here.'

'What *is* in there?' Iris asked fearfully.

He winked. 'That'd be telling.' He removed a parcel

wrapped in brown paper from the bag. It was wound with brown sticky tape and sealed with blobs of red wax.

Iris looked worriedly both ways. 'Put it back in the bag,' she gasped. 'How long will I have to keep it? I mean, it might be months before the thief is caught.'

'The bobbies have got their eye on the culprit. They expect to catch him either this weekend or the next.' He looked grave. 'I hope you're not going to make any objections, Mrs Grant. I went out of me way to help you; I expect you to do the same for me.'

'I had no intention of making an objection,' Iris said stiffly. She was still curious, even after all this time, to know how he had scared Matthew Williams off. 'What did you say to the chap in the Sloane Hotel?'

'Took a copper friend of mine with me, an inspector, like. All he had to do was flash his badge and tell the chap to make hisself scarce and not come back again, and he was off like a bloody shot.' He laughed. 'Shaking like a leaf he was, too. Take it there's been so sign of him since?'

'You're right, there hasn't.' She was glad she hadn't tried to deny owing him a favour. He'd taken a policeman to the hotel and had no doubt told him who she was. He had proof that he'd acted on her behalf in the form of the law. Once again she looked from left to right. 'Put the bag in the pram, please.' It was safer that way, neither hidden or too exposed. There was nothing suspicious about a Henderson's carrier bag.

'In the bag, out the bag and shake it all about,' he chanted. 'Oh no you don't, young feller,' he said when William made a grab for it. 'It might explode.'

'It's not a bomb, surely!' Iris was horrified.

'Course it's not a bomb,' Alfred Desmond said playfully. 'I was only joking. Look, I'll be outside the Maypole at the same time next week, or it might possibly be the week after. Oh, and don't open it, whatever you do. If you open it, there'll be all hell to play and I might have to have you killed.'

Iris assumed he was joking again.

She crept home, wheeling the pram as carefully as she could, tipping it off pavements and on again with the greatest care, not wanting to disturb whatever was in the parcel. Morning surgery was in full swing when she arrived – Tom's load had lessened now that the National Health Service had been officially brought in and all doctors apart from a few like his brother Frank, had agreed to join. Adele was no longer his receptionist except in emergencies, and Iris hadn't done the job for years. Frances Blake, a widow in her thirties with two teenaged children, whose husband had died in the war, was now Tom's receptionist.

Iris wheeled the pram down the side of the house into the yard, lifted William out, picked up the bag and went into the kitchen, leaving Louise, who was still asleep, outside for now. Louise was a sweet baby with a lovely lazy smile who slept a lot. Tom kept remarking on the fact that his real child wasn't as clever or lively as William, who had Nell for a mother and a father who was unknown.

'I wouldn't be surprised if our Frank wasn't the father,' he said once.

Iris was so angry at the implication that William's intelligence could only be due to the presence of Grant blood that she had thrown the tea cosy at him, only wishing the teapot had been inside. She was expecting another child, and as long as it was happy and healthy, she didn't give a damn how bright he or she was.

William made straight for the stairs, but was thwarted by the gate at the bottom. He rattled it, but it stayed in place, much to his annoyance. There was no doubt he was a real handful, but Iris never allowed herself to complain, not even to herself. Getting him had been such a dramatically unpleasant experience that she felt she had no right to. His real mother would never have found fault with her little boy, of that Iris felt quite sure.

She stared at the Henderson's bag, picked it up, but didn't remove the parcel. It wasn't heavy, so it couldn't contain expensive – stolen? – jewellery or gold bars. Maybe there was money inside, a few hundred five-pound notes – stolen, of course. She picked at one of the blobs of sealing wax. It fell off and she panicked briefly, but realised there were loads more blobs and the missing one wouldn't be noticed.

Where was she to hide it? There were plenty of places where Tom would never look, but there was always a first time when he might search for something under the sink or look on the top shelf of the cupboard in the hall or beneath their bed or in the wardrobe in the guest room.

In the end, she decided to put it in the outhouse, which had never been used for any reason at all since they'd come to live there. What was more, she would put it in the old rusty boiler. If Tom should discover it there, she would claim she knew nothing about it.

Over the next seven days, Iris never forgot for a single minute about the parcel. A few times, when Tom was out, she went into the outhouse to check it was still there, though there was hardly a chance on earth that it would have been taken.

The following Friday she set off to do the weekly shopping with William and Louise in the pram and the parcel tucked at the foot. It dawned on her that Alfred Desmond must have known about her movements to have been waiting outside the Friday before and to have known that she would be there at the same time this week. She shivered, hating the idea of being spied on by such an odious creature. She resolved to change her shopping habits from now on and go at different times each week.

She bought the groceries, went outside and looked for the

man she was beginning to think of as her tormentor. There was no sign of him. William was kicking the pram with his heels and had woken Louise, who smiled when Iris looked down at her.

'Poor darling, did your horrible big brother spoil your beauty sleep?' She reached inside and sat her daughter up against the pillow.

'What a lovely family you have,' a passing woman remarked.

'Why, thank you.' She enjoyed the moment, but sighed when she realised that Alfred Desmond wasn't coming. He had said it might be two weeks until he would want the parcel back. She released the brake on the pram and went home.

She suffered another week of worry. Her nerves were on edge, half expecting the police to turn up and search the house, having heard there were stolen goods on the premises – or money. If money, it might be counterfeit. She imagined Alfred Desmond denying all knowledge of the parcel. Her heart almost leapt out of her body when she imagined him having known all along that William was the grandson that Tom and Iris had virtually stolen from his daughter. Blackmail or revenge of some sort might well be on the cards in the future.

To her relief, when she emerged from the Maypole the following Friday, he was outside talking to William.

'Got it safe, kiddo?' he enquired.

'Yes,' Iris said through gritted teeth. *Kiddo!* She took the Henderson's bag out of the pram, gave it to him, and released the brake. She was about to hurry away, when he caught the pram handle.

'Half a mo,' he said. He removed the parcel from the bag and tore the paper off. William helpfully joined in. 'Here you are, little man.' William accepted the contents, a fluffy black and white panda, with delight. 'His name's Percy,' Alfred Desmond said. 'Percy Panda.'

'Percy!' William hugged the toy to his chest. 'Panda.'

'What was that all about?' Iris was enraged. 'You've had me terrified for the last two weeks, yet there was no need for it.'

He shrugged. 'Just didn't want to let a favour go to waste. If I'd left it any longer, it would've been too late to ask.'

'I would have been quite happy to do a normal favour for you.' She pushed the pram, but he was still holding the handle and walked along beside her.

He shrugged again. 'Couldn't think of one. Anyroad, it won't have hurt to keep you on your toes for a while. By the way, I thought you'd like to know, our Nellie's business is thriving; I think that's the word, thriving. Crown Caterers, it's called.'

'I know. My mother-in-law and some of her friends use her.'

'She's courting too, our Nellie. Nice chap, Red Finnegan, as Irish as they come. He's in show business,' he said proudly. 'Known as Flynn and Finnegan. He plays the fiddle like a dream, even writes his own music. You can buy it on records in Rushworth and Draper. They're getting wed come summer.'

'Really!' Iris was conscious of the longing in her voice. Oh, how she would love to listen to Nell talk about the man she intended to marry. She was glad Nell had a chap of her own, and hoped everything would go well for her in the future.

On the second Tuesday in May, a day that began with drizzly rain but turned into one ablaze with glorious sunshine, Maggie came to Liverpool for her friend Nell's wedding. It was a wrench leaving her girls behind, but Holly was only one and a half and Grace seven months, and she couldn't face the ordeal of taking them on the train, or, even worse, in the car – she'd passed her driving test the previous year.

'If I catch an early train there and a late one back, I can do it in a single day,' she said to Jack, who had promised to take the day off to look after their precious daughters.

She arrived at Lime Street station at eleven o'clock, caught the electric train to Bootle, then made her way to the O'Neills' house in Coral Street, where Rosie let her in and together they admired Rosie and Ryan's new baby, Peter, who had been born three months before.

'He's massive,' Maggie said. 'My girls are so small, yet it hurt so much when they were born. I've decided not to have any more.'

Rosie said she'd quite like another two. 'But it means finding a bigger house. As it is, we're all a bit squashed. Ryan's actually thinking of buying one.'

'We bought our house in London. Imagine what me mam'd think if she were alive and she knew me and Jack and you and our Ryan were buying our own houses!'

'D'you think your dad and Bridie would be all right on their own?' Rosie asked anxiously. 'If he preferred, we'd take Bridie with us. She feels like our little girl as it is. I'd be upset at leaving her behind.'

'I should be offering to do something like that.' Maggie felt ashamed that she saw so little of her small sister, who was now eight. 'But I get the impression she far prefers you to me. I bet the last thing she wants is to come and live with us in London. It'd upset her if I asked. She probably thinks of you as her mam, Rosie.' She scratched Tinker underneath his soft, furry chin. 'I expect Tinker thinks the same.'

'Whatever Bridie thinks, she's coming home from school in her dinner hour specially to see you,' Rosie said. 'If I were you, I'd get changed now so she can see you in your new outfit.'

The new outfit came from Selfridges in Oxford Street and had cost an arm and a leg: a shell-pink two-piece in a mixture of silk and linen. The top had pearl buttons and a frilly collar and

cuffs over a straight skirt. The hat to match was a little white
bonnet with a pink flower on the side.

'You look lovely, Auntie Maggie,' Bridie said when she
came home. She kissed Maggie shyly. She looked lovely
herself in her blue school frock, her dark hair tucked behind a
blue ribbon. She was the image of their mother.

'I'm not your auntie, sweetheart, I'm your sister.'

'I know that really, but somehow I always think of you as
me auntie.' The little girl blushed.

'Haven't you grown tall? I'm sure you must come nearly
up to me shoulder.' Maggie was upset at being called auntie.
She suggested that Bridie come to stay with the Kaminskis in
London during the summer holiday. Perhaps it was time they
got to know each other better.

Bridie looked a bit dismayed at this and didn't reply. Rosie
said to wait and see how she felt about it once the holidays had
started.

She managed to get to St James's church just before the bride
arrived. Mrs Desmond wore a stiff net cartwheel hat in a lovely
purple colour. Maggie could only assume it was part of a
collection that had fallen off the back of a lorry, as Nell's sisters
wore the same style of hat but in different colours. Their
husbands and their various children were also there. The only
relative absent was Nell's sister Theresa, who was working as a
stewardess on the *Queen Elizabeth*, sailing to and from New
York. On the groom's side of the church the guests included a
woman who was already crying copiously and three couples,
all young, who turned out to be the groom's friends.

It was really lovely to see Nell come walking up the aisle on
her dad's arm, looking so radiantly happy. She wore a simple
white knee-length frock and a circle of white flowers in her
hair. Alfred Desmond appeared to be wearing an evening suit
with a Paisley bow tie.

And Red, who Maggie had never seen before and who she

thought looked a little bit like a red-haired monkey, had a truly charming smile that nearly split his face in two when Nell joined him in front of the altar. His best man, Eamon Flynn, was tall and handsome in an offbeat sort of way – beanpole-thin with a tangle of black hair. The crying woman wept more and more loudly throughout the ceremony.

In no time at all, the couple were pronounced man and wife, by which time the woman's cries filled the church. Photographs were taken in the grounds, and the small party walked as far as the Bootle Arms in Marsh Lane, where the reception was being held in a room upstairs.

Maggie had hoped to see Iris in the church with all the other people at the back, mainly women, who'd come to watch. Iris was on the point of having her third baby. Although Maggie knew that years ago she and Nell had had a falling-out, a wedding seemed the ideal opportunity to mend things. But there'd been no sign of her in the church or outside. She resolved to do her best to call on Iris later, before she left Liverpool for London.

At the reception, Nell introduced Maggie to Red as 'my very, very best friend in the world'.

'Pleased to meet'cha, Maggie,' Red said, kissing her extravagantly on both cheeks. 'Any friend of Nell's is a friend of mine for life.' He introduced her to his best man.

'How d'you do?' Eamon Flynn shook her hand so hard it hurt. 'Are you aware, Maggie, that in Ireland we have this custom at weddings where the best man chooses any woman he fancies from the guests and she's obliged to spend the night with him?'

Maggie giggled. 'I wasn't aware of that, no.'

'Ignorance is no excuse,' he said severely. 'It's a custom approved of by the Pope himself. If a woman doesn't comply, she has to say five hundred Hail Marys once a day for the rest of her life.'

'Then I'm just going to have to say the Hail Marys, I'm afraid, seeing as how I'm a married woman with two children and me husband wouldn't approve. I'll start saying them on the way home on the train, though it won't be as interesting as reading a book.'

Eamon pretended to look as dejected as sin. 'Are you allowed to dance with me?' There was a piano in the corner of the room, and one of the guests was playing a selection of Irish songs. A few people had already started to dance.

'Indeed I am.' Maggie couldn't wait. She loved Jack to distraction, but couldn't see any harm in dancing a jig or two with a dashing musician with black curls and dark, sexy eyes.

'Before he whisks you away, Maggie, let me introduce you to me ma. She's the one who made a show of herself by sobbing her heart out in the church. Ma,' Red said fondly, putting his arm around his mother's shoulders, 'this is Maggie. Maggie, meet me ma, Eithne Finnegan, who came all the way over from Ireland to witness the last of her bairns get married.'

Eithne had once been pretty, but her worn, sad face showed evidence of having led a hard life back in Ireland. She started to cry again. 'Oh, it's lovely to meet you Maggie, darlin'. Isn't it a wonderful day for a wedding? Now I can die in peace knowing me baby boy is happily wedded to a good Catholic woman.'

'She wanted me to be a priest.' Red rolled his eyes, and Maggie, who felt embarrassed, was glad to be whisked away by Eamon, who flirted with her outrageously the entire afternoon. When it began to approach four o'clock, she made her excuses, saying she had to go home. She hadn't forgotten she wanted to see Iris before she caught the six o'clock train.

She was saying ta-ra to Nell when the door was flung open and a voice screamed, 'So you thought you'd get away from me, did ya, you fuckin' bitch? Well I followed you, and here I am, at me own son's wedding where I've every right to be.'

A man, middle-aged, grey-haired and unshaven, had burst

into the room. He wore a collarless shirt and a shabby navy suit. His wild eyes scanned the room until they lighted upon Eithne Finnegan. Before he could be stopped, he grabbed the woman by her hair, threw her to the floor and kicked her.

As quick as a flash, Red jumped over the table with the refreshments on and leapt upon his father, punching him so hard that he bounced off the wall.

'You bastard!' he roared. 'Can't she get away from you not even for a single day?' He was thumping the man with both fists, while Eamon tried to separate them.

In the end it was Alfred Desmond who lifted up the intruder and dragged him outside. He came back about ten minutes later to say he'd rung the bobbies from the telephone downstairs and they'd taken the bugger away.

Mrs Desmond, still wearing her wondrous cartwheel hat, offered to put Eithne up until Red and Nell returned from their honeymoon and sorted matters out. Eithne was bawling her head off while Nell bathed a bruise on her chin.

Maggie made her goodbyes, assuming that the reception was over, but she was going downstairs when the piano started again, someone began to sing 'It's a Long Way to Tipperary' and the guests joined in.

'Everyone's having babies,' Maggie remarked when Iris opened the door preceded by her enormous stomach. Sometimes she felt quite willing to put up with the pain again, but Jack refused to countenance the idea of another child. 'I couldn't stand it, even if you could, my dear Maggie,' he would say. 'When exactly is yours due?' she asked Iris.

'A week on Wednesday.' Iris's face had lit up at the sight of her visitor. 'Oh, it's lovely to see you, Maggie. What a beautiful costume. Have you been to Nell's wedding?'

'Yes. It went very well.' Out of loyalty to Nell, she didn't mention the fight. 'I thought you might have come at least to watch.'

'I really didn't feel up to it.'

Maggie could tell from her tone of voice that she was lying. 'I find it hard to believe that you and Nell are no longer friends,' she said irritably. She longed to know the reason for it. In the hope of receiving an explanation, she pressed on. 'You two became such good friends that I felt quite jealous.'

'We just didn't seem to get along when we were in Wales,' was all Iris said, which was more or less what Nell had said when Maggie had tried to get an explanation out of her.

It wasn't until that moment that Maggie noticed that Iris actually didn't look at all well, that her face was terribly pale. They'd been standing in the hallway all this time. Overcome with contrition, Maggie insisted on making the tea when it was offered. In the kitchen, she made Iris sit down while she put the kettle on and took the cups and saucers out of the cupboard where she remembered they were kept.

'Where are William and Louise?' she enquired. Iris already looked better just from sitting down.

'Tom's taken them for a walk so that I can have a rest.'

Maggie felt even more contrite. 'I hope he manages to get back before I leave; I'm catching the six o'clock train from Lime Street,' she explained, 'and I have to collect me suitcase from me dad's house on the way.'

'If Tom does get back soon, he'll take you in the car,' Iris said kindly. 'Save you having to rush.'

'That's awful nice of you.' Maggie felt close to tears. 'Sometimes I wish I'd never gone to London all those years ago,' she said quietly. 'I wish I still lived in Liverpool and could see you and Nell every day – well, nearly every day.' She would have done something to make sure they were all friends again, the three of them, just as they'd been in their army days.

'If you'd stayed in Liverpool, you wouldn't have met Jack,' Iris said, pointing out the obvious. 'You might have other children by now, but not your two little girls. Life would have been very different.'

Maggie was forced to acknowledge the truth of this. Iris asked about Rosie's baby and Maggie described her new nephew, and said that Rosie and Ryan were thinking about buying a bigger house as Rosie wanted more children.

Iris nodded and said she and Tom were thinking the same. 'This house is huge, the second floor is hardly ever used except for storage, but we have no garden and I do think children need a garden to play in.'

'We never had a garden to play in when we were growing up. Me and Nell – all the kids – played out in the street. We made swings on the lamp posts, played hopscotch on the pavement, and the lads drew goalposts and cricket stumps on the walls, but have you noticed the number of cars around these days?' Maggie went on indignantly. 'There were at least three parked in Coral Street earlier. It's no longer safe for kids to play in the street.'

They discussed the problem of ever-increasing traffic until Tom came back with the children. He was only too pleased to take Maggie to the station, after collecting her suitcase first.

Maggie felt the sort of sadness that was almost an ache after she had got on the train and found a seat. She *did* miss Liverpool, her friends, her relatives – she really should see more of Bridie. Sometimes she almost forgot she had a sister. Oh, and she missed Nell, always had. And she was worried about Iris, who looked so miserable yet should be excited at the thought of having her baby in a matter of days. Tom hadn't been quite himself either, a bit quiet really, not quite as friendly as she remembered.

But as the train passed through Crewe, then Stafford, followed by Birmingham, her spirits began to rise. She imagined Jack putting the girls to bed – he would sing to them, Polish lullabies, holding both of them in his arms, rocking them to and fro. She suddenly felt as if it was days, weeks since she'd last seen her family, yet it was only early that morning.

And tonight she would go to bed and lie in Jack's arms, they would make love, and it would be wonderful.

At Euston station she saw Drugi waiting on the far side of the barrier, as Jack had promised he would, to drive her home. Home! The very thought of it made her smile.

She hurried towards the exit, Liverpool forgotten. It wasn't until she woke up the following morning that she remembered where she'd been the day before and proceeded to tell Jack all about it.

Chapter 12

A week after Maggie's visit, Iris gave birth to a second daughter, Dorothy.

'I hope people don't call her Dottie,' grumbled Tom, who had been hoping for a boy. He showed no interest in suggesting names for girls.

'I think Dottie sounds all right,' Iris said. Though she'd rather they stuck to Dorothy. Despite her small build, she had little trouble having babies, hardly any pain at all. She had already decided that she would have one more child, then stop. Four children made the ideal family. She supposed it would be nice having two boys and two girls, but she really didn't mind what sex her children were. She wondered if Maggie's husband minded only having daughters.

When the new half-century was only a few months old, Britain found herself at war again. This time it was with North Korea, who, backed by Russia, had invaded the south. Kenny Desmond, who was too young to have fought in the war that had not long ended, was called up to fight. Yet again parents were forced to watch their young lads go off to battle, this time to a country that most had never heard of.

After Nell and Red had returned from their honeymoon in the Isle of Man, Red moved into the flat over the Labour Party offices and helped with Crown Caterers when he was home. Flynn and Finnegan performed regularly at working-men's clubs and ceilidhs. Their earnings varied from a few pounds one week to as much as twenty or thirty the next. Red would return from a performance laden with roses for his wife or whatever flowers happened to be in bloom at the time

Three months after the wedding, Red's mother, Eithne, returned to live in Ireland, with instructions to call in the Garda should her brutal husband come near once he was allowed out of prison for brawling.

In November, Nell realised she was pregnant. She had always known that she was lacking in certain ways, that she didn't experience the range of emotions of someone like Maggie who could move from a state of utter despair to one of total bliss within the space of minutes. But now, married to Red, with a baby on the way, she was as happy as she had ever been. She and Red began to look round at houses – the flat wasn't nearly big enough for two adults and a baby. Eventually they settled on a semi-detached house on a new estate being built close to the sands in Waterloo, a mere few miles away from Bootle.

And although she hadn't thought it possible to be happier than she already was, she felt happier still when she saw the wonderful modern kitchen with its black and white tiled floor and cream fitted units that would shortly be hers.

Quinn Finnegan kicked his merry way into the world almost a year after the wedding, by which time it was 1951 and Nell and Red were living in Waterloo. Quinn had his own room, hastily painted blue.

At about the same time, Iris Grant gave birth to another girl, Clare, and so did Rosie O'Neill, who called her daughter Laura after the picture of the same name starring Dana Andrews, who she claimed strongly resembled her Ryan. She, Ryan and their children moved into a modern house in Lydiate, on the very outskirts of Liverpool, taking Bridie with them and leaving Paddy alone in the house in Coral Street, not that he minded. As agent for the Labour Party he was always busy, and was able to hold meetings whenever he pleased now that he had the house to himself.

Maggie wrote to Nell.

All these babies! Lots of my London friends are having them too. I'd love more, but Jack always puts me off. Secretly, I'm glad. Now that Grace is out of nappies and she and Holly can both walk and talk, I've realised that babies aren't nearly as much fun or as interesting as toddlers. You'll find that out soon.

I used to imagine us going for walks with our babies at the same time, taking them to school and chatting over a cup of tea in each other's kitchens, but that's not possible, is it? Did you know Iris and Tom have bought a big posh house in Balliol Road, Bootle? I'd love to see it. Tom's surgery will stay in their old house and they'll rent out the upstairs.

PS Tomorrow we are going to the Festival of Britain pleasure gardens. I understand they are truly beautiful. If only we could have gone together . . .

The Balliol Road house had been decorated from top to bottom. There were enough bedrooms for each child to eventually have his or her own. The kitchen was rather old-fashioned, but Iris had decided to leave the modernisation till later. There was a vast dining room that housed the big wooden table from their old house. The dream she had always had, of a table full of children demanding food or passing the jam and the toast to each other, would shortly come true. William and Louise were already old enough to sit there for their meals – Louise needed a cushion; that was all.

Tom was often home late for his evening meal, not that she minded. He kept all his notes and his medical library in the old house and stayed there to write prescriptions and keep the records up to date. Nowadays she found his presence rather inhibiting and preferred the place without him. He rarely smiled, and didn't show much interest in the children apart from William. He had even started to talk about Charlie, their little boy who had died in his sleep all those years ago. She guessed it was because he wasn't pleased to have so many daughters. For some silly reason, it must make him feel less of a man.

Iris was glad they had moved. She felt happier in this house and was sure the older children did too. Within a few weeks, their faces had acquired a far healthier colour from playing in the big garden full of mature trees with a vegetable patch in a corner at the bottom. With memories of Maggie saying she had swung from a lamp post when she was a child, Iris had bought a stout rope and hung it from an equally stout branch of a leafy elm tree. William loved it.

Another advantage was that there was a little independent school further along the road where the children could go – William was due to start school next year. Tom was determined that they be educated privately. Honestly, Iris thought impatiently, the older he got, the stuffier he became. It was almost like being married to his brother, the revolting Frank.

There had been a general election in 1950 and Labour had emerged with a majority of a mere six seats. The people were restless. Food rationing was still in force, there was a desperate shortage of houses along with building materials and thousands of people had resorted to squatting in no-longer-needed army and prisoner-of-war camps and empty properties of any sort. In central London, squatters took over a row of luxury flats that had been used as offices during the war. Sometimes it was possible to smell imminent revolution in the air.

Maggie's Auntie Kath became a well-known supporter of squatters' rights, attending rallies, waving banners and making speeches all over the country. Her photograph was frequently to be seen in the newspapers, and she was termed a 'heroine' or a 'troublemaker', depending on which political view the paper supported.

The country was hard up. The United States had lent money to help fight the war, but now demanded it back. Politicians on the other side of the Atlantic weren't too pleased at the idea of supporting a left-wing government, despite it having been elected by the people.

Late in 1951, another election was called in the hope of Labour increasing its majority. Instead it lost even more seats, despite achieving almost a quarter of a million more votes than the Conservative opposition. The Member for Bootle Docklands increased her already massive majority by more than ten per cent. Kathleen Curran was loved by the left and hated by the right, which she considered was exactly as it should be.

Early in the following year, when King George VI died of cancer, Auntie Kath publicly conceded that just because a person was royal it didn't mean they were automatically bad. The late King had been a gentle, modest man who had shared the privations of the war with his people. Although he and his family could have gone to live in Canada, he insisted they stay in London and live on ordinary rations like everyone else.

His daughter, Elizabeth was crowned Queen in June 1953. Unlike virtually the entire population of the United Kingdom, Auntie Kath declined to watch the coronation on television – many thousands of sets having been purchased beforehand for that very purpose.

Nell's neighbours on one side were an elderly couple, Maude and Edwin Carter, who had grown-up children and several grandchildren. On the other joined-on side lived Susan and Harold Ramsey, who'd only recently been married. The older couple adored Nell's little boys, Quinn, who was now four, and Kevin, who was three. The pair were admittedly a handful, and the Ramseys complained bitterly about the noise the boys made both inside and outside the house. They remonstrated with them for peering through the hedge into their garden or climbing trees to do the same thing. They kept any balls that happened to land anywhere on their property and even accused Nell of allowing her lads to wee on the flowers in their front garden and make them die.

'I saw them with my own eyes,' Susan Ramsey raged.

'You can't have done,' Nell stammered. Quinn and Kevin could do many things, but they couldn't have got out of the house on their own.

She was incapable of answering back or losing her temper, but she was deeply upset by the Ramseys' attitude, which she considered unreasonable. She hoped that when Susan Ramsey became pregnant, she would have twins or even triplets.

'Let's see how she copes then,' she would say to Red when he came home. Red got his own back by playing his fiddle and singing as loudly as he could, ignoring the furious knocking on the door when one of the Ramseys came to complain. Some days Eamon would drop round and they would play together. Eamon had lodgings in Seaforth. His landlady made him huge meals because she claimed he needed filling out a bit. She was also doing her utmost to seduce him.

The Finnegans were a popular couple on the little estate in Waterloo. In his own way, Red was a minor celebrity. Few people had heard of Flynn and Finnegan, but it was known that they travelled about the country entertaining miners and the like. Once they had actually appeared on television, though only to accompany a troupe of Irish dancers, and their records were on sale in town.

When Red came home, Nell would yelp with delight and fling her arms around him, and all four Finnegans would sit on the big settee kissing and cuddling till they got fed up and went their various ways.

★

In December 1955, Maggie sent a letter with the Christmas card made from a new photograph of her and Jack and their growing daughters.

Do you realise, Nell, she wrote in her barely readable scrawl, *that it's ten years since the three of us returned to Liverpool after the army. Just think how our lives have changed since then. Eight children between us, husbands for you and me, a lovely house each. It's an awful pity that Iris and Tom have broken up. At least I think so. She hardly ever mentions him in her letters, and Rosie reports that Tom seems to live permanently in their old house in Rimrose Road. What's more, there's a woman living there too, though maybe she just rents the flat upstairs and people are spreading nasty gossip – me included!*

It had started with Tom coming home late most nights, or sometimes staying overnight in Rimrose Road. When he did come home, he mumbled something about being overladen with work, being at his desk till all hours, bringing the filing up to date and all sorts of other excuses that Iris found difficult to believe – he'd never had to work late before.

Iris just mumbled something back. It was horrible to think the way she did, but the less she saw of him, the better. Now she had enough children, she no longer wanted to sleep with him, not even if he used a French letter or she one of those horrible rubber caps women were supposed to insert inside themselves. It was ages since she'd had pleasure from sex.

She had come to the unwelcome realisation that she no longer loved her husband, though she remained fond of him. It had taken her a long time to reach that conclusion. Since coming home, she had tolerated him and, in a way that she was very ashamed of, used him merely as a means of achieving a family.

Even when she discovered he was having an affair with Frances Blake, the receptionist who'd been there for years, she didn't mind. In fact, she was glad. It meant he had a woman who had taken on Iris's role as a wife, making her own behaviour seem less selfish.

He still turned up to take eight-year-old William out to museums, football matches, the pictures – they were both fans of Tarzan films.

'Why don't you ever take the girls with you?' Iris once asked.

'They squeal too much,' he claimed.

And that was that.

In the Kaminski family, all was sweetness and light. Jack could not possibly have loved his girls more than he already did. Holly was the sweetest little thing, a real daddy's girl, all sugar and spice and able to twist Jack around her little white finger with her captivating smile.

Maggie was also her elder daughter's willing slave. At seven, Holly was the prettiest girl in her class, if not the entire school. She had her father's fair hair and the same steady blue eyes.

'You spoil her,' people remarked from time to time, in particular Rosie when the Kaminskis went on their yearly visit to Liverpool, staying in one of the best hotels.

'We love her,' Maggie would say simply. 'Too much love can't possibly spoil a child.'

It was a statement with which Rosie couldn't disagree. 'Poor Grace must feel neglected,' she said once.

'Grace hates to be made a fuss of,' Maggie would say confidently. She regarded herself as a perfect mother to her perfect children, as well as a perfect wife to Jack.

Grace was possibly too independent for her own good. She insisted on tying her own shoelaces from an early age, resulting in several nasty falls when they came loose.

'Don't help me,' she would snap when Maggie went to put on her coat or cut up the food on her plate. Her features were too strong to be classed as pretty; more striking. She had

Maggie's black curls and blue eyes with a touch of lilac. Jack admired her enormously, calling her his 'little brick', which was how Greek generals referred to their heroic soldiers, he maintained. Even when she was very young, she refused to sit on his – or anybody's – knee, though she condescended to listen to the stories that he told, sitting sternly beside him on the settee, while Holly curled up in his arms, the adoring daughter.

If Jack had a fault, it was a minor one. He was intent on tracking down his relatives who had disappeared from Poland during the war, a task that took up many hours of his time – too many as far as Maggie was concerned. He would sit well into the night in the dining room, only used to eat in at weekends, and which he regarded as his study, the table covered with papers. They had been married a few years before Maggie realised that the Kaminskis had been a rich, highly respected family in the small town in Poland where Jack was born. They had owned acres of forests and farming land as well as dozens of cottages.

The Polish set in London that Jack was part of had in the main been servants or neighbours of his family. Some of these people were also trying to find family members who had disappeared. They could well be dead, but it was not certain.

Letters often arrived at the Kaminski house from countries all over the world, though mainly from the United States, addressed to Jacek Kaminski. The envelopes contained many sheets of paper full of strange handwriting, rarely in English. Phone calls would come at all times of the day, providing bits of information as to where a certain person might be.

'Who are you trying to find?' Maggie had asked more than once. She knew his parents were dead, and his sister was married and living in Russian-occupied Poland. They had no idea when they would see each other.

'Cousins,' Jack would answer vaguely. 'Aunts and uncles, friends.'

Maggie hoped that one day soon he would discover relatives living in America, and that she, Jack and the girls could cross the Atlantic in one of the big liners and visit them.

The Finnegan brothers were ear-achingly loud, they laughed too much, were too darned happy, couldn't keep still, and were too clever by half. Aged five and six, they didn't exactly terrorise the school, had never bullied a soul, yet they just seemed to dominate the place. When a Finnegan laughed, it could be heard in every corner.

Everyone felt sorry for the mother. She seemed such a nice quiet woman, who didn't deserve to have two such rowdy lads. And their dad was that singer chap who could occasionally be seen on telly playing the fiddle and singing Irish songs.

'I suppose that explains it,' some people said. 'The kids are Irish.'

Nell would have been upset had she known that people felt sympathy for her. As far as she was concerned, she was mother to two exceptional little boys who were the most popular in the school – with the other pupils, that is, if not their parents and the teachers. Scarcely a week would pass without them being invited to a birthday party somewhere in Waterloo. The party might turn into chaos, but the young guests would have a good time, having battled with Red Indians or won the war a second time under the leadership of General Quinn or King Kev Finnegan. Quinn could do a perfect imitation of Winston Churchill making a speech while smoking a big cigar, and Kev could stand on his head and do the splits upside down.

One Monday, Red came home after a tour of concerts in Yorkshire.

'I've written you a song – or I should say I've written a song about you,' Red said in between kisses. 'I sang it twice, and each time I was asked for an encore. It's called "Ode to Nell".'

'Sing it to me,' a dazzled Nell requested. She'd like to bet she was the only woman in Liverpool whose husband had written a song for her.

Nell, sang Red, looking at her adoringly, *my darling Nell,*
When you smile, a bell chimes in my heart.
In my heart.
Nell, my dearest Nell
If you should leave, hot tears will blind my eyes.
My eyes.
You are the light of my life,
And I want you for my wife.
Oh Nell, my sweet Nell,
Please be mine.

'That's lovely, Red. I'm flattered beyond belief.' Nell burst out laughing and they collapsed together on to the settee. 'I really love my song.'

'It still needs a bit of polishing,' Red said modestly. 'But I expect the record to come top of the charts one day soon.'

He sang the song to the lads when they came home from school, and they sang it to their mother, then gave an exhibition of Irish dancing that they'd been taught that afternoon. (The Ramseys next door now had two children of their own and had stopped complaining.)

The memory of that very ordinary Monday, the day when her husband first sang her song and her children danced for her, would remain at the forefront of Nell's mind throughout her life. Even when she was an old, old woman, she would smile as she remembered her little boys in their jerseys and shorts dancing in unison, lifting their scarred knees, shoulders back, hands on hips, solemn expressions on their tough little faces, red hair bouncing – they took after their da in that respect – while Red played the fiddle like a madman.

When they finished, Nell was moved to tears, as if she was aware that she had just experienced a remarkable event.

Seeing the tears that they'd never known their normally happy ma shed before, the lads launched themselves upon her, stroking her cheeks, kissing her ears, patting her head.

'Don't cry, Ma,' Quinn ordered.

'We'll kiss you better, Ma,' Kev offered.

'But I'm all right.' Nell tried to laugh, but the boys were stuck to her like limpets and it only made her cry more.

'Your ma's okay, lads.' Red attempted to lift the boys off, but they refused to let go until Nell promised never to cry again.

'Not for as long as I live,' Nell vowed, though she thought that most unlikely.

Some weeks later, 'Ode to Nell' reached number twenty-eight in the charts. The following week it went down and continued to do so. Red was disappointed, but Nell didn't care. It was *her* song, nobody else's, and would always be number one as far as she was concerned.

In March of 1959, Jack received an extra-thick letter from Boston in the United States. Maggie was fast asleep by the time he came to bed on the day it arrived after spending the entire evening in his study.

'You must have read it a dozen times,' she remarked next morning as they were having breakfast. The girls weren't due to come down for another half-hour.

'I think I might well have done,' Jack said gravely.

'Did it contain lots of new information?'

'It did indeed.' He nodded. 'I might be late home tonight. I've arranged to see a few people at the Red Pepper.' This was the restaurant in Soho owned by Drugi's uncle that the Polish contingent, as Maggie thought of them, used as a meeting place.

'What time do you think you'll be back?'

'I don't know, darling.' He looked at her absently. Maggie went cold, realising that this was the first time in their relationship that he wasn't concentrating wholly on either her or their daughters. Right now, he had other things on his mind, and it rather upset her. He blinked, as if suddenly remembering she was there. 'Don't do me a meal,' he said. 'I'll eat at the restaurant.'

It was ten o'clock when he arrived home. He'd brought her flowers; daffodils, that were merely hard green buds. It would be a while before the yellow petals appeared.

'Thank you,' she said, trying to sound grateful – she couldn't have explained why she wasn't. It was as if a little cloud had appeared in their lives, a ridiculous thing to think when all he'd done was get a letter from America, something that had happened loads of times before.

'I might go away for a while,' he said when they were in bed.

'To America?' she enquired.

'Yes, Washington. I need to see people.'

'Is it an aunt or an uncle who's been found?' Perhaps it was a cousin.

'No one's been found, not exactly. It's more information as to where someone might be. I need to go myself to make sure.'

Maggie could tell he wouldn't countenance taking her and the children with him. She decided not to make a fool of herself by asking.

'Good night, darling,' he said, turning over.

Maggie went cold again. *He hadn't kissed her good night!* It wasn't deliberate, she could tell that; it was merely because he'd forgotten, which was much, much worse. 'Who's the someone you've had information about?' she asked in a loud voice.

But Jack didn't reply. He was fast asleep. Or pretending to be.

A few days later, he came home and announced that he was flying to America at the weekend.

'How long will you be away?' Maggie asked. She did her best not to sound bad-tempered.

'I've arranged with the bank to take a month's leave, though I may not need that much.'

'A month!' How could he think of leaving his family for an entire month?

He smiled and took her in his arms, as if the enormity of what he was doing had suddenly dawned on him. 'I'll miss you,' he said, holding her close. 'In fact, I don't know how I'll live without you for such a long time.'

Maggie started to cry. She couldn't begin to explain just how distant from her he had felt recently. Those damn letters, they took him back to a time before they'd met and she'd become part of his life. She resented every minute he spent with them, dredging up old memories. She wondered how he would feel if she did the same thing. Some wives would have made a real fuss. Maggie felt the urge to do the same, but he'd always been such a good husband. 'Until now,' a little voice said, but she ignored it.

'I think,' he said tenderly, 'that seeing as how it's Easter next week, you should go and stay with Nell.'

She'd been looking forward to spending Easter with him. 'It's always so noisy at Nell's.' Holly was actually frightened of the Finnegan boys, though Grace got on with them like a house on fire and had once asked if they could become her brothers. 'I'll think about it,' she said, trying to sound positive. 'Oh!' She remembered something. 'If you're not home by the twentieth of April, you'll miss my birthday!'

'Then I shall do my very best to be here.' He was still holding her in his arms and began to rock to and fro. 'If I can't be here, then I shall send you tons and tons of flowers all the way from America.'

He left early on Monday, which meant she was unable to go to the airport with him as she had to get the girls to school. After they'd gone, the house felt extraordinarily quiet, although on a normal day Jack wouldn't have been there. It felt even quieter during the afternoon knowing she didn't have to make him dinner, and again when he didn't come home in the evening. At about half past six, the telephone rang and it was Jack saying he'd just arrived in Washington and it was raining.

'What's the weather like there?' he asked, and she wondered why he should care – or was he just trying to think of something to say?

She couldn't remember. She had to look out of the window, and discovered it was sunny and had probably been sunny all day and she hadn't noticed.

He told her that he loved her, they said goodbye, and she put down the receiver.

'Was that Daddy?' Ten-year-old Grace looked extremely cross. 'I wanted to speak to him – you promised I could.'

'I forgot, love.'

'And I wanted to, Mummy.' Holly came out of the living room, where she'd been watching television.

'I'm so sorry, both of you.' Maggie longed to burst into tears, but the children were already upset at their father going away; she didn't want to make it worse.

And it could actually be like this for an entire month!

Jack was still away on her birthday. There were cards from friends and relatives in Liverpool and London. Auntie Kath sent a birthday cake, her father sent flowers, Nell telephoned in the afternoon and they had a long talk. Maggie promised to come and stay for the weekend. Easter had been the week before, and she would prefer to only be away for two days.

But there was nothing from Jack, not even a phone call wishing her happy birthday, let alone the tons of flowers he'd promised. For the first time ever, he had forgotten her birthday; he had forgotten *her*.

The weekend in Liverpool wasn't a success. Maggie had never thought it could happen, but she actually felt jealous of Nell. She hadn't realised just how much Nell and Red were in love, how well they got on, what fun they had together. Until a few weeks ago, she and Jack had got on wonderfully together too. She hadn't imagined other couples could be as happy as they were, but now she felt as if they would never be that happy again, that she and Jack were less exceptional than she'd thought. She told herself she was being foolish, exaggerating the way she always did. The tiniest bad thing could happen and she'd think it the end of the world. All marriages must have their ups and downs. They'd been married for twelve years, and this was the first of the downs.

The Finnegan lads were driving her wild. They were so noisy, uncontrolled. Grace was having a wonderful time galloping around with them, while Holly remained close to her mother's side, terrified of going near them.

On Sunday morning, Maggie went to see Iris, taking Holly with her – Grace flatly refused to go. Iris seemed perfectly happy living without a man in the house. She saw Tom once or twice a week, and that was enough, she said with a grin. The house wasn't exactly peaceful, the three girls arguing all the time, but Maggie was impressed with William, nearly thirteen, who was growing into a lovely young man; very gentlemanly, very handsome. Maggie found it strange that he bore no resemblance at all to Iris or Tom.

'He takes after Tom's side of the family,' Iris explained

when Maggie remarked on this. 'Tom has a cousin, Robin, and William is the spitting image of him.'

William pushed Holly gently on the swing and she looked at him adoringly. They'd often met before, but this time Maggie reckoned her daughter was getting her first big crush. As long as it wasn't one of the Finnegans, she quite liked the idea of Holly finding out what it was like to be in love. She'd felt the same about some lad in Pearl Street when she'd been eleven; she couldn't remember his name.

She and Holly were glad to be home again. Grace was angry. Where Holly would cry, Grace became cross. She missed the Finnegans. 'Why don't we live in a noisy house?' she asked. 'And where's Daddy? He's been away *years*.'

'It's only three weeks, luv.' It seemed like years to Maggie, too.

After taking the girls to school, she made coffee and sat slumped over the table in the kitchen, thinking how miserable she was. After a while she started to feel ashamed that she'd allowed herself to get into such a wretched state just because her husband had gone away for a few weeks. What if Jack's plane crashed on the way home and he was killed? It had happened to loads of women during the war and they'd survived. And she would survive too – she would have to for the sake of the children, and she would certainly survive one more week before Jack came home. She recalled that she and Jack had only met that New Year's Eve because she was upset at being by herself. It really was time she got over it.

Maggie jumped to her feet. She'd go shopping, buy something new from the big C&A Modes in Oxford Street where she'd gone with Nell when she'd come to stay in London. She could afford to go somewhere posher, but she was fond of C&A; 'Coats an' 'Ats', as the bus conductors used to say in Liverpool when the bus stopped outside. She'd buy something for the girls, too. Cheer them all up.

Jack returned home on Monday, four weeks to the day that he'd left. He'd rung the day before, so Maggie was expecting him.

She and the girls were waiting in the parlour window, all wearing their pretty new frocks, when Drugi's car drew up outside and he and Jack got out. The girls rushed out screaming, 'Daddy!' Even Grace allowed herself to be picked up.

Inside, Jack slowly let them slide to the floor before kissing Maggie warmly on the lips. She touched his cheek in response, unable for some reason to throw her arms around his neck as she would normally have done – perhaps because Drugi was still there. Jack looked rather thin and hollow-eyed, as if he hadn't eaten or slept much while he was away.

Drugi stayed for tea. Holly and Grace had known him all their lives and loved him. They called him 'Uncle Drugi', and he made faces at them and told them silly stories. Jack described some of the interesting people he had met in Boston and New York.

'New York!' Maggie exclaimed. 'I didn't know you'd been to New York.'

'My last week, that's all. I spent the first three weeks in Boston.'

Well, you might have told me, Maggie thought. 'I see,' was all she said.

'Sorry, darling, I forgot.' He smiled apologetically. 'Oh, and I also forgot your birthday, didn't I? But not to worry, I've bought you something nice to make up for it.'

'I'm dying to see it,' she lied. No matter how nice it was, she would have preferred tons of flowers.

Drugi left, the girls went to bed, Holly nursing the doll and Grace the American football that Daddy had bought them.

'This is for you, darling.' Jack sat beside Maggie on the settee and handed her a velvet box. She opened it and stared at little chunky diamond earrings that must have cost a bomb. 'Do you like them?' he asked eagerly.

'They're lovely,' she said dutifully, not adding that the earrings were for pierced ears and she wore the sort with clips. One day soon she would quietly have her ears pierced, wear the jewels, and Jack would never know. 'Thank you,' she said, kissing his chin. 'Thank you very much.' There was a short silence, which Maggie broke. 'Was your trip successful?' she asked. 'Did you find who you wanted to find?'

'Yes, I did,' he replied after another pause. 'I found my wife.'

Afterwards, Maggie thought she might have fainted when she heard Jack's words, because when she came to, he was in the middle of explaining exactly why he had a wife, but she couldn't remember what he had said when he started.

She gathered that someone in Washington knew someone who had seen her, the wife, in a hospital in New York, and told someone else in Washington who told someone else. The final someone else knew that Jacek Kaminski lived somewhere in London, and got his address off one of the other someone elses and wrote to him.

'The big fat letter that came six or seven weeks ago,' Jack explained.

Maggie discovered she was leaning against him on the settee and he had his arm around her shoulders. She wanted to move away as much as she wanted to stay.

He'd thought she was dead, his wife, Jack said; was absolutely convinced. And she'd thought the same about him. 'I left Poland for England to join the Royal Air Force, and about a year later she was told I'd been killed in a raid over Berlin. I was informed she'd been sent to a labour camp in Germany and had died there.'

'Aren't there such things as death certificates?' Maggie asked.

'Not always in wartime. The circumstances were often chaotic and confused.' He shook his head and she felt his chin rub against her scalp. He needed a shave. 'And Aniela had always been very frail. I couldn't imagine her lasting long in a labour camp, but it turns out she was there for five whole years. I'd always been absolutely convinced that she was dead.'

Aniela! It was a pretty name. 'She must have been tougher than you thought.'

'Oh, she has always been tough.' It was like a criticism, as if Maggie had spoken unkindly of his wife.

'What was she doing in hospital in New York?' she asked.

His face became grim. 'She has TB, tuberculosis, and is likely to die very soon. Maggie, darling,' he cupped her face with his free hand, 'would you mind if I went back to New York to be with her at the end? It would mean to much to her. She has no one over there, not even a friend. She was in some terrible charity hospital, but I had her moved to a much better place.'

'Of course I don't mind.' She minded terribly, so much that she wanted to scream the house down, curse him for going to America and finding his bloody wife.

Wife! She sat up sharply and his arm fell from her shoulders. 'It means we're not married.' She gasped in horror. 'We aren't man and wife.' She turned on him angrily. 'What's going to happen to me – to us? And why didn't you tell me you'd been married before?' She began to hit him with her fists. 'I hate you.' She burst into tears and he pulled her into his arms, but she pushed him away. 'Don't *touch* me! I don't want you any more. I don't love you. In fact, I hate you, Jack.'

She got up, but had no idea where to go, what to do. This was all too much. She had no idea how to deal with it.

'Aniela is dying, Maggie,' he said gently. 'She has only a few more weeks to live, possibly days. I found her just in time. Is it too much to ask that I sit with her during her dying days?'

'Yes,' Maggie insisted. 'Yes, it is too much.' She began to

cry again. 'No, of course it isn't. Someone should be with her. I'm glad you found her in time. But it's so unfair, Jack, springing something like this on me without warning. I'd sooner you hadn't said anything, that you had made some excuse for going back to America again. I'd sooner have never known about your wife.' She left the room, saying, 'I'm going to make coffee.'

She returned minutes later with two cups and put his on the hearth near where he was sitting. 'It wouldn't have been such a shock,' she said, 'if you'd told me right from the start that you'd been married before.'

He smiled a trifle coldly. 'You came into our marriage with secrets of your own, my dear. I could tell the first night we slept together.'

She looked at him just as coldly. He'd never called her 'my dear' in such a way before. 'I had an affair,' she conceded. 'One affair. It's hardly the same as being married.' Though she'd very nearly got married; she remembered the day quite vividly. She'd nearly married a bigamist; this time she actually had. 'You could have had dozens of affairs and I wouldn't have cared. It was *me* you wanted to marry.'

He collapsed back on the settee looking stricken. 'What a fool I've been! You're right, Maggie. I should have told you straight away that I'd been married before. And I should have told you it was Aniela I was going to the States to look for. I shouldn't have sprung this on you the way I did.' He reached for her hand and pulled her down beside him. 'I'm sorry. *Dead* sorry, as you would say. You know what it means, don't you? We're going to have to get married again,' he put a finger to his lips, 'but let's not tell anyone. We'll have a second honeymoon, and this time we've got the whole wide world to choose from. Let's ask someone to look after Holly and Grace and we'll go, just the two of us, to any place you want.'

'I'll think of somewhere,' she promised with a sigh.

After a few long kisses, more apologies, a groan, followed by

'I bought you the wrong sort of earrings, didn't I?' and more kisses, he seemed to think everything was back to the way it had always been.

But Maggie knew it wasn't. Something had happened to her love for Jack; it had altered course slightly, like a train travelling through points. He was no longer perfect in her eyes; he was an ordinary man with faults like other men.

They didn't have a perfect marriage any more, more a perfectly ordinary one, and she would have to be satisfied with that.

Jack returned to America, to New York, from where he sent her flowers every other day. But it made her feel awful for having complained so much. There he was, attending to his dying wife, which must have been a terribly upsetting experience, while having to remember to regularly send flowers to his other 'wife' back home. She was glad when it was all over and he returned.

'What was it like?' she asked in a low voice.

'Pretty awful,' he replied, tight-lipped. 'At the end she was in a great deal of pain.'

'I'm sorry.' She stroked his brow. 'And sorry for Aniela too.' She wished she was a better person. Being nice was a terrible battle, and it wasn't often that she won.

It wasn't long before everything felt normal again. They drove to a place called King's Lynn in Norfolk, where Jack had arranged for them to marry in a registry office. It was a place where no one was likely to recognise their names. They returned home straight away. Neither had felt like leaving the girls behind to enjoy a second honeymoon only because Aniela had died. All Maggie wanted was to be the wife of Jack Kaminski, and that would never change. She didn't speculate what would have happened had Aniela been found alive and well. It was much too frightening to consider.

Chapter 13

William Grant's twenty-first birthday party in May 1968 was a rowdy affair, much rowdier than his parents had envisaged. His actual birthday had been a few days earlier, but the party was held the following Saturday. Fellow students from the University of East Anglia in Norwich, where he was coming to the end of his studies for a degree in maths, were there, as well as friends he'd had at Merchant Taylors' school in Crosby, and more friends that he'd made on his travels around India the summer before, and in Australia the summer before that.

Drugs were smoked – 'Christ almighty, it smells like there's pot in there,' Tom said, aghast, to Iris after passing through the breakfast room.

'What's pot?' Iris enquired.

'Grass, marijuana, whatever,' Tom explained, shrugging helplessly. 'Let's hope none of the other guests have joined the police force.'

'I quite like the smell,' Iris said, drifting towards it. 'Is William in there?'

'No. He's in the garden. I don't like making a fuss, creating an atmosphere, perhaps spoiling the party. Anyroad, on reflection, I don't mind all that much. It's what young people do these days.'

Iris said she didn't mind all that much either. In fact, she would quite like to have a few puffs. They trusted William completely. After all, he couldn't be expected to monitor every one of his fifty or sixty guests.

It was a fragrant spring evening, still light at nine o'clock, still warm. Music blasted through the open French windows into the garden: the Beatles, the Rolling Stones, the Who, the Animals, Freddie and the Dreamers . . .

'I wish there'd been music like this when I was in the army,' Iris remarked. 'The dances would have been really great with the band playing "Love Me Do" or something equally catchy.'

'You mean you prefer the Beatles to Glenn Miller or Tommy Dorsey or good old Bing Crosby! Shame on you, Iris Grant! That's real music, not this new tuneless stuff.'

'I really like it.' The Beatles had made the city of Liverpool world-famous.

Iris and Tom were in the kitchen keeping an eye on the drinks. They didn't mind mild inebriation, but wanted to avoid anyone getting plastered and wrecking the furniture – or risking a visit from the police. As soon as it was midnight, they would turn down the noise.

'All we have to do,' Iris said, 'is close the French windows. This is a detached house and the music won't bother the neighbours.'

Tom agreed and asked if she'd like another sherry – they were the only ones drinking it. Most of the boys were consuming beer out of cans, the girls Babycham, Cherry B, or mild shandy. They were asked for the occasional orange juice.

Their daughters, Louise, Dorothy and Clare, were having a wonderful time, as there were more men at the party than women. Louise, at twenty, had turned out to be a terrific flirt. Iris had invited Maggie's girls, Holly and Grace, but they had another party that night closer to home.

'I wonder if Nell remembers what day it is?' she said to Tom. It was marvellous how well they got on together these days. They'd never even discussed getting divorced and saw each other two or three times a week. Tom still lived above the surgery in Rimrose Road.

'Eh?' Tom looked at her vacantly.

'Nell is William's mother.'

'Yes, of course!' He slapped his forehead. 'Sometimes – no, most of the time – I forget he isn't ours. Well, he *is* ours, but you know what I mean.'

'I'm glad Nell has another two boys; that she isn't all by herself knowing William is probably having a party and she isn't there.' She swiftly changed the subject, wishing she hadn't mentioned Nell in the first place. It was the sort of remark Tom hated; anything that suggested that Nell might have rights over William, even so much as that she might *think* about her son, he found extremely irritating. 'Is that girl with the blonde hair William's girlfriend or not?' she asked.

'Not. She came with someone else.'

'I hope whoever-it-is doesn't mind William dancing with her all the time.'

'He's the birthday boy, isn't he? He's allowed to dance with anyone he fancies.'

Iris laughed. 'Don't be daft, Tom. Anyroad, I don't like her much. She's wearing too much eyeshadow.'

In Waterloo, Nell thought about William while she waited for Quinn and Kev to come home from a disco in Southport. Flynn and Finnegan were playing at a holiday camp in Wales and wouldn't be home until tomorrow. Normally she didn't think about William much, just remembered how he'd looked and felt in her arms the day he was born. Waterloo was several miles from Bootle and she'd never so much as glimpsed him since that day, had actually gone out of her way to make sure she and Iris never came face to face. Today, though, she wondered what he looked like now that he was twenty-one, and if he was having a party seeing as how it was a Saturday. She also wondered how he would feel if he knew that Iris and

Tom weren't his mam and dad and his real mother lived in the vicinity.

It was well past midnight by the time the lads arrived home, having got a lift in someone's van. There was the noise of doors slamming, shouts of 'See you next Sat'day' and 'Ta-ra, mate.'

Nell winced. Would the time ever come when they stopped making so much noise? Well, she hoped not.

She opened the door to let them in. They were a hefty pair these days, with even more growing to do, sixteen and seventeen, with long hair just as red as the day they were born. They were often taken for twins. They wore jeans and checked shirts. 'You look as if you're off to chop down a few trees,' she'd told them earlier when they were about to leave.

'Why aren't you in bed, Ma?' Quinn said now. He lifted her up a bit and kissed her nose.

'Hi, Ma.' Kev ruffled her hair. 'Is there any tea made?'

'No, but I'll make some.' She hurried into the kitchen. 'Did you have a nice time?' she called.

'It was okay,' Quinn shouted back. 'Lousy music, not nearly as good as me dad's. Just wait until me and our Kev's group is ready to swing.' He had learned to play the fiddle and Kev the piano in the front room. They had played professionally a few times and were preparing to launch themselves on the world of show business in the forthcoming summer holidays.

A few minutes later, Nell went in with a tray of tea and an unopened packet of ginger biscuits – every biscuit would have gone by the time they went to bed. Kev leapt up and took the tray from her.

'Ta, Ma,' he said.

They all sat down, and Nell surveyed her two lovely red-headed lads and forgot all about the other son, who could well be celebrating his birthday not all that far away.

★

William's party broke up at about two in the morning. Most of the guests went home, but a handful stayed, having brought sleeping bags and intending to sleep on the living room floor. The girls had gone to bed. Tom had gone back to Rimrose Road. Iris had been tempted to ask him to stay – but only for the company.

Tomorrow, Sunday, he was coming early to help clear up after the party and to talk to William about what he wanted to do after he'd taken his finals in a few weeks' time.

'Of course, I'll pass,' William said indignantly the next day.

'You can't take that for granted, son, until your results come through,' Tom argued. 'You haven't even sat the exams yet.'

'I shall pass, Dad. I assure you. And I shall get a good degree, I know that too. I've always done well in exams – you already know that,' he said accusingly.

'I've never believed in counting my chickens before they're hatched.' Tom sounded like a grouchy old man, Iris thought.

'Neither have I, but I'm taking mathematics. My answers will be either right or wrong and I'm smart enough to know the right ones. I'm not going to be subjected to someone's judgement on whether I've understood the meaning of a poem or a novel or some historical fact.'

'Oh, all right,' Tom said testily. 'Let's say you pass with flying colours, you have an excellent degree, what do you want to do then?'

'Go into politics.' William's face shone with enthusiasm. He was such a handsome young man, Iris thought. Not exotically handsome like Maggie's husband Jack, just plain ordinary down-to-earth good-looking, with steady brown eyes and a lovely honest face – just like his mother's. The thought came from nowhere and took her aback.

'Become a Member of Parliament?' Tom was badly shocked.

'Hell, no!' William shook his head. 'No. Join a ministry; Defence, say, or the Treasury. The Board of Trade, perhaps.

Work with figures. I really fancy being connected to government.'

Tom's mind had changed. 'I really approve of that,' he said warmly. 'You'll become a civil servant and end up with a knighthood.'

'Well, I certainly don't want one of those. I'm not sure if I believe in that sort of thing.'

Iris spoke for the first time. 'What are your politics, William?' It wasn't something they'd discussed before.

William leant back in the chair and frowned. 'I'm not really sure. I'm not right-wing, and I don't think I'm left, either. Somewhere in the fluid centre, probably, wobbling a bit either way – more to the left than to the right.'

Iris and Tom laughed. 'That needs some working out, son,' Tom remarked. 'It sounds a bit uncomfortable to me, but as long as you don't fall off, I don't suppose it matters.'

William returned to Norwich on Monday. A few weeks later he rang home and informed his mother that all his exams had been taken and he was convinced he'd done well.

'That's really good, love,' she said warmly.

'I don't suppose Dad'll believe me till I get my results,' he grumbled.

'Oh, don't take any notice of your father, William. What do you intend doing when you finish uni?' she asked. She hoped he would just stay at home for a few weeks and she could make a fuss of him.

'Go to London, I think, find a bedsit, or maybe share a place with some blokes from here. I'd like to have a good look around the House of Commons, actually, attend a few sittings, see what goes on.'

Iris hid her disappointment. 'I'm terribly envious,' she said. 'I'm sure you'll have a very exciting time.'

They rang off and she returned to the housework. The place was very quiet these days. Louise and Dorothy had gone to work and Clare was in the sixth form at school and would shortly leave. Iris began to wish she'd had more children, another three, maybe. After all, seven wasn't an excessive number. In the old days, loads of women had double figures. But even with a bigger family, she thought dolefully, they too would inevitably grow up and she'd end up with a quiet house. Anyway, she was fifty-one and it was too late now.

William came home a few weeks later, after finishing university for good.

'I had a brilliant idea the other day,' Iris told him. 'You know young people sometimes work for Members of Parliament for a couple of months, perhaps as long as a year. I'm not sure what they do and I don't think they get paid much.'

William looked interested. 'They mostly do research,' he said.

'Well, I know an MP you could approach for a job: Kathleen Curran, she's the member for Bootle Docklands. She and I are sort of friends. Whenever there was a general election, we'd have her poster in the window of our old house, but she doesn't represent this part of Bootle. I'll write to her if you like, tell her about your interest in politics, see if she'll take you on. Would you like that?'

'I'd love it, Mum. Thank you. I didn't realise my mother had friends in high places!'

'I've only got one friend in a high place, William.'

Iris had always been proud of her connection with the famous, some considered notorious, Kathleen Curran. Although she had never actually joined the Labour Party, Kathleen had often invited her to the occasional event and they always exchanged Christmas cards.

She wrote to her friend straight away, and Kath wrote back just as promptly and invited William to come for interview.

When Tom was told, he groaned. 'I don't like the idea of

William being associated with such an infamous figure. He'll be tarred as a rabid left-winger from the start.'

'Oh, don't be silly, Tom,' Iris said impatiently. Sometimes he could be such a pain. 'When he's finished with Kathleen, he can go and work for some rabid right-winger and even things out.'

Had Kathleen Curran been younger and William older, he could well have fallen for her straight away. She was a magnificent woman, fifty-nine years old, with long black hair streaked with white secured in an untidy knot at the back of her neck. She wore a bright scarlet dress and he was rarely to see her in any other colour apart from the occasional black skirt or coat.

'So, you want to go into politics, William?' was the first thing she said. They were in her tiny office in the House of Commons, where the walls were stacked almost to the ceiling with files and books and old newspapers and magazines. She shared the office with another Member, whose chair was empty.

'I don't want to become an MP,' William said hurriedly.

'I understand. Your mam said as much in her letter. Well, you look a nice enough young lad. When can you start?'

William was astonished. 'But aren't you going to interview me? You haven't asked any questions.'

'The less I know about you the better, lad. People don't normally tell the truth in interviews. They give answers they think the interviewer wants, which can lead to all sorts of complications and possibly lies.' She gave him a truly wonderful smile. 'As I said, I like the look of you; I've known your mam for more than twenty years and I like her too. Your dad could do with a firework up his arse from time to time, but he's a decent enough chap. So, what d'you say, William? Do you want to work for me or not? The pay's five hundred pounds a year, which'll just about cover your expenses.'

'Oh, I do, I do,' William stammered. 'And the pay is fine.'
He was to discover later that she only took half her salary as an
MP and gave the rest to charity.

'Good.' She smiled again. 'I hope you don't mind, but I
find William a bit of a mouthful and am going to call you Will.
Is that all right?'

'It's what I was called at uni.' Sometimes he was called
Willy, but he wasn't going to tell her that.

'You can call me Kath,' she told him. 'Now, Will. Shortly,
Parliament will break up for the holidays, just like school. I
am visiting various African countries to write a report on the
poverty there. You can stay and tidy up this office. Get rid of
most of the papers, only keep the ones that look important.
Can you type?'

'A bit.' It was an awful little bit.

'Well, you can get some practice in on this ancient
machine.' She laid her hand on a dust-covered typewriter. 'It
has difficulty typing "e". Perhaps you can see a way of fixing
it.'

'I'll do my best,' William promised. 'More than my best.'

'Well I can't ask for more than a person's best. Oh, there's
another thing. There's no need to dress so formally.' She
nodded at his well-cut charcoal-grey suit, sparkling white
shirt and mildly patterned tie. 'Jeans and a T-shirt will do, but
be careful with the message – on the T-shirt, that is. Nothing
rude about the Pope or the royal family, otherwise it might get
in the papers that me researcher is a bolshie bastard and me
reputation will go even further down the pan.' She got to her
feet and William did the same, just as a woman knocked on
the open door.

'Morning, Auntie Kath,' the woman sang, followed by a
gasp of 'William Grant, what on earth are you doing here?'

'Will is my new assistant,' Kath said. 'Of course, you two
know each other, don't you? I first met your mam,' she said to
William, 'at Maggie's mother's funeral.'

William shook hands politely with the newcomer. He remembered her well from over the years. She was a cracker like her aunt, and, he recalled, had an extremely pretty daughter called Holly. He accepted with alacrity when she invited him to tea on Sunday. London was turning out to be a pretty wonderful place.

He returned to the tall, shabby house in Islington that he was renting along with four other students whom he'd been with at university; two boys and two girls. He'd been the first to arrive yesterday and had taken the first-floor front room after touring the house and deciding it was the best. The room below was bigger, but it was by the front door and the occupier might feel obliged to answer every knock.

After unpacking a few more things and hanging them in the wardrobe that could have accommodated at least half a dozen adults, he lay on the bed, stared at the ceiling, and wondered how many other young men would look forward with such heady anticipation to the idea of tidying up an office. Tomorrow he would buy some jeans and T-shirts – his parents had never approved of either – and he vowed never to iron a shirt again.

The weather was glorious that summer, continually warm and sunny, only raining during the night, when it refreshed the earth and plants and didn't inconvenience anybody. William realised that until he'd come to live in London, he'd only been half alive. At university, he'd mixed with the earnest hard workers, studied a lot, drank little, and only bothered with girls who felt the same. Mind you, he had lost his virginity a long time ago. Studying hard didn't stop a chap from having sex.

Having three sisters, he got on well with girls and didn't feel embarrassed as many of his friends did who'd had no experience of the opposite sex. In the pubs, clubs and dark coffee shops where he spent most of his evenings, he met new girls every night. They were usually the sort who were familiar with politics and what was happening in the world. Discussions raged well into the night. They argued about the war in Vietnam, the race riots in the Deep South of the United States, the terrible, dreadful, unbelievable tragedy of the assassinations of Jack Kennedy and Martin Luther King, and then, only a few weeks ago, the killing of Robert Kennedy after he'd won an important primary on his way to becoming the second Kennedy to be president of that strange country where heroes died and bad people thrived – the Mafia being only one example.

His favourite girl, though, was Maggie Kaminski's daughter, Holly. At twenty, she was such a delicate little thing, an incredibly pretty blonde with the most astonishing blue eyes. She was so very different to the other girls William associated with, who regarded themselves as beatniks and wore slacks and shapeless sweaters and occasionally hobnail boots. They used either no make-up or far too much so that their faces were dead white and their eyes looked like cockroaches. Sometimes their lips were painted black.

In contrast, Holly wore soft, feminine clothes and her face was discreetly made up. Her soft, breathy voice reminded him a little of Marilyn Monroe, who most men he knew were madly in love with. Holly had had a crush on him – it was impossible not to have noticed – for as long as he could remember. She was a receptionist in a beauty salon in Bond Street, whereas the other girls he knew lived on the dole or served in bars and were constantly looking for good causes to march for and bad issues to march against.

He hadn't yet asked her out. He had the feeling, with Holly, that asking for a date was almost akin to a proposal of marriage. She would take it very seriously, not casually like the other girls, and in view of her relationship to his employer – she was Kath's great-niece – he didn't want to blot his copybook by ditching her if he discovered they weren't made for each other.

The problem was solved one Sunday when Holly's dad, a charismatic individual with an important job in a Polish bank, produced a pair of tickets for *There's a Girl in My Soup* starring Donald Sinden, which was on at the Globe Theatre in the West End on Wednesday. He suggested William take Holly to see it. At this, Grace, the other daughter, looked amused. She was as different from Holly as chalk from cheese. Dark-haired like her mother, darker blue eyes, argumentative, wilful, quite rude – at least he thought so, the way she made fun of his opinions and told him to his face that he was full of hot air. Out of the hearing of her parents, she made liberal use of four-letter words.

The show was really good. William enjoyed it, particularly the way Holly kept her hand tucked in his throughout the performance. He was a little perturbed when they came out and she assumed they would take a taxi back to where she lived in Coriander Close in Finchley. He had only a few pounds in his pocket and was terrified he wouldn't have enough for the fare. Holly had requested a Tom Collins in both intervals, and the drinks had cost a bomb. He had to concede it was hot in the theatre, though lemonade had been enough for him. The cost of the taxi virtually cleaned him out, and he used his last few shillings to get back to Islington on the tube. If he couldn't borrow money in the morning, he'd have to walk to the House of Commons.

By the time William eventually laid his head on the pillow, he had quite gone off Holly Kaminski. The other girls he knew would never have done that to a fellow. They wouldn't have expected a taxi or, if they'd wanted one, would have paid for it themselves. And it was boring talking to Holly, who hadn't a clue what was going on in the world. He would have liked to discuss the end of the Prague Spring in Czecho-slovakia and the overthrow of Alexander Dubček, who had wanted to turn his country into a democracy. But Holly had never heard of Czechoslovakia or Alexander Dubček and preferred to talk about things like the latest shoes and *The Sound of Music*, a film she'd seen five times and which William wouldn't have wanted to see had he lived to be a hundred.

He groaned into the pillow, having remembered that the following night, Thursday, he had promised to take Holly to a disco in Covent Garden, and for lunch in Hampstead on Sunday, followed by a walk on the Heath. It meant he'd have to withdraw two or three times as much cash as he normally did. Even if he really fancied her for a girlfriend, he couldn't afford her.

Next day, he forgot about Holly while he continued with the tidying of Kath's office. Some of the newspapers were more than twenty years old. They were mainly left-wing: the *Daily Mirror*, the *Daily Herald*, the *Daily Worker*. The headlines fascinated him: *Rationing Ends – AT LAST! Britain Occupies Suez Canal. Death of a President.* Wars started, wars ended, trains and planes crashed, there were floods and fires, countries had famines and people died in their millions, rarely from natural causes. He cut out everything to do with politics and put them in box files.

William became lost in the history of his country and the world until he realised it was time to go home and change for the disco tonight. He had an almost waist-high heap of news-papers to throw away when he came in on Monday. He would be glad when the weekend was over and his life would be Holly-free and his money his own again. It hadn't taken long for him to realise that she wasn't made for him after all.

Maggie smiled benignly through the window as Holly linked William's arm and they made their way to the station. They were going to a disco in a pub somewhere.

'She's been mad about him from when she was about ten,' she said to Jack, who was watching the news on television.

'Since he's come to live in London, I could tell he was longing to ask her out. I'm glad you got those theatre tickets. It's really brought them together.'

'Seemed a bit mean to me,' Jack said. It had been Maggie's idea for him to give William the tickets as a way of getting him and Holly to go out together. 'He was put in a position where he couldn't very well refuse.'

'But he looked pleased when he saw them, not at all put out or anything. They're going out again on Sunday. Oh Jack, wouldn't it be wonderful if they got married? Between us, the Kaminskis and the Grants, we could have a really big wedding.' Maggie rubbed her hands together gleefully. Nell would come to the wedding, and she and Iris might become friends again.

'Don't get all worked up about it,' Jack warned. 'It might not happen.'

'On the other hand, it might.'

She saw his lips tighten just a little and recognised the sign. She was getting on his nerves. 'You always have to have the last word,' he'd said once.

It had happened gradually over the years, loving each other less and less until one day they wouldn't love each other at all. She'd had a long conversation about it with Nell over the phone. 'Maybe you're just getting used to each other,' Nell had suggested. 'Maybe you love each other just as much, but in a different way. It's just not so passionate any more.'

Maggie hoped that Nell was right; she usually was. She didn't want to not love Jack any more. She had dramatic visions of him dying, watching his eyes close for the final time, knowing that he would never open them again, never speak, not even breathe. She was surprised when it brought tears to her own eyes.

Maybe she still loved him just as much as ever. She hoped he wouldn't have to die before she found out for sure.

'I think I'll give Nell a ring,' she said now. 'She'll be really thrilled to know that our Holly and William Grant might get married.'

She decided to call Nell from the bedroom, where there was a telephone and she could sit comfortably on the bed instead of the hard seat in the hall. Before sitting, she opened the window and breathed in the cool evening air, then dialled Nell's number in Waterloo.

Five minutes later, she came downstairs, her face ashen. 'Can we please go to Liverpool in the car tomorrow, Jack?'

He must have noticed the trembling urgency in her voice. He turned down the television and looked dismayed. 'Oh darling, you know I can't. There's this chap coming from the States and I've promised to look after him for the day. I did tell you.'

'Of course you did, but I'd forgotten.' It would be unreasonable to expect him to back out at the last minute.

'What on earth's the matter, Maggie? You've gone terribly pale.'

'Nell has just told me the most awful thing . . .'

'Sit down,' he urged. He got up and pulled her to an armchair, where she sat and he dropped on to his knees beside her. 'What awful thing, darling?'

She was so outraged, so disbelieving, that she could hardly speak. 'According to Nell, William isn't Iris's child, but hers, and his father is an O'Neill. It can only be our Ryan – she never said anything, but I could always tell she was really keen on him. She only told me now because I said that Holly and William were getting serious about each other and there was a possibility they'd get married. But they can't, because they're related to each other; blood relatives, I think it's called.'

'And why must you go to Liverpool tomorrow, Maggie?' He stroked her face. 'Don't you know enough already?'

'I need to speak to Iris about it, face to face, make sure that what Nell said is true. And I'd like to talk to Nell again;

properly, this time. Before, she was so upset I could hardly understand what she was saying.'

'They must have kept the truth from William,' Jack said thoughtfully.

'Oh lord,' Maggie sobbed. 'What a terrible mess. And you know, Jack, I had always thought Nell was a virgin until she married Red, yet she'd actually had a *baby*! And before I'd had Holly, too.'

Maggie was a reasonably good driver, but she baulked at the idea of driving her new red Mini all the way to Liverpool by herself. She was considering going by train, and was pleased when Grace, who had passed her driving test with flying colours a year ago, offered to take her on condition her father allowed her the day off work – she worked as a clerk in his bank. He graciously gave his permission.

'That's really nice of you, love,' her mother said gratefully. 'But I'd appreciate it if you kept to forty miles an hour.'

'Don't be daft, Mum,' Grace snorted. 'It'd take all day. I promise not to go more than sixty. Anyway, what's the reason for going to Liverpool all of a sudden?'

'I'll tell you later.' Well, she might. It all depended what the truth was. It wasn't like Nell to exaggerate or tell lies, but the idea of William being her son was so improbable. 'I have to speak to Nell first, then Iris Grant, William's mother,' she told her daughter.

'Why not telephone?'

'It's something that has to be done face to face. I've rung Nell and told her to expect me about midday.' Iris was expecting her later in the afternoon.

'It sounds incredibly mysterious.'

Maggie sighed. 'It's more tragic than mysterious, love.'

It was a perfect day for driving; not too bright and not too hot. They didn't talk much. For all her outward confidence, Grace was rather nervous of driving so far, and on a motorway too. Maggie was immersed in trying to work out what had happened twenty-one years ago – no, it would be nearly twenty-two since William was conceived. She recalled that Iris had been ill when she was pregnant, blood pressure or something, and had gone to live in Wales for peace and quiet – and Nell had gone with her! Well, that fitted in with what Nell claimed had happened; that it was she who'd had the baby, not Iris.

'Holy Mary, Mother of God,' she whispered.

'What, Mum?'

'Nothing, I'm just remembering things, that's all.' Not only was she desperate for an explanation, by the time they reached the motorway services at Keele, she was just as desperate for a cup of tea. They stopped for half an hour in the restaurant so Grace could rest her legs, which were aching badly.

'This is the furthest I've ever driven a car,' she told her mother.

'You *are* a brick, love. That's what your dad used to call you, his "little brick".' She really was a wonderful daughter: reliable, helpful, the sort of person you would trust with your life. Whereas Holly . . . She recalled her sister-in-law's warning that Holly was being spoiled, and Maggie saying back something like 'A child can't be given too much love, Rosie.'

Well, that wasn't true, Maggie realised now, too many years later. Maybe her brain was clearer today, because she wouldn't normally have acknowledged, not even to herself, that Holly had grown up vain and empty-headed, concerned with no one but herself. That morning, she hadn't even noticed her mother was upset and had spent half an hour in front of the mirror making up her face before going to work.

Neither woman spoke for the remainder of the journey, not until they came off the M6 on to the East Lancashire Road and Maggie studied the map and instructed Grace how to get to Waterloo.

★

Music was throbbing out of the open windows of Nell's house, Irish music, the sort that Maggie loved but wasn't in the mood for right now. Nell must have been looking out for her, because she opened the front door and Maggie and her daughter went in. Grace made a beeline for the source of the music in a room upstairs. She still got on well with Nell's lads.

'Let's sit out here,' Nell said to Maggie. They went into the kitchen, which was badly in need of decoration. She closed the door and put the kettle on.

'Doesn't anyone ever complain about the noise?' Maggie asked.

'They did at first, but they seem to have got used to it. Some people come and sit on the wall outside just to listen.'

'Who's that playing now?'

'Quinn and Kev. They're quite good. They're off to London tomorrow to play at a club there. Red and Eamon are on their way to Ireland.'

'Hmm.' Maggie stared at her friend, wondering how to begin. She was acutely aware that while both women were forty-three, Nell appeared much younger than herself, despite the expensive creams that Maggie smoothed on to her face night and morning, the facials and the face packs, the stylish haircuts. Nell's skin, bare of make-up, was beautifully clear, her brown hair casually cut and terribly smart. She wore a plain red sweater and black slacks that looked very elegant, no doubt unintentionally. In her flowered sundress and frilly bolero, Maggie felt overdressed and over-made-up.

Nell suddenly said, quite sharply, 'Don't look at me like that, Maggie, as if you're sitting in judgement. I have done absolutely nothing wrong.'

Maggie spluttered, taken aback. 'My daughter is madly in love with William Grant. Whose fault is that?'

'Hardly mine. The last time I saw him, he was only a few hours old.'

It sounded so terribly sad. 'I'm sorry, but why didn't you tell me you'd had a child, a son?' She felt deeply hurt. 'I thought we were supposed to be friends.'

'We *are* friends, but it was none of your business. Just like what happened between you and Chris Conway was none of mine.'

Chris Conway was so far from Maggie's mind at the moment that she couldn't even remember who he was. 'Does our Ryan know about William?' she asked. 'I'll have a bone to pick with him next time I see him.' She might even go to Lydiate and do it today.

'That's just like you, Maggie,' Nell said scornfully, 'to go barging in when you don't know the truth about anything. Do you think that'd be fair on Rosie? Anyroad, your Ryan has nothing to do with it. William is your father's son.'

'My father!' Maggie put her hands over her ears, as if the music had suddenly become too loud or she didn't want to hear the truth. 'You mean me dad?' she whispered. 'Are you saying me dad raped you?'

'I'm saying no such thing. Your dad was drunk. It wasn't all that long since your mam had died and he was still mourning her.' Nell's lips actually curled into a slight, sad smile. 'He thought it was her, your mam, he was making love to, he said the most loving things in me ear.' There were tears in her eyes. 'Afterwards, I bet he never remembered a thing about it – or thought it'd been a dream. He never mentioned it, anyroad.'

'You should've stopped him,' Maggie cried.

'I wanted to, honest, but I couldn't. I couldn't move. I'd drunk vodka, you see; someone spiked the punch. Tom told me some people have an intolerance to alcohol. They have a sort of fit – the first time it happened was in the army. Remember?' She spoke matter-of-factly; not hesitantly or in the least bit embarrassed. 'I know it sounds daft, but I didn't mind what was happening. I mean, I didn't feel as if I was being raped.'

'I remember when you drank alcohol in the army.' Maggie nodded. 'Oh, but Nell, you should've told me dad what he'd done later.'

Nell threw back her shoulders, pulled herself together, as it were. 'Not then, not now, not ever,' she said firmly. 'Imagine how he would have felt had I told him. He was out of this world, Maggie, making love to your mam for the very last time, not that he knew it.'

'Oh Nell!' Maggie burst into tears.

'You must never tell him.' She looked so kind, so earnest, so caring that Maggie almost wanted to genuflect to her friend. 'You must promise me that, Maggie. And it's time Iris and Tom told William the truth. He's twenty-one and has a right to know the identity of his real mother and father. I know you'll want to tell Jack, but no one else, please; not your girls, or Iris's girls. I won't breathe a word to me mam and dad. If mam knew William was her grandson, it'd be all over Bootle before the day was out. Red knows I've had a baby, but not the details. I'll tell him now, though. So, only six people in the world will know: you and Jack, Tom and Iris, and me and Red. Oh, and William, of course.'

Maggie nodded. 'I agree.' When it came to Holly and Grace, she'd just have to think up a suitable lie.

'It's ages since the kettle switched itself off,' Nell got to her feet, 'and about time I made the tea.'

With her mother ensconced in the living room with Iris Grant, Grace attempted to eavesdrop, but the door and walls of the old house were too thick and all she could hear was a mumble. She wandered into the garden, where a young woman was swinging idly on a rope suspended from a tree.

'Hello,' Grace said. 'I'm Grace Kaminski, Maggie's daughter.'

The girl grinned and stopped swinging. She was small, neat, blonde and pretty. Grace liked her straight away. 'I'm Louise

Grant, Iris's daughter. Why is it I've never seen you before, yet I've met your sister Holly?'

'Because when we come to Liverpool Mum usually spends most of her time at Nell's house, and she has these great sons, Quinn and Kev. I've always preferred to stay with them than come here. We've just been there now. Have you ever met the Finnegans?'

'No. My mum isn't a friend of Nell, but she talks about her sometimes.'

'The Finnegan brothers are dead interesting,' Grace said fervently. 'I wish they lived in London or I lived here.'

'I wouldn't mind living in London either,' Louise said wistfully. 'It's dead boring here. I was too young to experience the excitement when the Cavern opened and the Beatles came down to visit us on earth.'

'Don't you go to work? I mean, it's Friday afternoon.'

'I work as a receptionist for my Uncle Frank – he's a doctor. I've got to back in a few hours for evening surgery. As I said, it's dead boring.'

Grace made a horrible face. 'I work in my father's bank, and that's dead boring too.'

'Do you think it'll be just as boring being married?'

'Probably,' Grace said gloomily. 'Mind you, our mums and Nell weren't bored when they were young and in the army.'

'Could we start a war, do you think?' the other girl suggested hopefully.

'Oh don't say that. Think of all the people who died – and the ones dying now in Vietnam. What we need is permanent peace. Why don't we join the Campaign for Nuclear Disarmament, they're always having marches and some of them get arrested, or there's Amnesty International?'

'I'd do it if I had someone to join with. Oh, wouldn't it be the gear to be arrested?'

'We could join together. Be sent to prison and insist we share a cell.'

250

Louise raised her pale eyebrows. 'That would be great, except I live in Liverpool and you live in London.'

'One of us could always move.'

'That would have to be me. My brother William lives in London in a really big house and there might be enough room there.'

'And hopefully enough for me! I know I live in London already, but it's about time I left home and took control of my own life,' Grace said a trifle pompously. Raised voices were coming from the other room and she thought it wise not to discuss the subject with her mother today. It was obvious she had other things on her mind. 'What a pity,' she said, 'that you have to work later. Otherwise you could have come back to London with me and Mum. The Finnegan lads have got a gig there tomorrow and I promised to go. They gave me two tickets, one for a friend.' She grinned. 'It would be nice if the friend was you.'

'I could always ring and ask my auntie to take over my shift for once.' Louise got to her feet, her face full of hope. She looked as if she'd just won a million pounds on the pools, Grace thought.

Maggie emerged not long afterwards, slamming the door behind her. 'Come on,' she said shortly to Grace. 'We're going home.'

'Can Louise come with us, Mum? She can sleep in our spare room. It's only for tonight – and maybe tomorrow night too,' she added as an afterthought.

'She'd better ask her mother first,' Maggie snapped. She walked down the path and got into the Mini, which was parked in the road. 'Come on,' she shouted to Grace.

'We're waiting for Louise,' Grace pointed out. Her mother had forgotten about Louise straight away. Gosh, something really big must have happened today.

Louise emerged, slamming the front door triumphantly, a

paper carrier bag stuffed with clothes in her hand. Maggie climbed out of the car and suggested she get in the front with Grace.

'I'll sit in the back where I can think me own thoughts without interruption,' she muttered, more to herself than anyone else.

So it was true! William Grant was Nell's son. Not that she'd doubted it by then, but Iris confirming it had put a sort of stamp on it, like a bank acknowledging that a payment had been received or a legal document had been made official.

There were bits Maggie hadn't known, that she hadn't thought to ask Nell. It had happened, Nell becoming pregnant, at the big party, Tom's parents' wedding anniversary.

'She wouldn't tell us who the father was,' Iris said. 'Though she swore she hadn't been raped. I'd often wondered if it was Frank, Tom's brother, who was responsible. He was always keen on Nell.'

'And I took for granted it was our Ryan when Nell told me last night,' Maggie said. 'But it turned out to be me dad.'

'Your father!' Iris's jaw had fallen. 'Paddy O'Neill?'

'Exactly,' Maggie had cried.

What was more, poor William didn't know that Iris and Tom weren't his real parents. 'But that's terrible,' Maggie raged. 'These days people are strongly advised to tell children if they are adopted.'

'These days, yes, but not then. And William wasn't adopted in a normal way,' Iris pointed out. She was angry at the way the truth had come out. 'My name and Tom's are on his birth certificate. We are officially his parents and it never crossed our minds that anyone would find out that we weren't. We trusted Nell completely. If William hadn't formed a relationship with your daughter, then nobody would ever have known.'

'It's still not right,' Maggie said tightly. 'He should have been told. Imagine the shock it will be when he finds out now.'

Iris had blanched. She looked sick and awfully old, Maggie thought. A little overweight, very ordinary, yet she'd been quite beautiful in the army. 'Why will he have to be told?' she asked in a raw voice.

'Because he and Holly are madly in love,' Maggie said, exaggerating more than a little. 'The relationship must stop here and now and they'll want to know the reason why. They've arranged to go out again tomorrow.' She recalled that Nell wanted as few people as possible to know. 'I'll tell Holly a lie,' she said. 'I'll say William telephoned and doesn't want to see her again. And Nell doesn't want your girls to know.' She hadn't thought it possible for Iris to look even sicker, but she did now.

'I hadn't thought about it, but I suppose it would be best if they didn't.' She rubbed her forehead tiredly. 'It's as if everything is collapsing around me,' she muttered.

Maggie had wanted to ask more questions. Why had Iris and Nell fallen out? They'd been such good friends, but Iris hadn't been invited to Nell's wedding. She positively refused to think that it was Nell's fault. Iris must have done something wrong – or Tom had.

She was so upset that she couldn't remember the rest of the conversation all that clearly, but at some point she had walked out of the house. It would be a long time before she spoke to Iris Grant again, she thought as she sat in the back of the Mini, listening to Grace and Iris's daughter chattering inanely. It felt like an entire lifetime ago since she'd felt that carefree.

Iris was writing a note to her daughters to leave on the kitchen table. Dorothy and Clare were due home at around five, and she was telling them that there was ham salad in the fridge. She had nearly addressed it to Louise too, but remembered just in time that she had gone with Grace Kaminski to London. The

253

note was to tell them that their mum and dad were going to London too.

Something really important has come up, she wrote, thinking how formal that sounded. *We might not be back until the early hours.*

Tom came into the room; he had been to fill the car with petrol. 'Are you ready?' He looked terribly cross, not just with her, but with the entire world, furious to learn of Maggie's visit and of Nell having revealed the truth about William's birth after all this time. He slammed the petrol receipt on the table and his cross face crumpled. 'He *is* our son, isn't he, Iris? No parents could love him more than we do.'

'Of course he is, darling.' Iris put her arms around him for the first time in many years. William might not have come from her womb, but he would always be their dearest, darling son.

Chapter 14

William felt as if he was suspended in mid-air. There was nothing holding him up and any minute he might fall to the ground with an almighty crash. It made him feel very tense, yet he was floating. It was an altogether horrible sensation, his body all crunched up, yet unsupported.

The front doorbell rang. He jumped and discovered he was lying on the bed in his room in London.

His parents had not long gone, leaving a piece of paper with the name and address of his real mother on. Her name was Nell, and she lived in Waterloo in Liverpool. It would seem his parents were no longer his parents, just two people who had no real claim on him other than having brought him up.

'Perhaps you'd like to write to her,' one of the people had said, 'your real mother, that is.' William didn't think he'd manage to come to terms with it for as long as he lived. His sisters weren't his sisters, either!

'You should have told me before,' he'd said – or wailed or cried or something terribly dramatic and tearful, because the bottom had quite literally dropped out of his world, which was the reason he'd been floating. 'You should have told me before.'

They'd only told him the truth now because they'd heard he'd fallen in love with Holly Kaminski and she and he were related, not through his mother, but through his father. It was vital the relationship be stopped before it went any further.

'I'm sorry, darling,' his fake mother wept – she had cried non-stop the entire time they'd been there. 'Nell, your mother, wouldn't tell us who your father was, but apparently it's Paddy O'Neill, Maggie Kaminski's father.'

'Then he must be really old!' Old enough to be his grandfather. Oh my God, this was so *awful*. And what made them think he was in love with Holly Kaminski? Last night they had gone to the disco in Covent Garden and she had driven him insane with her silly chatter. At least this terrible, horrible, unbelievable thing that had happened meant he didn't have to take her to Hampstead Heath tomorrow. Hopefully he would never see her again.

His mother – the woman who had been pretending to be his mother for the past twenty-one years – wanted to stay, but his father – Tom, Mr Grant, his pretend mother's husband – thought they should go back to Liverpool. 'Let William get used to the new, er, conditions,' he said.

Conditions! William turned over and buried his face in the pillow, just as someone knocked on the door, then opened it.

'Fancy going for a drink, Will?' a voice asked.

'Sod off,' William snarled.

'Are you all right, old man?'

'Sod *off*,' William shouted.

'Oh, all right.' The voice was hurt. 'There's no need to take that tone.'

The door closed. William staggered over and locked it. He couldn't imagine talking to another human being again.

Holly fucking Kaminski! If it hadn't been for her, he might never have been told that his parents weren't his parents, that instead they were a woman called Nell and a really old man called Paddy O'Neill who probably had grey hair and walked with a stick.

He tried to calm his thoughts. He would have *had* to know sometime. It wouldn't have been right to go through his entire life without knowing who his real mother and father were. In fact, his pretend parents really, really should have told him years ago, right from the start, not sprung it on him when he was a grown man and it would come as an appalling shock. He couldn't visualise ever getting used to it, he thought fretfully.

He beat the pillow with his fist. What the hell was he supposed to do now?

Sunday afternoon. Nell had been to midday Mass, having slept in for a change. The bells were still ringing; she loved the sound of church bells.

Red was still in bed fast asleep, having travelled back from Ireland on the overnight boat. He and Eamon had entertained the passengers. Eamon hadn't a piano, but he could get really haunting music that brought tears to the eyes out of a simple hornpipe. 'Danny Boy' sounded totally heart-rending.

Yesterday, Quinn and Kev had gone to London in Red's van. They were meeting up with Grace Kaminski and Louise Grant, Iris's eldest girl, spending the weekend together, the lads sleeping in the van.

Nell hoped there'd be no hanky-panky, or at least only mild hanky-panky, nothing serious. After all, Kev was only seventeen.

Bits of yesterday kept flashing through her mind: Maggie's anger, her own refusal to be bullied, relief that the truth was at last coming out. She wondered when William would be told that Iris and Tom weren't his parents.

She washed a few clothes and hung them on the line – not all that long ago, Sunday had been regarded as a day of rest, and it was frowned on for Catholic women to do housework, but fortunately those days had passed.

When she came in, she switched the radio on, turning the dial until she found music, any music, she didn't care what sort. Since marrying Red, she couldn't stand a silent house. It was a lovely sunny day – though one degree more and it would be too hot for comfort.

The kitchen clean and tidy, she put the kettle on for tea, wondering how many pots of tea most women made throughout a lifetime. Thousands and thousands, she reckoned.

There was a knock on the door and she went to answer it. A young man was standing outside and she knew who it was straight away. Ever since Maggie's visit it had been on the cards that this might happen. Iris and Tom had told him that he wasn't their child.

'William,' she whispered shakily. Poor lad, he looked at the end of his tether: red-eyed, white-faced, so obviously tired. She reached for his hand and pulled him inside. 'Come on in, luv.'

The door closed, they stood staring at each other, Nell marvelling at how tall he was, how handsome, despite his drawn features, how desperately unhappy.

'Didn't you know?' she asked, and he shook his head miserably. 'It must have come as a terrible shock.'

'It did,' he mumbled. 'Are you Nell?'

'Yes, luv.' There were pains in her stomach, contractions, the sort she'd had in Caerdovey the day he was born. But they were satisfying pains, pleasurable almost. 'Let's sit down,' she said.

They sat on the lumpy settee – she kept meaning to suggest to Red that they bought a new one. 'I'll make a cup of tea in a minute,' she promised. The kettle was already on.

'Thank you.'

'I don't suppose you know what to do with yourself. How did you get here?'

'I caught the first Liverpool train from Euston.' He sighed. 'I didn't sleep a wink last night.' He closed his eyes, and she thought he was about to drop off there and then.

'Perhaps you'd like to have forty winks later. We have a spare room.'

'I think I might,' he muttered.

The estate agent had referred to it as a box room. Eamon

258

slept there from time to time. There were hooks behind the door to hang clothes. She'd change the bedding later.

'Did Iris and Tom tell you who your father is?' she asked.

He sighed. 'Yes, someone called Paddy O'Neill.'

She patted his arm. 'It's not fair, is it? People get up to all sorts, and years later other people have to put up with the consequences. Anyroad, luv, Paddy O'Neill is a really lovely man. And what happened was more or less a case of mistaken identity. I won't go into more detail, if you don't mind.'

'I don't mind,' he said weakly.

'Yesterday, Maggie and me, we agreed only to tell our immediate families, otherwise you'd have dozens of half–brothers and sisters wanting to get to know you.'

'I see.' He sighed deeply.

She got the impression it was a load off his mind, but realised if him and her lads came face to face she would feel obliged to tell them he was their half-brother. She hadn't imagined him turning up here and all three were entitled to know the truth.

When she told him about Quinn and Kev he just looked resigned, as if by now everything was quite beyond him. 'Is Paddy O'Neill Kathleen Curran's agent?' he asked tiredly.

'Yes, you'll probably meet him one of these days. And Kath is Paddy's sister-in-law. It's all desperately complicated.' Nell rose to her feet. 'I'll go and make that tea now. Would you like something to eat?'

'I wouldn't mind a sandwich.'

'Won't be a mo. I've got a tin of corned beef open.'

It was all terribly surreal. Not only had he been starving hungry when he'd thought he'd never eat again, but now William felt quite calm as he waited for the tea and a corned–beef sandwich, as if somewhere deep down inside he knew that everything was going to be all right. He liked his real mother. He liked the way she didn't fuss or cry or drool over him, just accepted that fact that he was there. He liked the way she'd sat beside him and held his hand, patting it gently from time to time. And perhaps he was being prejudiced, but he thought her truly beautiful, with her gentle brown eyes and smooth forehead. He also liked her plain clothes and un-affected manner. And he liked her house, which was tidy but full of books, pictures and photographs. It was also very colourful, and there was an old piano against the wall with sheet music on the stand.

There were footsteps on the stairs and a man came into the room. He was as thin as a stick, fortyish, not very tall, and his hair was the reddest William had ever seen.

'Hello, there,' the man said. 'Are you the one that knocked?'

'Yes,' William conceded. 'I hope I didn't disturb you.'

'No, I was already awake. I'm Red Finnegan, Nell's hus-band.' The man approached and shook his hand. He had a strong grip and a marked Irish accent.

William, who'd never had anything to do with Ireland in his life before, suddenly found himself with Paddy O'Neill for a father and Red Finnegan as a stepfather of sorts, probably both Catholics, while he had never been near a Catholic church in his life. 'I'm William Grant,' he said. He wondered, panic-stricken, if Nell had told this man that she'd had a child – long before they were married, he assumed.

'Aha!' Red's green eyes lit up. '*That* William!'

'I hope you don't mind my coming.'

Red Finnegan spread his arms in a generous gesture. 'Glory be to God, no. I couldn't be more pleased that you're here.'

All the bits of William's body that had fallen awkwardly out of place slowly began to settle back to where they should be, and he found himself breathing evenly again.

William slept for hours in the little narrow bed in his mother's spare room. He still felt strange, would do for a long time, but yesterday had had a bad side and today a good side, and he couldn't help but feel grateful that things had turned out the way they had.

He woke up from time to time and could hear noises downstairs, people talking, the piano being played, a violin – a *violin*! He was tempted to go downstairs and investigate, but felt too sleepy, though he did venture down later when a car drew up outside and several people came in, amongst them a girl who sounded very much like his sister Louise, though it couldn't possibly be.

It turned out that it *was* Louise, who was even more surprised to see him than he was her.

'*William!*' she cried when he appeared. 'What on earth are you doing here? I didn't know you knew the Finnegans.'

'I've only known them for a little while,' he said.

It was Maggie who summed up the various events later in the week.

'In a matter of days, so many lives have changed,' she said to Jack one night after they'd had dinner. She was no longer speaking to Iris or Tom Grant, who she was convinced had tricked poor Nell out of her baby. She would have liked to fall out with Nell, too, for keeping the baby secret, but she didn't want to cut off too many ties. 'Our Holly's got a broken heart, claiming that she was madly in love with William; William's left London and gone to live with Nell in Liverpool; and Louise has left Liverpool and taken over William's bedsit in London.' She put her finger to her lips and glanced at her husband. 'Is that everything?'

Jack smiled. 'Not quite everything. This morning Grace gave in her notice at the bank. It appears she's going to live in the bedsit with Louise.'

Maggie's face turned beetroot red. 'Over my dead body,' she said threateningly.

'It's no good trying to stop her,' Jack said easily. 'What's more, her notice has been accepted. She's leaving at the end of the month.'

'But Jack, she has a really good job at the bank.'

'It was as dull as ditchwater. Young people need a bit of adventure before they settle down. You had it in the army and I did in the RAF. She won't be stopped, Maggie,' he warned, 'and I shall be on her side if there's an argument.'

Maggie was silent for a while. 'I expect you're right,' she said with a sigh. 'We had a great time in the army.'

'I didn't exactly have a great time in the RAF, but I wouldn't have missed it for worlds. It helped me grow up.'

'Well all I can say,' Tom muttered bitterly, 'is that Nell is certainly taking her pound of flesh. She must think we treated her very badly. It can only be due to her that William hasn't been in touch.' There had been neither sight nor sound of William for more than a fortnight. Louise had told them he was living with the Finnegans in Waterloo, which she considered mighty odd.

Iris drew in an exasperated breath. 'We *did* treat her badly,' she snapped. 'At least *you* did.' She couldn't be bothered going over the details again so many years later. 'And it just shows how little you know Nell if you seriously think her capable of taking some sort of revenge for what happened with William. Even if she could stop him from seeing us, she wouldn't. In fact, she's more likely to encourage him. We've seen nothing of William because he doesn't want to see *us*.'

If only she'd gone to visit Nell years and years ago, assured her that she still wanted to be friends, but she'd felt so ashamed of Tom's behaviour. Eventually, too much time had passed and it was too late. It was frightening the way life could change, completely alter course, over the space of a day or so – even a few hours. Who would have thought that William, who she loved with all her heart and soul, would no longer be her son? What was more, as a result of all the upset, Louise, her eldest daughter, had gone to live in London with Grace Kaminski, with whom she'd become as thick as thieves.

Tom began to cry, but Iris felt no sympathy for him. She left her husband to get on with it and went upstairs to cry alone.

William had always loved music. Ever since the Beatles had burst out of Liverpool on to the world, he'd been particularly drawn to rock 'n' roll. Though never, in the wildest of his dreams, had he imagined joining a group and playing on stage, as he had over the last two weekends.

Quinn and Kev Finnegan had accepted him as their half-brother with such ease and lack of formality that you'd have thought strange relatives turned up out of the blue on a regular basis. He'd been co-opted into their act playing the tambourine at a working men's club in Wigan last weekend, and a wedding reception the week before. Quinn and Kev played guitars and sang. William discovered he had quite a pleasant voice and sang with them, mostly songs they'd written themselves or that had been composed by their father, who was moderately well known along with his friend Eamon as a double act who played wild Irish music at places all over the British Isles and sometimes on the radio.

It was an odd world in which he now lived, on an entirely different plane from the one in which he'd lived before.

'What were you planning on doing with your life, William?' Nell asked him one day.

'I wanted to get involved with politics,' he told her. 'It was why I was working for Kathleen Curran, learning from the bottom up.'

'I hope you haven't given up on that idea. It sounds dead interesting to me. You don't want to let what's happened knock you off course, as it were.'

William grinned. 'Is that a roundabout way of telling me I'm a lousy tambourine player?'

'No, luv. You play really well, but being a musician is a hard

263

life if it's not in your blood like it is with Red and the lads, and it's not what you really want to do, is it?'

She was looking at him with understanding in her steady brown eyes. It was what William loved about her: she never pretended to be annoyed, never did anything for effect. She was just herself, completely honest and down-to-earth without being hurtful. Her husband and sons loved her to death. It was a very happy home that he'd wandered into.

'I don't really know what I want to do at the moment,' he confessed. He'd already written to Auntie Kath – she genuinely was his auntie now, though she didn't know it – to inform her he didn't want to work for her any more. He hadn't given a reason.

'Well, there's no need to hurry. You're only young, there's plenty of time to make up your mind.'

September came. Kev returned to school to study for his A levels and Quinn retired to his bedroom to compose new songs. Red and Eamon continued to tour with their frenetic act.

William was wondering what sort of job he could get that wouldn't interfere with his own musical career, which he intended to continue with despite Nell's words, yet would give him enough to pay her for his keep, when Auntie Kath came to see him. To his surprise, she threw her arms around his neck and kissed him on both cheeks. She looked very sunburnt and fit after spending the summer travelling around Africa, where, she said, the poverty was heartbreaking.

She either hadn't received his resignation letter or had decided to ignore it. 'I've come to sort out the dates for the Labour Party conference, Will,' she said cheerfully. 'It's being held in Blackpool this year and I'd like us to go together on the train, so we can have a talk about this and that.'

'But I'm part of a group now,' William stammered. 'I'm with Quinn and Kev.'

She patted his arm. 'I know, lad, and you play the tambourine.' There was a touch of humour in the way she said this. 'You'd only be in Blackpool for seven days at the most. I'm sure Quinn and Kev can manage without you if they have a concert during that time. You'll have to leave a week on Friday.' She nudged him playfully. 'That letter you wrote, giving in your notice, like, I tore it up.' She chattered on about how interesting he would find the conference, the speakers there would be, the fringe meetings that would be held in clubs, pubs and odd places all over Blackpool. He would have the time of his life, she assured him. By the end of the week, there'd be politics coming out of his ears.

'Oh, all right, I'll go,' he said eventually, if only to get rid of her. If he could, he'd wriggle out of it over the forthcoming days. And she needn't think he was going back to work for her when the week was over.

There was no opportunity to wriggle out of it. Two days later, an envelope addressed to him arrived containing a return train ticket to Blackpool, a hotel reservation, a conference programme and a pass with his name on, along with details of some of the fringe meetings Auntie Kath had mentioned that he had to concede sounded really fascinating; on Northern Ireland, for instance, the invasion of Czechoslovakia, the war in Vietnam, the future of the National Health Service and numerous other interesting subjects.

He sighed. It was too late to refuse, and should he try, Kath would kill him.

Before leaving for Blackpool, William went to see his first parents – this seemed a sensible way to think of them. They hadn't met since the day in London when they'd told him that Nell was his mother.

He felt embarrassed and stiff and didn't know what to say. But it had to be done. He had to admit that the love they had given him had been unstinting, and there had always been a happy atmosphere in the house. Even though Iris and Tom hadn't lived together for a long time, there hadn't been any rows and their relationship was amicable. He had loved his sisters and they'd loved him.

'So, you're going away?' his first mother said, looking close to tears.

'Only to Blackpool,' William said, 'and only for a week.'

He could tell there were questions they badly wanted to ask but didn't like to. He imagined they would like to know if he would ever live at home again; would he come and see his sisters – not his *real* sisters, mind – or could they come and see him?

William didn't give them the opportunity. He kissed them awkwardly and went home to Nell.

Next day he caught the train to Blackpool.

'Do you really need to take that with you?' Maggie asked when Grace threw a heavy suede coat lined with lambs wool on to the bed. Jack was taking Grace and some of her belongings to Islington later that night. 'I thought you and Louise were sharing a wardrobe. You'll be using up your entire half with that.' She nodded bitterly at the coat. She was annoyed that Grace was moving to the bedsit before the end of the month when she finished work in the bank. It was as if she couldn't wait to get out of the house in which she'd lived her entire life. 'You can always leave the coat and come back and get it in the winter,' she went on. 'I mean, I take it you intend coming back to see us from time to time?'

'Of course, Mum.' Grace laughed. 'I mean, it's not as if I'm leaving under a cloud, is it?' She wiggled her eyebrows.

'Then leave the coat for now and take more sensible clothes with you.' They were only halfway through September, and autumn had been lovely so far.

'All right, Mum. Anything to please you.' Her daughter hung the coat back in the wardrobe and surveyed the contents,

266

eventually removing two summer frocks. 'I can wear these with cardies,' she muttered.

'I can't understand how anyone in their right mind can bring themselves to leave such a lovely room.' Maggie sniffed. The wallpaper was lilac with tiny white flowers and the frilly curtains had the same pattern. The furniture was cream with fancy gold handles, and on the bedside cabinet was a pretty white lamp with a lacy shade that Grace had chosen herself. 'My room in Bootle was less than half the size of this and had lino on the floor. I mean, nobody had carpet in the bedroom in those days.' The carpet here was cream. Holly's room was just as nice. 'And I had to share it with your Auntie Bridie.'

'Is that why you left to come and live in London, Mum?' Grace asked.

'Well, no,' Maggie conceded, 'but if I'd had a room like this, I'd've found it hard to leave. It was probably the miserable bedroom that drove me out of the house.' That wasn't true and she knew it. She'd left in search of adventure, as Grace was doing now, and nothing Maggie could say would stop her.

'Well *I'm* being driven out by my horrible grumpy old mother.'

'You're not, are you, love?' Maggie was suddenly anxious. Jack had said the other day that she'd lost her girlish love of life.

'That's because I'm now a woman,' she'd said to him crossly. 'Anyroad, you've lost your . . .' She'd stopped, unable to think of anything Jack had lost. In fact, he had hardly changed at all, still as charming as he had always been. He took her out regularly: to the theatre, the cinema, to dinner. Some nights she went reluctantly; she would have preferred to stay in and watch television. His looks had changed, naturally. After all, he was fifty-three and there were glints of silver in his blond hair, but he hadn't put on an ounce of weight and the lines on his face made him look a trifle worn and terrifically handsome. There'd been a time when strangers used to give the pair of them admiring glances, but nowadays the glances were only directed at Jack. Maggie patted her expanding waistline. She really must go on a diet.

Jack drove her and Grace and her belongings to Islington that evening. Holly wanted to come with them, but there wasn't room in the car. Holly was understandably upset that her sister was moving. Nobody liked change apart from the people who were changing. Grace was happy to be leaving, making everyone else sad. Even Jack was sorry to be losing a daughter, though he was all for the idea.

When they arrived, Louise was attempting, not very successfully, to put together the single bed, which had arrived in pieces. Jack immediately took over and had it done in no time.

Maggie examined the room. It was at least clean, and the furniture was old but decent. It was rather better and much bigger than the room she'd had in Shepherd's Bush, but not as cosy.

Louise asked if Maggie would please telephone or write to her mother and inform her that where her daughter was living was perfectly respectable. 'She's worried I'm starting out on a life of utter depravity,' she said. 'It would help if you could assure her I'm not living in a brothel or anywhere nasty like that.'

'I'll get in touch tomorrow,' Maggie promised. She'd vowed not to contact Iris again, but that would have been mean. Louise was a nice young woman and Iris had far more reason to worry about her welfare from far away in Liverpool than Maggie had about Grace, who was only a few miles away.

On the other side of the country in Blackpool, William was having the time of his life. It was possible to be somewhere exciting and thoroughly enjoyable for almost twenty-four hours a day, leaving hardly any time for sleep. There were fringe meetings before conference began in the beautiful Tower ballroom, more meetings at lunchtime and after conference finished. The bars were packed, and after they closed there were Irish nights, where the sort of music he'd become so familiar with of late was played well into the early hours of the next day.

He had never talked so much or argued with so many people. Even when he was totally sober, he felt drunk. One night he went on stage during Irish night and played the tambourine and sang. Another night a girl called Sara came back with him to the hotel. They had hardly finished making love when it was time to get up for conference. He looked everywhere for her throughout the day, but couldn't find her anywhere. He didn't even know her surname. They never met again.

At one social event, he stood right next to the prime minister, Harold Wilson, and watched him smoke his famous pipe. At conference, he listened to a speech from Barbara Castle, a striking and wholly inspiring female politician who made his heart lift and the blood race through his body. He rubbed shoulders with Roy Jenkins and Jennie Lee and other famous representatives of Labour politics.

On the final day, he sang *'The people's flag is deepest red, It shrouded oft our mortal dead'* while holding hands with his neighbours on either side.

But even that wasn't the end of it. On the Blackpool train, William spoke to Stuart George, editor of a small-circulation magazine based in London. He only employed a handful of staff, he told William. 'But occasionally I commission freelancers to write articles. Would you like to do one on the conference? It would be interesting to have a fresh eye. You'll be paid, of course, though not very much.'

'Willingly,' William replied. He would have written it for nothing.

Chapter 15

William wasn't surprised as he approached Nell's house in Waterloo to see a small crowd outside. Even from so far away he could hear music – guitars being played very loudly – coming from inside. It sometimes happened that an audience would gather during rehearsals.

The front door was open. The lovely weather of the past seven days had changed; now, a cold wind blew and there was rain in the air. As soon as he could manage it, he intended shutting himself in his bedroom and translating the copious scribbled notes he'd made in Blackpool into clear English.

When he went in, the place was full of people he'd never seen before. It turned out later that most were Nell's relatives, her sisters, their husbands, their children and their children's children. Being Saturday, nobody had to be at work or school. There was no sign of Nell.

'What's going on?' he asked a thin, starved-looking chap who happened to be passing.

'It's Red,' the man explained. 'The other night he was leaving this club in Manchester and was knocked down by a drunken driver.'

'He's not dead?' William's voice came out in a croak, as if all the breath had left his body. 'He can't be dead!'

'Killed outright, poor sod. Our Nell's heartbroken.' The chap turned out to be Nell's brother, Kenny. 'Red Finnegan was a really decent bloke.'

'One of the best,' William gulped. He hadn't known Red for long, but he was one of the nicest people he'd ever met. 'Where is Nell?'

'In the dining room with Red,' Kenny replied somewhat mysteriously.

The mystery was explained when William went into the room where Red Finnegan lay in his coffin, his long red hair spread like a fan on the white satin pillow. One of the fiddles that he had played with such brilliant dexterity throughout his too-short life lay at an angle upon his breast. There was a scent in the air that William at first couldn't recognise. It turned out to be partly incense and partly the candles that were flickering madly on the mantelpiece. It was the first time in his life that he'd seen a dead person.

It was in this room that Quinn and Kev were loudly strumming their guitars, their eyes closed, quite lost in the music, and Nell was seated beside the coffin, where she seemed to be carrying on a conversation with her dead husband. She was leaning over and touching his face, an expression of such tenderness on her own face that all William wanted to do was rush upstairs to his room to escape from these alien beings with their strange religious habits and rituals.

He went over, touched Nell's hand, mouthed, 'I'm sorry,' and fled.

Halfway upstairs, he bumped into an elderly man wearing an atrocious cream and brown checked suit. The man caught his arm, blocking his way, and growled suspiciously, 'Who are you when you're at home?'

'I'm William, a friend,' William said raggedly.

'Oh, aye. Our Nell spoke about you. I'm Alfred Desmond, her dad.' He stood aside to let William pass. 'She was wondering when you'd be home.'

'I need to go to the bathroom.'

'I'll see you later, lad.'

William bolted the door of his bedroom and sat on the bed.

He was shaking. Just then, what he wanted more than any-thing was to be in his old house with his old parents. They would want to know every detail of his time at the conference in Blackpool, hanging on his every word. They would be thrilled to bits to hear about the offer from Stuart George to write an article for his magazine. His father would grumble about it sounding a bit left-wing. Then his sisters would come in and they'd all sit down to tea together, laughing and joking.

That was his world, the one he was used to, not this other *Catholic* one with candles and dead bodies and incense. He was used to going to church once or twice a year, at Easter and Christmas, and the house had been completely free of holy statues and pictures.

And those people downstairs, most were now his relations; half-brothers and half-sisters. Alfred Desmond was his *grand-father*, for God's sake; his genuine maternal grandfather. He recalled his other grandfather, Cyril, who had died about five years ago. He'd been very much a gentleman, courteous and kind. Nell had remarked that her father was a crook.

'During the war he was what's called a spiv. Do you know what a spiv is, William?'

He'd said that he did. He'd seen spivs in the cinema, read about them in books, and now he had one for a grandfather. He badly wanted to get away from the house, although he really should stay and comfort Nell, but not in front of so many people who would want to know who he was. Just imagine if they discovered he was a relative! They would want to shake his hand, possibly kiss him, possibly hate him. They would want to know his story – and Nell's story. Where had he come from? As far as he knew, only a handful of people were aware of who he really was. The longer it stayed that way, the better.

Not even his own father knew he had another son. He wasn't to be told. Apparently, it would upset him. Tough! William thought cynically. If he wasn't to be upset, then he shouldn't go around impregnating young, innocent women. A case of mistaken identity, according to Nell. He squirmed at the thought of how casually he seemed to have come into the world.

He left the room, crept quietly down the stairs and out of the house. He knew exactly where he wanted to go.

'William!' exclaimed Addy when she opened the door of her little house in Woolton. Addy was the name he'd given Grandma Adele when he'd first learnt to talk. His sisters had followed his lead and called her by the same name. She was sweet and gentle and thought he could do no wrong. 'Come in, darling. It's ages since I've seen you.'

He followed her down the hall. Nowadays, she needed a stick just to get around the house. Her health had deteriorated swiftly after Cyril had died. She was little more than a bag of ancient bones, and he got the feeling she herself was waiting patiently to die.

They sat in her sitting room in front of a small fire. The book she'd been reading was laid face down on the table beside her chair. It was by Agatha Christie. The wireless was on low, a medley of old songs.

'I would have the world on a string, do anything, if I had you,' a man with a haunting voice was singing. The tuneful music and wistful words caught at his heart in the way that rock' n' roll never had. The words actually *meant* something.

'You look awfully unhappy, darling,' Addy said. Her face was vastly more wrinkled than he remembered.

William had no idea what to say to this. He felt as he must look. 'I don't know where I belong any more,' he gasped, and felt tears come to his eyes.

'Your mother told me you'd left home, but not why.' Addy shrugged. 'I could tell she was more upset than she need be, and was left to guess the truth for myself. She thought knowing would upset me, but I've known the truth all along. I've always worried that one day you'd find out and it'd come as a terrible shock.'

He was astonished. 'You mean you've always known I was adopted?'

Addy nodded. 'Not exactly adopted, darling; I don't know what the actual arrangements were.' Her forehead furrowed in an effort to find the right words. 'Let's say Nell handed you over with a great deal of reluctance. But you were better off with Iris and my son,' she hastened to assure him. 'Nell was a lovely young woman, but she was single and that father of hers was a terrible man, still might be for all I know. Lord knows what would have happened if he'd discovered his girl was pregnant. She could have ended up giving birth in one of those awful homes for unmarried women, for instance, and you might have been brought up in an institution run by nuns or sent to Australia, or something horrible like that.'

William felt more confused than ever. The only world he'd ever known had been comfortably middle class, but could easily have been so very different. And rather nasty, he realised.

'Iris and Tom couldn't possibly have loved you more,' Addy continued. 'They'd been desperate for another child since Charlie died—'

'Charlie?' William interrupted.

Addy sighed. 'Of course, you don't know about Charlie, do you? Charlie was born just before the war, nineteen thirty-eight or nine. He was only a few months old when he died in his sleep. Afterwards, Iris and Tom tried for years to have a baby until by chance, like a miracle, you came along, though in a most unexpected way. You brought joy into all our lives, William love.'

William ran his fingers through his already tousled hair. Nowadays he was forever learning things that surprised him, not always welcome.

'I've got all these relatives,' he mumbled. 'Nell's husband's died and the house is like a church. His body's there,' he gulped, 'lying in a coffin.'

'Nell's husband,' Addy gasped. 'That lovely red-haired man who sang Irish songs! Oh, what a shame. I shall go and see her soon. She won't mind my coming, even after all this time. We got on really well in the old days. Would you like some tea or coffee, darling? Or a drink? I still have some of Cyril's whisky. I expect it must taste better with age, though I can't stand it myself.'

'Whisky, please.' Perhaps this was one of those times when it would be good to get a little bit drunk.

William stayed the next two nights with his grandmother. She was the only relative from his old life to whom he felt he belonged. He slept in a narrow bed under a patchwork quilt and stared at the moon through cream lace curtains.

Sunday, Addy made a trifle, his favourite pudding, while he swept up the leaves in her garden, trimmed the hedge ready for winter and hoped Iris and Tom wouldn't turn up for a visit.

Next morning she woke him with a cup of milky tea and told him it was Red Finnegan's funeral that afternoon. 'It's in St Helen's church in Waterloo at two o'clock. I telephoned the house and someone told me. They didn't want to know who I was. I think you should go, darling.'

'Of course I should.' William sat up and took the tea. 'And I should take flowers; a wreath or something.'

'There's a florist not far from here,' Addy told him. 'I'll give you the money and you can get a wreath from me too. And if you have the chance, darling, tell Nell I'll come and see her soon.'

'I will,' William promised.

The funeral wasn't as sad as he had expected. Perhaps Catholics really did expect to meet the dead person in heaven one day so that they didn't get as upset as those who thought they'd lost their loved one for ever.

Maggie was there with Grace and Louise and asked how he'd got on at the Labour Party conference. William had forgotten that he'd been there. It felt hardly credible that a week ago he'd been embroiled in political debates, either listening in the conference hall or arguing in the bars and cafés.

Perhaps it was to be expected that music, none of it holy except in the church, played a big part in the proceedings. Red's mother had returned to live in Ireland years ago when her husband had died. She was over for the funeral and looked almost starry-eyed as she sang 'Ave Maria' and 'Your Tiny Hand is Frozen', in a quivery soprano voice. Red's friends from long ago played his favourite tunes; his sons sang a song they had just written dedicated to their father. Instead of making everyone cry, it made them laugh.

Early in the evening, William packed his suitcase, looked for Nell, and told her he was leaving.

'I knew you wouldn't stay for long,' she said. She wore a green dress, her husband's favourite colour. 'But you'll come back and see us from time to time, won't you? I don't want to lose you, William, as well as Red.'

'And I don't want to lose you. I promise I'll come back often. But I need to learn to live on my own.' He had just started to do so when the secret of his birth had been revealed and all hell had broken loose – or so it seemed to William. He had lost his place in the world and needed to find it again. He wished he hadn't given up the bedsit in Islington. Now Louise and Grace were living there.

'Where will you sleep tonight?' Nell asked. She was bearing up remarkably well.

'With my grandmother, Addy.' He had the strongest feeling that she wasn't long for this world.

'Adele!' She smiled fondly. 'I always loved Adele.'

'She intends to come and see you, but it mightn't be a bad idea if you went to see her instead.'

'I'll do that.' Nell kissed him on both cheeks. 'Ta-ra, my lovely lad,' she whispered.

'Ta-ra, Nell.'

That night in his grandmother's house, William cried himself to sleep.

Grace and Louise were having the time of their lives in the flat in Islington. Both worked as barmaids in a pub called the Green Man off Holloway Road, a huge place that catered for hundreds of customers. The pay was derisory, but the tips were enormous.

They only worked nights. The pub was supposed to close at ten, but it was well gone eleven by the time it emptied, the tables were cleared and the glasses washed. One of the barmen usually gave them a lift home. If none were about, then the landlady, Phyllis Goddard, would pay for a taxi. She was a glamorous blonde in her fifties who was reputed to have been a prostitute in a previous life. Some people said she was a widow, others that her husband was serving life for a horrific murder. Her apartment on the top floor was full of pink mirrors and white carpets.

The girls slept till late. By the time they got up, most of the other tenants in the house had either left or were staying in bed even later, so they had the shared bathroom to themselves. They indulged in long, leisurely baths wearing face packs and slices of cucumber on their eyes, after which they would do their hair. It was essential that Grace's natural dark curls be straightened a little so it didn't look as if they'd been permed to death, and Louise experimented with her long blonde tresses, arranging them in different styles decorated with coloured slides, flowers and ribbons.

Afternoons, they went to the West End or one of the

numerous markets, on the lookout for cheap clothes and shoes.

'I never thought I could be so happy,' one of them would say from time to time, or something like it, accompanied by a blissful sigh.

'You're wasting your life,' Grace's mother, Maggie, would say on the occasions she came to visit, usually in the morning when they were having baths, doing their hair, or trying on the clothes they'd bought the day before. Only occasionally did they remember to eat. They consumed coffee by the gallon.

'When I was your age,' Maggie said only a few days after Red Finnegan's funeral, 'there was a war on and I was in the army toiling away on behalf of my country.'

'Toiling!' Grace hooted. 'You've always claimed you had a marvellous time in the army. And if there was a war on, we'd join the forces, wouldn't we, Lou?'

'Mmm,' Louise agreed through the hairpins stored in her mouth while she tried to twist her hair into a chignon or a topknot or something equally complicated. At other times she might be experimenting with black lipstick or seeing how thickly she could apply eyeliner without looking like a clown or a crazy woman.

'I suppose you could say I'm wasting me own life,' Maggie said thoughtfully. 'After all, I'm doing nothing with it. I need something useful to occupy me time. Or a hobby, a useful hobby, not like flower-arranging or collecting thimbles.' While she spoke, she was wandering around the room picking up clothes off the floor, the bed, the chairs, and putting them away in the wrong drawers or hanging them in the wrong place – the coats went behind the door, not in the wardrobe.

'Have you bought any furniture polish yet?' she enquired when she found a mark on the table.

'Not yet, Mum.' The girls rolled their eyes at each other. Grace usually got rid of marks with spit and the corner of her hanky. Louise didn't even notice them. Housework wasn't on their agenda.

'Would you like me to see if there's a job going in the pub, Mam?' Grace enquired. She winked at her friend and Louise grinned.

'Don't be daft, girl. Though I wouldn't mind working for a charity, like. I mean, it's not as if your dad and I need the money.'

'My mum has got a job,' Louise announced. 'She works Fridays and Saturdays in Owen Owen's ladies' clothes department.'

'Does she really!' Maggie was genuinely interested. 'Owen Owen's was one of our favourite shops when we were young. Sometimes we'd have afternoon tea in the restaurant, Nell and all. Ah, those were the days,' she said nostalgically. 'You girls,' she went on changing tack completely, 'you're doing the right thing. Enjoy yourselves while you can. I'm lucky having such good times to look back on. Would you like me to make you some coffee? I wouldn't mind a cup meself.'

'Yes please,' the girls chorused. Once she'd drunk the coffee, she would go away and leave them in peace.

William had returned to London. He was in Auntie Kath's office in the House of Commons somewhat painfully typing the report he'd written on the Labour Party conference while staying with Addy. Last week, the Conservatives had held their conference in Brighton. Next Monday, Members of Parliament would return and the house would sit again with a full programme of legislation to debate and possibly pass.

A Labour government was currently in power, the prime minister, Harold Wilson, a bluff Yorkshireman who made something of a show about being seen puffing his pipe.

Despite all William's current problems, his worries, his concern about who exactly he was, he was looking forward to working for Kathleen Curran, who swept into the office at that very moment. She wore a scarlet cloak and a white knitted beret. She didn't exactly resemble Little Red Riding Hood, but could easily have been taken for a character out of a children's story or a nursery rhyme. She kissed him on the cheek.

'Did you have a good time in Blackpool, darlin'?' she asked. 'These days I miss all the fringe meetings, and I particularly miss the Irish nights. Unfortunately I feel obliged to attend the events that people tell me are more important.'

'It was great. I loved every minute,' William assured her.

'Where are you living nowadays?' she asked. 'Didn't you give up your room for some reason?'

'I'm staying at a cheap hotel,' he told her.

'You won't manage that for long on the money I pay you,' she said bluntly. 'You'd better stay in the flat for now.'

The flat, it appeared, was where her agent, Paddy O'Neill, stayed when he was in London. William swallowed hard.

'Paddy's getting on a bit and he doesn't come to London all that often these days, so *he* can stay at a cheap hotel in future. It's across the bridge in Lambeth, just two rooms, kitchen and bathroom, the flat, that is.'

'Is it very expensive?' At Red's funeral, after acknowledging that William would only earn peanuts working for her aunt, Maggie had suggested she ask her husband if there were any vacancies at his bank.

'I mean, you've got a degree in mathematics, haven't you? Perfect for a bank.'

'Not really. It's a different sort of figures altogether,' William had said at the time. He shuddered at the notion of being a bank clerk. It really wasn't his cup of tea. He wanted more from figures than putting them in columns and adding them up.

'The flat's rent-free, lad,' Auntie Kath said now. 'It comes with the job. After all, you've got to eat and treat yourself to a drink now'n again. I'll give you the key before you leave.'

William heaved a sigh of relief. His life would never return to normal, but bit by bit it was feeling less strange.

When he saw the flat, he felt even more pleased with the way things were going. It was the top floor of a Dickensian house in a street of similar three-storey houses. Self-contained, it was exactly as Kath had described: kitchen, bedroom, living room and bathroom. Everything about it was miserable: dark, dusky wallpaper, yellowing ceilings, cracked linoleum on the floor, tattered curtains. The furniture was cheap, modern stuff.

But William couldn't have been more pleased had he been looking around an apartment in Mayfair. Despite never having had to so much as think about decorating before, he began to look forward to painting the walls nice bright colours and replacing the linoleum and curtains. He'd been given money for his twenty-first so could afford to pay for a few improvements, though not new furniture. Hopefully the current lot would improve with a good polish. Once everything was done, he would look up some of his mates from university and invite them round for a drink. He recalled Kath saying that the flat would do 'for now', but as long as he worked for her, surely she wouldn't dream of chucking him out!

Oh, and he must write to Nell, tonight, as soon as he had unpacked his bag. Write and tell her how much he missed her, but that it had been important for him to get away.

'What's she doing now?' Quinn Finnegan asked his brother. They were in the hallway of the house in Waterloo.

Kev peered through the slightly open door of the living room to where his mother was sitting on the settee. 'She's reading me da's old letters,' he whispered. 'The ones he used to send if he was away for more than a few days.'

'I thought as much.' Quinn's brow darkened. 'If we go in, she'll stuff them under the cushion and pretend to be reading a book. She doesn't want us to know how much she misses him.'

'She's a stoic,' Kev opined. 'That's what Grandad said when he came round the other day. He said she's always been a stoic. She doesn't want to make a nuisance of herself by weeping and wailing all over the place.'

'I'd prefer it if she did.'

'Me too. Shall we make her a cup of tea?'

'I think so. And something to eat. I've noticed she's hardly eating.' It was a month since their da's tragic death. Quinn opened the door and sauntered into the room. 'Fancy a cuppa, Ma?'

Nell pushed the papers she was holding down the side of the settee. 'I wouldn't say no, son.'

'I'll put the kettle on.' He went into the kitchen. 'D'you fancy a cuppa, Kev?' he shouted.

'Wouldn't mind.' Kev came into the room just as casually as his brother. 'I'll warm the pot, shall I?'

'If you don't mind, kiddo.'

Minutes later, Quinn brought in three mugs on a tray. Kev followed with a plate of bread and jam, the bread almost an inch thick and the jam piled on. They sat one each side of their mother on the settee.

'That looks nice,' Nell remarked. She picked up a piece of bread and began to nibble at it. 'Mmm!' she said appreciatively. She could tell they were worried about her. Perhaps it was time she told them what she had planned. There was bound to be an argument, and best get it over with. 'I'm looking for a job,' she told them. 'I'd quite like to be a cook – you know how much I enjoy cooking.'

'We don't want you going to work,' Quinn spluttered through a mouthful of bread and jam. 'I'll go to the labour exchange tomorrow and get a job meself.'

Kev missed his mouth with the tea and it went down the

front of his shirt. 'And I'll go with our Quinn, Ma. There's no need for me to stay at school. I'll be eighteen at Christmas.'

'Neither of you will do any such thing,' Nell said as loudly and as authoritatively as she could. If she spoke in her 'won't take no for an answer' voice, they might be persuaded to agree. 'Your da would have wanted you to stay at school, Kevin, you know he would.' She turned to her other son. 'And Quinn, you have to stay home and write loads of music and songs and rehearse ready for when you both turn professional and follow in your da's footsteps. That's the most important thing of all, taking over from your da.'

She hoped the time would come when they'd make more money than Red, who'd just earned enough to make life comfortable. They'd saved very little over the years, and she'd let Eamon, Red's partner, have half the money in the bank, as he hadn't saved a penny. Poor Eamon was gutted by the loss of his partner. After the funeral, he'd returned to Ireland and she hadn't heard from him since.

'Who would you cook for?' Kev asked sternly.

Nell shrugged. 'A restaurant, maybe. Or perhaps a big factory with a canteen – I'd quite like that, it would be just like I did in the army. Or some posh family that wants a cook of their own.'

Quinn shook his head. 'Not a posh family, Ma. A restaurant'd be okay, or a factory. But it's only to be for a year. In the meantime, me and Kev'll practise like mad and do as many gigs as we can at weekends. When Kev leaves school,' he said boastfully, 'we're going to take the music world by storm.'

'It'll do her good going to work,' he said to Kev later. 'She's bound to be lonely without me da at home. There'll be people for her to talk to and everyone'll like her. People always do.'

'We'll make a fortune one day and buy her a bigger house and a new car – a Mini, she likes Minis. We'll get a yellow one. Yellow is her favourite colour.'

283

Grace and Louise had discovered that working for up to six hours a night for six nights a week in a public house whose clientele was at least three quarters male meant it was hard to keep the men at bay. Although the bar itself served as a barrier, at least half their time was spent collecting glasses and wiping tables. There were a handful of customers who seemed to regard the barmaids – there were five altogether – as part of the service, available for them to grope whenever they went near.

By now, both Grace and Louise were skilled at repelling attempts to pinch their bottoms or squeeze their breasts.

'Don't you *dare* do that!' they would hiss, eyes flashing angrily, whenever a customer got too fresh. If the man persisted, with Phyllis Goddard's encouragement they would dig a sharp elbow into the most convenient place on his anatomy. By then, most chaps would have given up, might even have apologised, but should they still not be put off, then Trevor, the doorman who was built like a brick wall as wide as it was high, would be called upon to deal with the matter and the customer would be thrown out.

Possibly most men – women too – thought that two young women working in such an environment couldn't possibly be virgins, but they were wrong.

In the liberated sixties, it had become fashionable to sleep around, but Grace and Louise had resisted. In fact, they hadn't even felt tempted. They were old-fashioned girls from good families who between them had determined that the first man they would sleep with would have to be special. In fact, he might possibly be the *only* man, the one they would marry. They couldn't imagine their mothers sleeping with a man other than their fathers – they would never know just how wrong this assumption was.

It was Christmas. Phyllis, expecting massive business, had offered the bar staff double pay over the holiday.

Maggie was aggrieved that Grace would only be present for Christmas dinner. She was bringing Louise with her – poor Iris wouldn't even glimpse her daughter on Christmas Day. William was going back to Liverpool to spend the day with the Finnegans.

The Green Man was opening at six. 'When I was young,' Maggie grumbled when the girls were ready to leave, 'barmaids were regarded as no better than they ought to be. No respectable girl worked behind a bar.'

'Things have changed since then, Mum.' Grace patted her mother's head. 'Anyway, you won't be here tonight. Aren't you going to a party in Soho?'

'Yes, but you and Holly are invited too. And Louise could have come, of course. They're your dad's friends. He'd love you to be there.'

'No I wouldn't,' Jack put in. 'It'll be as boring as hell. I'm not looking forward to it myself. The old people will talk about old times – in Polish. Grace and Louise will have a much better time in a pub with loads of young men.'

'I love going to parties in Soho,' Holly said unctuously.

'That's because you are a saint, Holly, and your sister is a little devil.' Jack bestowed smiles on both his daughters. 'And I love you both very much. Let me know when you're ready to leave and I'll give you a lift home. There won't be much in the way of public transport on Christmas Day.'

'Your dad is positively gorgeous,' Louise said when they were back in Islington and getting changed ready for work. 'He's as handsome as a film star. I could quite easily fall madly in love with him.'

'You'd better not, or my mum will scratch your eyes out.'

'If I were a lesbian, I could fall in love with her too. She's terribly pretty for an older woman. How old is she?'

'Forty-three.'

'My mum's older than that; she's in her fifties, and my dad's ancient. He's going on for sixty. What's the matter?' she asked, alarmed. 'Why did you pull that awful face?'

'I got a twinge in my tummy.' Grace sat gingerly on the end of the bed. 'It really hurt. I hope I'm not coming down with something. It can't be my period, I'm not due yet.'

'Whenever you're ill it starts in your tummy. It might be flu. Loads of people have got flu. Would you like some medicine?' Louise opened the drawer that served as a medicine cabinet. 'We've got Beecham's Powders, cough medicine, aspirin, and some dirty bandage.'

'A Beecham's Powder, please.' Grace had gone quite pale.

'When you've had it, I'll make some tea. I'll put sugar in and it'll help settle your tummy.'

Grace said she felt better after the powder and the tea. Both girls struggled into jeans. Although they adored high heels and lace stockings, the sight only drove some of the male customers to distraction, and the girls were inundated with unwelcome advances. Jeans, training shoes and a loose sweater was not only the most comfortable outfit for a barmaid, but the safest and most sensible too.

They took a taxi to the Green Man – Phyllis had given them the authority – and arrived to find long queues outside the doors. Customers anticipated spending the entire evening there, some getting drunker and drunker until they hardly knew who they were.

Grace and Louise looked at each other and shrugged, then linked arms and marched through the staff door together.

Things were hectic from the minute the doors opened and the customers poured in. Huge crowds formed at the bars. Although the staff worked tirelessly, the crowds never seemed to get smaller. As soon as people were served, more joined the queue, and by the time they had been seen to, the people served first were ready to order again.

Christmas songs blared from loudspeakers overhead, every-one was forced to shout at the top of their voices, the smell of beer was gradually taken over by the smell of perspiration, and numerous sprigs of mistletoe were held over the girls' heads and desperate attempts made to kiss them.

Grace noticed that a rather nice-looking blond chap with an enviable tan had stationed himself in front of Louise and seemed to have no intention of budging.

'He's an American and his name is Gary,' Louise managed to tell her when they were both waiting by the optics for vodka. 'Oh lord, Grace, are you sure you're okay?'

One of the barmen managed to catch her friend before she hit the floor after fainting dead away.

Phyllis called a taxi to take her home. The house in Islington was completely quiet; everyone must be out. Grace removed her jeans and shoes and got into bed. She supposed she could have got in touch with her mother in Soho and asked her to come round, but it hardly seemed fair on Christmas Day. Anyway, Mum would fuss no end and blame the pains on working in a bar, say it was due to the unhealthy atmosphere or something.

Oh, but she would love a hot-water bottle to put on her aching tummy. For the first time she wished she wore pyjamas, as her legs were freezing cold.

'Oh Mum!' She sniffed dejectedly and listened to the silence until eventually she fell asleep.

Louise didn't come home until after three o'clock. It was the sound of the door being unlocked that woke Grace. She looked blearily at the clock and sat up. 'You can put the light on,' she said. 'I'm awake and I'd love a cup of tea.'

But the light didn't go on. Instead, Louise said dully, 'Oh Grace, something terrible has happened. That man, the American, he raped me.'

Chapter 16

Somewhat miraculously, Grace felt better. She didn't exactly leap out of bed, but managed to get out and make her way to the light and switch it on. She led Louise to a chair by the table and sat her down. Next, she filled the kettle and put it on the tiny gas ring. It was important that Louise, and she herself, had tea. Making tea was the first thing her mother did in a crisis.

Leaving the kettle to boil, she went to the table, sat down, and put her arm around her friend's shoulder. 'What happened?' she asked gently.

Louise's tragic face aside, the rest of her was remarkably tidy. Her clothes weren't torn and her hair was only slightly mussed, though she was shaking badly. 'That chap, that Gary,' she said in a rushed whisper. 'He invited me back to his hotel. It was dead posh. We sat in the bar and he bought champagne. I think I drank half the bottle . . .'

'*Louise!* Oh, if only I'd been there.' If she had, they would have come home together. 'Louise, we always swore we would never go out with a chap when our shift was over, not even if he looked like Warren Beatty.' She recalled that the American in the Green Man earlier had been exceptionally attractive.

Louise started to cry. 'He seemed so nice,' she wept. 'After the champagne, I felt quite sick and he took me up to his room. I think I lay on the bed. It must have been the drink that made me fall asleep. When I woke up, I had hardly any clothes on and neither had . . . had he, and I just knew I'd been raped. He'd taken advantage of me, Grace. I was hurting and bleeding.'

The kettle boiled. Grace made two mugs of tea and returned to the table. 'Drink this,' she said, her voice still gentle, but terribly shocked at her friend's behaviour. It really wasn't like Louise to act so irresponsibly. 'Would you like me to telephone the police?' she asked. There was a phone with a coin box down in the hall.

'*No!* Oh God, no,' Louise gasped. 'I'm too ashamed to tell anyone apart from you. I'd sooner die than tell a policeman. Anyroad, I'm still all in one piece. He wasn't rough or anything.' She picked up the tea, and Grace had to help hold it to her lips because her hands were so unsteady.

'Would you like to have a bath? Though the water's not likely to be hot at this hour.'

'No thank you. I'll drink this and get washed in here with a flannel, then go to bed.' There was a sink in the corner. 'I'll take some aspirin, too.' Her voice and her hands were becoming steadier.

Grace fetched the tablets and shook two out of the bottle and another couple for herself. Her tummy had begun to hurt again. She helped Louise out of her clothes and into a nightdress, noting that none of the clothes had been torn. 'How did you get home?' she asked.

'He asked my address and put me in a taxi. He must have paid because the driver didn't ask for money when I got out.'

'Well at least he had the decency to do that.'

Grace helped Louise into bed and tucked the eiderdown around her shoulders. She sat on the edge and stayed until Louise's breathing became steady and she was asleep. Then she got into her own bed, but it was a long time before she fell asleep herself.

Next day, neither girl got up until after midday. Grace made tea, and Louise sat up in bed to drink it. She looked a bit dead-eyed, but that was all. 'I never want to go back to the Green Man,' she said with a shudder. 'That chap could come back again any time – he might even be there tonight.'

'If you'll be all right on your own, I'd like to do my shift tonight, but I'll give my notice in and we'll get jobs in another pub in another part of London.' It was Boxing Day and Grace didn't like letting Phyllis down, not at such a busy period. She didn't feel terribly well, but it was probably due to lack of sleep.

'What if Gary comes here? He knows my address, remember.'

'Yes, but he doesn't know what room you're in. Keep the door locked and I'll be back as soon as I can.'

Phyllis Goddard's office was lined with dark wood and hung with elaborate metal shields and swords with jewelled handles that were actually made out of plastic. Although her age was supposedly fifty, she was rumoured to be well into her sixties. Today, she wore a tiger-print jersey dress stretched tightly over her curvaceous bosom.

She looked up impatiently from behind a beautiful old desk when Grace entered her office, and appeared to be highly annoyed when her barmaid told her she was handing in her notice. 'What about your friend?' She was hopeless with names; understandably, as staff left and new people started by the minute.

'Louise was – well Louise was raped last night.' Quite un-expectedly, Grace burst into tears. 'I'm sorry,' she said, wiping her eyes. 'It's really upset me, but Louise was upset enough herself, I couldn't very well start crying too.'

To her astonishment, Phyllis got up, opened a cocktail cabinet with marquetry doors, and poured a small whisky.

'Here, drink this,' she said kindly. 'And tell me what happened.'

Grace described Louise's experience the night before.

'Stupid girl!' Phyllis snorted. 'I warned the pair of you about doing anything as silly as that when you started. What got into her?'

'I have no idea,' Grace confessed. 'Absolutely no idea.' She'd tried, but couldn't think of an explanation for Louise's behaviour.

'How do you feel?' Phyllis enquired. 'Didn't you faint or something last night?'

Grace nodded. 'I had stomach ache.'

'Is it better?'

'Not really, but,' she added hastily, 'I'm well enough to work my notice out.'

'Well you're not going to.' Phyllis removed a tin cash box from the drawer beside her and took out a handful of notes. 'Here is double pay for this week as promised, but your friend can have her usual wages. I hope for her sake she hasn't caught something disgusting. As for you, you look as pale as a ghost. I am grateful that you are willing to work while feeling ill – not many people would and I appreciate loyalty – but I'd sooner manage without you. If I were you, I'd see a doctor about that stomach of yours.' She shook Grace's hand. 'Just let me know if you need a reference. And good luck.'

William supposed that the best way to describe the Christmas spent with his mother and half-brothers was musical. Apart from when everyone was asleep, music in one form or another filled the house every minute of the day, whether it was from the record player, the wireless, the television or played by Quinn and Kevin with himself rattling a tambourine.

Nell stated quite solemnly that Red would be looking down on them from heaven, tapping his foot or clapping his hands or possibly even playing a sublime fiddle. Her faith was so sure, so rock solid, and so was that of her lads, that William himself almost became convinced that Red was spiritually involved in the proceedings being enacted in his old home on earth.

'He'll be pleased you came to stay with us for Christmas,' Nell said with quiet satisfaction.

William gave her an emotional hug. He wanted to say 'I love you', but felt too embarrassed.

Before returning to London, he felt bound to drop in on his old family in Balliol Road. When he called the day after Boxing Day, the house was deathly quiet. Tom had reopened his surgery after the Christmas break and had been inundated with patients so couldn't be there; Dorothy and Clare, William's former sisters, had gone to the pictures in town, and Iris was in the house alone.

'Hello, William.' Her lips twisted in a tired smile.

'Hello.' He brushed his cheek against hers; it was the least he could do. He felt overcome with guilt: that he hadn't stayed at his old home for Christmas, that it was due to him that Louise had gone to live in London, that he was responsible for breaking up his family. But it was *them,* Iris and Tom, who had betrayed *him*, he reminded himself. It was Iris and Tom who had torn his life apart, so that he didn't know if he was coming or going – or who exactly he was – for quite a long time, though he was all right now; well, more or less.

'How is Addy?' he enquired.

'Poorly,' Iris said with a shrug. 'We went to see her yesterday, but she wasn't up to making anything to eat. Tom thinks she'll have to go in a home quite soon.'

William resolved to stay another night and visit his grandmother in the morning. He'd take her flowers, which reminded him that he had presents in his coat pockets for everyone.

He gave Iris a paperback copy of the latest novel by Margaret Drabble.

'*Jerusalem the Golden!*' she exclaimed. 'I've been longing to read this.' She stroked the front of the book and said to him shyly, 'Fancy you remembering that Margaret Drabble is my favourite author.'

'I doubt if it's something I shall ever forget,' he said with his best smile. After all, she had been his mother for twenty-one years. From another pocket he produced a box of cigars for Tom and fancy pens for Dorothy and Clare.

'I'm sure they'll love them,' Iris said when he told her what the small parcels contained. 'They talk about you all the time, William.'

When he knocked on the door of Addy's house, there was no reply. A woman from across the road came and told him that an ambulance had arrived early that morning and taken Mrs Grant away.

'The people next door have been keeping an eye on her,' she explained. 'She was unconscious when they went in earlier. They called her doctor and it was him who sent for the ambulance.'

Addy was dead by the time William arrived at the hospital.

'Old age,' Tom said gruffly when he and William came face to face. 'She had a good stout heart, but it just got tired of beating.'

Uncle Frank was there − ex-Uncle Frank. William had never liked him − not many people did − but he seemed devastated by his mother's death. They shook hands and he held William close for a few seconds.

'I'll never understand life,' he remarked. 'One morning you wake up and without warning everything has changed. I doubt if I'll ever get used to not having a mother.'

'I remember Adele Grant,' Aunt Kath remarked when William returned to London and told her what had happened. 'She was a really sweet person, ever so kind and quite left-wing without realising it. Are you going to the funeral?'

'If you don't mind me taking the day off, it's next Tuesday.'

'Of course I don't mind. How could I possibly refuse to let you go to a funeral?'

'I still haven't finished searching through your old news-papers for articles that might be relevant some time in the future.' He had developed a complicated filing system so the cuttings could easily be located.

Maggie and Jack threw a party on New Year's Eve. 'Have I ever told you how I met your dad on this day twenty-one years ago?' Maggie asked her daughters before the party was due to start.

Holly groaned. 'You tell us every year, Mum, and at other times too.'

'We're sick of hearing about it,' Grace complained. 'And about the new years you spent in the army.'

'Those memories are very dear to me.' Maggie flounced out of the room in her red chiffon dress.

'She looked like Scarlett O'Hara in *Gone With the Wind* just then,' Louise commented. She was still feeling very down and Grace had spent ages persuading her to come to the party. The Soho contingent would be there, as well as Auntie Kath. Her grandad, of whom she was extremely fond, had been staying upstairs in the spare room over Christmas. Oh, and William was expected; she was looking forward to seeing him. It seemed ages since they'd last met.

Maggie's house reflected her personality, William thought; the decoration and the furniture all slightly over the top. The walls were full of paintings that seemed to have been chosen for their bright colours rather than their content. Cezanne's fruit mingled with Van Gogh's fields and Gauguin's Tahitian beau-ties. Wallpaper dazzled, carpets looked too pretty to walk on, photos in a variety of frames stood on every windowsill and shelf. He had never seen such a voluptuously padded three-piece before, its shapeliness emphasised by the oyster satin material that covered it. Everywhere smelled of perfume. He doubted if Jack had had a say in anything. He had a study somewhere that William would like to bet had sober walls and was full of books.

He went upstairs in search of a lavatory, and on the way back was passing a bedroom when his name was called.

'Louise!' he said with pleasure when he went in and saw the girl who had been his favourite sister sitting on the bed. Grace was seated in front of the dressing table doing something to her hair. She waved at him in the glass.

Louise held out her arms and they embraced. She was only eleven months younger than him, and as small children they had shared baths and even the giant pram they'd been pushed around in.

'How are you, William?' To his surprise, she looked quite tearful. He assured her he was fine. 'It wasn't until I saw you that I realised how much I missed you,' she went on. She clung to his hand and pulled him on to the bed beside her.

'How are *you*?' he asked. There were shadows beneath her eyes and she looked quite drawn. 'Are you looking after yourself, Louise?' he asked angrily. These days his life consisted of worry after worry. 'Are you eating properly? Perhaps it's time you went back to Liverpool.'

Grace turned round to face them. She didn't look all that well herself. 'She's all right. We worked in this really busy pub over Christmas and we're both exhausted. We've left,' she assured him hastily. 'In a few days we'll look for somewhere new.'

'Perhaps you should give bar work a miss,' he suggested. 'It's not a very healthy atmosphere, all that smoke.'

'Perhaps we should.' Grace nodded.

'William! There you are,' Maggie said from the door. 'My dad's downstairs. I thought you'd like to meet him.'

He got up, and she took his hand and squeezed it. 'He doesn't know,' she whispered. 'He'll never know that he's your dad too.'

★

Paddy O'Neill looked young and old; young from a distance, relatively unwrinkled, a full head of iron-grey hair, but close up his watery eyes and rather vague expression were indicative of a genuinely old man.

'This is William, Dad, he works for Auntie Kath,' Maggie said. She pushed William forward, and he and his father touched for the first and only time in their lives. The older man's grip was limp, without any pressure.

'How d'you do, William,' he said warmly. Auntie Kath had said that Paddy was getting too old to be her agent, but he'd have to leave of his own volition; she had no intention of sacking him.

'I'm very well, thank you.'

Auntie Kath approached. 'Will is the best researcher in the House of Commons, Paddy,' she said in a loud voice – she appeared to be incapable of talking in a quiet one.

William managed to escape from the party an hour before the clock struck midnight and 1969 was upon them. He felt very emotional, what with Addy's death and the funeral to come the day after tomorrow, Louise looking so unhappy, and encountering his father for the first time.

He travelled to his flat in Lambeth on the Underground and reached it just in time to hear Big Ben toll in the new year, not on the wireless or television as he had done before, but from across the river, where it could be heard quite clearly. Cheers followed from all directions, fireworks burst into the sky. Unfortunately, William had no alcohol on the premises. He made a mug of tea and held it aloft.

'Happy New Year,' he said to the empty room.

Addy's funeral was a sad, dignified affair with an air of inevitability about it. Unlike Red Finnegan, she hadn't been a young person who'd had her life taken away years too soon. She'd lived happily for more than eight decades; had married a doctor and raised two doctor sons; been greatly loved as a mother and a grandmother. She died because her time had come. Iris said it would have been impossible to have had a more perfect mother-in-law.

Nell attended the funeral. She buried her head in her hands and didn't speak to anyone. It wasn't all that long since she'd buried her husband.

When it was over, William wasn't sure whether to leave with Nell, or go back to Balliol Road for refreshments. In the end, he left alone and caught the train back to London.

Grace collapsed on Tottenham Court Road underground station and was taken to the nearest hospital by ambulance.

She had arranged to meet her mother for lunch in a nearby restaurant. Maggie waited for ages before going home in disgust, calling her daughter all the names under the sun on the way, at the same time feeling just slightly worried. At home, the telephone was ringing and she answered to discover that the Middlesex Hospital had been trying to get in touch for ages. Grace's appendix had burst and she was about to have it out.

After calling Jack, Maggie rushed to the hospital. Grace's bothersome appendix had been removed and she was lying smiling in bed, glad it was all over and apologising for letting her mother down.

'Don't worry about it, luv. As soon as you're better, I'll treat you to lunch somewhere dead posh.' Maggie regretted having called her daughter so many names, even if they had been inside her head. She might have known that Grace would never miss an appointment if it wasn't an emergency.

Grace came home from hospital several days later with a hideous scar on the right side of her stomach.

'I'll never be able to wear a bikini,' she complained bitterly to her mother.

'It'll soon fade,' Maggie said complacently.

'It won't fade altogether, Mum. In fact, I might not be able to get married.'

'Oh, don't be such a silly girl, Grace.' Maggie had already forgotten the silent vow she'd made to treat her daughter with saintly patience from now on. 'In future, only go out with chaps who've had *their* appendix out, and you'll both have scars to match.'

A week later, the two girls started work in Selfridges' restaurant in Oxford Street. The pay was slightly better than in the Green Man, but the tips were not nearly as good. The hours were much better, though, as they worked during the day and had the evenings free to sample clubs, see films and window-shop in the West End, dropping in somewhere beatniky or terribly avant-garde for a coffee afterwards.

This agreeable new life had only existed for four weeks, and they were staring at a mouth-watering display of glamorous evening dresses in Liberty's window when Louise said, 'I've just thought of something: I haven't had the curse for ages.'

'But you're often late,' Grace pointed out.

'I know that, but I'm never so late that I miss a period altogether. I should have started one about mid-January; now it's mid-February.' She looked at Grace, the words hanging in the air between them.

'Oh, Louise,' Grace said weakly. 'What on earth are we going to do now?'

Louise was positive she wouldn't have an abortion. 'There's a living, breathing thing, a little baby, lying all curled up in my womb waiting to be born. I couldn't possibly kill it.'

Grace, a Catholic, couldn't have agreed more. 'Would your mother look after it?' she wondered aloud.

'She might, but she's just gone back to work, hasn't she, after raising four children. Anyroad, how do I explain what happened? They'll want to know who the father is.'

'You know who the father is.'

'Yes, a man I'd met a couple of hours before in a bar, a man who raped me and I haven't seen since.' Louise aimed a kick at Liberty's wall. 'Sometimes I feel really disgusted with myself. Oh, and I don't want it adopted, either. It's my baby and I shall keep it.' She beamed at her friend. 'On reflection, I shall have it and I don't care what anyone thinks or says.'

The weeks passed. Louise was aware of her waist thickening, but otherwise felt perfectly well. 'It's going to be an easy pregnancy,' she announced one day. 'I hope it's an easy birth.'

Grace didn't answer, mainly because she couldn't think of anything to say. It was Sunday afternoon and she was darning tights when the front doorbell rang. She jumped slightly, piercing her finger, when someone knocked loudly on the room door and shouted that they had a visitor. 'He's rather gorgeous, actually,' the someone, a girl who lived downstairs, said.

Louise got to her feet and offered to see who it was. Grace assumed it must be a stranger; friends and relatives knew to give one long ring and two short ones on the bell. She grew more and more surprised after quite a long time had elapsed and Louise hadn't come back. Laying down the tights, she went over to the window and looked out.

Afterwards, she was never sure why she wasn't surprised to see her friend standing by the front door in earnest conversation with the young man she'd met in the Green Man on Christmas Day, the man who had allegedly raped her, who she wasn't beating with both fists and screaming insults at, but speaking to in a perfectly friendly manner. Or slightly more than friendly, the way she had her hand on his arm and the way they were looking at each other so passionately.

Grace picked up her handbag and sped out of the house.

'Grace!' Louise tried and failed to grab her friend as she rushed blindly past.

Half an hour later she was in her parents' house, being

interrogated by her mother. Hadn't it entered her head to comb her hair before coming out? Why was she without coat or cardigan when, although it might well be April, today was extremely chilly?

'Dad,' Grace said desperately, 'will you please tell Mum to shut up.'

'Shush, darling,' her father said mildly, 'and leave our daughter alone.'

Maggie muttered something about Holly having a new boyfriend coming to tea and what on earth would he think of her sister, after which she obediently shut up.

It wasn't until late that night that Grace returned to the flat. She would have waited and gone back in the morning, but it would have meant a relentless third degree from her mother once her father had gone to work.

She found Louise sitting fully dressed on the bed. 'You weren't raped, were you?' Grace said angrily. 'Why couldn't you have told the truth? Why on earth claim to be raped when you weren't?'

'I've no idea,' Louise said dreamily, a sickly expression on her face. 'When it was over, I felt terrible about the whole thing, cheap and nasty. I was a virgin and I'd just lost my virginity to a stranger who I'd fallen in love with at first sight. The thing is, though, it was absolutely wonderful, gentle and romantic and passionate, truly lovely, but I imagined him thinking I was "easy virtue", as they say. When it was over, I just panicked and insisted on leaving.'

'I see,' Grace said, though she didn't. 'Where's he been all this time? And what's happening now?'

'He was on his way home to the States after doing some business in London for his father, but was held up getting a signature on a contract when he found the person had gone away for Christmas. On Boxing Day, he tracked him down, then flew home.'

'And didn't give you a second thought.' Grace threw herself on to the bed, leant against the headboard, and sternly folded her arms.

'He did, actually, lots of second thoughts. But I'd behaved like a lunatic, hadn't I? I mean, when we went into his bedroom, I'd *wanted* him to make love to me, really wanted him to. I'm not sure, I was sozzled at the time, but I might even have initiated it. Then when it was over I had hysterics.'

'So why did he come back?'

Louise sighed, one of those lovely, long, pleasurable sighs that so far Grace had only made when she bit into a particularly scrumptious chocolate. 'Because he couldn't forget me. He could tell it was my first time and understood why I panicked. His name's Gary Dixon, by the way.'

'So what's happening now?'

'We're getting married.'

'When?'

'On Saturday. Gary's getting an emergency licence or something.' Another long, ecstatic sigh. 'Will you be my bridesmaid, Grace?'

It wasn't the path that Grace had imagined their lives would take. She had assumed the two of them would continue to have a good time for the next two or three years without any intention of getting married. The arrival of a baby on the scene had already put a spoke in this vision of a future, but they could have worked alternate shifts and taken turns looking after the baby. Or her mother might have been willing to look after it from time to time; after all, she was on the lookout for a worthwhile job, and it would almost be like working for a charity.

But now, not only was Louise getting married, but she was going to live in America; in Boston, Massachusetts. Her mother, Iris, was telephoning Grace's mother several times a day wanting to know what Gary was like. Where did Louise meet him? How long had they known each other? Did he come from a good family?

'Well I don't know, do I?' Maggie said reasonably to Grace. 'I mean, I haven't set eyes on him, and *you* hardly know a thing about him, so I'm not likely to know anything, am I? I must say, it *is* rather sudden and I feel sorry for Iris, I really do. I hope you don't go off and do something like this.' She paused for breath. 'Thank goodness Holly is getting engaged at Easter and by this time next year she'll be off me and your dad's hands and someone else's responsibility.'

'Am I a responsibility too?' Grace asked, hurt.

'No, of course you're not, luv,' her mother gushed. 'And Holly isn't either. Don't take any notice of me. Most of the time I haven't a clue what I'm saying.'

Gary's parents – or 'folks', as he called them – were unable to travel from Boston for the wedding, and another ceremony would take place there the following week.

Iris and Tom Grant and their two other daughters, Dorothy and Clare, were staying at a hotel in Islington for a few days. They didn't meet their prospective son-in-law and his best man, an old friend from college who lived in London, until the day before the wedding. They all sat through a stiff, uncomfortable meal during which Iris kept trying to start a conversation but no one helped continue it.

Grace didn't go to the meal. She was fed up with the entire situation and couldn't wait for everything to be over. Next day, her mother, unaware that she herself hadn't been invited to the wedding, assumed that she had and managed to stop things falling apart by making a huge amount of noise that covered up the awful silences and other embarrassments.

In the middle of it all, Iris, exhausted from the strain, burst into tears. 'Oh, I can't stand it,' she wailed.

'It'll be all right, old girl,' Tom said, as if he was comforting a dog.

Gary, who was as handsome as that new film star, Robert Redford, looked extremely uncomfortable throughout the brief ceremony.

The atmosphere improved slightly after the wedding, when they went to a restaurant for a meal. It was an expensive place, Gary was paying, and the wine flowed liberally. His father, Gary explained, owned a bank. It had been started by his great-grandfather at the end of the last century and, unlike so many banks, had managed to survive the depression.

At five o'clock Grace decided it was time to go and leave Gary and the Grants to get to know each other. Her mother left with her.

'Me and your dad are going out to dinner tonight – why don't you come with us, love?'

Grace went because she didn't like the idea of being alone. She didn't fancy living in the room in Islington on her own, but she fancied even less finding someone else to share it with.

The following Monday, she acquired a passport application form, completed it, and took it to the office in Victoria where passports could be obtained over the counter rather than waiting weeks for them to come by post. She joined the Youth Hostel Association and studied maps, deciding where to go.

Louise and Gary left for America, to live in his parents' big house in the West End area, the best and richest part of Boston.

'I'll come and visit you when the baby is born,' Grace promised.

'Oh will you? I know I love Gary, but I wish we could have lived in London.' Louise clung tearfully to her friend. 'I feel awful leaving Mum and Dad, my sisters and William. I wonder why he didn't come to the wedding.'

'It was very short notice. Perhaps he had something important to do.' Grace looked tearfully at her friend. 'Goodbye, Lou.'

'Ta-ra, Grace.' The girls embraced and swore it wouldn't be for the last time.

Maggie screamed when Grace announced her plan to hitch-hike as far as France and from there to wherever her spirit might take her.

'Kids! They break your heart,' she wept into Jack's shoulder when her daughter was leaving.

Grace just thought it typical of her mother to behave in such an exaggerated way, but after she'd gone, Maggie cried herself to sleep for weeks, while up in Liverpool Louise's mother was doing the same thing. Fathers might be sad when their children leave, Maggie thought, but mothers feel as if they are losing part of themselves, creating a wound that will never heal.

Chapter 17

The telephone rang at three minutes after eight. Jack, who was about to leave for work, picked up the receiver and reeled off the Kaminskis' number.

'Oh, hello,' he said warmly after a pause. 'And what can I do for you?'

He listened, nodding from time to time, frowning slightly, before telling the caller that he'd look into it that very day and ring back when he came home from work. 'Bye, Nell,' he said, before replacing the receiver.

'Why on earth is Nell calling you?' Maggie said, aware that she sounded unreasonably bad-tempered.

Jack opened the front door. 'Because she wanted to speak to me,' he said. 'Farewell, my darling.' He stepped outside, grinning, and closed the door.

'Huh!' Maggie snorted. She thought about ringing Nell, but it didn't seem right somehow. If her friend had wanted to speak to her, she'd only had to ask.

She went into the kitchen. It was Monday. Mam had always done the washing on Mondays, and Maggie still did, even if it only meant throwing the dirty clothes into the automatic washing machine and switching it on. No more dolly tubs, mangles and having things soaking in bowls for days to get the stains out. If it was raining, the contents were merely trans-ferred to the tumble dryer, a piece of equipment that she used rather more often than she should, including on lovely sunny days when there wasn't a cloud in sight – she loathed hanging washing on the line. The role of women was gradually being sidelined, she thought darkly, though she wouldn't have had it any other way.

In an office in St John's Street, in the centre of Liverpool, Nell Finnegan was peeling onions, a metal spoon clamped between her teeth. It was probably an old wives' tale, but some women swore their eyes didn't water if they held something metal in their mouth while handling onions. Nell had been doing it for years, but still couldn't be sure if it helped.

She spread the chopped onions over the pieces of sirloin steak at the bottom of the large metal casserole dish, added the carrots and a final layer of thick sliced potatoes. She made a gravy of Bisto and various spices, poured it over, put the lid on, and moved the dish out of the way for now. At eleven o'clock, it would go in the oven.

It was nearly ten and time to make a morning drink for the staff of Gregory, Forrester and Turnbull, a firm of solicitors that had practised in Liverpool for almost fifty years. The first Mr Gregory had died before the war and his place had been taken by his son, young Mr Gregory, who was nearly seventy. Mr Forrester only came in on Mondays and Fridays, and Mr Turnbull was in a home for the elderly in Birkdale and not expected to last much longer.

There were other solicitors in the firm who would no doubt appear on the headed notepaper at some time in the future, five altogether, and it was for these gentlemen, plus Mr Gregory and, twice a week, Mr Forrester, that Nell cooked lunch, which they ate in the conference room off a massive oval oak table with claw legs.

It wasn't exactly a taxing job. The hours were nine thirty to four, and all Nell was required to do was make a different type of casserole for each day of the week, followed by a simple pudding of something like stewed apple or pears or fresh fruit trifle.

The second, slightly less important part of her job was to make morning and afternoon drinks for the other staff, twenty-two altogether – secretaries, typists, clerks, and an office boy – and take them round on a tray.

Everyone was terribly grateful and painfully polite. Nell bearing trays of tea and coffee was a welcome sight in their otherwise terribly dull and boring lives. Fridays, she was often presented with flowers and chocolates. Miss Stokes, Mr Gregory's secretary, was knitting her a stole.

Her lads came into the office from time to time to make sure she wasn't being exploited or overworked. It was June, and Kev had already taken his A levels and would leave school soon. Quinn had acquired a part-time job in a supermarket. What with occasional royalties from Red's records and Nell and Quinn's wages, the Finnegans weren't doing at all badly financially.

Once the Finnegan Brothers, as they had decided to call themselves, had launched themselves professionally on to the world, they expected to make their fortune and their ma would never have to work again.

The drinks seen to, the casserole in the oven, Nell made herself a cup of tea, sat on the hard chair in the small, basic kitchen and took out of her apron pocket the letter that had arrived that morning from a film company she'd never heard of in Los Angeles. Cerulean Productions intended making a movie in the near future called *Lost in Paradise* and wished to use the song 'Ode to Nell'. They understood that the composer, Red Finnegan, had died the previous year, and as his next of kin, would she agree to the use of the song. They offered a five-thousand-dollar fee for the privilege and hoped to hear soon that she approved.

If Red were alive he would be so thrilled; over the moon, in fact. She smiled at the thought and remembered the first time he'd sung 'Ode to Nell' to her, in the living room, making the words up as he went along. She closed her eyes, visualising the scene. It would be so easy to cry and get furiously angry at the way he had been taken away from her and his lads, killed by a drunken driver.

The song hadn't done particularly well. She felt a sudden urge to keep it to herself, her and Red's song, but he hadn't written it just for her, but for the world, for everyone who wanted to listen to it.

And the money would come in useful. Five thousand dollars was the equivalent of two thousand five hundred pounds. She could pay off the mortgage so there wouldn't be any more monthly instalments to find.

She wasn't sure why she'd telephoned Jack Kaminski. She assumed that working in a bank he knew all about money. Saying yes to the letter seemed the obvious decision to make, but was it the right one? She fancied some advice first.

Jack telephoned that night, and was of the opinion that saying yes might be a mistake.

'Why?' Nell asked.

'Well, first of all, Nell,' Jack said in his lovely warm voice with only the faintest hint of a foreign accent, 'the bank has a branch in Los Angeles. I phoned an acquaintance there and he advised me that Cerulean Productions are a very prestigious company. They rarely produce more than one picture a year and always get excellent reviews.'

He listed three pictures, but Nell had to admit she hadn't seen any of them. 'Red and I never seemed to have time for the cinema, though I used to love going with Maggie.'

'Anyway,' Jack went on, 'I then talked to someone else here and they said you might be better asking for a share of the profits. If the picture does well, you'd earn massively more than five thousand dollars, though you'd have to wait a while before you got it.'

'And if it doesn't do well?'

'You'll get hardly anything!' It was like a bet, he told her. And it all depended on how much she needed the money. If she was hard up, then accept it, but if she was willing to take the risk . . . 'Think about it, Nell,' he advised. If she took the second option, she would need to get further advice from an accountant who was familiar with the ins and outs of show business. 'I will find the right person for you,' he promised.

'I'll talk to the lads about it,' Nell said. She'd do it straight away.

'Take the chance, Ma,' Quinn said firmly. 'Take the chance, not the money. It's what me da would've done.'

Kev agreed. 'I think so too, Ma. Our da always loved a bet.'

There seemed no more need for discussion. Nell telephoned Jack there and then and told him what they had decided, and he said he would set the ball rolling in the morning.

Half an hour later, Maggie rang. 'Nell, you are not under any circumstances to turn down that money,' she said in a bullying tone. 'I mean, five thousand dollars is a small fortune. Jack doesn't realise just how hard up you are. The advice he gave you was very irresponsible. Don't take any notice of him.'

Nell wasn't prepared for an argument. She informed her friend that she wasn't hard up, that she liked the idea of getting a share of the film's profit, even if turned out to be only a very small one, and she was grateful to Jack for adding a touch of spice and excitement to her rather dull life. 'Ta-ra, Maggie.'

She rang off with a flourish and grinned at her lads. She would probably have to sign one or two things in the future, but they decided not to talk about the matter, not even in passing, until after the film was made.

'How's your son getting on in London, Iris?' Blanche Woods enquired. 'Is he still working for that woman MP?'

'Kathleen Curran. Oh yes,' Iris confirmed. 'We had a letter from him only the other day.' It had been a postcard of the Houses of Parliament, actually, and Iris knew why William had sent it. It meant he didn't have to write 'Dear Mum and Dad' as he would on a letter. He clearly found it uncomfortable associating with the couple who had raised him since he was a few hours old. She smiled and sighed at the same time. Nowadays, she was able to accept the way things had gone with William and her daughter, Louise, without wanting to scream and burst into tears. When Louise's baby was born in September, she and Tom were going to Boston to see their first grandchild.

'Would you like to deal with this customer, or shall I?' she said to Blanche. It was Saturday afternoon and they were in Owen Owen's ladies' coat department, where Iris had worked two days a week, Fridays and Saturdays, for almost a year. It had seemed only fair that she earn some money once the children had grown and she had time to spare, rather than depend for everything on Tom.

'I'll see to her,' Blanche said. 'I like the look of the chap she's with, don't you? He's dead handsome, and I reckon he's much younger than she is.'

Iris glanced briefly at the tall, dark-haired man, elegantly dressed, accompanying the rather dowdy little woman wishing to buy a coat. 'He's not bad,' she muttered. She hadn't been interested in men for a long time.

She wandered away, pretending to tidy a row of jackets, taking the hangers off the rail and shaking the garments, rather than stand looking as if she had nothing to do. She finished the row and caught sight of herself in a mirror. When she'd started looking for work, she'd had her greying hair dyed to its original blonde, lost weight, and bought smarter clothes – including two pairs of high-heeled shoes. She'd actually forgotten how flattering high heels were, and the lovely feeling she got from wearing them with gleaming silk stockings.

She smoothed the black material of her skirt over her hips and adjusted the collar of her white silk blouse, pleased with her reflection.

'Is it just a coincidence,' a voice said, 'or do you spend most of your time in this shop?'

In the mirror, she saw that the dark-haired man was watching her with admiration. Closer up, she could see that his hair was sprinkled with silver. 'What do you mean?' She had no idea what he was talking about.

'When we last spoke, it was in this shop, in the restaurant, actually.' He shook his head. 'Oh no it wasn't. We last spoke in the waiting room of your husband's surgery. You set the police on to me – or is that putting it a trifle coarsely? The police came to see me on your behalf. There, that sounds better.'

'Captain Williams!' She hoped she didn't look as shocked as she felt. She couldn't remember his first name.

'It was Major, actually.'

She wasn't going to apologise, not for anything; certainly not for setting the police on to him, as he put it. 'I'm surprised you've got the cheek to speak to me,' she said tartly. 'I'm sure most people would sooner forget they'd behaved so despicably, not remind someone about it after so many years.' She saw that Blanche was helping the woman he was with, presumably his wife, into a bright red coat that didn't remotely suit her.

'Just now, when I saw you,' he said, 'my first impulse was to run a mile.'

'Why didn't you?'

'Because I had a second impulse, and that was to say how sorry I was. You're right, I behaved despicably. You wouldn't believe the times I've thought about it and felt ashamed.' He genuinely did look mortified. 'I was a total cad, a complete mess. I'd had a hard time during the war, not that I'm complaining about it,' he said hastily, 'but when I arrived home my wife had left me for my brother and I no longer had a house. I think I might already have told you that. I couldn't get work. I was desperate. I was turned down for the job I'd come to Liverpool to be interviewed for, came across you in the restaurant here and saw you as an answer to my prayers.'

'You saw blackmail as an answer to your prayers,' she reminded him.

His face flushed and he literally hung his head. She suspected he was genuinely sorry, but she still had no intention of forgiving him. What he had done, tried to do, had been truly vile. 'Your wife wants to speak to you. I think she would like your opinion on her coat. I thought the black one looked best on her,' she added. The woman looked dumpy in the red coat, which she was trying on for the second time. Blanche, a ruthless saleswoman, was probably trying to talk her into it because it was considerably more expensive than the black and she'd earn a higher commission.

'I haven't got a wife. The lady's name is Sarah Holmes and she's my housekeeper.'

He went over and spoke to the woman. She removed the red coat and put on the black. He nodded approvingly, produced a chequebook, and the coat was folded and put in an Owen Owen's carrier bag. Iris noticed that his lightweight cream jacket held a hint of silk and his trousers were linen, very well cut. He returned to her. 'She has been my housekeeper for over twenty years,' he said. 'The coat is a sixtieth birthday present. We are now about to have tea in the Adelphi.' He smiled, and she remembered noticing what an attractive blue his eyes were even though he had been in the process of trying to get money off her in such an appalling way. 'You see, it turned out to be a good thing I came to Liverpool all those years ago. That night in the hotel, I met a chap about to open a garage in Southport selling antique and vintage cars. He took me on as manager and I have never looked back since. When he retired, I bought the place off him. We remain the greatest of friends. After that meeting, I had no intention of calling on you again on the Monday as I had said I would.'

'As you had *threatened* you would,' she reminded him.

His lips twisted. 'As I said, I'm sorry. Could I possibly take you to dinner sometime and plead for your forgiveness?'

'I will never forgive you,' Iris said flatly. 'Never.'

She thought about him frequently over the weekend, though she hadn't wanted to. He had been shut out of her mind years ago and she was cross that he had re-entered. She was even more cross that the memories weren't of his blackmailing activities, but of the times in the army when they had made love. He had been a gentle, thrilling lover. Afterwards, he had held her for a long time in his arms, stroking her face, kissing her softly, touching her again, making her come over and over. He had been perhaps the best of the numerous men she had made love with in the hope of conceiving a child. His name, she recalled eventually, was Matthew.

Thinking about it now, all these years later, Iris caught her breath. It was so long since she and Tom had made love, and by the end it had become more irritating than enjoyable. She had lost interest, and it was only now she realised what she was missing.

On Monday, Tom's receptionist telephoned Iris at her house in Balliol Road. Nicola was twenty-one and planning to get married the following year.

'Mrs Grant,' she said brightly. 'There's a chap with a gorgeous bunch of red roses on his way to see you. He thought you still lived here, but I told him you'd moved. He should be there any minute. He's driving a super royal blue Jaguar. He said the flowers were to thank you for looking after his housekeeper in Owen Owen's the other day.'

'Thank you, Nicola,' Iris said faintly. The message was an

313

innocent one, nothing to raise suspicion if Tom had heard it and they had still been a proper man and wife. She hadn't looked after his housekeeper, but only the two of them knew that.

She replaced the receiver and stood in the hallway of the quiet house. The girls were out; she wasn't expecting visitors. Her heart was beating frantically in her chest. He had referred to himself as a cad, yet a cad wouldn't buy his housekeeper a coat and take her to tea at the Adelphi.

He had badly wanted to apologise for his behaviour all those years ago. After a whole weekend thinking about little but him, how could she possibly refuse to accept his apology – or the roses!

The house in Beacon Hill, Boston, where the Dixons lived must have contained at least twenty rooms. Every piece of expensive furniture looked as if it had been made especially for its place against the wall, or in its own special corner, or underneath one of the beautiful curved stained-glass windows with their silk or velvet fully lined, deeply frilled curtains. Iris admired it, but wouldn't have wanted to live there. It would have felt like living in a museum. There was nothing warm or homely about it.

It was the nursery that she particularly disliked. It was too white, there was too much lace, the century-old crib was too fussy by a mile. It was the sort of nursery a little girl would like for her favourite doll, not a real live baby, not Iris and Tom's handsome little grandson George.

'How our Louise stands that woman, I do not know,' Iris said to Tom in their ornate green-themed bedroom on the second floor – she'd asked Louise to make sure that they had single beds.

'That woman' was Monica Dixon, Louise's mother-in-law, a small, quiet woman with a will of iron who dominated the house and everyone in it. Iris had actually been rebuked, albeit quietly, for picking George up out of his frothy crib in his frothy gown even when he was wide awake and in need of company. He might only be a fortnight old, but Iris could tell he wanted to be held in someone's arms and be told in a gooey voice what a smart little chap he was. She had always believed that babies should be fed on demand and never under any circumstances be left to cry themselves to sleep when they badly wanted a cuddle, as had happened with George.

'Louise seems to get on with Monica all right,' Tom commented. 'Have you spoken to her about it?'

'I don't like to, Tom. I don't want her to know that we detest the woman. After all, we're going back home. Louise has to live here. You'd never think she was George's mother. Monica has completely taken over.'

'Is there any suggestion of her and Gary getting their own house?' Tom asked.

'Not that I've heard,' Iris said darkly. She powdered her nose and combed her hair in the dressing table mirror and they left the room.

The carpets were like thick velvet. A woman dressed plainly in grey with beautiful blonde hair was standing outside a door on the floor below. As they approached, she put her hand on the gleaming brass knob. The gesture was to stop them going in. The door was to the nursery and the woman was Monica Dixon, who looked young from a distance but was deeply wrinkled close up. Iris was overcome with a feeling of deep loathing.

'Louise is feeding baby,' Monica said in her odd, expressionless voice. 'Please don't go in.'

Iris had several answers to this request. We are Louise's parents, she wanted to scream. Tom is a doctor and it's perfectly all right for him to see his daughter breastfeeding. If we were at home, Louise would be feeding George in the living room surrounded by the entire family. Oh, and George is *our* first grandchild too. You are a bitch, Monica, and I hate you.

But she didn't say a word. Tom said politely, 'Good morning,' and Iris echoed it with a smile that she hoped couldn't be read as a grimace. They made their way downstairs to the breakfast room, where the food was laid out on a side table: eggs, hash browns, ham, toast, fresh tomatoes, a pot of coffee, a jug of orange juice and a bowl of assorted tea bags. If they wanted pancakes, all they had to do was ring the bell and Alma, the lovely black woman who worked in the kitchen, would come and take their order.

Louise and George apart, Alma was the only normal human being in the house. Gary, Louise's husband, had seemed quite a nice young chap at the wedding in London, but he was in fact in thrall to his mother, her willing slave, and would do anything in his power to please her. His father, Mervyn, was just as obedient. There was a daughter, Roberta, at university, and another son, Hank, who managed the New York branch of the bank. There was also a grandfather who they had yet to come face to face with and who had so far only been seen at a distance in the garden.

Iris had imagined the Dixons' bank to be a small operation, but she had been amazed by the size of the impressive building in Custom House Street with its beautiful marble floors. If it hadn't been for Monica, she would have considered her daughter had fallen on her feet by marrying Gary Dixon.

'The Dixons must be millionaires,' she said to Tom.

He contradicted her. 'You mean multi-millionaires.'

A beaming Alma entered the room when Tom rang. 'What can I get you folks?' she said cheerfully.

'Some of your delicious pancakes with syrup.' Tom patted his stomach. 'I'll be a stone heavier by the time we get home.'

'I'd like just one pancake, Alma.' Iris was watching her figure.

'What shall we do today?' Tom asked when Alma had gone.

They'd been there three days, and Monica had made no attempt to entertain them. They usually went sightseeing by themselves. Once Louise had taken them shopping, but George had been left at home and she'd missed him.

Boston was a beautiful city, steeped in history, particularly attractive in autumn with the fallen leaves dancing in the breeze. So far, they had visited the site of the original Boston Tea Party, been on a sunset cruise, and visited the Old State House.

Monica entered the room. 'What are you two doing with yourselves today?' she asked briskly.

'We might go on a walking tour of the city,' Iris said on the spur of the moment.

'That's a good idea. We are having guests this evening for dinner, so don't tire yourselves out.'

'We won't,' Iris promised.

'I have appointments for most of the day, so won't be around.' She left the room with a brief smile, just as Alma came in with the pancakes.

'I suggest,' Iris said in a low voice, 'that once madam has gone, we take Louise and George out with us. He must have a pram and there are bound to be parks where we can take him. We can stop for coffee and even have lunch somewhere.'

George's giant pram was in the triple garage, the bedding in the nursery. Louise seemed keen on the idea of taking him out, and once everything had been put together, they left the house.

'This feels very strange,' Louise said from behind the pram. She was clutching the handles nervously.

'Haven't you and George been out together before?' Iris asked.

'Monica's worried he'll catch a cold.' Louise tucked the little eiderdown further around the baby's shoulders.

'But the weather's lovely and mild.'

'I know, Mum. And I know Monica's a bit of a fusspot, but she means well.'

'George is your baby, love, not Monica's. It's up to you whether he goes out or not.' At this, Tom dug his elbow into Iris's side. Shut up, he was saying. Don't turn her against the woman. Iris obediently shut up, and Louise either didn't hear what her mother had said, or affected not to.

The morning was pleasant. They strolled around Boston Common, and Louise lifted George out of his pram and showed him what grass and trees looked like, and that was the sky overhead and the sun over there, and there was a little white dog sniffing the wheels of his pram. Tom chased the dog away before he weed on one of the front wheels. He fetched coffee in cardboard cups from a refreshment stall, and later they had lunch on the way home in an open-air restaurant where quite a few people stopped to admire the baby.

Later, Louise looked worried. 'I hope they didn't breathe germs on him.'

'He's a baby, love, not a rare flower,' said Tom, the doctor. 'If no one's allowed to breathe on him, he'll grow up without any resistance to germs and start catching things at the drop of a hat.'

Once again, Louise didn't answer. Iris said, 'Remember what I was like, Tom, when we had babies? It upset me taking them for walks and people sticking their heads under the hood of the pram to have a look.' She squeezed Louise's hand and nudged Tom to shut up. It was her turn to warn that it was no use frightening their daughter. If she wanted to stay on good terms with her mother-in-law, it'd be best not to argue and just let the awful woman have her own way.

Next day, Iris and Tom went to lunch in Macy's department store in Washington Street. It was busy, noisy and full of tantalising smells. They ordered ravioli from the pasta stall and a tiny bottle of red wine each. They listened to the other customers discussing their problems, their marriages, their clothes, their health, all sounding much more interesting

318

when related in an American accent. They smiled at each other.

Iris thought what a nice relationship she had with Tom these days; they could actually sleep in the same room together without sex, without arguing and without embarrassment. She loved him as much as she would have done a brother or a best friend.

Tom must have been thinking along the same lines. 'Would things have ended up between us this way if Charlie hadn't died?' he mused aloud.

Iris shrugged. 'Who can say? Do you realise that if he'd lived, Charlie would have been thirty this year?'

'I hadn't forgotten.' He looked at her searchingly. 'You look so much better since you met that chap, ten years younger and quite beautiful.'

'Thank you.' She'd told him about Matthew and their affair, but hadn't mentioned their previous relationship. She'd met him in Owen Owen's and had known him slightly in the army was all she'd said.

'Are you likely to want a divorce one of these days?'

'Oh, no.' She finished her wine. Although there hadn't been much of it, she felt quite heady. 'It's an affair, not a marriage.'

It was a very passionate affair. They met in hotels and occasionally in the house in Balliol Road if Dorothy and Clare were out. They were in love, and what made it so utterly perfect was that she was fifty-three and he was two years older. It added piquancy to it, like old wine, the discovery of something unexpectedly precious at an age when making love with such sublime delight she had assumed was long over.

Back at the Dixons' house, Monica was out and Louise and her parents were in the garden with George and Gary's grandfather, Leonard, who was eighty and had fought in the First World War. He'd retired from the bank twenty years before. He kept them entertained with tales of how things had been in Boston early in the twentieth century. It was all really fascinating, and Alma brought them tea and made a small stack of pancakes especially for Tom.

All too soon it was time to return to Liverpool. Tom had engaged a locum to look after his practice, and Iris was worried about what Dorothy and Clare might be getting up to in the house on their own. She imagined wild parties and the place being wrecked.

Oh, but it was a wrench leaving Louise and George behind. Although her daughter hadn't shown it, she strongly suspected she wasn't happy living with her husband and his family.

And how old would George be before they saw him again? It was silly, but she imagined Monica Dixon having him dressed like Little Lord Fauntleroy in a velvet suit with a lace collar. She felt a lump come to her throat.

They were due to leave at half past three in the afternoon, and were having breakfast, Tom eating the last of Alma's pancakes, when the doorbell chimed – the chimes were similar to Big Ben. One of the maids must have answered it – Monica had gone to the hairdresser's. There was silence for a little while, then a scream from Louise.

'Grace! Grace Kaminski. Oh, am I pleased to see you.'

It turned out that Grace had worked her way across the Atlantic as a waitress on a cruise boat. She had then hitch-hiked to Boston from New York. In her jeans and checked shirt she looked bronzed and healthy and was smiling broadly. She smiled even more broadly when she discovered Iris and Tom were there.

'I promised Louise I would come and visit the baby when he was born,' she said. 'No way was I going to let her down.'

'I'm so glad you're here,' Iris said emotionally. At least Louise would have company for another few weeks, or however long Grace intended staying.

'It doesn't seem so bad leaving her and George behind when Grace is there, does it?' she said to Tom that afternoon in the taxi.

'No.' Tom sniffed and looked quite tearful. 'Monica didn't look all that pleased to see her; Grace, that is.' Monica had deigned to come back to say goodbye to the visitors and found Grace there.

'Grace won't care,' Iris said tersely. 'As for Monica, she can go and jump in the lake.'

It was late. Everyone in the house was asleep apart from Louise. Beside her, Gary lay as still as a log, breathing evenly. He rarely woke during the night. Louise slid carefully out of bed, as she did every night, and crept along the corridor to the nursery. She opened the door and went in. It terrified her every time she looked at her baby asleep in his crib. He was so still and white and she was fearful that he had died, all alone and motherless.

She pulled a chair up to the crib and sat beside it, holding her son's tiny hand, whispering a lullaby. *'Rock-a-bye baby, in the treetop, When the wind blows, the cradle will rock . . .'*

She stayed for half an hour, then kissed his cheek, sighed, and left the room. But instead of returning to her own bed to lie beside Gary, she went up a flight of stairs to a room next to the one where her mum and dad had slept. Knocking softly on the door, she went in.

'Grace,' she said in a low voice.

Her friend woke up instantly. 'What's wrong? Are you all right?'

'No,' Louise said hoarsely. 'I am not all right. I'm desperately unhappy, more than I've ever been in my entire life. Oh Grace, you've got to help me get out of here before I go stark raving mad.'

Chapter 18

It wasn't until she was on the crowded train into town that Nell had time to open the letter with the London postmark that had come that morning.

It was a cutting from an American show-business magazine attached to a compliment slip from Jack Kaminski with a message in Jack's incredibly neat writing.

Thought you might find this interesting, Nell. I wonder if this is the one with Red's song and they've changed the title from Lost in Paradise?

The interesting bit had been circled in red and it announced that the film company Cerulean Productions would shortly commence work on a movie called *Raining Flowers*, starring one-time matinee idol Hugo Swann and newcomer Naomi Vaughan. The company hadn't revealed any more details.

Nell's lips curled into a delighted smile. She'd always loved Hugo Swann. Putting aside Red coming back to life, she couldn't think of anything more wonderful to look forward to than a picture starring one of her favourite film stars and featuring her beloved husband's music.

In London, Maggie Kaminski faced the morning with a vinegary smile. The night before, their elder daughter Holly had informed her mother and father that she was getting married at Easter next year to Dennis Walker.

'But we don't want a big fuss,' she said in the hoity-toity

voice she used sometimes. 'What Dennis and I would prefer is that instead of spending loads of money on the wedding, you give it to us for a deposit on a house.'

'And how much are Dennis's parents coughing up towards this house?' Maggie had demanded in the hoity-toity voice she sometimes used herself. She didn't like Dennis, or his family. They were ordinary people who'd made loads of money with a couple of cheap furniture shops and had lost touch with their roots. Maggie was working class and proud of it.

'It's the bride's family who traditionally pay for the wedding reception and stuff,' Holly informed her.

'But not for the house. That is considered the job of the husband, who earns the money by going to work.'

Maggie half listened to Holly's reply and decided she couldn't be bothered arguing further. Later, she went to bed and read until Jack came up. 'What she doesn't seem to realise,' she said at once, 'is that *I* want a big do, even if she doesn't. *I* want her to have a posh dress and posh cars and millions of flowers. *I* want a slap-up sit-down meal at the reception with loads of guests. What do we do, Jack, show them a photo of the bloody house instead? I suppose we could have a house-shaped cake.'

'What we can do, darling,' Jack said patiently, 'is have a posh do with all the trimmings for you, and give Holly money as well. We can afford it, don't worry.'

'It doesn't seem right.' Maggie smouldered. 'I'll only agree to give her money if Dennis's mum and dad put up a similar amount. I don't want those horrible people sponging off us.'

She was still smouldering the following morning. It didn't help when a letter with an airmail sticker dropped on to the mat. It had been written three days ago by her other daughter, Grace, who had arrived in Boston.

Louise has had a gorgeous little boy called George, she wrote. *But she also has this absolutely monstrous mother-in-law.* She went on to describe the beautiful house, finishing, *Mr and Mrs Grant were there when I arrived, but flew home the same day.*

'Children!' Maggie spluttered to her own empty house. Poor Iris, having her daughter and first grandchild living thousands of miles away. In fact, she'd give Iris a call, sympathise with her. She recalled having resolved never to speak to Iris again after learning what had happened with Nell and William. There and then she decided to forgive her. Anyroad, she'd gone to Louise's wedding and she and Iris had spoken to each other normally then. It was a long, long time since William had been born, more than twenty-two years.

Another thing, Maggie was fast running out of friends to chat to, either in person or on the telephone. The members of the ex-servicewomen's club had moved away or just lost touch. Same with the Soho contingent, the younger ones having moved out to the suburbs or even further afield. Nell was at work, Rosie, her sister-in-law, was also working. And she may as well not have a sister for all she saw of Bridie.

Maggie dialled Iris's number and sat on the stairs prepared for a long jangle. There was no reply, and she recalled that it was Friday, one of the days Iris worked in Owen Owen's. It reminded her that she still hadn't found a job herself. Life would be considerably less boring if she had somewhere to go a few times a week. She decided to ring Auntie Kath and suggest they have lunch, and telephone Iris on Monday.

William answered. 'She's at a committee meeting,' he said. He seemed extremely fed up.

'Are *you* free for lunch,' Maggie enquired. He was, after all, her half-brother, and it was time they became better acquainted.

'Why not?' he said tiredly. 'Where shall we meet?'

She recalled the hotel not far from Westminster where Jack had taken her the magic night he'd proposed. They'd just come away from seeing Auntie Kath. 'What about the Meredith?'

'Isn't that very expensive?' William sounded alarmed.

'My treat,' Maggie said. 'Anyroad, it would hardly be fair to invite you to lunch and expect you to pay, would it?'

'No, it wouldn't.'

It turned out that William was genuinely fed up. Auntie Kath hadn't exactly sacked him, but she had suggested he find another job. 'She said it was for my own good, as it was time I got a proper job with a proper wage.'

'Is she right?' Maggie asked.

'Well, yes,' William said gloomily. 'I've worked as a researcher for Kath for a year and it will look good on my CV, but it wouldn't do to stay too long or it will start to look bad, show I have no ambition, no "get up and go", as she put it. Trouble is, I have neither of those things.' He sighed deeply. 'If it were up to me, I'd stay with Kath until I retired. But the pay's lousy. My gran – the person I'd always thought was my gran – left me a bit of money when she died last year, but it won't last for ever, will it?'

'No,' Maggie agreed. She studied his handsome features. He had the O'Neills' good looks and Nell's lovely brown eyes. She felt as if she were seeing him properly for the first time, that it was only now she truly appreciated how lost he must feel; one minute the much-loved son of a close family with three sisters, then all of a sudden entirely on his own. She'd heard from Grace that he rarely went home to Bootle. He had no father to ask advice from about his future. Nell must love him, but she already had Quinn and Kev and their futures to think of.

The waiter arrived with the starters. 'You must come to dinner one night soon,' she told William. Jack would be only too willing to advise him about his career. Just discussing things with someone else might help him make up his mind. 'Oh, and I had a letter from Grace this morning. She's in Boston. Did you know Louise has had her baby, a little boy called George?'

'No, I didn't.' He brightened up slightly. 'Will you let me have the address in Boston and I'll send a card. And something for the baby. Louise was always my favourite sister,' he said wistfully. 'I miss her.'

Maggie put her hand over his. 'I'm sure she'd love to hear from you. And although she's no longer your sister, you don't love her any less, do you?'

William looked thoughtful. 'I've probably really hurt her. And Dorothy and Clare. They don't know about this other stuff, do they? I mean about me being adopted. They must think it's a case of . . . how do you put it?'

'Out of sight, out of mind?'

'Yes, that's it. Yet I think about them all the time.'

'Then write to Louise and go and see Dorothy and Clare.' Iris and Tom would be thrilled to see him too. Crikey, she thought, life wasn't half complicated.

Iris left Owen Owen's through the staff door only minutes after the shop had closed. She hurried around the corner and met Matthew outside the Cups, a small pub in Williamson Square. Tall and devastatingly attractive, he was moving im-patiently from one foot to the other. He picked her up and kissed her hard and greedily before they went inside, where he ordered her a gin and lime and a whisky for himself. They sat in a corner, just looking at each other and holding hands. It was the first time they'd met since she and Tom had returned from Boston. It was now seventeen days since they'd seen each other.

'How are your daughter and her baby?' he asked. Iris could tell he was only being polite, that he really wanted to tell her how much he'd missed her and hear her say the same to him.

She told him about Louise and George, about the house on Beacon Hill, and Monica Dixon. 'She's a dreadful woman,' she said. 'Of course, now Tom and I are really worried about our daughter.'

She'd forgotten he didn't like her mentioning Tom. A few times he'd tried to talk her into getting a divorce so that they could get married, but she'd refused to discuss it. She had no intention of breaking up her family.

'I missed you terribly,' he said huskily. He put his finger beneath her chin and raised her face so they could kiss.

'And I missed you,' she assured him. She was longing for them to make love. Some nights they didn't bother having a drink, going straight to the hotel instead because they couldn't wait to be in bed together. This seemed to be one of those nights.

'I thought about you all the time,' he whispered. 'It was strange, but I kept thinking of when we were in the army and we made love in the back of your car. It was the best I'd ever known, far better than with my wife.' He frowned slightly and said almost petulantly, 'You had quite a reputation. I suppose I was just one in a long line of lovers.'

'You are the only one I remember,' she said. It wasn't strictly true, but he'd been the best. She decided to tell him the truth, why she'd allowed so many men to make love to her. 'Before I joined up, I lost a baby. Tom and I tried, but I never had another. That's why I slept around, as it's called. I was trying to get pregnant.'

He thought about this for a while, before saying, 'But you eventually did?'

'William, our eldest, is adopted. By then, the war was over and Tom and I managed to have three daughters of our own.'

'I see.' He leaned forward and kissed her on the forehead, running his hand through her hair. 'You are a remarkable woman, Iris Grant, and I can't wait to make love to you. I have booked us a room in The Temple hotel by the Town Hall. I suggest we leave this very minute and get a taxi there.'

Iris finished her drink in a single swallow. She couldn't wait either.

★

His car, the blue Jaguar, had been left in St John's car park. They strolled towards it after leaving the hotel at ten, exhausted from lovemaking, but deliriously happy too. He drove her home and dropped her at the top of Balliol Road. Neither said much on the way. Iris rested her head on his shoulder. She was already thinking about tomorrow, Saturday, when the same pattern would be repeated. She told him she preferred them not to waste time by going to the pub first.

Matthew said he couldn't agree more. He would reserve a room at the Temple and meet her there instead. 'I shall have a bottle of champagne on ice waiting for you.'

She went into the house expecting it to be completely quiet – Dorothy had gone to her friend Rachel's house with the intention of staying the night, and Clare to the hen party of a girl she worked with who was getting married tomorrow. She wasn't expected home until late. But Iris could hear Dorothy's distressed voice coming from the living room followed by Tom's quiet one.

Dorothy, it appeared, had arrived at Rachel's only to find she had started her period a day early. She usually had very heavy periods. Neither she nor Rachel had a sanitary towel, all the chemists were closed, and as Rachel lived quite close, she returned home for a towel.

'But then she fainted,' Tom said, 'in the bathroom, and banged her head on the rim of the bath. When she came to, she managed to crawl downstairs and ring me. She's hurt her knee really badly too.'

'I'm going to have a horrible bruise, Mum.' Dorothy touched the pink swelling above her right eye. She was lying on the settee with Tom sitting beside her. Her knee was heavily bandaged. The room reeked of disinfectant. 'I thought you'd be in,' she said accusingly to her mother. 'Where on earth were you?'

'I've been to the theatre with Blanche,' Iris lied. She'd

become best friends with Blanche Woods, or so she told her girls, to explain away the time she spent with Matthew. She and Blanche often visited the theatre together or went for a meal after work. Her children had grown up aware that their parents didn't live together, but she knew they would be upset if they discovered she was going out with another man. Tom was always there when they needed him. He no longer showed a preference for William over his daughters.

'I'll make a hot drink.' Minutes later, she returned with three cups of tea. She gave one to her daughter. 'There's two heaped spoons of sugar in there. It should make you feel better.'

'I'm worried she's anaemic,' Tom said. 'I'll give her a blood test next week.'

'I won't go to work tomorrow.' Iris didn't like letting people down, but Dorothy couldn't be left on her own all day in the state she was in, and Clare would be going to the wedding.

'I haven't got surgery in the morning. I'll look after her.'

'It's all right, Tom.'

'There's no need to fight over me.' Dorothy chuckled. For all her injuries, she seemed in a very good mood. She was the most easy-going of the Grants' daughters. Louise was over-sensitive, Clare demanding, but Dorothy had always been very laid-back. Perhaps, just now, she was enjoying being made a fuss of. 'I'll manage on my own.'

Tom said she'd do no such thing. 'You might have difficulty walking when you get up. No, your mother will go to work and I'll come and read you some of those super Enid Blyton books you had when you were little. I've noticed they're still around. I really miss those books. I think I enjoyed them more than you girls did.'

Early next morning, Iris telephoned Matthew at home to say she couldn't meet him that night. Sarah Holmes, his housekeeper, answered. 'He's gone to Chester for the day.' It appeared there was to be an auction of old cars at the home of Lord Something-or-other.

'Will you please tell him Mrs Grant won't be able to meet him as arranged and I'll telephone on Sunday?'

'Yes, Mrs Grant, I'll do that.'

At work, Iris found herself far more worried about her daughter than she was about missing her date with Matthew. Why had she fainted? It was worrying. Even in the army, living among hundreds of women, she'd never known one to faint because of a period. *Feel* faint, yes, but not drop unconscious to the floor. Hopefully it was just anaemia as Tom had suspected, and all their daughter needed was a course of iron tablets.

Even travelling home on the train rather than catching a taxi down to the Temple where Matthew would have been waiting with a bottle of champagne, she found she wasn't exactly bothered. In fact, she would sooner see Dorothy than her handsome, passionate lover. She couldn't love him as much as she'd thought, she concluded. Or it was a case of loving him with her body, whereas Dorothy she loved with all her heart and soul, as she did all her children.

Her daughter looked pale when she went in, but still managed to sound cheerful. Tom was in the kitchen making tea.

'Did your father seriously read you the Enid Blyton books?' Iris enquired.

'He read all three of the *Faraway Trees* and both *Wishing Chairs*,' Dorothy confirmed, 'and some *Mr Meddles*.'

'Silly idiots, the pair of you,' Iris said fondly.

Tom came in with drinks. 'We had a lovely time,' he commented. 'Very nostalgic.' He glanced at her. 'Are you going out tonight?'

'Of course not. I wouldn't dream of going out again and

leaving Dorothy. What about you? Are you and Frank going for a drink?' He sometimes went to the pub at weekends with his brother.

'I wouldn't dream of leaving Dorothy either. I suggest we ring that rather nice Indian restaurant in Stanley Road and order a takeaway, then sprawl on the settee and watch television. It's a very unhealthy way of spending the evening, but it won't hurt for once.'

'Goody!' Dorothy rubbed her hands. 'I love curry.'

Matthew telephoned just after nine the next morning. 'What happened?' he snapped. 'I sat in that hotel for nearly an hour, unsure whether you were coming or not. It so happened I called home about something and Sarah said you'd left a message. That was pretty sudden, wasn't it? Why couldn't you have let me know sooner?'

'It was very early when I phoned. Sarah said you'd gone out for the day; that you wouldn't even be at work. I wasn't to know you'd go straight to the hotel, was I?' Poor Matthew! She felt upset at the idea that he'd been sitting there waiting for her to arrive. 'I'm so sorry,' she said, filled with remorse. 'I'd have phoned the Temple if I'd known you hadn't got my message.'

'I know you would,' he conceded. 'Look, when can I see you again?' His voice dropped. 'I love you, you know, but you spent a whole fortnight with your other daughter. I was really looking forward to last night.'

'So was I.' Yet she'd had a very nice night without him. Dorothy had sat between her and Tom, shoulders touching, while they watched television. Clare had come home from the wedding with a hilarious tale about an aunt who'd got drunk and done a genuine striptease. It had only needed William and Louise to be there and the evening would have been perfect.

She didn't like to suggest to Matthew that they leave it until Friday before they met again. 'Can you take a few hours off on

Tuesday afternoon and we can meet in the Temple?' He had an assistant in his garage.

'Yes,' he said eagerly. 'That would be wonderful.'

He told her again how much he loved her and they rang off.

On Friday night, William was in a cinema in Leicester Square watching a very dull picture with a very dull friend from the House of Commons. Douglas Meredith was possibly the most tedious chap alive, obsessed with detail, never using one word when three, four or even five would do.

The picture finished, Douglas began to dissect it frame by frame, droning on and on as they left the cinema. William knew he would continue in the same dreary voice when they went to the pub or for a coffee. He decided he couldn't stand it another minute and made an excuse that he was expecting a telephone call from the United States and had to rush home straight away. 'It's from my sister, she's in Boston,' he explained.

'You've never mentioned you had a sister,' Douglas remarked. He was incapable of sounding surprised.

'I have three, old man.' They shook hands and William hurried back to his flat in Lambeth. He'd sooner talk to himself than Douglas. And although it had been a lie that he was waiting for a call, he'd actually heard from Louise in Boston only the other day.

After sending her a card and a teddy bear for George, she'd telephoned him in his flat late one evening. She'd thanked him for the things. 'We seem to have lost touch over the last year,' she said. 'You went off to London and forgot all about us, Mum and Dad too. What's more, William Grant,' she said accusingly, 'you didn't come to my wedding.'

'I'm sorry, I've been frantically busy.' William felt awful. In fact, he couldn't remember having received an invitation. He changed the subject. 'How's married life?'

'Not so hot, bruv,' she said unexpectedly.

He was slightly shocked. 'But someone told me,' he couldn't remember who, 'that you'd fallen madly in love with this chap.'

'Oh, I did, I did,' she assured him. 'Trouble is, his slavish attitude to his horrid mother has completely put me off him. He loves her more than he does me.'

'Oh, Louise.' He wished he'd known before, not that there was anything he could have done about it. 'You must feel very lonely over there.'

'Grace Kaminski is here. She stayed at the house for a while, then got a job in a diner and went to live in a hostel. We manage to see each other every day. Anyroad, William, I'd better ring off. I'd like to bet that Monica, my blessed mother-in-law, goes through the phone bill with a fine-tooth comb and I'll be told to go easy if she finds I've spent ages tele-phoning England.'

The news that Louise was unhappy had upset him, but at least he felt slightly engaged with his family again. On Satur-day, he decided, he'd catch an early train to Liverpool, spend the day with his real mother in Waterloo, and the next day with his other mother in Bootle – no, with *Iris*. From now on, he'd think of them as Iris and Tom; it would make things so much easier.

He could really do with a car, but would never be able to afford one with the money he earned as Kath's researcher. She was right, it was time he moved on, got a proper job, wore proper clothes and earned a proper wage.

Nell held his face in her hands for a few seconds before kissing him on both cheeks. 'It's really lovely to see you, William,' she said tenderly.

He'd already been told about the Hollywood film producers who were using Red's music in a film, and she showed him the cutting from Jack Kaminski. 'I hope you're getting a nice fat fee,' he said. She could do with some money. The house looked run-down and he'd like to bet she didn't earn much in that job of hers. Quinn and Kev made peanuts from their occasional gigs.

'Oh, I'm not getting a fee, but a share of the profits,' she told him. 'Jack thought it the best thing to do. It's like gambling in a way, and Red was always a bit of a gambler himself. Well, more than a bit,' she added. 'He would have approved.'

William considered it too damned risky. She might end up with nothing at all.

Quinn and Kev were still in bed and pleased to find their half-brother present when they came downstairs. William took them all into town for lunch. That night, the lads had a gig over the water in Birkenhead. He went with them in their van with his tambourine and was a member of the Finnegan Brothers for two highly enjoyable hours.

Next morning, all four of them went to nine o'clock Mass. William couldn't think why, but Nell liked him to go with her. Maybe she thought she'd convert him to Catholicism in the course of time, but he knew there was no chance of that.

After a massive fried breakfast, he caught the bus to Balliol Road to see Iris and Tom.

Both his sisters were sitting on him, Dorothy on one knee, Clare on the other. Each was twisting one of his ears. 'You're hurting,' he yelled. 'Tickling and hurting. I can't stand it.'

Dorothy stopped. 'We thought you'd left us altogether,' she said. 'That we'd never see you again. This is punishment.'

'You won't see me again if you don't stop twisting my ears.' They both stopped.

'Do you mean that?' Clare looked as if she might cry.

'Of course I don't mean it, no,' William said good-naturedly, 'but you really are making me feel ill.'

Iris came into the room. 'Leave William alone, girls. You're behaving like little children.'

They slid off his knees and leaned against him instead. 'We've missed you,' Clare sighed. 'We thought you'd given up being our brother and would never come back again.'

'I have been back a few times.'

Dorothy poked him. 'But not when we were in. If we'd known you were coming we would have been in, wouldn't we, Clare?'

'Of course. In fact, if we'd known you were coming, we'd have baked a cake.'

'Ha, ha, very funny.' William heard the front door open and close. Someone had come in, probably Tom. He'd heard Iris phone him earlier. 'William's here,' she'd hissed.

'Hello there, son.' Tom beamed at him. 'How's the world of politics?'

'It's pretty fine,' William said, 'though I'm thinking of making a move soon. I've been long enough in my present job.'

'That's probably true.' Tom sat opposite him and Iris and the girls went into the kitchen to prepare lunch. 'Good to get as much experience as you can while you're young. You can't hop about changing jobs once you're in your thirties.'

'That's right,' William agreed. 'I'm just not sure which way to go next.'

'I suppose,' Tom mused, frowning thoughtfully, 'you could always work for a Tory for a while, see what it's like on the other side of the fence sort of thing. Or what about that magazine you wrote the article for about a year ago? Did you do any more?'

'About half a dozen or so. They bought them all.'

'Maybe they would take you on their permanent staff. Or you could submit articles on a freelance basis to the press in general. I understand they pay quite well.'

That was three ideas in the space of just three minutes. William was glad he'd come.

★

A month later, William went to work as bag-carrier, speech-writer, secretary and chauffeur to Sir Roland White, a gentle, old-fashioned Tory whose father and grandfather before him had held the same seat in Devon for more than sixty years. His salary doubled, though Auntie Kath reminded him he couldn't have the flat in Lambeth for ever. He bought a guitar and signed up for a course of lessons.

Meanwhile, as he gradually settled into his new job and practised the guitar, Christmas approached. He would be spending half the time with Nell in Waterloo and the other half with Iris and Tom in Bootle. He had been invited to Devon for a few days with Sir Roland and his family – he had a real cracker of a granddaughter called Sophie – but perhaps another time.

Life was turning out to be pretty good again. He knew where he stood, though not exactly what he wanted from the future. But that would come with time.

New Year's Eve, another year gone, people exclaimed in surprise. Nineteen seventy was a matter of hours away. The Grants, including William, Dorothy and Clare, sat down to a dinner of bits and pieces left over from Christmas. A chicken pie that had been frozen, a tin of ham, Brussels sprouts, the last of the stuffing, dates, a giant trifle, half a Christmas pudding, some crumbling Christmas cake and a Yule log that nobody liked.

'Well, I'm glad we got rid of that lot,' Iris said when the meal was over. The Yule log could go out for the birds. She would never buy one again.

The dishes washed, the family settled in front of the television to watch a film. Tom started to fall asleep, but was startled awake by the sound of a car hooting its horn repeatedly outside.

'Is that someone calling on us?' Iris muttered.

William got to his feet and went to look out of the window,

following by the girls. A white Hillman Imp was parked outside and people were climbing out; two women, he noted, one carrying a baby.

'It's our Louise!' Clare squeaked. 'And she's brought the baby.'

The other young woman, the driver, William noted, was Grace Kaminski. She opened the car boot and began to remove suitcases. Dorothy and Clare were already running down the path to greet them, screaming mightily and disturbing the peace on what was an unusually quiet day in Balliol Road.

Iris was beside herself. All her children, a baby, and her husband together under one roof on New Year's Eve! Although it was many years since she and Tom had been proper man and wife, it seemed only right that he be there. The house had rarely been so noisy and full of happiness and high spirits.

Louise was describing how they'd managed to leave Boston with George. 'Both parents are supposed to sign an application for their child's passport. Grace asked a friend to pretend to be Gary and he forged his signature, otherwise I would never have got away.'

At this, Tom was both shocked and worried. 'But that's a crime, love. You could get into serious trouble.'

'Only in the States, Mr Grant,' Grace Kaminski pointed out. 'And I'm sure the Dixons wouldn't go to court or anything like that. It would look very bad on the family.'

Iris watched Louise and William with their heads together, obviously really pleased to see each other. She remembered when they were little, less than a year apart in age, inseparable, and Louise at about five declaring that she wanted to marry her big brother when she grew up. Iris and Tom had laughed, though it actually was a possibility. Her heart quickened. Once Louise was divorced – she intended to start proceedings in the New Year – she would be free to marry again, and William was already free. She couldn't think of a single thing more wonderful than the two of them getting married.

Hints would have to be dropped, the truth about William's birth revealed – if he agreed, of course – and Iris would have what had suddenly become her heart's desire.

Chapter 19

The first event of any importance to take place in the new year was the death of Paddy O'Neill. He had drunk to excess ever since his beloved wife had died at such a relatively young age, and everyone considered it was a miracle he had lasted as long as he had.

It was hard to be sad at the funeral, where so many jokes were told about Paddy's drinking prowess, the Finnegan Brothers played all his favourite Irish tunes and the mourners danced a mad jig and became pleasantly drunk themselves.

William felt obliged to attend; after all, Paddy had been his father, even if he'd never known. He didn't like attending these Catholic rituals, where he felt desperately out of place, and unable to reveal his true relationship to the likes of Ryan O'Neill, his half-brother, whom he liked instantly, and Bridie, his half-sister, a little mousy woman who seemed a bit stuck up if the truth be known. According to Maggie she was twenty-eight, but she looked more like a teenager.

Auntie Kath made a speech, astonishing everyone by announcing that she would retire from Parliament before the next election so that someone younger could take her place.

'You're little more than a slip of a girl, Kathleen,' someone shouted.

'Yes, lad, but I've got things to do. As soon as I stand down, I'm getting married, but I'll remain in gainful employment. I'll be working for a charity. I decided I needed a change.'

A voice came from the back of the room, a woman's voice, loud and determined; a voice that demanded respect. 'I'd like to declare meself a prospective parliamentary candidate to stand for the seat of Bootle Docklands,' it declared. 'The constituency needs an heir to Kathleen who will fight as she did for the rights of the people, the trade unions, the weak and the poor, the sick and the old.'

There was a burst of applause and the speaker turned out to be Bridie O'Neill, who no one had thought would say boo to a goose, but who was obviously very different when it came to politics.

'Who's Auntie Kath marrying?' Maggie demanded of William. 'I didn't know she had that sort of relationship with a man.'

'Neither did I.' William claimed total surprise. 'They must be doing their courting in secret.'

They all had such a good time that it was hard to feel sorry about Paddy having died.

'Well, that's the way it should be,' Jack said later to Maggie, who complained she hadn't cried once at the funeral. 'We should be celebrating the person's life, not weeping and wailing.'

'I'll never stop weeping and wailing if you die before me,' Maggie said soberly.

'Don't be daft, darling.' He stroked her hair. 'You're a fighter. You'll soon get over losing me.'

'No I won't,' Maggie shook her head. 'In fact I hope I'm the one who dies first, so *you* can jolly well get over *me*.'

At Easter, Holly Kaminski married Dennis Walker. The winter had been harsh, but the weather obligingly improved in time for the occasion and the day was sunny and warm. Maggie hadn't gone as mad as she would have liked with the arrangements. Holly's wedding dress had been made by a local dressmaker, Grace had bought her pretty cotton bridesmaid's dress at John Lewis, and Maggie's smart ice-blue outfit came from Marks & Spencer. There was a buffet rather than a sit-down meal, served in a marquee in the garden.

It had seemed wrong to waste money on a slap-up wedding that the young couple didn't want. Maggie hoped that when Grace was married, it'd be an opportunity to go to town with a really grand affair. On the other hand, Grace, who'd been living at home since returning from Boston with Louise and her baby after getting up to all sorts of shenanigans – taking the baby out of the country illegally, from what she could gather – was quite likely to get married, if she ever did, wearing jeans and halfway up a mountain somewhere like Nepal. Her mum and dad wouldn't even know until they received a telegram afterwards.

Maggie circulated among the guests, shaking hands or kissing cheeks, whichever was appropriate. She hugged Nell, who looked lovely in pale green, a touch of grey already in her smooth brown hair.

'Your Quinn or Kev are likely to be the next to get married,' Maggie said. Grace had insisted on inviting them, but Holly had refused to let them play.

'There'll be no rowdy Irish jigs at *my* wedding, if you don't mind,' she had said in the hoity-toity voice that nowadays she used virtually all the time.

Maggie sat beside her friend. 'I'll be glad when all this is over,' she whispered. 'I must be getting old. There was a time when I used to love this sort of thing.' Both she and Nell would be forty-five that year.

'You'd enjoy it if it was someone else's wedding,' Nell advised. 'As it is, you feel responsible for everyone else having a good time and nothing going wrong.'

'Oh Nell,' Maggie said fervently. 'I wish you lived here. I'm forever getting meself in a state when there's no need to. Jack's always telling me to calm down.'

Nell smiled. 'Well, if you've got Jack to tell you, why do you need me?'

'Because I don't take any notice of him, but I do of you.'

A week later, in Liverpool, Iris Grant was telling Matthew Williams yet again that she couldn't see him any more. Her life was too full for an affair. She would have given up her job in Owen Owen's had she not needed the money. Tom was incredibly generous, but she felt obliged to contribute something to the household expenses.

The trouble with her job was that Matthew knew exactly where to find her on Friday and Saturday nights and he refused to listen when she tried to tell him their affair was over.

'Things have changed,' she would explain. 'I have so much to do nowadays. My daughter has a baby to look after and she needs help, and my son comes home most weekends. I feel obliged to be there.' She *wanted* to be there. When William was home, Iris didn't want to be anywhere else. And because he was there as well as Louise and George, Tom was coming round more often. The house was full of noise, laughter and the sound of a baby. It was exactly what Iris had hoped for back in those quiet, empty years when she'd longed for a baby of her own.

'But I love you,' Matthew would say tetchily, as if that was all that mattered.

Iris would insist on going home when she came out of work, but find herself agreeing to see him one afternoon in the Temple the following week. Today, though, she was determined to finish it. It was Wednesday, and he was driving her back to Balliol Road from the hotel in his Jaguar when she told him the relationship must definitely end.

He became angry. 'Are you saying our affair merely helped fill in the time before your daughter came home?'

'No, no, of course not. I loved you.' She realised her mistake straight away.

'Loved!' he snapped. '*Loved!* Are you saying you no longer do?'

'In a way. All good things come to an end,' she said weakly.

He stopped the car, braking sharply. They were barely halfway home. 'Get out,' he hissed. 'Get out. I never want to see you again.'

'Matthew . . . let's not finish like this,' she protested.

He leaned across and opened the passenger door. 'Get *out!*'

It wasn't the end. Next day, he phoned and pleaded for forgiveness. 'I was upset, I'm sorry. Let's meet again, please.'

Iris flatly refused. Last night she'd had to get the bus home from where he'd ordered her out of his car. 'No, Matthew,' she said firmly.

He lost his temper, calling her a bitch, saying she was wicked to have led him on. She was reminded of the time more than twenty years ago when he'd tried to blackmail her. She put down the receiver. He phoned again a few days later. This time he cried and she listened, feeling miserable, because she really had loved him for a while.

'Matthew, darling,' she whispered. 'It really is over.' She held on until he stopped crying and had replaced the receiver without saying another word. Then she hung up and started to cry too.

A general election in June that year saw a Conservative government returned to power and the genial Edward Heath became prime minister.

Auntie Kath retired from politics and Bridget O'Neill was elected the Member for Bootle Docklands. Over the course of the last few months, Bridie the mouse had become Bridget the lion.

Auntie Kath became the public spokesperson for the charity Famine Awareness and also married Mick Baker, a widower and journalist with well-known left-wing views.

A remarkable and honourable political career had come to an end and a new one had begun.

One rainy August morning, a casually, though expensively dressed young man knocked on the door of the Grants' house in Balliol Road. Iris answered.

'Mrs Grant.' He touched his gabardine cap. 'Is Louise here?' he asked courteously.

Iris resisted the urge to scream. The exceptionally good-looking caller was Gary Dixon, Louise's husband and father of George. She took a long time trying to think what to say. She was about to deny Louise's presence in the house, or indeed that particular part of the world, when George shouted, 'Blah!' and Louise cried, 'What's the matter, sweetheart?'

'You'd better come in,' Iris said warily. They hadn't exactly become friends with Gary when she and Tom had stayed in Boston.

Gary managed a smile. 'I come in peace,' he told her, raising a hand in what she supposed was a conciliatory gesture.

She took him into the living room, where twelve-month-old George was seated on the floor opposite his mother, who was clapping her hands and teaching him how to count. She went pale. 'Gary!' she gasped.

'Hello, sweetheart.'

Iris waited to see how her daughter would respond to this. When she got to her feet, burst into tears and ran into her husband's arms, Iris went into the kitchen.

For the last eight months, ever since she had arrived back from Boston, Louise had been on edge, waiting for Gary to turn up and demand George's return. Even worse, she had half expected representatives of the law to arrive and take her in chains back to the United States, where George would be handed over to Monica to raise as she pleased. In vain did Tom and Iris assure her that the second of her fears would never

345

happen, though there was always the chance that the first might.

Iris rang Tom, who was in the middle of morning surgery, and told him what had occurred. It sounded as if war had been declared at the other end of the line. 'It's bedlam here,' Tom said. 'I've no idea what time I'll be able to get there.'

There was no shouting coming from the living room, just the faint murmur of voices and George's occasional chuckle.

Gary had written numerous letters over the intervening months. It had become quite normal to find an airmail letter on the mat when the post came in the morning. He had also telephoned frequently. He wanted his wife and son back, had vowed he would buy them their own house; that his mother would only be allowed to visit if Louise gave her permission.

'But,' Louise had said to Iris, 'I don't want to live on the same land mass as Monica Dixon. Gary can come and live here if he likes, but that's as far as I'm prepared to go.'

What are they talking about now? Iris wondered. The voices had become no louder. She didn't want Louise and George to go back to America. It wasn't just selfishness, but worry that her daughter would find it impossible to escape the claws of her mother-in-law, no matter what Gary promised.

Louise appeared looking very grave and asked her mother if she would please make coffee.

'Of course, love.' Iris got out the best china and searched for a tray cloth. She opened a packet of chocolate biscuits and arranged them on a plate.

Gary jumped to his feet when she went in and took the tray from her.

Back in the kitchen, she chewed her nails for the first time in many years, longing to know what was going on.

An hour passed before Louise appeared again, this time to ask if it was all right for Gary to stay the night.

'Gary is your husband. He can stay for as long as he wants,'

Iris said. She felt unreasonably irritated. 'There's no need to ask.'

It turned out that Gary had been called upon to fight in Vietnam. His parents quite understandably didn't want him to go – it was possibly the only matter on which Iris and Monica Dixon shared the same view; Iris wouldn't have wanted William to go off and fight. It was relatively easy in the United States for the sons of the wealthy to avoid military service by joining the National Guard or the Peace Corps.

But Gary was determined to do his bit. And once he had served his time, he wanted Louise and George to return to Boston. 'He promised that his mother wouldn't come near us,' Louise said. 'He knows he behaved badly when I went to live there, but he concedes he was completely underneath his mother's thumb.' She smiled grimly. 'But now he's come to his senses. If I insist, then he'll even get a job in this country.'

Why did I want children? Iris wondered when she was in bed that night. They cause nothing but heartbreak. They're either going away or coming home, or going away again. You worry about them all the time – even on your dying day you'll worry how they'll get on without you. And stupid me, I actually wish I'd had a couple more!

Another Easter; another wedding. It came as a surprise to everyone when an invitation to William Grant's wedding arrived in the post. He was marrying Sophie Eaves, grand-daughter of Sir Roland White, Member of Parliament for the seat of Devon Coastal, for whom he now worked. No one was even aware that they'd been courting.

The day when it came started off with a soft wet mist, but had improved by midday, when it was time for the wedding. The flowers in the grounds of the ancient village church sparkled in the suddenly brilliant sunshine, giving off a fresh, heavenly scent, or so claimed Maggie Kaminski to her handsome husband as they walked along the grassy path into the church.

Both mothers of the groom were seated in the front pew, she noted; Nell in blue and Iris wearing cream, William's real mother and his adoptive one. And they were talking to each other, which really was the gear. As far as she knew, Nell and Iris hadn't spoken since the day William had been born. It was only right that they start again today of all days.

William had announced the identity of his real parents to the world in general, and had found himself related in one way or another to virtually half of Bootle. He didn't care any more, he told Maggie, now officially his half-sister. He wasn't embarrassed about anything.

His maternal grandparents, the Desmonds, had been invited to the wedding. Mabel, in yellow net, looked very much like an aged bridesmaid, while Alfred next to her cut an imposing figure in a black velvet suit and scarlet cravat.

There were about fifty people there; it was a small wedding, so Maggie had been advised. She thought fifty relatively large. She was also warned that Sophie's mother and father were divorced and were likely to indulge in a fist fight if they were together under the same roof for too long.

The bride was a dear little thing with a heart-shaped face, white-blonde hair and dark brown eyes. Her dress was made of layers and layers of stiff organdie like the petals of a flower.

The ceremony was short and sweet, nothing like a Nuptial Mass that you could really get your teeth into. Perhaps that too had been arranged with Sophie's parents in mind.

The ceremony over, the newly married couple, the two tiny bridesmaids in frilly pink and the guests poured out of the church and posed for photographs. Quite a crowd had gathered in the churchyard to watch. More people applauded from outside their little stone houses as the wedding party, William and Sophie in the lead, made their way through the village to the pleasant old house where Sir Roland's family lived. The reception was being held in a converted barn.

'It's all terribly medieval,' Maggie whispered to Jack. 'They're like serfs kowtowing to their betters. I half expect the women to curtsey. I'm glad Auntie Kath couldn't come. She might have said something rude.'

'You've just said something rude yourself, darling,' Jack reminded her.

'Yes, but not in a foghorn voice like Auntie Kath.'

The sit-down meal was delicious: the chickens had only been slaughtered the day before, and the pigs (supplying the ham) had been hand-reared on the farm next door.

The bride was a vegetarian and had a salad for her meal. Thinking about the hens that had been happily running round twenty-four hours before, Maggie thought that she might well become a vegetarian too. Sophie was also a feminist and a member of the Campaign for Nuclear Disarmament, and disagreed with her politician grandfather on most things.

The speeches were terribly funny, in particular the offering from Quinn Finnegan, William's half-brother, which was full of rude Irish jokes that no one seemed to mind.

When everything was over, the guests took themselves into the house, the pretty garden, or stayed in the barn, where there was a bar.

Maggie steered Nell and Iris into a little square of lawn surrounded by a hedge on all four sides, where they seated themselves on a collection of garden furniture in various stages of antiquity. She was determined to keep her friends together for as long as possible so there would be no chance they'd drift apart again. She parked herself on a bench and placed her champagne glass on top of a wrought-iron table that had once been painted white. A bee buzzed noisily nearby and birds fluttered madly in the hedge in which there were glimpses of a nest.

'That was lovely,' she said. 'The ceremony, the meal, the

atmosphere – everything. I really enjoyed it. Sophie seems a lovely girl. I'm sure she and William are going to be very happy.'

'I'm sure too.' Nell sipped her orange juice. 'She told me she wants at least five children.'

Iris nodded approvingly. 'William will make a good father. He was always very patient with the girls. You know,' she said contemplatively, 'I rather wanted him to marry Louise. They always got on really well together. He was fonder of her than the other girls.'

'I would have been very much against that.' Nell sounded uncommonly forceful. 'I know they're not related, but it sounds faintly indecent, and it was important for William to get away from the Grants, the Finnegans, the Desmonds and the Kaminskis and start a new life with new people somewhere other than Liverpool. Now he can be himself. It's what he deserves.'

'I agree with Nell.' Maggie picked up a white cat that had wandered into their leafy hideaway and began to stroke it. 'Don't you think she's right, Iris?'

Iris conceded this with a little nod. 'I suppose his life would have been rather claustrophobic otherwise.'

Jack poked his head around the hedge. 'Oh, there you are,' he said. 'I was wondering where you'd gone.' He went away again.

Minutes later, Tom came to check where Iris was and Kevin Finnegan to make sure his mother was all right. After-wards, they disappeared.

Maggie was conscious of the sun sinking lower in the sky and the hedge beginning to rustle from a slight breeze. A waiter appeared with a tray of champagne and she and Iris took a glass each. Nell said she was perfectly happy with orange juice, though she hoped there would be tea or coffee later. 'No, not just later; quite soon.'

'How long is it since the three of us were together like this, just talking, like?' Maggie mused. She was pleased that there seemed to be no animosity between Nell and Iris. They were getting on fine, though they should have been mingling with the other wedding guests, making themselves known.

'About a quarter of a century, I reckon,' Iris said.

'It can't possibly be that long, surely!'

'It is, Maggie, I can assure you.' It was before William had appeared on the scene, Iris recalled, and he would be twenty-four in a few months' time.

'Oh lord, Iris! That makes me feel really old. Twenty-five years doesn't sound nearly as long as a quarter of a century.'

'Twenty-five years, then.'

'Anyroad, we must get together again quite soon. I can always come to Liverpool and stay overnight with one of you.'

'Don't forget, I go to work,' Nell reminded her friend.

'I had forgotten, Nell. I don't like coming of a weekend and leaving Jack by himself.'

'We'll think of something,' Nell assured her. 'It won't be another twenty-five years before we talk again.' She smiled at Iris, who smiled back, and both women felt as if something very wrong had been mended.

From the other side of the hedge there was the murmur of voices, and further away two women began to laugh.

'Has that picture with Red's song in been released yet?' Iris enquired.

'It came out in America only the other day. It won't be shown in this country for another few months yet.'

'These things take ages,' Maggie remarked, as if she was an expert on the making of films and their distribution. 'I'm going to start praying it will be top of the pops.'

'The Long and Winding Road' was being played by a group of imitation Beatles in the barn, disturbing the birds, which fluttered in protest. The women sang along to the first two lines: *The long and winding road that leads to your door* . . . Their voices faded when they couldn't remember any more of the words.

It was time for the dancing to start. Maggie didn't think she could be bothered, and neither did Iris. Nell said she hadn't danced with a man since Red had died and had no intention of going near the barn just in case someone asked her.

'Anyroad, I like being here with youse two,' she said comfortably. 'Eh! Remember that dance in the army, Maggie? It was held on Ash Wednesday and the band played nothing but hymns. They must have all been Catholics.'

'Did we dance to the hymns or not?' Maggie asked.

'We thought it'd be sacrilegious, so we sang them instead.'

Iris hadn't been at the dance; she'd probably been involved in some activity they'd never known about.

They continued to sit there until the sky grew dark and the air turned cold; old friends talking about old times, remembering this and remembering that, as old friends do.

Epilogue

A few hours after the wedding
(Liverpool)

Louise was in bed in Balliol Road when the telephone rang downstairs in the hall. She was eight months pregnant and hadn't felt up to attending William's wedding. Her sister, Dorothy, who'd badly wanted to go, had insisted on staying home instead and keeping an eye on her and George.

Dorothy, already in bed, shouted, 'I'll get that, sis. It's probably Mum or Dad to say they're on their way home.'

But Louise was already pushing her feet into slippers. 'It's okay, I'll answer it,' she shouted back. Her parents would never ring so late, and she had a feeling what the call was about. In the corner of the room, George was fast asleep in his cot, snoring slightly. She felt a rush of love that almost choked her.

'Is that Mrs Louise Dixon?' a man's voice with an American accent enquired when she picked up the receiver.

'Speaking.' She'd had a funny sensation all day that something was wrong.

'I'm so sorry, ma'am, about calling you like this, but we weren't too sure if you'd be there to accept a telegram. There's another address in Boston, you see.'

'I'm Gary Dixon's wife if that's who you want.'

'I'm so sorry, ma'am,' the voice said again, 'but I have to inform you that Private Gary Dixon lost his life yesterday at Song Ve Valley. He was a good, brave soldier. My commiserations, ma'am.'

'Thank you for telling me,' Louise whispered. She replaced the receiver. She and Gary hadn't had much time together. It didn't seem fair that she should lose him so soon. But was it ever fair that a man could die before he had even set eyes on one of his children?

Dorothy had come halfway down the stairs in her night-dress. 'What is it, Lou?'

'Gary's dead.'

'Gosh, I'm sorry.' Her sister looked stricken. She ran down the rest of the stairs and flung her arms around her. 'Shall I make tea?'

'Please.' Louise stood helplessly in the hall, feeling lost and alone, despite having Dorothy with her and her son only upstairs. She badly wanted Mum and Dad. She looked at the telephone; there was something she must do. There'd be time to cry later. She picked up the phone and dialled a number. It would be afternoon in Boston.

Monica Dixon answered with her name followed by the telephone number. Her voice was thin and frail and full of despair.

Louise swallowed. 'Hello, this is Louise. Have you heard about Gary?'

'Yes, a friend rang.'

'I'm sorry.'

'I think I want to die,' Monica Dixon said wretchedly.

'Please don't. Do you know I'm expecting another baby? Did Gary tell you?'

'Yes. How are you feeling?' The question was clearly an effort of will.

Louise could hear dishes rattling in the kitchen where her sister was making tea. 'Not so well, but as soon as the baby is born I'll come and see you. I'll bring George too.'

'Would it be all right if I came and saw you? Soon, very soon. Tomorrow, in fact.'

'You'd be very welcome. Good night, Monica.'

'Goodbye, Louise.'

Dorothy was taking the tea into the living room. 'Was that your horrible mother-in-law?'

'Yes, she's coming tomorrow.'

'You poor thing.' Her sister looked troubled. 'I bet she's the last person you want to see.'

'She's Gary's mother, sis. We've both lost him. We should mourn him together.'

It was the right thing to do.

Epilogue 2

Two days after the wedding
(New York)

Raoul and Lucia Perez emerged from the cinema off Times Square. As ever in this area, the sidewalks teemed with people.

Lucia linked her husband's arm, worried she might lose him in the crowd. 'Well, that was a really rapturous movie, honey.' It was her favourite word: rapturous. '*Raining Flowers*. I love the title.'

'My mom was in love with Hugo Swann when she was a girl,' Raoul remarked. 'She told me so before we left the apartment.' His mom was babysitting their two little boys.

'Maybe I could take her to see it next week. I wouldn't mind seeing it again.'

'Mom'd like that. Thanks, hon.'

'We could go Thursday. You could look after the kids.'

'It's a deal.' He squeezed her arm. 'Shall we stop for a coffee?'

'Yeah, I'd like that. Next diner we come to, we go in.' She began to hum a tune in order to express just how happy she felt, linking her husband's arm, going home to the cutest couple of kids in the entire world.

'What's that tune?' Raoul asked.

'It's from the movie. I dunno if it had a name. It's – what d'you call it? Catchy. It sounds Irish.'

'So it does. I like it too. Tell you what, hon. Tomorrow I'll see if I can buy the record.'

He began to whistle the tune along with her.